Cyril Cook was born in Easton, Hampshire, but at the age of five was brought to live on a farm in Mottingham, Kent. Educated at Eltham College, he matriculated in 1939, joined The Rifle Brigade in 1940, and was commissioned and transferred to The Parachute Regiment in 1943. He saw considerable service in the 6th Airborne Division in Europe and the Far East where for a period he commanded, at the age of 22, a company of some 220 men of the Malay Regiment.

His working life was spent mainly as the proprietor of an engineering business which he founded, until he retired to start the really serious business of writing the six volumes of The Chandlers.

By the same author

THE CHANDLERS

VOLUME ONE – THE YOUNG CHANDLERS
Published in 2005 (Vanguard Press)
ISBN 1 84386 199 2

VOLUME TWO – THE CHANDLERS AT WAR
Published in 2006 (Vanguard Press)
ISBN-13: 978 1 84386 292 5
ISBN-10: 1 84386 292 1

THE CHANDLERS

Volume 3

The Chandlers Fight Back

Cyril Cook

THE CHANDLERS

Volume 3

The Chandlers Fight Back

Vanguard Press

VANGUARD PAPERBACK

© Copyright 2006
Cyril Cook

The right of Cyril Cook to be identified as author of
this work has been asserted by him in accordance with the
Copyright, Designs and Patents Act 1988

All Rights Reserved

No reproduction, copy or transmission of this publication
may be made without written permission.
No paragraph of this publication may be reproduced,
copied or transmitted save with the written permission of the
publisher, or in accordance with the provisions
of the Copyright Act 1956 (as amended).

Any person who does any unauthorised act in relation to
this publication may be liable to criminal
prosecution and civil claims for damage.

A CIP catalogue record for this title is
available from the British Library

ISBN-13: 978 1 84386 293 2
ISBN-10: 1 84386 293 X

*Vanguard Press is an imprint of
Pegasus Elliot MacKenzie Publishers Ltd.*
www.pegasuspublishers.com

First Published in 2006

**Vanguard Press
Sheraton House Castle Park
Cambridge England**

Printed & Bound in Great Britain

This book is dedicated to my late sister

JOAN DEVERILL

She was the youngest of the family.

Whilst her six brothers were away on active service during World War Two, Joan, only fourteen years old when war broke out, looked after our Mother: she was badly crippled with arthritis and unable to get into Anderson shelter. Together they sat under the stairs through the London bombings and the V.I. attacks. They were both symptomatic of the bravery of those who can only wait.

Joan, whose smile lightened any room she entered, died much too young, as bravely as she lived.

MAIN CHARACTERS AND EVENTS FROM BOOKS ONE AND TWO:- "THE YOUNG CHANDLERS" AND "THE CHANDLERS AT WAR"

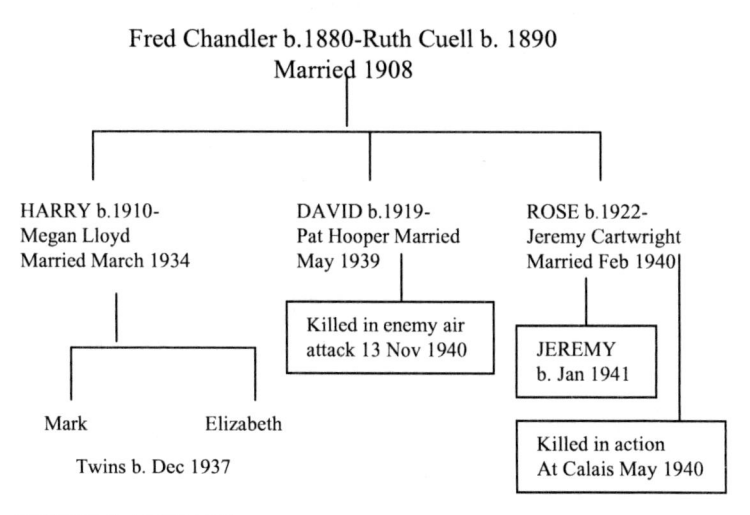

Fred Chandler b.1880-Ruth Cuell b. 1890
Married 1908

HARRY b.1910-
Megan Lloyd
Married March 1934

DAVID b.1919-
Pat Hooper Married
May 1939

Killed in enemy air attack 13 Nov 1940

ROSE b.1922-
Jeremy Cartwright
Married Feb 1940

JEREMY
b. Jan 1941

Killed in action
At Calais May 1940

Mark   Elizabeth

Twins b. Dec 1937

OTHER FAMILIES

JACK HOOPER — David's father-in-law. Divorced Pat's mother. Married MOIRA EVANS, Megan's Aunt. Moira is a Top Civil Servant involved in the Atom Bomb project. They have a son JOHN born August 1937.

TREFOR LLOYD and Elizabeth. Megan's parents.

BUFFY CARTWRIGHT and Rita. Jeremy's parents – Rose's "in-laws."

KARL REISNER Refugee from Nazi Germany. Father of ANNI married to ERNIE BOLTON, David's friend from boyhood and now the Works Director at Sandbury Engineering.

DR KONRAD VON HASSELLBEK and wife. Parents of DIETER, David's great pre-war friend now in a panzer division of the German Army. All fervent anti-Nazis. Also Daughter INGE, ardent Nazi married to Himmler's nephew. DIETER married his cousin ROSA in April 1940.

Chapter One

It was Wednesday the 3rd of September 1941, the second anniversary of the declaration of war on Germany. Those two years had seen the Wehrmacht's crushing invasion of Poland in 1939, their humiliating victory over France and Britain in Western Europe in 1940, resulting in the miracle of Dunkirk and the heroic defence of Calais, and finally their headlong invasion of Russia in June 1941. It seemed that nothing could stop this mighty force. Deutschland really was 'über alles' as their national anthem boastfully claimed.

Ruth Chandler sat in front of the Aga in the large kitchen at Chandlers Lodge in the small Kentish town of Sandbury. It was half-past seven in the morning. Her husband Fred had just left – on a bicycle, petrol was very precious! – to run the engineering factory he and his friend, Jack Hooper, owned and which was flat out on war production. Finishing her cup of tea, her reverie was shattered by the obscene wailing of the air raid siren mounted on the roof of the Sandbury police station a quarter of a mile away, and sounding as if it were in their back garden.

"Oh no! Not again," she exclaimed to the world in general, and calling up the stairs, "Rose, get ready to go to the shelter – I've got the emergency bag here." The emergency bag contained mainly sundry accessories designed to cater for Rose's baby son, Jeremy, now eight months old and to quote his grandmother – 'A proper handful.'

They had suffered eight alerts in the past week, bombs being dropped only once during these attacks. Although Sandbury did have an attractive target in the form of an R.A.F. air field one mile out towards Maidstone, the town itself was not exactly a massive enough industrial complex by any means to draw the attention of enemy bombs. That said, stray bombs had fallen, the airfield had been attacked on numerous occasions, and there had been a number of casualties over the past year, one of which being her beloved daughter-in-law Pat, David's wife.

The routine followed on these occasions was that if you heard the heavy guns firing from the Maidstone direction it usually meant the planes were heading towards Biggin Hill or South London and would probably fly over Sandbury, therefore it would be expedient to take cover in the Anderson shelter in the garden. There was no such activity this morning and after half an hour the 'all-clear' sounded.

Ruth was depressed by the fact that her son David, a captain in the prestigious City Rifles, was not only going back off leave, but of all things had been posted to a parachute training centre. David had recently completed a mission in occupied France for the Special Operations Department, where he was flown in and out by an R.A.F Lysander, now he was being prepared for a further project which would entail his having to parachute in. That's all the family knew. Where he was going, what he was doing, when he was going, how long he would be gone was all unknown to them as it was to David, and it was the not knowing which added to the depression she felt.

"The raid didn't come to anything then," came a cheery voice from the doorway. It was David, being even a little more cheerful than his normal cheerful self, suspecting that his mother would be feeling a bit low with his going away today.

"No thank goodness. Now what are you going to have for breakfast?"

This was really a question with very few possible answers. The days of eggs and bacon, kippers, kedgeree and so on were long gone. Most tinned goods were rationed, or 'on points' as it was generally known, so even such mouth watering sustenance as Spam or corned beef had to be queued for. With a ration of one egg per person per week, two ounces of butter and two rashers of bacon, a mini feast could be enjoyed on Sunday morning followed by porridge and toast during the rest of the week. At least there was plenty of bread.

"I'll just have some Shredded Wheat and toast afterwards please Mum."

"What time is Paddy coming for you?"

Paddy was David's batman, a regular soldier of long service who also had been on leave and was joining David on the parachuting course.

"He's picking the P.U. up in London at eight o'clock which means he'll be here about nine-thirty. By the time we've loaded up and had a cup of tea we should be away by about ten. Paddy's got to dump our kit at Euston where I understand someone else will collect the P.U. from him. We should be in Manchester by about five o'clock, where we will be met. I will give you a ring sometime after seven, I should get through reasonably quickly at that time."

Almost too casually a voice from the doorway asked "And when do you start jumping?" It was Rose, carrying a gurgling little Jeremy who was punching at the air with both fists like a miniature Jack Dempsey. David took him up.

Working on the premise that the more he talked about parachuting the more familiar, and therefore less frightening it would be to his mother and sister, he replied, "I've no idea. I would think we would have several weeks' groundwork to do before we jump. Anyway the first two jumps are out of a balloon, not from an aeroplane." (As if that makes any blooming difference he thought – you're still seven hundred feet up with only a thin sheet of nylon to ensure you get down again, but it sounded less frightening.) He continued, "I understand that by the time you've done all the groundwork the actual jumping is child's play." (And that's the biggest blooming whopper I've told in years he said to himself, feeling the tightening in the pit of his stomach as he thought of it.)

As he said this, so young Jeremy landed him a beautiful right-hander right on the tip of his nose. "Ouch, you bully, I'm supposed to be your best friend, didn't you know that?" Jeremy gurgled even more, Ruth and Rose laughed, the tension at the thought of jumping was forgotten for the time being.

Paddy duly arrived just before nine-thirty and loaded all David's kit into the pick-up. He had been on leave at the same time as David, part of which he had spent at the home of a young woman, Mary Maguire at Aylesbury. He had met Mary, a corporal in the A.T.S. on the catering staff, at the covert operations training centre where he had been employed whilst David was away on his three months operation in France. Both Mary and Paddy had been sworn under the Official Secrets Act. Up until now Paddy, at 37, was a confirmed bachelor, with nineteen years service in the Rifles, but he had indicated to David before he went on leave that he found Mary Maguire 'very comely,' which David said sounded somewhat old fashioned. To this Paddy had replied that he was an old fashioned sort of chap, all of which had left David acutely anxious to know what had happened when Paddy at last had his 'feet under the table' at Aylesbury.

They said their goodbyes to the family, Fred, David's father, unexpectedly coming back to wish them a safe journey. They headed away up Wrotham Hill and over the Downs, were waived through at the military check point on the A20 at Swanley, and then found themselves sliding at times, on the wet tram lines in South London.

As soon as they cleared Sandbury, David, with a quizzical look to Paddy said, "Well?"

"Yes Sir, very well, everything went very well Sir."

"You know what I mean you lummock – how did you get on at Aylesbury?"

"Well Sir, they were a little bit what you might call restrained at first. Mary's father is the manager of a local insurance company, so they're fairly well off you understand. I think they were a bit worried that I was eleven years older than her, a regular soldier and all, and although they're Irish they were born in England, so they didn't know what sort of a bog-trotter I might turn out to be. I was there for three nights and on the second night her father said, 'Do you fancy a quick drink at the Rising Sun Paddy?' I replied, 'That would be very nice Mr Maguire.' 'Oh forget the bloody Mr Maguire business Paddy, my names Eamonn.' So off we went and got on like a house on fire."

"So, when's the wedding?"

"Well, I didn't quite get to making a proposal as you might say. I wanted to have a word with you first. After all, I might be dead tomorrow, and if I'm not, what sort of future does a time served soldier offer to a young woman brought up in the sort of comfort she's been used to?"

David was silent for a while. Being still a young man, worrying about the future did not rate highly on his list of priorities. He might meet a violent death as a soldier, that he accepted, but beyond that the future was too far away to lose any sleep over. On the other hand Paddy was getting on toward the forty mark, which to David, and people of a like age, was almost reaching the edge of senility. He could have given a flippant answer, but he sensed that Paddy was seriously concerned about the problem.

"I'll say what my mother would say to you Paddy. You, me, Mary, even Mr Maguire might be dead tomorrow and there's absolutely bugger all that anyone can do about that. Therefore it can be discounted. When you come out of the army you're the sort of bloke who will be invaluable to any firm or business, in addition to which you'll have a decent pension to back you up. So I say, pop the question, and I'll be your best man! I've just thought, on reflection, my mother wouldn't have said bugger all. Anyway apart from that it's as plain as a pikestaff to me that you forget all your little worries and ask the girl. She would be stark raving mad to say no and what I've seen and heard of Mary Maguire she's far from being stark raving mad."

"I'll write to her tonight Sir. There is one other thing that worries me a bit though. She's a good pure Catholic girl and I've been around a bit during my service. I've dipped my wick in a good many places over the years so I'm hardly what you might call unspoilt goods. What's she going to think about that?"

"God, now you're asking me. She's far too intelligent to think you're still a virgin at your age. What you think of each other now and how straight you are after you're married is what counts. If you're really concerned on that score, and I don't think you should be, have a word with the R.C. padre at Ringway – he'll put you straight. But as far as I can guess, the subject will never come up."

They drove on in silence for a while until they were crossing Waterloo Bridge, when Paddy voiced the phrase that all would-be suitors say aloud, or to themselves – "Well, she can always say no." David grinned at him.

The journey from Euston was slow but uneventful. At Manchester Piccadilly a young A.T.S. lance corporal was waiting at the barrier anxiously endeavouring to pick out a captain in the Rifles from among the throng of soldiers in every regiment from the Grenadier Guards to the Pay Corps. Spotting David's black pips and buttons she said "Captain Chandler, Sir?" And continued, "Have you got kit with you Sir?"

"I would estimate around about half a ton, at the last count," smiled David. "My batman has just won a trolley in a close contest with a gentleman from the Devonshire Regiment so he should be here at any minute." She smiled at his friendly answer.

Having loaded the kit on to the P.U. they threaded their way south through the Manchester suburbs to the R.A.F. airfield at Ringway. Having passed through the main guard the driver pulled up outside a Nissen hut with the notice 'adjutant' on the door.

"You're to see the adjutant Sir, and then I've to take you to your quarters," and then added, "I shall be your permanent driver I believe."

David went into the office wondering why he would need a permanent driver if he was living on, eating at, and jumping from Ringway airfield, but he was long enough in the service not to try and understand the workings of military minds – particularly staff wallahs whose sole purpose in life was to make things difficult to understand, thereby justifying their own existence.

The adjutant was a genial R.A.F. flight lieutenant.

"So you're Captain Chandler are you?"

I wouldn't have said I was if I hadn't been thought David.

The adjutant continued. "Well, as I understand it you, unlike most of the paratrooping types we get here, or should I say the would-be paratrooping types, a lot of them don't make it, are a special, and living out."

"Living out?"

"Yes. You are billeted at a house at Wilmslow, about five miles away. Lance corporal Dudley is assigned as your driver. She will collect you and take you back; you will make arrangements with her as regards times in collaboration with your course instructor."

"Any particular reason for all this?" asked David.

"Reason? You've been long enough in the army to know the powers that be don't have to have a reason, although my tiny little mind tells me there must be one in your case, what it is I know not. I'd be the last to know, I'm only the adjutant," he added, grinning.

"Yes, and I've been in the service long enough to know that you probably know a hell of a lot more than you're letting on. Still, as long as this billet is provided with hot and cold running chambermaids I shall not complain."

"Off you go then, be here nine o'clock in denims, bring your P.T. kit, we'll fit you and O'Riordan out with lockers. By the way, there's not much in the way of rank here. The sticks are all mixed ranks, captains mix with corporals, even the odd brigadier graces us with his presence at times, to say nothing of mysterious looking civilians of all nationalities male and female."

"Sounds very interesting."

"When you first get on the fan you may have a different word for it." Both smiling they shook hands, David walking out thinking what the hell is the fan, and remembering the adjutant's words when he was eventually introduced to the beast.

Lance corporal Dudley has driven this journey more than once David thought, as she swiftly negotiated little used back lanes in as far as he could tell, a southerly direction. The farmers of the county of Cheshire have always prided themselves on their immaculately kept hedges, but by now, two years into the war, with many men called up, there were signs that the traditional late autumn jobs of hedging and ditching were having to take second place to more essential production tasks in helping to feed, and in particular in Cheshire, to provide milk for the nation. One day we'll have to design a machine to cut hedges and dig ditches working off a tractor, David mused. Then, that's not as daft as it sounds, I'll have a word with Dad the next time I'm home. Sandbury Engineering, his father and father-in-laws' business, was originally formed to make agricultural equipment, although now of course it was flat out on a multitude of projects for the government, ranging from mobile workshops to wooden tail sections for the beautiful Mosquito aeroplane, to disposable long-range fuel tanks for all manner of aircraft, and many other components and sub-assemblies.

Coming out of a particularly narrow lane on to a main road, they drove through Wilmslow and came to a driveway at the entrance to which was a lodge housing War Department police. The gatekeeper checked the names of the passengers, opened the back covers of the P.U. to ensure they were not smuggling in some female entertainment for the use of the licentious soldiery as David afterwards suggested was the purpose of their investigation, and then waved them on. Half a mile or so up the long sweeping drive they pulled up outside a large mansion, not unlike the one in which they had been billeted in Sussex a few months ago.

"I'll take you to the orderly room Sir," said the lance corporal, continuing with, "Paddy, will you unload the kit into the hall and I'll get you some help to take it to your rooms."

An A.T.S. sergeant in the orderly room checked Captain Chandler D.C.M. in, and then queried, "May I ask Sir, how a captain has the Distinguished Conduct Medal?" (The D.C.M. is a decoration given for bravery to other ranks, not to officers.)

"I got that as a corporal in the Great War, sergeant, I look a lot younger than I really am."

His driver indulged in a well concealed explosion of laughter, the sergeant searched his face to try and establish whether her leg was being well and truly pulled, but being unable to come to a firm conclusion said, "Will you go in to Room 2 Sir," pointing to a doorway in the far corner.

As David turned towards Room 2 so the door opened and to his total surprise two figures emerged talking animatedly to each other until they simultaneously spotted him coming towards them. The first he knew very well – it was 'Robin,' his guide and mentor in Sussex before he went to France and one of his interrogators when he returned. The second was Hilary Jarvis, looking even more stunning in her lieutenant's uniform than she did when he last saw her in her A.T.S. sergeant's regimentals, even in those she had been an eye stopper. Immaculately tailored now she was, well – stunning! In April the previous year, 1940, David and his brother-in-law Jeremy together went to Winchester to appear before a War Office selection board to hopefully become officers, this same Sergeant Jarvis had been in charge of their intake. Every potential cadet had drooled over this gorgeous piece of military perfection, but had to drool from afar. When David travelled back to London and then on to Sandbury however, he found himself seated next to her on an acutely crowded train, to the obvious envy of others in the compartment and of those standing in the corridor peering in. He established she was a graduate language student and was herself, at that time, applying for a commission. He told her he was married to a lovely girl named Pat, to which she replied that she knew – she'd looked at his papers. All this went through his mind in the few seconds it took to cross the room.

"David, how nice to see you again. This is Lieutenant Jarvis – David Chandler."

David took her outstretched hand. "Lieutenant Jarvis and I have met before," David replied, "not of course that she would remember such a trivial encounter with a mere would-be cadet."

"I remember it well," she rejoined." "I received a very

professional escort through the hazard of throngs of salacious representatives of His Majesty's forces congregated in Waterloo and Victoria stations, and as I recall you were on your way home to two women, one-your wife and two-a tortoiseshell cat called Susie. Now how's that for a good memory?"

She then noticed there was no answering smile on either David's or Robin's face.

"David, have I said something wrong?"

"You couldn't know, Pat was killed by an enemy fighter on Sandbury aerodrome last November. She was driving a Rotary Club mobile canteen around the perimeter. She and her friend Lady Halton were both killed."

"Oh, David how awful, I really am so sorry."

Robin took charge. "If you go on then David I'll be with you in a moment."

With the usual, "I'll see you later then" to Hilary, David made his way to Room 2. It was a magnificent room. It had been, in fact it still was, the library to the mansion. Whoever had loaned the property to the government had obviously come to some sort of agreement regarding its care and guardianship; its contents David conjectured, being worth a small fortune. It was about thirty feet square, and around twelve feet high. One wall was shelved almost to the ceiling; each shelf containing a mass of leather bound volumes, most of which appeared very old. On the second wall, in the middle of which was the door through which one entered the room, were shelves of more modern works, encyclopaedias and so on, and on the third wall two distinct sections, one containing works of reference in respect of the world of engineering, the second a massive collection of books covering four centuries of art and music. The fourth wall housed a large fireplace on either side of which were large picture windows looking out on to the garden at the rear of the house – well maintained David noted, I bet the army doesn't see to that.

As he stood in the middle of the room taking all this in, Robin rejoined him.

"Robin – you can leave me in here for the rest of the war – please. What a room!! Who on earth was mad enough to allow the common military person access to such surroundings? In most places I've been to which have been requisitioned, the owners have even removed the lamp shades!"

"Ah, well you see David, in this instance as I'm not a common military man they were assured nothing would be disturbed."

"So you are here permanently then?"

"Yes, this station is new, and I am the first commandant. And those are all the questions you're going to get answered on the subject, which won't surprise you."

David grinned.

"Now, they'll be serving supper in a few minutes. After supper come and see me in here and I'll fill you in on a number of details regarding your course, O'Riordan, Hilary and several other matters. The sergeant at the desk will point you in the direction of the dining room."

In fact she didn't need to – Paddy was waiting in the hall. In typical Paddy style he told David he'd done a quick recce of the building after he and a couple of mess waiters had taken David's kit to his room. "I'll sort it out after dinner Sir, so I will." It was a beautiful place, the only concession to its being occupied by men in hobnailed boots being the provision of long thick jute runners in all the corridors and thin protective boards on all stairs except the servants' stairway at the back.

Arranging to meet Paddy in his, David's room after his meeting with Robin, they parted and went off to their respective dining places, in David's case a magnificently corniced room provided with a huge mahogany table which would be capable of accommodating thirty people, and in Paddy's case an even larger deal table in which used to be the 'downstairs' dining room catering for a staff of forty or more. On entering the dining room, Hilary, who was talking to a lofty looking guards major at a small bar in the far corner, came across to meet him and holding his arm announced to the dozen or so people standing chatting whilst they waited for dinner to be served, that this was David who was here for the parachuting course at Ringway. He received the usual quota of nods, smiles and hello's common on this sort of introduction, and assumed that as he was not on an operation he would not be given a pseudonym as he had at Sussex. The others there, with the exception possibly of Hilary Jarvis, about whom he would most certainly be cross-examining Robin later that evening, would know nothing of him, as he would know nothing of them.

A well-prepared dinner was served by polite and efficient A.T.S. staff, during which David was seated between Hilary and the lofty major. As the meal progressed David found the major, despite having the plumiest, most drawling voice he had ever heard, and he had heard a few, and the most immaculately manicured hands he had ever seen on a man, let alone on a soldier, had an extremely droll sense of humour and was in fact a superb conversationalist. The general view about guards officers among the commissioned ranks of the rest of the army was that they were a mixture of 'being there because Daddy got them there' or their great-great-great-grandmother slept with King Charles or some other monarch, and that most of them were too thick to be let loose in any other regiment. It was generally assumed that sergeants ran the guards while the officers ran the nightclubs. All probably scurrilously untrue thought David, grinning as he turned towards Hilary.

"And what are you grinning at?" she asked. The grin froze on his face. Pat had said those very words to him when they were driving along one day with his pal Charlie Crew. He had replied 'Nothing much.' She had then said 'People get put away for grinning at nothing much.' It seemed so long ago and yet it was less than a year.

"I'm sorry – it's just that Pat said those exact words to me a short while before she was killed. I said 'nothing much.' She replied that people in white coats came for people who grin at nothing much, or words to that effect."

Hilary said nothing, put her hand on his arm, and then said, "Poor David."

Dinner over, David said, "Well I must go and see the headmaster in his study – see you later," and with that he made his way to Room 2 wondering what the next hour was going to bring. One or two surprises, I've no doubt, went through his mind. He was not to be disappointed.

Chapter Two

On the 3rd of September 1941, Company Sergeant major Harry Chandler MBE stood on the dockside at Keppel Harbour, Singapore watching the unloading of his unit's vehicles from a large, somewhat rusty tramp steamer. A similar ship was waiting out in the roads to bring in the second batch. Once all the vehicles were ashore they would all move to a new park which had been created for them in the rubber beyond Bukit Timah in the north of the island. And the quicker we get up there the better I'll be pleased, Harry had said to himself. Since landing from their troop ship two weeks ago, his company had been based in Alexandra Barracks, a regular army establishment with more bull than a Chicago stockyard. After a long, and to make matters worse, totally dry voyage from Liverpool, except for a week's stopover in Cape Town – the less said about that the better – the men had gone haywire in the bars, taxi dancing joints and brothels of Singapore, rapidly spending the two months pay due to them after their voyage. These activities had frequently resulted in inevitable punch-ups with all manner of people, service personnel, civilians, military and municipal police, as a result of which he constantly had people unavailable for duty through either being in the nick, waiting to go in the nick, or in some cases having ended up in hospital.

Harry, a quartermaster and two H.Q. N.C.O.'s checked each vehicle as it was off loaded to ensure it had suffered no damage in transit and above all to make sure that all its full complement of ancillary components was present. The slight breeze blowing in off the harbour alleviated only to a small extent the discomfort of working in a temperature way up to the 90° mark with a humidity level approaching that of a Turkish bath most of the time. He was not sorry when the last of the vehicles was swung off, pushed into the holding area and left under guard until the morrow. In common with all service personnel on Singapore Island, he had swiftly learned that everything moveable had to be nailed down to prevent the Chinese nicking it, up to and including 3 ton lorries.

During the two weeks whilst they were awaiting the arrival of their trucks, he had been very busy up at the new depot, allocating living quarters, offices, workshop areas, parking areas, and making a hundred other minor decisions a good company sergeant major does to reduce the load on the company commander. Major Deveson was always available to give an opinion should Harry require one, but in the main was only too happy to let him 'get on with it,' having, in the past, suffered badly from senior N.C.O.'s and sergeant majors who 'wouldn't scratch their arses without first asking me.'

In his spare time, having the use of a motorcycle and the freedom to go from the top of the island to the bottom without let or hindrance, he had explored the island itself, in the north the causeway and palace at Johore Bahru, the jungle and mangrove swamps in the west of Jurong, the grim walls of Changi Jail in the east, and finally in the south, the town of Singapore itself, probably the most fascinating city in the world, the crossroads of the east, Singapura – 'the Lion City,' founded by the Sumatran Prince Parameswara in 1392 shortly to sink into oblivion for 400 years until it was colonised by Stamford Raffles in 1819 to become one of the busiest ports in the world.

In the course of his exploration of this unique island, Harry found himself forming a deep bond with it and the people who lived there. The Malays he saw in the kampongs he rode through on his travels in the back areas were all so friendly, the children immaculately clean, wide eyed and fun loving, the women walked with a grace he never tired of watching and on the occasions upon which he had to stop to study his map, he would immediately be surrounded by a merry throng until the advance of an elder hushed the noise whilst he was directed on his way.

He saw the very best of Singapore, it would never ever be the same again, after being under the heel of the most evil conquerors since Genghis Khan for three and a half years, to be followed over time by the builders of sky scrapers, cross island freeways, industrial parks, shopping malls and convention centres. No longer would you drive through dusty kampongs with chickens scurrying out of the way and children waving happily, soon they would no longer exist. That was the price of economic success, of being one of the four 'Dragons' of the east. But terrible things were to happen to Harry, his comrades and all the other Singaporeans before that transformation came about.

When he got back to Alexandra Barracks late that afternoon, he reported to Major Deveson, and then went on to the sergeant's mess to get some tea before going on to his room to shower and change before the evening meal. He was delighted to find several letters awaiting him. Three were from Megan, mainly chat, a good deal of 'luvvy duvvy' as he always called the more intimate pages, news of the twins Mark and Elizabeth, now nearly four years old, and above all, of the new little one ('or ones – twins run in my family' Megan had said), due in November, and last but not least, news of the Lloyds in Carmarthen, Megan's family. There was a letter from David (that's my ration for another month he said to himself, David never did overdo the writing stakes) and of course the regular weekly letters from his mother and from Ernie Bolton at the factory, keeping him in touch, as far as security allowed, with the happenings at the factory and with his family, wife Anni, baby David, and Karl, his German refugee father-in-law, now released from internment.

The working days followed this same pattern until finally all the trucks arrived. With 160 x 3 tonners, 8 x 15 cwt trucks, four of which fitted up as anti-aircraft vehicles for use in convoys against low flying attackers, 8 motorcycles for convoy control and D.R. work, and finally sundry P.U.'s, recovery vehicles and a mobile workshop all lined up on the new park, all brand spanking new, it was an extremely impressive sight.

"You look a mite serious, sergeant major."

It was Major Deveson. Harry saluted.

"Well Sir, I was thinking what a lovely target it would make for the Jap bombers."

"So you think the Japs might start something?"

"I'm guided by one of my directors back home Sir. He is pretty well up in City and government circles, and there was no doubt in his mind they would join in as soon as they were ready. Perhaps it would have been as well if they hadn't cut all the rubber down to make this an open park, but had cut say every other one down and put the vehicles underneath the canopy of the trees."

"Now you know only too well Mr Chandler, that that sort of thinking doesn't exist in the army book of rules, staff wallahs for the use of. Anyway let's assume that most of the time these blighters will be out working and not present such a beautifully pristine target as they do today." Nevertheless he thought to himself as he walked away, I've struck oil here, a thinking sergeant major, and he's far from being wrong!

The main task for Harry's company was the carriage of loads of four-gallon cans of petrol to the various depots up country. There were two main hazards involved. Firstly the distances. From the park to Kuala Lumpur for example was some 200 miles, and although the roads were very good, convoy speed increased the travel time to around fifteen-sixteen hours, involving an overnight stop. This provided the second hazard, namely how to guard say twenty-odd lorries containing the most enticing of cargoes. It was still peacetime therefore the thought of armed guards shooting at would be thieves was unthinkable. In the main they endeavoured to 'overnight' in military, or in the more remote areas, police compounds. Each convoy had to take an emergency breakdown truck, but again that had to be kept guarded in view of the valuable collection of tools and spares it carried.

One drawback to life Harry found as a C.S.M. was that he had no equals in the company. True, there was a company quartermaster sergeant – C.Q.M.S. – he too was a warrant officer class II as was Harry, but he was so dour that trying to have a conversation with him was like pulling teeth. Harry had given up even before they left England, not that he disliked the man, but having to make a conscious effort to get beyond 'Good morning' proved to be beyond even his undoubted ability in communication skills. The strange thing was the man was married to a really charming looking woman if the photos in his bunk were anything to go by, and had a couple of nice looking kids! This set Harry's mind working as to how he had said enough to get her to fancy him in the first place and secondly whether his demeanour altered at least when he was on the job. 'No, I reckon he must have some hidden talents', was Harry's concluding thought on the subject.

The days rolled by. Once you got used to it the weather was bearable. Harry had a 'boy', in fact a thirty-two-year-old man, all male servants, waiters, and so on of no matter what age, were called 'boy' and though it sounded absurd at first, he soon got used to it. His name was Osman; he had been working for British warrant officers since he was twelve. In a climate where you may well need four or five shirts a day, he was always busy keeping Harry looking as immaculate as a sergeant major should look, and took a personal pride in so doing.

Before he came abroad, Jack Hooper, the 'director' he had referred to when talking to Major Deveson, had asked him, if he had the opportunity, to try and find out whether his first wife was alright. He had no feelings for her any more; after all she had left him and her little six-year-old daughter Pat many years ago for Jack to bring up on his own. On the other hand, he wouldn't want her to be 'in penury' as he put it. She was last known, some years ago to be living in Muar with a planter named Rowlands, a right shit of a man by all accounts, with whom she had decamped. At the end of October, Harry's company had orders to stock a new petrol depot at Muar, which would involve a number of convoys covering the 150 mile journey over the period of nearly a week. Major Deveson suggested that Harry should billet himself up there until the job was finished, along with the company second in command Captain Bailey, and then go on to Kuala Lumpur for a few days well deserved leave. In the event, Captain Bailey went down with dengue fever so the major told Harry to manage on his own, thinking to himself 'he'll do a better job anyway,' he wasn't over-enamoured of his second in command's organisational powers.

Harry settled in at the Rest House in Muar ready for the first convoy to arrive on the morrow. The dump was to be guarded by a detachment of Ghurkhas, so he had no worries on that score, nevertheless when he arrived he made his first job an inspection of the perimeter fencing along with a young second Lieutenant straight from the OCTU at Bangalore, pointing out one or two weak spots which the young subaltern agreed would need to be attended to. As it was late afternoon he wandered past the padang on the edge of which youngsters were playing a knock-about game of cricket, until the road came to a low wall, on the other side of which flowed the River Muar. There was a breeze coming in off the sea just a couple of miles away, it was shady where he was standing, everything was peaceful, even the birds seemed to have taken time off for a late afternoon snooze. In contrast the river, tidal at this point and with it being low tide showing a wide expanse of thick black evil looking mud, flowed sluggishly on its oily, menacing way. He calculated in his mind what time it was back at Sandbury, trying to guess what Megan and the twins would be doing. She would either be on night shift or in bed he concluded. If she was on night shift the twins would be with Nanny at Mr Hooper's place with young John, otherwise... a voice at his elbow broke his reverie.

"Thinking of having a swim sergeant major?"

Harry turned, to see a very well groomed man of about forty he would guess, dressed in a medium grey tropical worsted suit, white shirt and striped tie and wearing a white panama hat. He spoke in a well modulated, cultured voice; in fact Harry's first thought was that he sounded very much like Jack Hooper back in Sandbury.

"Well, Sir, I've seen a few rivers in my time, including the Thames at its filthy worst, but I think this one is the most sinister looking one ever. I certainly wouldn't like to fall in it."

"I agree, you'd be very much advised not to. Of course it looks like this because at this point it drains from the mangrove swamps to the north – they are not among the nicer places to be found." He then noticed Harry's MBE medal ribbon and Mention in Dispatches oak leaf, along with his Jubilee and Coronation medals. "You have a mention. Now you are far too young to have been in the last lot so in which theatre did you get that?"

"I was in the B.E.F. in France from the beginning Sir, and came out at Dunkirk."

"Did you by Jove. Now what's your name, I can't keep calling you sergeant major."

"Chandler, Sir, Harry Chandler."

"I'm Nigel Coates – can I suggest we cut all the 'Sir' business?"

"Well, its second nature in the army to call distinguished looking gentlemen 'Sir' I suppose" replied Harry with a grin, "you never know when they are in mufti that they're not generals or something in disguise."

"You can satisfy yourself I'm not a General, except perhaps a general nuisance to my ever suffering wife. Look' he went on 'if you are free why don't you come and have a drink with us, it will soon be dark. I'd like to talk to you about Dunkirk, my younger brother was there in the Durham Light Infantry, and although I've had a couple of letters from him, he's not exactly the world's best at descriptive writing. My wife and I would like to know more about it."

"Thank you, that is very kind of you," Harry replied, nearly putting the inevitable 'Sir' on the end, but then thinking I wonder what the good lady is going to think when hubby trails a company sergeant major in with him. A captain or a major perhaps would contribute to, even add to the standing of the company, but a sergeant major?

The Coates' house was only a short distance away, a large, well proportioned building with a sweeping drive up to the porticoed front door and having a low stone wall surrounding the property. At the rear Harry glimpsed a row of singly storey dwellings, obviously the living quarters of the household staff, and at the very end a large double garage. This bloke's got a bob or two, thought Harry.

As they approached the front door it was opened by a middle-aged, immaculately clothed Malay servant, who took Nigel's panama and malacca cane, and Harry's service hat. Nigel led the way through the marble tiled hallway into a large drawing room, which, in turn, opened on to a veranda looking out over the padang. As Nigel was saying, "We watch the cricket from here," they were joined by an extremely attractive lady of 'around the forty mark' in Harry's estimation, a young lad of about fifteen and a girl of about thirteen, all three looking newly showered and dressed for the evening.

"Darling, this is Company Sergeant Major Harry Chandler. Harry was at Dunkirk."

Harry studied her face to see if there was any sign of condescension in either her attitude or reply. His previous misgivings were quite dashed when she shook hands firmly, gave a welcoming smile and said, "Welcome to Muar, Mr Chandler. You see I know that sergeant majors are called mister, just like subalterns, because my father was a sergeant major in the Gordon Highlanders in the Great War. Now, these are our children, Oliver and Greta, though I'm afraid we shall be losing them in a few days when they go off to England to school."

"Right now, drinks. Your usual stengah dear? What will you have Harry?"

"Excuse my ignorance – what's a stengah?"

They both smiled. "It's a long drink of a soupcon of whisky filled up with soda water, keeps you from being dehydrated."

"I think then I might prefer a beer if that's possible."

"Not only possible, I'll join you."

The Malay servant, having been given his instructions, returned with the drinks, including lime juice and sodas for the two youngsters, and having settled themselves in comfortable rattan chairs on the veranda, Nigel proposed the good health of their guest. Harry, in turn, thanked them for welcoming him to their beautiful home. None of them could possibly have a thought pass through their minds that in a few short weeks this very house would be the centre point of one of the bitterest and bloodiest battles in the whole of the campaign in Malaya and Singapore.

"Harry, I hope you don't mind our asking you about Dunkirk," Nigel again broached the subject. "In fact, not only for the benefit of Cecely and myself but also for the children, who being out here were quite divorced from it all. I wondered that if you were to tell us about it from your own personal experiences from the time you first went out until you landed back again it will give all of us a clearer picture of exactly what happened there."

"I'll gladly do that, but of course you have to appreciate firstly as a sergeant I was not exactly included in the general staff's planning sessions, secondly I was not a front line fighting soldier, being in the Royal Army Service Corps. However, one of the advantages of being in the RASC is that you do move about a lot, therefore you do get a clearer picture of what is going on than you would possibly as an infantryman in a front line slit trench."

With this introduction he commenced his story of how he was sent first to Le Mans with frequent journeys to the Maginot Line. Then they were moved to Bergue, near Dunkirk, where they were based when the 'phoney war' ended in May 1940. They were then engaged in moving ammunition from Calais up to the British Expeditionary Force reserve dumps, being constantly attacked by enemy aircraft. After Calais was captured 'my brother-in-law was killed there and my brother was one of the few that got away,' he was involved in transporting wounded from the front line back to the dunes at Dunkirk. He had three lorries allocated to him for this job, the rest of the company having been sent back to England. Two of the lorries were put out of action, he being left on his own when the driver of the remaining vehicle became wounded. He was buttonholed by a captain in the Royal Engineers whose vehicle, loaded with explosives to blow two bridges and thus prevent Jerry from getting round the northern flank of the Dunkirk salient, had broken down. They loaded Harry's vehicle with the explosive, blew the first bridge and then moved on to the second where they ran into trouble.

Cecely broke in on the narrative.

"Do forgive me Harry, but dinner is ready to be served. Would you care to join us and then perhaps you could carry on with this fascinating account after the meal."

Thanking her profusely, Harry readily agreed with her suggestion, with the two offspring proclaiming that they be allowed to stay up afterwards to hear the remainder of Mr Chandler's story.

The dinner was an experience which lived on in Harry's memory, particularly during the years soon to come when he had, at times, to live daily on only a tenth of the amount he had tucked away this evening. They started with a delicious duck and yam soup, followed by an individual papaya and crab salad. This was followed by a main course of highly spiced lamb meat balls in a superb curry sauce, served with white rice, and after a short break the meal ended with fresh pineapple soaked in rum and lime juice and covered in whipped cream.

Sitting back enjoying their coffee, the two men sipping a brandy apiece, Harry said, "That was the most memorable meal Mrs Coates, it was superb. Tell me, would it be in order for me to ask you to pass my compliments on to your cook, and to tell him that he is not just a cook – he's an artist."

They all laughed at this, Cecely repeating Harry's comments to the servant. The Malay disappeared into the kitchen and in a short while re-appeared followed by a diminutive, smiling Chinese man of uncertain age but certainly well past the first flush of youth, who bowed three times quickly in succession, turned and hustled back through the kitchen door.

"You realise that Ah Sin will now almost certainly want a rise in wages," laughed Nigel, "now let's hear the rest of this story. You said that at the second bridge you ran into trouble."

Harry described how they were fitting the gelignite on to the girders when they heard something approaching. Because the river banks were high and there was a dog-leg in the road after it went over the bridge, they couldn't see down the road towards Poperinghe. He ran up on the bank to where he had sited a Bren gun, saw two Germans on a motorcycle combination coming towards them stop and callously shoot a single retreating British soldier standing with his hands up. When the combination reached the bend approaching the bridge, He gave them a burst from the Bren. "I acted as judge, jury and executioner," he said. "They deserved it." There was a moment of silence. He then continued saying they were ready to blow the bridge when a Messerschmitt spotted their lorry and fired a long burst at it. The lorry still had explosives and detonators on it, which promptly blew up as the plane flew over it, bringing the plane down. As far as he knew, it was the only instance of a 3 tonner shooting down a Messerschmitt! The captain said that it was all very well but now they had to walk to Dunkirk. Not if I can help it he had replied, ran over the bridge, started the motorbike and brought it back saying, "My Lord, your carriage awaits." Telling him to get clear, the captain then blew the bridge, in the process getting hit on his steel helmet with a lump of metal.

Harry concluded his story with:-

"I loaded the unconscious captain into the sidecar and tied him in. I found a Red Cross flag off my 3 tonner which I stuck in the tube on the sidecar normally used for a Nazi banner, and went back to Dunkirk, picking up a couple of wounded chaps on the way."

At this point Cecely put her hand to her mouth and was about to exclaim something to Nigel, who indicated to her not to say anything.

"Well after that for the next eight days I worked for the major at the casualty clearing station by going out on my motorbike, with Red Cross flag flying I might add – I didn't fancy someone letting off a burst at me thinking I was a Jerry – and on the last day the major ordered me to get in the queue. And that was that."

There was a total and complete silence at the end of the story until Nigel got up, went to a bureau and took a letter from it. "This was from my brother." He began to read.

Dated 14th July 1940. Kent and Canterbury Hospital, Canterbury, Kent.

Dear Nigel

Sorry to have been so long in writing but have had a bit of a rough time just lately. However, I'm recovering well now and able to take short walks with the aid of a simply scrumptious staff nurse who I've asked to marry me several times, so far she's leaving me out of luck. I got wounded in the chest and the M.O. patched me up and pointed me in the direction of Dunkirk saying, "Try and make it old son," and that was that. There were no ambulances and we were under heavy shellfire.

I must have walked for about an hour when I laid back against a bank for a rest. Some shells came over; one hit the pave, a piece of stone thumped into my thigh, and another into my shoulder. I put my field dressing on the thigh, it was bleeding like mad but I could do nothing about the shoulder. I must have passed out for a bit. Anyway I awakened to hear the putt-putting of a motorcycle engine and there in front of me was this German motorbike. I thought oh God, I'm going to be a prisoner of war, but to my astonishment a sergeant in the Service Corps dismounted saying, "Hello Sir, looks as though you could do with a bit of help." With that he took his own field dressing out, sliced my uniform with his clasp knife and bound up my shoulder as best he could to arrest, if not to stop, the bleeding. Another casualty who was riding on the pillion, also with a shoulder wound and with one arm strapped across his chest, got off the pillion and between them they lifted me up and wedged me into the sidecar against a tank corps sergeant who was badly burnt. He then tied us in with a length of rope, and that's the last I remember until I came to in the casualty clearing station on the dunes at Dunkirk. They put me on the urgent queue apparently and I ended up here.

The man saved my life (Nigel commented – he has underlined that) and the terrible thing is I don't even know his name, why a Service Corps sergeant was collecting wounded in the first place, and what the devil he was doing with a German motorcycle combination. I didn't even have the opportunity to thank him. I would have bled to death from the shoulder wound alone if he hadn't got me to the beaches.

Nigel paused, "The rest is just family chat," he said, a noticeable catch in his throat. Harry looked across at Cecely, she was quietly weeping at the emotion of it all, Oliver sat enthralled at this real life drama whereas Greta, after a minute or so of silence, got up from her chair, ran round the table, threw her arms around Harry's neck and kissed him firmly on the cheek.

"That's for saving my darling Uncle James," she cried, which action brought smiles to the faces of the others, and for Harry to jest –

"Well, it looks as though I had one satisfied customer."

"If you did that for eight days how many do you think you saved?" queried Cecely, eyes shining through the tears.

"I truly didn't keep count," Harry answered, "but the RAMC major told me they kept a record and he made it a hundred and ninety two. Some of the journeys were comparatively short, only two or three miles. The sad thing was that nine of those died and were buried in the dunes, or so I was told."

"How did you get back?" It was the first question Oliver had put.

"On HMS Shikari, the last ship away, though how she made it I don't know, there must have been thousands crammed on to her."

There was a silence for quite a while, broken eventually by Cecely telling the two youngsters to get off to bed. At this, Greta ran again to Harry and put her arms round him saying, "You will come and see us again, before we go won't you Mr Chandler?" Giving him another kiss on the cheek, and with Oliver having shaken hands, they went off to their respective rooms.

When they had gone Harry said, "I should get back to the Rest House or they will lock me out."

"I'll come and help you batter the door down if they do," Nigel joked, and continued "now Harry, we're having some people in on Saturday evening for a buffet supper to say goodbye to Cecely and the children before they go off to England on Monday. Do you think you could come? We would like that very much."

Harry accepted the kind invitation saying he would be finished at Muar by Friday night and then intended to go on leave on Sunday to K.L. for four or five days. It would be a very great pleasure to visit their lovely house again. He paused for a moment, "I wonder if you can help me with some information for my father's co-director back in England. His name is Jack Hooper, a real gentleman. His wife left him many years ago. They had a daughter, Pat, who married my brother David. Pat was killed by enemy aircraft last November. Mr Hooper has no feelings for his ex-wife, in fact he is happily married again and has a little boy, but he said he would not like to see her in straightened circumstances."

"Do you know her name?" Cecely asked.

"The chap she went off with was called Rowlands I believe," replied Harry.

"Oh my God," Cecely obviously knew her or knew of her very well. She continued, "To answer your question, she is far from being in straightened circumstances, she is very well off. Rowlands is one of the wealthiest planters in Malaya, but he treats her like a chattel. He is a known womaniser, has households with mistresses in both Singapore and K.L. and as far as we, and most of our friends are concerned, is completely cut, despite his money. Marian comes to see us occasionally, she is a very pleasant woman, she leads a lonely life, but as she has said 'I made my bed, I must lie in it.' She finished vehemently, "He's a first class pig."

Harry apologized for having ended the evening on such an unpleasant topic, which apology they swiftly brushed aside saying they looked forward to seeing him again on Saturday.

In the short walk back to the Rest House, he mulled over the happenings of what was to have been just another ordinary day and which ended up the way it did. If he had possessed an insight into the future he would have known that the next visit to the Coates' home would prove in an entirely different way, even more memorable, and not just for him.

Chapter Three

Just after Paddy and David had left Chandlers Lodge, so named long before the Chandlers moved in, the postman arrived. Ruth met him at the door commenting he was late today, to be told that the Maidstone main office was damaged in the previous day's raid, which delayed the Sandbury area distribution. Sifting through she found no fewer than four letters for Rose. With a knowing little smile on her face she walked back into the kitchen where Rose was feeding Cow and Gate to baby Jeremy.

"Someone's very popular today. Now this first one would appear to be in an artistic hand, probably a tall, elegant, black buttoned person. The second is a bit ink smudged denoting, I would say, perhaps an old Etonian or someone of that breed. Now the next one is written in broad determined unflinching strokes indicating someone of Herculean stature. Lastly, this one is written by someone with a technical background as can be readily seen by the meticulous spacing of the letters. Now am I right or am I right?"

Ruth passed the letters over, but before Rose could answer she continued, "If you had got one from Tim you would have had a full house!"

Rose laughed. "You're only jealous," she joked.

It was now over fifteen months since her darling Jeremy was killed in action at Calais. The letters were from various friends, some, if not all, of whom would like to become more than friends. The 'artistic hand' was Major Mark Laurenson, David's old company commander who had taken her out on occasion and was deeply attached to her. The Old Etonian was Charlie Crew, David's pal at OCTU, whose father Lord Ramsford, was the brigadier commanding the special operations organisation David was now working for. Charlie was young, the grandson of an Earl, and very attached to Rose. The 'Herculean' contender for her affections was Major Ivan Sopwith of the Royal Marines who had been billeted on the Chandlers when he came to teach the Canadian battalion stationed at Sandbury how to use assault boats, and from then on, despite his previous committed bachelorhood, worshipped at her feet. Finally, the technical contender was Ray Osbourne, the captain of the Royal Engineers Harry had worked with on the bridges in France and who had become a great friend of the family. 'Tim' was the colonel commanding the Canadian Infantry battalion stationed locally who had become almost part of the family as a result of two of his majors being billeted on the Chandlers for several months after their first arrival in England. Mark Laurenson was the only active suitor but he had made it clear to Ruth that he respected Rose's situation being newly widowed, and would let time take its course.

That evening after they had finished their Home Guard duties, Jack Hooper and Fred came back to Chandlers Lodge for supper. As usual talk about the war was given reliability and accuracy by the considerable inside knowledge that Jack picked up in his dealings with the top civil servants and others in the City. This evening, whilst Ruth and Rose were in the sitting room talking to a neighbour who had called, Jack said he was very concerned about Japan's movements in the Far East. The Nazis had leaned on Vichy France to allow Japanese forces to occupy strategic bases in Indo China, which meant that warships would be only seven hundred miles from Singapore.

"Not only that," continued Jack, "most people think of Japs being experienced in fighting in the jungle. This is absolute nonsense. They are urban and agricultural people like us. Their fighting in Manchuria and China has virtually all been in open areas, they are no more jungle fighters than we are. You can bet your bottom dollar therefore they are going to use the Indo-China jungle as a training ground for the invasion of Malaya, the Philippines and so on. I'll say no more for now," he said, noticing Ruth and Rose coming towards the kitchen where he and Fred were seated, he had no desire to worry them with such observations.

When Harry was first told he was going to Singapore, Megan had expressed the view, "Well, it's better than going to the desert." No one could have foreseen how dreadfully wrong that sentiment was to turn out.

"Well Jack, how are things in Paddock Wood these days," asked Ruth. Jack's business in the City had been bombed out during the blitz and he had re-established it in the small Kentish town some ten miles away.

"Running itself as usual – they don't really need me except as a frontman to deal with all these insufferable ministry types," laughed Jack. "Do you know, I heard of one ministry chap who applied to run one of the new shadow factories in his particular county. One of his colleagues asked him what he knew about factories to which he seriously replied he was well qualified as he had been involved in the opening ceremony on three separate occasions of similar works."

"Did you read the report on road accidents for last year?" asked Fred. He continued, "There were nearly nine thousand killed in 1940, seventy five per cent of them in the blackout. I can't understand why we can't have a system whereby streetlights are left on until an advance warning of approaching aircraft is given. Nine thousand seems an enormous number when you think how few cars there are on the road."

They talked on for a short while until Jack took his leave. "Back to my lonely couch," as he put it. Moira, his wife, was still in America and not expected back until the end of the year.

"Doesn't the house seem empty to you Ruth," he asked on leaving, "now that you've lost your service people?"

"To be truthful, although I've loved having them for the past eighteen months, it has been a nice break to be on our own for a little while. Now I've said that, the billeting officer will probably be knocking on my door tomorrow morning!"

And sure enough, so he did.

"Good morning major – you're bright and early," Ruth greeted him almost like an old friend now.

"Usual request Mrs Chandler, I've got two Canadian officers who will be working with Colonel McEwan for a few weeks. He hasn't got room for them in his mess apparently so they've got to live out. Can you cope with them? I know you're a Canadian expert."

"Yes of course, when will they be arriving?"

"Tomorrow sometime, but I'll telephone you in the morning, to confirm it" and with the pleasantry that – 'it looks like being a nice day' – he drove off.

Ruth mulled over the thought of getting used to new faces and wondered if these new Canadians would be part of the family as Alec and Jim, both majors in Colonel Tim's battalion, had become. Mrs Cloke, the daily help arrived and between them they soon had the bedrooms ready and on the following morning the promised telephone call from the billeting officer duly informed Ruth that Captains Grant and Lefevre would be arriving around midday. When they arrived, Ruth and Rose were surprised to see that in addition to the Dodge they were travelling in, they were accompanied by a 3 ton lorry.

"I'm Ray Grant," the first officer said, striding towards Ruth with hand outstretched, "and this is Pierre Lefevre," and having been introduced to Rose and seeing their eyes taking in the 3-tonner, "Oh, don't worry, we're not off-loading that here, that's going on to the camp – when we've found the camp that is.

Like Alex Fraser and Jim Napier before them they were totally unalike. Ray was a very stocky red-haired fresh complexioned twenty-five year old, Ruth guessed, whilst Pierre was nearly six feet, slimly built, sallow complexioned with very dark brown hair, about the same age.

They off-loaded their kit, the two drivers carrying it into the hall and having been given directions to the camp by Rose took themselves off.

"Well, they seem nice chaps," Rose declared; "we've been very lucky with the people we've had here. The Australians didn't fit in very much but were no trouble, the others have more or less been family. But, then again, they've been jolly lucky to have landed in such a comfortable berth so I suppose it's a two way thing." She paused, "it's alright mother dear, I'm just having one of my philosophical mornings."

When the newcomers returned that evening they were accompanied by Alex and Jim. "We thought we'd better guide them back," Alex informed them, "you see they're in the Intelligence Corps which means they are almost permanently lost."

"The Intelligence Corps?" queried Rose, "now mother dear, we know why they're here! You see Ray, we were saddled with these two for months, as a result we got to teach them how to speak proper, to do joined up writing and to add up without using their fingers, but we didn't have time to get any further. I assume therefore that you have come to remedy this."

"Well, since they are our superior officers I feel rather constrained in answering that in their presence. Perhaps we can discuss it further later on."

"I agree," said Pierre.

These two are going to fit in nicely Ruth thought to herself.

"You now have a slight inclination of what you are going to have to put up with from this young lady in particular whilst you are here," Jim pronounced, "and in due course you will meet the other members of the family – ah, here's one of them now." Fred appeared from the back porch having put his bicycle away in the garage.

Jim continued, "With a bit of luck we shall all now sample a nectar known as Whitbreads' Light Ale which will appear out of that bottomless cupboard under the stairway."

Fred was duly introduced to the new arrivals, a crate of Jim's 'nectar' was brought from the cupboard and the men all sat around the kitchen table rather more than sampling it. A cry from the sitting room meant that baby Jeremy had wakened; he was therefore brought into the company which he viewed one by one with obvious interest until his eyes lighted on Fred when he burst into a frenzy of chortling and punching the air, struggling to go to his grandfather.

The two captains soon settled in and proved to be as amenable as Alec and Jim had been. The next evening Rose asked, provided it would not land them all in the Tower, if they could explain what the Intelligence Corps did and how it connected with an infantry battalion like Colonel Tim's.

They explained that in general, every battalion had its own intelligence section which analysed air photos of areas of proposed operations, analysed maps and made sand tables indicating the actual topography shown on the map, for the use of the battalion to which they belonged. The Intelligence Corps liased with the battalions in a division, but in the main were concerned with the larger picture. They were required to provide the senior commanders with up to date information about all manner of things so that they, in turn, would be able to make their battle plan.

"Does this mean Colonel McEwan's men will be going into battle then?" asked Rose, her stomach tightening at the thought of Alex, Jim and Tim himself, along with the other officers they had met at mess parties, facing danger.

The two captains exchanged glances trying to arrive at a suitable answer. After a short pause Pierre replied:- "I think it will not be too long before we all go into battle. That, after all, is what we are here for."

In the fifteen months since her beloved Jeremy was killed and her life had been shattered, Rose had gradually regained her old vivacious self, modulated a little perhaps, by motherhood, but assisted by the certain knowledge that Jeremy had not left her but was there, around her, all the time, watching over her, protecting her. She didn't expect others, even her close family, to fully understand this, but she herself knew it for a fact. It was at moments like this when the prospect of others near and dear to her were made to appear insecure that this protection deserted her momentarily. The thought that Charlie, Mark, Tim, Alex, Jim, even her brothers Harry and David would be soon putting their lives in jeopardy was too horrific to contemplate. They had lost Jeremy, they had lost Pat, dear dear Pat, more of a sister to her than many blood sisters are to each other, how could she face the loss of anyone else?

Ruth, realising Rose had naturally associated the talk of battle with her own deep tragedy for ever lying near the surface of her thoughts, broke in:- "I wonder if we could have a little get-together to introduce our new friends to everybody?" and after putting the idea to Fred when he came in from Home Guard duties a little later, it was agreed for Saturday week – "Though what the devil I'm going to give them to eat I don't know," was Ruth's afterthought. She need not have worried too much. Jim and Alex raided their equivalent of a Naafi and brought boxes of crisps, and other nibbles, which combined with vol-au-vents made from non-rationed bits and pieces from their family butcher, toasted bites with indeterminate but nevertheless tasty morsels on them, all washed down mainly with beer, spirits being in short supply, made it a very successful evening. The newcomers were surprised to meet their brigadier there, he being a close friend of the family. It was his wife, Lady Halton, who was with Pat when they were both killed by an enemy aircraft whilst driving their canteen on the local aerodrome. Furthermore they were intrigued at talking to a German, namely Anni's father, whose wife had been killed in Dachau. As had been said before by one of their compatriots, 'this gives us a clearer picture as to why we are here.'

The next morning, Sunday, they were sitting around the big deal table in the kitchen when the telephone rang. Ruth answered it and came back in from the hall saying to Rose, "It's the galloping major."

Rose departed to take the call. When she eventually returned she announced to all present, "Mark sends his kind regards."

Fred turned to Ray.

"Ray, will you repeat, 'Mark sends his kind regards'."

Ray did as requested. Fred continued, "Now Pierre, how long did it take Ray to say 'Mark sends his kind regards.'"

"I should think about five seconds at the most."

Fred again addressed the whole company, "Eighteen and a half minutes he's been pouring his money into the telephone company and all he has said is 'Mark sends his kind regards' – not very good value for money is it?"

"Ah, but Mr Chandler," Pierre began, "you do realise that in a telephone conversation between a male and a female it's not level pegging. By that I mean, as is normally the case in all such discourses, the male part of the equation has difficulty in getting a word in edgeways. So let's take a standard chat. If the fellow gets thirty percent of the action he's lucky. Therefore thirty percent of eighteen minutes is, according to my lightning mental arithmetic about five and a half minutes. If we deduct from that the five seconds for the 'kind regards' palliative, the poor chap had little over five minutes – and in stating that I'm being generous."

"There's a flaw in that argument," Rose responded, "when you go to a theatre you pay to hear someone else speaking. When a gentleman telephones a lady it is roughly the same thing. He pays a call to get away from the brutish male voices constantly around him so as to hear the soft gentle dulcet tones of the fairer sex. They tell me that some men even dial the lady on the speaking clock just to hear a female voice – did you know that?"

"There are some funny people about in that case," was Fred's opinion.

As they were talking Ruth, who had been in the garden picking vegetables for Sunday dinner during this discourse, arrived with Jack, who was joining them for the meal.

"Ruth love – Mark sends his kind regards" from Fred, and then,

"Oh hello Jack – Mark sends his kind regards."

Not being in on the joke they both smiled vaguely at the receipt of the message. Fred followed with, "Do you think we should drop a line to David and Harry and tell them too?"

Rose looked at the two Canadians who were grinning hugely. "Don't you worry," she said, "I'll pay him back."

With that they all sat talking, inevitably about the war. Jack told them he had heard the official figures for air losses in the two years since the war started. The R.A.F. had lost 3087 aircraft of all types. The figures for German losses were a little over 8000, whilst it was estimated they had lost a further 4000 on the Russian front. Both of those last two figures were probably somewhat exaggerated but even if they were, they were still not sustainable.

"We talk of aircraft losses," said Ruth sadly, "what of the people in them, English and German and their families. Oh how I hate this man Hitler."

Chapter Four

David's visit to the 'Headmaster's Study' was most interesting. Robin opened the conversation by saying how pleased he was to be working with David again, asked him if he had seen anything of Brigadier Halton while he was on leave (Robin and the brigadier were at school together), asked after the family, particularly the new baby, and ended the preliminaries with the statement that nothing of David's proposed operation would be gone into at least until Christmas. What the hell do I do in the meantime was David's immediate thought.

"However," he went on, "in the meantime you will be busy. You will carry out your parachuting course, which takes three weeks or so, depending on the weather. You will then have a week's leave. When you return you will have a series of courses designed to equip you to stay alive when you eventually get to your destination. In addition, you and Hilary will be receiving intensive tuition in Swiss-German along with the current social, political, and economic situation in Switzerland. Finally you will receive training in cipher work and in the operation of a short wave radio. Any questions so far?"

"No, except about Hilary."

"I'm coming on to Hilary later."

He then went on to talk about Paddy, who had 'done some jobs in Ireland' while David was on his previous operation in France.

"Paddy did extraordinarily well on the projects I gave him in Ireland. Whilst you are in - wherever it is you may be – I want him to do some more for me. In his previous op he not only found out all I asked him to find out, he also gleaned a couple of nuggets of information I was able to pass on to a certain other department and this information subsequently turned out to be absolutely copper-bottomed. From what he told me I deduced that his intelligence intake did not suffer pro-rata to his alcohol intake as was the case with the people with whom he was having what he called 'a bit of a session.' Suffice it to say he appears to be a natural for work in dockyards and such places."

They both sat grinning at each other at the thought of Paddy drinking some unwitting informant under the table – and being paid for it!

Robin continued. "As a result I would like your opinion as to rewarding him. It occurred to me that the best and most permanent way was to have him promoted to sergeant. That way he would be paid more and have more prestige which would serve the purpose admirably. Can you see any objection to that?"

"The obvious one is I shall probably have to find a new batman –

as far as I know only generals merit sergeants as batmen. The second is that Paddy has had a pathological antipathy to sergeants for the past eighteen years, will he be able to reconcile himself with being one?"

"There's no reason he cannot stay on as your batman. In fact I wouldn't mind betting my next months salary, little though it is, that rather than be a sergeant, he would much rather stay your batman. I see no reason why he can't be both, it's not as though you are in a service battalion and if you ever are, then you can cross that bridge when you come to it."

"I'll put it to him tonight. Incidentally you mentioned betting a months' salary – did you notice that we poor brown jobs, as the R.A.F. wallahs at Highmere call us, only get pay. Class distinction, that's what it is."

They grinned again. Again Robin continued.

"Regarding Hilary. Once you have completed your parachuting courses and leave allowances, you will both study with a Swiss tutor. Hilary will be going with you to Switzerland, where subsequently you will eventually split up. That's as much as I can tell you at the moment in that respect. I have to add that if you both turn out to be duffers in the cipher lark and so on, or jib on the jumps, neither of you will go anywhere. I will bet my salary for the following month that that will not happen."

"I have a strong suspicion that the loss of two months pay, sorry salary, would make little difference to your financial stability," quipped David as he stood up, shook hands and walked back to his room, having first been given an envelope with the lettering 'Sgt. O'Riordan' on the front.

Paddy was sitting in an armchair in David's room as he walked in. He jumped to his feet saying, "Everything's put away Sir, I'll have a bit of pressing to do as soon as I can organise an ironing board, otherwise everything's in good shape."

"Jolly good" replied David, "the only thing is you may possibly not be a batman for much longer."

"Jesus Christ – you're not sending me back to the battalion are you Sir? What about the jumps, I've set my heart on getting a paratrooper's wings! Oh, come on Sir, you're pulling my pisser aren't you Sir? What good would I be back at the battalion, and anyway, how would you manage, you've got to have somebody so why not me. Bloody hell."

"Now don't get your knickers in a twist, it's just that we have a problem," and with that he tossed the envelope to Paddy. Paddy reached into the envelope and pulled out a set of gold and black sergeant's stripes. David resumed his statement 'The powers that be wish to show their appreciation of the sterling work you did in the land of your birth and have, as from six o'clock this evening, promoted you to sergeant. Having reached this exalted rank it was considered it would be beneath your dignity to serve as a batman. If I were a major general it might be a different thing altogether, he would merit a sergeant as batman, but as a humble three pip captain it presents a different picture altogether."

Paddy digested all these arguments but before he could reply David put another point to him, rather slyly, "Of course, when you get married on your next leave, it would be as a sergeant, and of course your new wife would get the marriage allowance of a sergeant."

"Are you saying I can't stay as a batman and be a sergeant at the same time Sir?"

"I'm not saying that at all. We're not attached to a service battalion where it might make a difference. Robin said we could cross that bridge when we come to it."

There was silence for a short while, while Paddy digested all this mayhem.

"In that case Sir, stripes or no bloody stripes I'm staying with you." He paused for a moment, "Won't Mary be surprised – and pleased – and what's more when I pop the question she can't say no to a superior rank can she?" They both laughed heartily "Do you know Sir, I'm bloody glad I got you at Winchester."

"That's mutual Paddy."

"I could have got that Brindlesby-Gore – they told me he was a right miserable ......" he was on the point of doubting that officer's parentage. When David first arrived at the Winchester depot as a new second lieutenant straight from the officer cadet training unit, Paddy had been delegated to look after him. When he left to go to a service battalion, Paddy had asked the depot R.S.M. to be allowed to go with him and he'd been looking after him ever since.

"Right now that's all settled. Tomorrow we start the real business. I fancy we shall have a few bumps and bruises to compare over the next few days." He was not far wrong. "Now, what are your quarters like?"

"I have a room at the top where the skivvies used to be housed." Paddy described it as being light and airy and comfortably furnished with the original civilian bed, wardrobe etc. "Do you know Sir, thousands of Irish girls used to come over here to work in service in these big houses. They had to work hard, they'd always been used to that anyway, but for the first time in their lives they had a clean, comfortable room of their own, sleeping in a bed with sheets, on their own, instead of with one or two or more sisters, good food got for them, and even if the wages were low they must have thought they were in heaven."

"How about if the housekeeper was an old cow or the butler couldn't keep his hands off them, or young Master Herbert crept up the back stairs at night?"

"Well I suppose that was the case sometimes, but generally they had some sort of safety in numbers. All in all, they had a better chance than being stuck in some godforsaken hovel out in the bogs somewhere, or in the Dublin slums."

"Well, all I can say is, don't dream about them when you go to bed tonight – you'll need all your strength tomorrow."

As it happened, the morrow was far from easy. Having been allocated their lockers they were told to join Stick 42, in the main hangar. Stick 42 was commanded by an R.A.F. physical training instructor, a flight sergeant. David's first thought on seeing him was, 'God he looks disgustingly athletic,' and felt immediately a sense of inferiority at his own rather lapsed state of fitness.

There were ten in the stick, all ranks, all sizes, all arms of the service. No Hilary, David thought – I wonder where she is. The flight sergeant explained what was going to happen. Today they would do a short road run (around the airfield actually), followed by some P.T. in the hangar designed to get them loosened up for the more strenuous exercises. The road run turned out to be about five miles, the P.T. lasted nearly an hour, at the end of which most of them had found muscles they had neglected or didn't even know existed. They broke off for the midday meal. In the afternoon they were introduced to the equipment they would start work on the next morning. Slides and chutes similar to those you see in a children's playground but ending about six feet off the floor, parachute harnesses hanging from the roof and again positioned so that the boots of the man suspended would be six feet off the floor, and on the floor, thick coir mats seen in gymnasiums everywhere. David could readily see that his 'bumps and bruises' prophecy was not long to be delayed.

Having examined the various pieces of equipment in this hanger, the instructor took them to an annexe, which had nothing in it except a number of large floor mats. They were told to line up, and were issued with round protective headwear, which tied under the chin. David and Paddy, being old soldiers compared to most of the stick, automatically fell in the centre of the line knowing that if an instructor was going to call someone out to demonstrate something he would usually pick on the one at the end. Not this time.

"Out here please Sir," pointing to David. David walked out. "Back again please Sir, every movement while you are here is carried out at the double." David returned to his place, then returned at the double.

"Right now, I would like you to fall over."

David just stood there, slightly bemused.

"Go on, fall over."

Because it is such an unnatural thing for the mind to initiate and for the body to execute, to purposely fall over is an extremely difficult movement to carry out. From the time you start to walk your whole being is dragooned into staying upright, not to fall over. There is no drill for falling over. If you do fall over, it's by accident not design. What is more, if you do fall over, you often hurt yourself, so falling over is something your body avoids doing at all costs. David could feel the instructor and the squad watching him. He buckled his knees, fell forward on them and put his hands out to take his weight at the conclusion of his fall.

"Thank you Sir, rejoin the squad."

David scrambled up and doubled back to his place.

"Now you've seen what the officer did, and what is natural for anybody to do – go on to your knees and put your hands out to break your fall. That is the last time the officer will ever fall in that manner, none of you will ever fall in that manner," his voice reached a crescendo, "and if you do, I'll send you back to your units."

After a silence, for effect thought David, he began to give them their first lessons in falling over. "I keep my feet together, I keep my knees together, I keep my elbows into my sides (they'll be holding the harness when I land from a jump) and when I land I do this." He made a little jump into the air, landed on both feet and immediately buckled over to the left in a kind of role which transferred his weight rapidly from his feet to the outside of his leg, to his hip, and then his shoulder. "You can see what I've done, I've transferred the force of the impact when I landed, so that the whole of, in this case, the left-hand side of the body, has accepted part of it. Now I'll do it again." He repeated the demonstration. "The golden rule is 'Feet and knees together,' now I want you to shout it out. Ready? 'Feet and knees together.' Terrible, terrible, shout it I said. Ready. 'Feet and knees together.' LOUDER. 'Feet and knees together.'" The stick were now smiling at each other. "Remember that and it will save you a broken leg or worse," he warned them.

Each trainee was then directed to his own mat and told to carry out six landings to the left and six more to the right. When he had completed them, the instructor would come and view his progress. Having had pointed out any failings, real and imaginary, they all found themselves doing another dozen rolls, until most of them, if they had not entirely conquered the reluctance to leave the vertical, at least knew what to do when it happened. Knees, ankles and particularly elbows suffered in the process but at four o'clock they heard the welcome announcement, "That's it for today. 9.15 here tomorrow and we'll have a bash at the chute."

As they walked off to the locker room Paddy confided, "I feel like I've had a punch up in a Bombay brothel with a gang of sailors."

"You and me both," laughed David. "I wonder if Robin has got any Goddard's Embrocation?"

As they spoke, the instructor overtook them. "You know Sir, you and the sergeant here are the two biggest blokes in the stick. It's much harder for the bigger people all the way through this course. Smaller people fall over easier, get through the apertures easier, and land that much lighter. Not that I'm trying to put you off at all!" and saying this he loped off grinning all over his face.

"Cheerful bastard isn't he Sir?"

The next day, after their five mile run and P.T. session, they moved back into the hangar, which housed the slides. Told to do a forward left or forward right landing as he flew off the end of the slide six feet up, David found, gave very little time to think. However, he did remember 'Feet and knees together,' as a result he escaped the verbal chastisement freely given to those who landed like a sack of potatoes. Four o'clock came. It being Friday they were told that on the Monday they would be let loose on the harnesses and learn backward landings. This led an extremely scholarly looking young man from the Royal Signals to observe that he understood Kings Regulations positively forbade torture of any kind, even to one's own soldiers, in reply to which one of his companions reminded him he volunteered for this – with a heavy accent on the 'volunteered.' This was true. Every parachutist or would-be parachutist was a volunteer, but this fact did not lessen the privilege of every self-respecting soldier to moan if he felt like it, even if what he was moaning at was of his own making.

When David arrived back at Wilmslow, the Sergeant at the reception desk called out, "There's a telegram for you Sir." David took it with a degree of trepidation. Telegrams were almost always bearers of bad news. If someone wished to send you a message that quickly it usually signified an emergency, emergencies usually spelt crisis, and crises were rarely events to be looked forward to.

He slit the envelope open and read: AM STAYING AT QUEENS HOTEL STOP. PLEASE COME ON SATURDAY FOR ST. LEGER.

STOP. AND DINNER STOP. HAVE MISSED YOU. PAMELA. TELEPHONE MANCHESTER PICCADILLY 4000. ROOM 410.

Paddy was standing nearby, looking very concerned. He too assumed "telegram = bad news.'

"Any trouble Sir?"

"Quite the contrary Paddy. I've been invited to the races tomorrow and dinner in the evening."

"I'll have to arrange to borrow a P.U. to take you in and pick you up, shouldn't be difficult." Nor was it.

David telephoned the number given and was told Miss Sherbourne would not be arriving until eight o'clock. How then did she know her room number he wondered. He rejoined Paddy.

"You know about this racing lark Paddy. I always thought the St. Leger was run at Doncaster or some such place. I know my brother won a sweepstake before the war when Barham came in first. How then is it that it's now at Manchester? And another thing, where's the racecourse at Manchester?"

Paddy was unable to answer either point but presumed the new venue was 'due to the war,' and continued, "What will you wear Sir?" the age old batman's question.

"I'll talk to Pamela this evening and let you know later."

Paddy's eyebrows raised perceptibly. "Oh, so it's a lady you'll be seeing is it Sir?" His speech was noticeably more Irish.

"I expect her brother will be with her," replied David quite innocently.

"And if he isn't will you be requiring the P.U. tonight Sir, do you think?"

"I don't have that sort of luck." They laughed together.

Later that evening David contacted Pamela. They had first met when David was stationed at Highmere airfield in Norfolk, his company being responsible for guarding this R.A.F. station. Pamela and her brother Reggie owned a beautiful old moated manor house out on the Cromer Road near Aylsham and were very considerable land owners. Since their last meeting they had corresponded regularly, but as David had said to Rose in reply to her teasing him with 'She's struck on you, you know."

"With her wealth and good looks she is probably chased by all the eligible gentry in East Anglia."

"Even if she is, she's still struck on you."

David smiled at the thought of this sisterly observation.

When he at last contacted Pamela she told him she and Reggie were coming for the races. They had no horse in 'the big one,' but Reggie had a horse, which was highly fancied in a novice race, and a miler, which stood a good chance. David said he hadn't realised Reggie was a racing man and was told that he was only in division four in the owners stakes. His horses were trained at Newmarket where he could go and visit them occasionally, but it was more of a hobby than a serious business.

They arranged to meet at The Queens at eleven o'clock, have an early lunch and then go on to the racing. David asked what he should wear and was told 'anything,' so he decided on civvies. Having resolved that, he had the thought that he had no hat. In all the pictures one sees in the Tatler and so on, the obviously affluent devotees of the sport of kings wear an almost uniform trilby-type headgear, never worn on the side of the head, that would be common, but worn slightly forward as if they were guards officers having to look out from under fringes of bearskin. He had left the telephone booth and was standing at the foot of the stairs pondering where he could get such an article when the guards major appeared from the ante-room.

"Hello old boy – lost something?"

David explained his predicament.

"I've a couple in my kit; you can borrow one of those if it suits you."

"You are kind, thank you very much."

They ascended the stairs to the major's room. A first glance at the dressing table provided immediate evidence that major 'X' –

"Do you know major; I don't even know your name."

"Geoffrey – Geoffrey Cheshire, Coldstream Guards, at your service."

"As you probably may have heard, Hilary announced me as David Chandler. I'm City Rifles, and before you say it, yes a black-buttoned mob."

The dressing table David has espied contained silver backed brushes all laid out in the sort of regimental manner one, I suppose, should expect of a guards officer or more probably a guards officer's servant. The silver seemed to be an inch thick, the monograms on each piece beautifully engraved with a coat of arms and initial G.W.B.C., they were obviously not the possessions of someone on the bread line.

"A friend of our family was a Coldstreamer, now a brigadier, Brigadier Halton."

"Halton? My father was with him in the last lot, he always speaks very highly of him, in fact he was the best man at my parents wedding in 1914. He married that ghastly man Oxleas' daughter. She, I recall, is utterly charming.

"I'm afraid she died. She was killed last November by an M.E. 109 along with my wife when they were operating a canteen vehicle on Sandbury air station."

"I didn't know. I was months without news at that time where I was. I really am so dreadfully sorry. Are you coping alright? – Silly question I suppose. How can one fully cope with a tragedy like that, it must take a lifetime. You really do have my sincere condolences."

"Thank you, thank you very much," he paused, and took the trilby, walked over to the dressing table and tried it on, looking at his reflection in the mirror. It was just a trifle small, but the major remarked that wouldn't matter because at the races it is worn to the front of the head, one of the reasons on a windy day why it is not uncommon to see headgear bowling across the greensward.

"Well, if it's at all windy tomorrow I'll make sure I jam it on firmly. Now let me buy you a drink."

"No need to old boy – I've got some here," and he walked to a wardrobe in the bottom of which was a galvanised iron bucket, obviously containing ice, out of which he pulled a bottle of Moet and Chandon. Taking two highly polished fluted glasses from a side cabinet and putting them on the dressing table, he took a cloth and, covering the cork, gently eased it out with just a gentle 'pop.' Having charged the two glasses he handed one to David.

"Your very good health dear boy, and good luck tomorrow."

They sat chatting; the glasses were refilled until the bottle was upended in the bucket. David expressed his thanks again to his host, firstly for the loan of the hat and secondly for the hospitality he had received, then took his leave.

He fell asleep that night wondering what the morrow might bring. Paddy's words about not needing the P.U. back to Wilmslow started him on a flight of fancy. After all, Pamela was twenty-five/twenty six-ish, she could well expect an escort not to leave her on the doorstep, on the other hand if she was struck on him, as Rose had insisted, it could well be that she would not want to give him the impression that she was 'fast.' On the other hand – Christ, here I go again – how many hands have I got?

He came to the conclusion that if he were given the offer he would accept it. On the other hand she might expect him to make the running – oh, bloody hell, go to sleep you silly sod. So he did.

When he met Pamela at The Queens the next morning, having arranged with Paddy to pick him up at 11.30, and with an answer that, 'if you don't turn up by midnight I'll bugger off back to Wilmslow,' he was greeted with this elegantly clad, strikingly good looking young woman throwing her arms round his neck and planting a lingering kiss on him, much to the benign amusement of several prosperous looking middle-aged couples, the standard clientele of The Queens, standing nearby. She held him at arms length.

"You've lost a little weight."

"By the time this parachuting lark is over I've a firm belief I shall have lost a lot more."

"I don't care, it suits you, you look gorgeous."

"Not a fraction as gorgeous as you do, you're an absolute picture." He looked her up and down, "As my friend Charlie Crew would say, you're an absolutely copper-bottomed corker."

"You leave my bottom out of this conversation."

He pulled her to him and gave her a little kiss on the forehead, to the continuing amusement of the aforementioned prosperous looking middle-aged couples.

"Now, we're having an early lunch all laid on in our suite. When we come to Manchester we always have the Lancastrian suite." That's how she knew her room number David decided. They went up in the lift, which they had to operate themselves. "This is a sign of the times," Pamela observed, "When I came here up until a few months ago there was a young man in white gloves who worked this thing."

The suite comprised three rooms. A centre sitting room with a bedroom off to each side. The table was laid up for three, which immediately put a blight on David's romantic aspirations.

"Reggie is having lunch with us and then taking us to the race course. After the meeting he has to go on up to Preston to see some people tomorrow morning. We then go back tomorrow afternoon."

David's romantic aspirations moved into a much higher gear.

Reggie arrived, they had lunch together, all then bundled into a hire car to the races. It was a great afternoon. Thousands of people out to enjoy themselves after a week of long hours and hard work at the dozens of armament and aircraft factories in and around Manchester, along with a nucleus of well fed, extremely well clothed people who obviously had not had to exist on two ounces of butter a week nor clothing coupons enough to provide one suit a year. Finally there were the spivs, flashily dressed, some obviously deserters, thriving on the black market and seemingly able to get away with it, despite their calling being so obvious.

From the time they left the car until they reached their seats,

Pamela held herself close to David's arm. She had looked up at him, "I don't want to lose you in the crowd," she had explained. His aspirations remained at a high level.

They had modest bets on each race. Reggie's novice was disappointing, coming in in the second half of the field, but the miler romped home at 8/1, which recouped their previous losses. The big race, the St. Leger, was won by Lord Portal's 'Sun Castle,' ridden by G. Bridgland, but as none of them had backed it they lost out. It was a lovely day out. As a result of some sort of Mancunian meteorological miracle the sun actually shone all the afternoon, making it a special day whether you won or lost.

"Now we'll find the car, then if you will drop me at Victoria Station I'll catch my train to Preston and you can go on back to the hotel. It's been grand seeing you again David, give my love to Rose. We see quite a bit of Charlie and Mark Laurenson so we do get the news from Sandbury. I think Mark is very struck on Rose, can't say I blame him, I think she's rather gorgeous myself," and with these words Reggie led them off to the car park. David's thoughts were threefold. One, so Rose has yet another admirer. Two, it looks as though my luck's in. Three, Reggie didn't have an overnight bag.

Having dropped Reggie off, they drove back to the city centre. As they cleared the station forecourt David looked at Pamela, smiled and said "Alone at last." She picked up his hand, kissed it lightly and held it close to her breast until they drew up at The Queens.

Chapter Five

Harry was kept extremely busy during the next few days at Muar. Lorry after lorry arrived, each carrying fifty four-gallon cans of petrol, each can so made that one could stack on top of another. The Ghurkhas provided fatigue parties to unload and stack the cans, four high in blocks of around twenty feet by eight, with suitable gaps in between. The dump had been positioned in an area of old rubber so that natural camouflage could be obtained, as Harry had suggested should have been the case in Singapore. However on the first day after his evening meal with Cecely and Nigel, he slipped away after work to a Chinese tailor's shop in Muar centre and was measured for a lightweight suit and half a dozen white shirts. The cutter having cut the cloth, the pieces having been lightly stitched, he went back the next day for a first fitting. This done, he went back the following day for another fitting and finally on the third day received his suit and shirts. A perfect fit ready in three days – that would be considered a miracle in England he said to the smiling tailor, who seemingly spent most of his life sitting cross-legged on the end of the cutting table.

They stacked the last of the petrol cans mid afternoon on the Friday. Harry made a point of thanking each one of the Ghurkha fatigue party for his hard work. Ghurkhas are cheerful, friendly, utterly loyal people, and superb soldiers as the Japanese were to find eventually to their cost. This unit however, in a few short weeks, would be one of the first to meet them, would be overwhelmed, and have all their wounded and prisoners bayoneted to death. The complete unit would no longer exist.

Saturday evening arrived and Harry set off on the short walk to the Coates residence. He was warmly welcomed by Cecely and Nigel and introduced to a number of people whose names he immediately forgot, then found he had a companion holding his arm in the person of thirteen year old Greta.
"Mr Chandler," she began.
"All beautiful young women call me Harry," he joked.
"Do you know lots of beautiful young women then?"
"Thousands, but they'd have to go a long way to compare with you," he replied gallantly.
"Anyway, I thought I might be able to help you remember all their names," she said. "It's always so confusing when you are plunged into a crowd of people for the first time," she paused for a minute, "that is

what is going to happen to me soon." Harry could feel this underlying apprehension, even fear, in the girl's voice.

"I can tell you this with absolute certainty, within half an hour of your arriving at wherever it is you are going,"

"Benenden."

"Right, within half an hour of your arriving at Benenden you will have made at least one friend. Within an hour – two, in a day – a dozen, and you'll wonder what the devil you ever had the wind up about, if you'll excuse my rough soldierly language." She squeezed his arm and planted a light kiss on his cheek.

"You've made me feel better already."

"I do that to all the girls."

They were both laughing at this sally, Greta probably for the first time feeling she was being treated as a grown-up. In the Colonies there was such a strict protocol of behaviour between and within the classes, the wealthy planters and mine owners, the government officials, the railway and utility managers and so on, each knew his or her place in the social scale and accepted or deferred to others above and below his level.

When all the party had arrived, other than the usual couple who were never early – if the party was at 7.30 you put 6.30 on their invitation knowing they would be there by eight o'clock – Nigel rapped on the table with a serving spoon and when hush ensued addressed his guests.

"Ladies and gentlemen. As you know, this is a going away gathering to wish Greta and Oliver Godspeed and our very best wishes to them as they take up residence at Benenden and Sevenoaks respectively." There were hear-hear's and applause from the assembly. "Secondly, to wish a safe journey to Cecely as she travels with them to see they are settled in, in war-torn Britain, and for her safe return in January."

He went on to say how much they would be missed by all their friends, but most of all by him.

"Finally," he continued, "I would like you to meet a new friend, Harry Chandler. Harry has newly arrived here, but previously was in the British expeditionary force in France, and was one of the very last to be evacuated from Dunkirk."

Harry felt very self-conscious at all the eyes upon him, but Greta squeezed his arm even more and, smiling, looked up at him.

"However, during his time there he was not only mentioned in despatches, but his selfless heroism won him an M.B.E. for sustained gallantry."

There was loud applause, which continued for some while.

"That isn't all. One of the nearly two hundred lives he saved was my brother James, who many of you know, and with your permission I will read part of James's letter describing this episode."

He read the passage of the letter describing James being wounded and his being saved by this unknown sergeant. During the reading Cecely again 'had a little weep' as she described it later. So too did several of the guests who knew James well and were caught up in the emotion of it all. Having finished the reading Nigel paused, continuing with, "Ladies and Gentlemen, please raise your glasses and drink a toast to our guest – Harry Chandler."

They all raised their glasses as commanded, followed immediately by long and sustained applause, until one bloody idiot, as Harry later reported to Megan in his next letter home, one bloody idiot called out "Speech, speech," which became a general chorus. The commotion died down as Harry, not normally lost for words, searched for something intelligent to say.

"I suppose I ought to start with 'unaccustomed as I am to public speaking'" he began. There was general amusement at this. "But as a company sergeant major spends a good deal of his time speaking publicly – ever so gently I hasten to add" – more chuckles, "that would not be strictly true. I've spent a good deal of my spare time here getting to know the country and the people. I have formed a profound regard for the gentle, friendly Malays and the industrious Chinese, even if we do get a little peeved sometimes with the latter's habit of nicking anything that isn't nailed down," (more chuckling) "and now this evening I have been introduced to, and been warmly welcomed by you all. I would like to thank Cecely and Nigel for their kindness to me, I shall always remember it, and I would like to thank you all for making me so welcome," and with a little semi-theatrical bow, which again produced chuckles, he signed off. There was loud applause, interrupted by the sounding of an enormous brass gong followed by the announcement from Haji Abdullah, the butler, that 'Supper was served."

During supper many people came up to Harry, most of them giving him an open invitation to call on them at any time he should be back in the district. His pocket gradually filled with cards, but he wondered whether the invitations were, in fact, just buoyed up with the unexpected drama of Nigel's announcement, or whether he would, in fact, be welcomed at 'Surrey House, near Milestone so and so on the Malacca Road,' should he call without warning. Greta must have read his thoughts. "They mean it you know. It is the custom here to give hospitality to travellers and friends. Many people live in very isolated places."

"You mean they would be glad to see even me on a dull day," quipped Harry.

Greta slapped him lightly on his shoulder.

"Now then, can't have you maltreating a poor defenceless soldier," came a hearty voice, "you could get five years in Outram Road for that."

"Uncle Charles, have you met Mr Chandler, I mean Harry."

"Very briefly, earlier on, when the throng arrived."

"Uncle Charles is a judge, so watch your p's and q's. He prides himself on filling up Outram Road, which as you will already know is the big civilian prison in Singapore."

"Ah but you have to do something criminal to get into gaol."

"Not necessarily with Uncle Charles."

The judge was standing listening and smiling at the banter going on between the two. "When you have finished your mendacious allegations young lady I would like a word with Harry. No, you can stay," he added quickly as Greta turned to leave.

"Now, I understand you are going on leave to K.L. tomorrow." Harry nodded. "Well, I have to go to Singapore for the rest of the week and the official car will collect me tomorrow. This means that my syce will be taking my car back to my apartment in K.L. Unless you've any arrangements to the contrary may I suggest he picks you up and that you stay at my apartment during your leave. My syce is John Chea, his brother Mark Chea is my butler and his wife is the housekeeper, so you would be well looked after. John will drive you to see any sights you want to see, and a few more that you would definitely not have seen if I know him. You see, Greta didn't say, but I am Nigel's elder brother, James is my youngest brother, and along with Nigel's family, my ultimate heir. I therefore am deeply in your debt."

Harry was completely taken aback, as he wrote to Megan later; it was a long time since his 'flabber had been so gasted.'

"That really is so very, very kind of you judge. Here I was expecting to hitch a lift on a three tonner and stay in some unknown hotel and I find I am being driven by a chauffeur and living in luxury."

The judge leaned over and whispered in his ear "Yes, and you bloody well deserve it." He stood back. "Right then that's settled. What time will you be off?"

"Would nine o'clock be alright?"

"For the next few days you decide everything and make the order accordingly. As a company sergeant major you will assuredly be an expert at that. So nine o'clock it is."

Cecely joined them. "What are you cooking up Charles?" she asked.

"Harry is going to use my car and stay in the apartment while he's in K.L."

"What a super idea. Mrs Chea is as good a cook as Ah Chin Harry, so you certainly won't go back to Singapore hungry. Now, if you two" (to Greta and Charles) "will excuse me, I want to whisk Harry away for a short while."

She led him across the veranda to a set of doors at right angles to the main part of the building. Pushing open the latticed door she led him into a largish room, obviously Nigel's study. Standing on a carpet in the centre of the marble tiled floor was a tall, slender, elegantly dressed woman, late forties Harry judged. Then with a shock, he instantly knew who it was.

Cecely was obviously a little discomfited as she began, "Harry I wonder if you would be so kind as to have a few words with Marian, I realise it's difficult but…"

Mindful of all the kindness Cecely and her family had shown him he could not, nor would not embarrass her by refusing. To be fair also, he was a little intrigued by this sudden situation, instantly reminding himself however that this was the woman who deserted their lovely Pat.

Cecely made the introduction. "Marian, this is Harry Chandler – Marian Rowlands."

She began to hold out her hand but recognising straight away Harry had no intention of shaking hands with her, immediately suppressed the movement. Cecely turned and left them.

"How can I help you Mrs Rowlands?"

"I wanted to see someone who knew and had spoken to my daughter. When I read in the Times of her death I realised even more what a hideous mess I had made of all our lives."

Harry was silent for a short while. He found it difficult to make up his mind whether to castigate this woman or, in view of her present background, to feel sorry for her. And then a little stab of anger ran through him.

"I've no wish to make you any more upset than you obviously already are. What I cannot understand is how you could leave a beautiful six-year-old child. The amount that child must have suffered long after you left, until in fact she grew up and met my brother, defies all belief. I can understand your being bored with your husband, although as far as I am concerned he is one of the finest men walking this earth. I could even understand if your husband wasn't satisfying you, putting it bluntly, you might want to have an affair on the side. So along comes this Rowlands who presumably does give you what you were missing and off you go. There is still such a thing as duty in this world, and no matter what sort of ecstasy you got with Rowlands; your duty was to your daughter, even if you could conveniently forget your husband. You just indulged yourself and damn everyone else. Perhaps you were just a selfish, self-centred, spoilt, upper class parasite, but you had been married for seven or eight years – you were no teenager, you were well past the irresponsible stage of life. Anyway, I've had my say. I shall report to Mr Hooper that you are in no way on the bread line, and if you've friends like these wonderful people here, you are not alone in the world."

Marian was quietly crying. Harry waited for her to give some sort of answer, but there was none forthcoming. She had spent years presenting herself time and again with exactly those censures with which Harry had just castigated her. She should not have asked to speak to Harry, she should have known that what she had done would be unforgivable in the eyes of the family and friends at Sandbury. At last she regained control and asked Harry quietly, "I have no grown up pictures of Pat. I've no right to ask you this but do you think you could get me one. Believe me, every word you said was true, what I did was terribly wrong and I have paid."

"Tell me, if this Rowlands treats you in the manner in which, I understand, he does why haven't you left him. I am well aware you have your own resources, you are from a wealthy background, why haven't you gone home?"

Again she took some little time in answering.

"I keep hoping everything will change back to the way it was at first."

Harry looked at her incredulously, but made no reply. He took out his wallet and took a postcard sized photograph from one of the divisions. It was of Pat and David on their wedding day. He handed it to her; she looked at it through her tears.

"Thank you, thank you so much," she paused, brushing away her tears with her hand until Harry offered her a handkerchief. She studied the picture closely. "She is so beautiful, David looks a nice boy, oh how much I have missed."

"I'll go back to the other guests Mrs Rowlands. Goodbye," and with that abrupt leave-taking, Harry pushed open the latticed door and rejoined the party. Meeting Cecely on the way he asked, "Will Rowlands be picking her up?"

"Good Lord no, he's probably with his Japanese cronies at his place in K.L."

"Japanese?"

"There are a number of Japanese owned tin mines scattered around his rubber holdings. The owners seem to possess the same sort of alley cat morals he has, that's why they get on so well. Their parties are quite notorious. We get to hear it all through the servant grapevine."

"But doesn't the man realise what the Japanese are up to? What they are occupying Indo-China for? What they have been doing in China?"

"That man thinks only of money and self-gratification. Anyway, to answer your first question one of the guests will take her home. It's not far, about twelve miles."

Harry rejoined the throng and was handed a drink by the judge, who then asked him about the Chandler family, about Sandbury, and the air raids. From time to time other people stopped to listen until a small crowd surrounded them. Harry recounting David's escapades at Calais, the tragic deaths of Jeremy and Pat, the ferocity of the air raids on London and how they spent the weeks before being posted to Singapore clearing up the bomb damage. He was asked whether Londoners' morale was as good as trumpeted in the newspapers, and was able to categorically state that despite the thousands of casualties and mile upon mile of devastation, Londoners' morale was supreme, there was absolutely no talk of defeatism or anything approaching it, there was nothing but cold-blooded anger and hatred of Hitler.

At last people began to drift away. Harry said his goodbyes to the judge, most of the other guests came to him in turn to say goodbye with the inevitable handing over of their card and the invitation to visit them at any time if or when he would next be in Muar. Harry had the great feeling that they all meant it. As someone said to him, "And they all mean it you know, colonial people are like that."

When, at last, he went to say goodbye to his hosts he asked Cecely where she would be staying whilst she was in England, and having been told she had booked lodgings at The Swan in Tunbridge Wells until the end of January, Harry said that she would be within easy travelling distance of Chandlers Lodge at Sandbury, he would tell his mother of all their kindness to him and she would make all three of them very welcome. He added, "Incidentally, how will you travel? I presume by boat from Singapore"

Greta, having re-established herself as the guardian of Harry's left arm excitedly chipped in, "No that's the most exciting part." She went on to tell him, the others amusedly listening to her obvious exhilaration regarding the forthcoming trip, which they were going by aeroplane.

"Daddy booked it a year ago. It's a Short flying boat. They call it the horseshoe route. It takes off from Singapore and goes to Colombo, Karachi, Basra and Cairo then down the Nile to Khartoum, Kampala and on to Durban. It stops at other places of course, but those are the main ones. We change at Kampala and fly west in another Short flying boat to Leopoldville, Lagos in West Africa, then follow the African coast up to Lisbon, again stopping at various places. From Lisbon we fly to Poole in Southern England. Isn't it marvellous?"

"And how long does it take to get to England from here?" asked Harry.

"Around about ten days, depending on the weather and the connection at Kampala being on time. We only fly in daylight of course, at I believe about 10,000 feet so you see lots of interesting things, and they say they even divert to a certain extent to show you any sights just off the direct route."

"So when you've taken off at Singapore you can ask the captain to fly over Nee Soon and I'll wave to you – do you think he'd do that? After all, I'm a bit of a sight don't you think?"

"I think you're lovely," she replied reaching up and planting a kiss on his cheek.

Harry looked at Cecely, raised his eyebrows, she smiled back.

"Well, when you get to England you go and see Megan and tell her that." He paused for a moment, "Just to think I could be back at Sandbury in ten days!"

It would be very very much longer than ten days before Harry saw Sandbury again.

The next morning the judge's syce, John Chea, arrived at the Rest House driving, as Harry later that day described in his letter to Megan, the most magnificent car he had ever had the privilege to travel in. It was a Railton, open-topped at the moment but speedily able to be enclosed with hood and side screens in the event of a downpour. The monsoon peters out in October, they could therefore, if lucky, get away with a dry run to K.L. John loaded Harry's case and travel bag into the rear locker, saw that Harry was about to sit in the front seat and swiftly moved around him opening the rear door so that he was marshalled on to the beautiful leather seats behind the driver. God, I shall have to practise my waving to the crowds at this rate he told himself. They took the coast road out of Muar past mile after mile of paddy fields to Malacca. Here they passed old Portuguese forts, Dutch churches and Hindu temples, honking their way through a veritable shoal of rickshaws and trishaws thronging the ancient city streets. Having negotiated Malacca, without killing at least half a dozen rickshaw coolies who transgressed into the path of the Railton and whose lives were saved only by John's superb and quite unruffled driving skills, they carried on along the coast for a while, then headed inland through mile after mile of rubber plantations to Seremban. As they approached the outskirts of K.L. John indicated a large house lying back off the main road, surrounded by a high wall. The iron front gates were manned by Sikh jaggers, obviously the owner did not intend all and sundry should be able to call upon him without warning.

"Mr Rowlands' residence Sir," John indicated.

"Oh, is it? Thank you John," and then Harry thought why should John associate him with Mr Rowlands? How would he know that I had ever heard of Mr Rowlands? Cecely's phrase flashed through his mind – 'we got to hear it through the servant grapevine.' This colonial servant business seems a bit like the Gestapo he thought. They relied on thousands of informers snooping on family, friends and neighbours. I suppose out here where everything is open, open doors, open windows, open access for servants; nothing is a secret, or very little.

The Railton turned off in the city centre to a quiet road leading to what was obviously a well-to-do suburb. On a curve in the road one hundred yards ahead Harry could see a pair of ornamental iron gates. John sounded his horn twice and flashed his lights at which two jaggers ran out, threw the gates open, the car passed through accompanied by deferential salutes from the two Sikhs, and Harry found himself in front of a substantial building in quite extensive grounds. He alighted, stretched, and thanked John for a very enjoyable drive, during which dialogue a Chinese lady and man appeared, obviously Mr & Mrs Mark Chea. From then on he was treated, as he wrote to Megan and to the folks at Sandbury, like a millionaire. He only had to look thirsty and a drink appeared, the food was superb, he only had to discard a shirt – or anything else – and Mark replaced it with newly laundered apparel. He went out for a day in the Railton to visit the enormous Batu Caves, followed by a drive through the mountains along roads with sheer unguarded precipices on one side. In one or two places they had to wait for half an hour for the 'down' traffic to appear- there would be nowhere in this section that two vehicles could pass so traffic, such as it was, flowed one way for one hour and the other way the next hour. It was an interesting day, at the end of which he was able to shower and swim in the well appointed communal pool of the apartment complex.

He intended to travel back to Singapore by train on the Friday, asking Mark if he could find out the train timings. He was sitting by the pool on the Thursday afternoon when Lucy Chea padded out to him.

"His Honour is on the telephone Sir."

Harry hurried into the apartment. After the usual enquiry, "Everything alright Harry?" the judge asked whether he would like to travel back to Singapore in the Railton. John could then drive him back to Muar on Saturday where he would spend the rest of the weekend. Harry jumped at the chance of, as he told himself, another bash at the Railton. He thanked the judge most profusely and went back to his life of luxury so soon to end when he came down to earth at Nee Soon garrison.

When, on Friday afternoon, the Railton approached the main gate to their company park, Harry was amused to see the guards racing out to lift the barrier and form a line to salute whichever V.I.P. was visiting them. They swept through and up to the Company Office, at the rear of which Harry and the C.Q.M.S. had their fairly spacious quarters. As they did so major Deveson appeared from the company office.

"Good gracious me, chauffeur driven C.S.M.'s – what's the army coming to? Don't tell me, you won it in a poker game, or perhaps you've been giving solace to a rich upcountry widow? Whatever it is you can't resign, as the song goes 'There's no discharge in the war.'"

"I'll tell you the story in a moment Sir," Harry replied, reaching on to the rear seat to extract a rectangular package neatly wrapped, which he handed to John.

"Thank you for all your kindness John. This is a small gift in appreciation of everything you have done."

"I suppose I couldn't have a peep at the engine," Major Deveson asked. Harry looked at John, who nodded vigorously, walked to the off side of the engine compartment, unhooked the spring loaded retaining mechanisms and lifted the hinged bonnet of that side of the compartment to reveal an immaculately clean straight eight cylinder motor of massive proportions. The two soldiers, whose every day was concerned with engines, marvelled at the symmetry and design of the various components making up this engine, surmounted as it was by a heavily chromed rocker cover stretching almost the full length of the engine compartment.

"But how do you get this beautiful machine serviced and maintained?" the major asked John.

"I do it Sir. His Honour sent me to Railton in England to learn."

"You mean to say you went to England just to learn how to service a motor car?"

"Yes, Sir, His Honour very particular man."

"I think he must be." He paused, looking hard again at this superb piece of machinery, and concluded, "You know Mr Chandler, it's a jolly good job the C.O. isn't here, the way he drools over engines he'd have an orgasm."

Laughing, they both shook hands with John who, climbing back into the beautiful car, departed for the city.

Harry followed the major back into the company office, reported the situation at Muar in respect of the dump, followed by the story of meeting Nigel and the coincidence of having had his brother as one of his 'sidecar guests' in France.

"You are, Mr Chandler, what the other ranks call 'a jammy sod.' You go to a backwater like Muar and end up being driven around like the governor himself. Nothing like that would ever happen to me, of that I am quite sure."

The next morning Harry came out on to the parade ground at nine o'clock, hoping he might see the Short flying boat fly over. His luck held. An easterly wind meant the boat had to take off into it, turn and fly back over the island. He looked up and waved; inside he felt a deep pang of envy to think that in a couple of weeks time his friends in that aircraft would, quite possibly, be talking to his nearest and dearest.

Chapter Six

The interior of the Short flying boat, forerunner of the famous Short Sunderland, was luxury itself. Even the covered launch that took the passengers out from the Imperial Airways landing stage to the aircraft was fitted with leather seats, padded leather on anything that stood out horizontally or vertically to prevent precious travellers bumping heads or elbows, and above all everything so immaculately clean as to be almost clinical. The Coates family, after tearful goodbyes to Nigel and the judge at the jetty, settled themselves in what were almost armchairs rather than seats. It was a way of travelling based on the luxury afforded to first class passengers on the great ocean liners, it was a way of travelling which very soon would be a thing of the past until the arrival of the first class lounges of the Jumbos, and even then the food and service would not even begin to compare.

At nine o'clock prompt, the airplane turned into the wind, and with its four engines whipping up the sea into a veritable mist of foam and spray, it roared across the water for what seemed an age to the three first time flyers, until the slapping of the waves on the fuselage was heard no more and gradually they gained height. Looking out Greta could see what looked like hundreds of ships of all types, from Chinese junks to two huge battleships, as the pilot made a gentle one hundred and eighty degree turn to fly back over the island and then to follow the coast north along the straits of Malacca to the first stop at Penang. It was at this point they passed over Nee Soon. Greta could easily see people on the ground and for a few seconds had a clear view of Harry waving from the centre of the parade ground.

"Mummy, there's Harry," she cried. By the time Cecely had leaned across Greta's seat, they were almost too far away to see him, but she did catch a glimpse.

"We must telephone his family after we arrive and let them know he's fit and well, and how very much we took to him," Cecely stated.

Their journey, although broken as it was at the end of each daylight period when they transferred to hotels and land for the night, by the time they reached Kampala was beginning to become wearing. They had to wait for two days at Kampala for the West African flying boat to arrive, and then a further two days whilst a repair was made to the hull caused by its hitting a piece of driftwood (or a crocodile?) on landing. By the time they reached Lagos they were distinctly travel weary, but then had to fly round the bulge of West Africa to Freetown.

When they eventually reached Lisbon they needed no second reminder to put on winter clothing for the remainder of their journey, getting off the aircraft for the short step on to the launch introduced them to a very chilly wind coming off the Atlantic, whipping the Tagus up into miniature waves.

Once they took off from Lisbon they were in a war zone. Life jackets had been issued in case they were forced to ditch by the Luftwaffe operating from airfields on the Atlantic coast of France. The pilot took a circuitous route due west at first and then swung north back towards Cornwall, eventually to land at Poole Harbour in the late afternoon of a murky October day, where they immediately perceived the necessity for thick winter clothing. Both of the youngsters were to suffer over the next few months from poorly heated dormitories and classrooms. It was a severe and sustained culture shock to switch in the matter of a few days some fifty degrees of Fahrenheit.

They stayed overnight at Bournemouth, the next day completing their journey to Tunbridge Wells, where the plan was to rest for a day or so, take Greta on to Benenden, and then install Oliver at Sevenoaks. When they arrived at the Swan at Tunbridge Wells, there was a letter awaiting them, postmarked Sandbury. It was from Ruth, saying they had received a cable from Harry telling them how kind they had been to him. Ruth concluded by saying that, 'as soon as you have got body and soul together after such a journey perhaps you will telephone us, and if there is anything that we can do to smooth your way, please do ask.'

Actually it was Megan who had received the cable, she suggesting that it would be better for Ruth to write since she was always, or nearly always, at home, whereas Megan was on duty or collecting the twins or at Chandlers Lodge – at the moment at any event. At the beginning of December she would be taking maternity leave, her baby being due in February, she would then be spending most of her time at home.

It was Sunday 2nd November 1941 that Chandlers Lodge received a whole string of telephone calls. Firstly, it was Charlie Crew, David's friend, fellow cadet and subsequently fellow subaltern in the Rifles. The battalion was going on leave on Friday, could he come and see them for a couple of days before he went on down to Worcester to his grandfather's estate on the Monday. Ruth had answered the phone and said of course, they would be delighted to see him. Ten minutes later there was a call from Mark Laurenson for Rose. He was going on leave on Friday. Would it be convenient to spend a few days at the Angel in

Sandbury so that he could see her, young Jeremy and the family before he went on to Shrewsbury to see his parents. Of course was the answer along with an offer to book the accommodation with John Tarrant at the Angel. Shortly after that Megan telephoned to say that Ray Osbourne had booked in at the Angel for the weekend and would very much like to see them all. As she said to her mother-in-law, she would offer to put him up at her house but it might make the neighbours talk!! Finally Cecely telephoned and asked if they would like to visit her on Sunday for lunch at Tunbridge Wells. When told of the mass of visitors who would be gathering at Chandlers Lodge, and being earnestly requested to join them – it was less than an hour's journey on the train – she readily agreed saying she was feeling rather lonesome without the children.

That evening Jack came for supper. He and Fred were both wondering why a complete battalion was going on leave, which appeared to be the case in respect of Mark and Charlie's visit. They came to the conclusion this could only mean an overseas posting, since leave in a battalion stationed in the U.K. was done on a rota system so that the battalion had a known strength at any one time, the battalion therefore rarely disappeared as a whole on leave. Rose overhearing this was quite upset.
"Where will they go do you think?" she asked her father.
"I would think, as they are nominally a motor battalion, they would send them to the army in Egypt; they would be of most use there. Knowing the army though, they could end up anywhere."

And so, on the following Sunday 9th November, there was a veritable house full. Luckily Charlie's grandfather had visited his cousin's estate in Scotland two weeks before and sent Ruth his customary box of grouse, venison and hares. With these subsidising her usual provisions she was able to use her normal rations to provide a buffet lunch, a task which would have defeated most people as more than one guest remarked. Cecely arrived at eleven o'clock, met at the station by Jack. He took advantage of the time spent in the short journey to Chandlers Lodge to tell her that he had had a letter from Harry describing the interview with Marian, thanking her for arranging it and requesting that there should be no further mention of the subject. Cecely fully agreed. She was warmly welcomed by the whole party, each asking after Harry, what did he look like, was he brown, how did he manage with all the creepy-crawlies which he always hated until every kernel of knowledge of Harry Chandler was extracted from her.

After lunch Rose asked Mark if he would care to stroll in the garden with her, baby Jeremy having been put down for his afternoon nap. The garden, as a garden, it should be said was no longer a nice rectangular lawn surrounded by herbaceous borders, but a flat expanse of vegetable patches, interspersed with narrow footpaths upon which it was difficult to walk side by side without being very close together. In addition, because one would not like to overbalance and inadvertently step on some of Mr Chandler's carrots, turnips et al, it became necessary for the male escort to place his arm around his companion's waist. They walked in this manner for a minute or two in silence until Rose looked up and said, "Are you going to Egypt?"

"Who gave you that idea?"

"Are you going to Egypt?"

"We are going away, I can't tell you where/"

"You are going abroad?"

"Yes."

Rose couldn't bring herself to say any more for the moment. She had known for some time now that she was in love with Mark but had that ever present nightmare feeling that he too might be snatched away as her darling Jeremy had been. She began quietly to cry. Mark led her into the little spinney in the far corner of the property, took her in his arms and just held her close for long minutes until eventually she quietened.

"Will David be going with you? And Charlie?"

"Charlie yes, David no, he has his own job to do," he continued, "Rose, I've loved you since our first conversation on the telephone before David went to France. I fell in love with you without even seeing you – that must be something a little out of the ordinary. And when I met you and your little boy I knew my original feelings, or instincts, or whatever it was were absolutely accurate, there is nothing in this world I want but to look after and love you and your son all my days. What I am trying to say is, will you marry me?"

Rose pressed her face into his tunic. She had known he would probably ask her during this visit. Over and over in her mind she had wrestled with which answer she would give. She couldn't get over what she considered would be the wrench of parting from her true love Jeremy, for she knew that even though his spirit would always be with her, she have to devote all her love and allegiance to her new husband, it would be deceitful not to do so. For his part, Mark fully appreciated her dilemma, he was a highly intelligent man who realised that the conflict of loyalties within her would be so terribly difficult for her to reconcile. His instinct was to try and persuade her to his way of thinking, but prudence prevailed and his sounder judgement in keeping silent proved to be the wiser path. After a while she looked up at him through the glistening traces of her tears and just whispered

"Yes."

He said nothing, kissed her gently and then held her close for long, long minutes.

"When do we tell everybody?"

Rose thought for a moment. "Since everybody, or almost everybody other than your family is here, I suppose there is no time like the present. But let us be practical. When do you go away?"

"In a little over a month. I would like to take you and Jeremy to meet my family next week. We could see Cannon Rosser tomorrow about a special licence and have the wedding say two weeks today. I know that is rushing you and under normal circumstances that would be the last thing I would want to do, but as everyone keeps telling me – 'there's a war on!'"

She took his hand, kissing it lightly, and softly said, "I'll be all I can be to you."

"I know my love, I know."

They walked back to the house through the kitchen door. Fortune favoured them in that Ruth and Fred were the only ones there. Rose looked up and said, "Shall I tell them or will you?"

Ruth had no need to be told. She ran to them both as Mark was about to delegate the announcement to his future bride, while Fred stood back, his immediate thoughts centring on the fact that his dear, beautiful daughter was again pledging her happiness in someone who very shortly would probably be leading troops into battle. If she became widowed for the second time who knows how her reason would suffer. Looking at Ruth and the young couple smiling, excited, thinking only of the moment, he brushed his fears aside and joined them with the down to earth statement, addressed to Mark, "Well, you had better come into the sitting room and tell everybody."

The announcement from the tall elegant major was simple and to the point. "I have the incredible privilege to announce to you that I am engaged to be married to Rose. As my unit is to be posted overseas in the not too distant future, I shall be seeking a special licence in the hope that our wedding will take place in two weeks, Saturday 22nd." There was silence for a moment or two. Mark continued quickly, "As we say in the army – message ends." There was then absolute hubbub, everyone crowding around to congratulate the couple.

Charlie, Ray and Tim, although each in his own way crestfallen by the announcement, were among the first to reach them, with Charlie being his usual cheery self saying, "Knowing him as I do, I don't know whether to offer congratulations or condolences," and then very softly to Rose, "Don't worry, I'll look after him," and it came to pass, as the Good Book says, that one day he did, nearly at the expense of his own life.

"We must telephone David to make sure he can be here," Ruth reminded Fred, her brain going into overdrive thinking of all the things there were to do in such a short space of time. The interview with Cannon Rosser provided no problems; Mark took Rose and Jeremy to his parents who welcomed them with open arms. They would only have five days for their honeymoon. All the coast resorts down as far as Cornwall were closed to civilian entry except resident pass holders, so it was decided they would spend it, since the bombing was, at least for the time being, no problem, in London. This left the decision as to what was to happen to Jeremy.

"Quite simple," pronounced Mark, "as he will then be my stepson he will come with us and I shall hire a Norland nanny to look after him when we go out in the evening and at night. During the day we shall look after him."

Mother and daughter looked at each other with amused surprise. Ruth broke the short silence. "You are taking your baby on your honeymoon?"

"We'll get to know each other that way."

There was really no answer to that piece of illogical logic. The fact that a nine-month-old baby would get to know somebody was arguable, although others would say there could be a 'bonding' take place, whatever that might mean. The second aspect was whether a nine-month-old baby would have any memory of this bonding in the months, possibly years to come, when his stepfather was no longer there. Well, thought Ruth, there are far more important things to worry about than that, the baby will go on the honeymoon! So that's that. In the event, it was a very sound move proving to Rose they were a family and that Jeremy was not just being accepted because he happened to be there. They had one or two embarrassing moments of course at first when well-meaning strangers remarked how much he took after his father, but they soon learnt to take it in their combined stride.

Rose had been a little apprehensive at meeting Mark's parents. She need not have been. Both she and Jeremy instantly captivated them, added to which they were beginning to get a little concerned that Mark was 'leaving it a little late to find someone nice.' Another cause of apprehension on Rose's part was the duty of appraising Rita and Buffy she intended to remarry. Again her unease was unnecessary. They had a long telephone conversation in the course of which both her parents-in-law wished her every happiness, being very complimentary about Mark, who although they had only met him once thought he was a most cultivated man. However, when the telephone conversation had ended and Rita and Buffy sat in front of the log fire, each preoccupied with the news they had just received, they simultaneously broke the silence with almost identical utterances – "God, I hope nothing happens to him." It was probably that many others that evening were harbouring the same fear, some things would doubtless be impossible to bear and in the view of many that would be one of them. In the midst of happiness there was anxiety, at a time of joy there was foreboding. War is a terrible thing in many ways.

Chapter Seven

Paddy waited at the Queens until ten minutes past twelve when, with a conspiratorial grin, he decided that it was highly unlikely that David would be requiring his services that evening. "Good luck to you my son," he announced to the windscreen of the P.U., which apart from misting up momentarily, said nothing in reply.

When David and Pamela had arrived back at the hotel there was no question of there being a lack of understanding nor strategy on the part of either of them. Pamela alighted from the hire car, strode across the reception hall to the lift, which was open, waited for David to catch up, pushed the button and away they went. When they reached their floor, she took his hand, led him to the Lancastrian suite, opened the door, hung the 'Do Not Disturb' sign on the outside, threw the key on to the wall table, drew the black out curtains, turned, walked to him, put her arms around him and, pressing herself hard against him whispered, "We have twelve lovely hours."

Pamela was, to say the least, an enthusiastic lover. She was ardent, vigorous, wholehearted, a sexual athlete in fact, but not in a wanton way. She enjoyed this coupling, it was not a means to an end, she was happy making love, very very happy. Every part of it, the touching, the caressing, the kissing, the exertion, the holding back and the letting go, it was all pure pleasure. Nor was she selfish. She played with David in a shameless unrestrained way without appearing anything but teasing and impish. David responding in a combination of simulated barbarity combined with tantalizing slow spells, making her almost scream with impatience and to sink her nails into him in desperation at being so tormented. It was around three o'clock before they eventually sunk into each other's arms falling into the sleep of the utterly exhausted. That did not prevent their waking again at first light renewing their pleasure, re-awaking with the clock telling them it was a quarter past ten. Pamela stretched her lissom body, pushed the sheet back from David as he lay on his back beside her and looked at him from top to toe, lightly running her fingers over him. "I didn't realize that Kent bred such magnificent stallions," she said, then laughingly rolled over him on to the carpet, ran to the bathroom, set the shower flowing, reappeared with half her naked body showing round the door frame saying, "Coming in?"

The shower took a little longer than a normal shower should take, even for two people. Pamela insisting that she soap David all over, in the process taking more time at some parts than at others. This inevitably led to the types of exercises not normally conducted in a shower and which required a certain amount of dexterity in their performance. Eventually they dried themselves, dressed and stood facing each other in the centre of the room. As they looked into each other's eyes they both saw happiness there. It was Pamela who started laughing, it was immediately contagious, they held each other close and laughed and laughed revelling in the pleasure they had given each other. At last Pamela held her companion at arms length. "May I suggest I call room service for breakfast Mr Chandler, sorry, Captain Chandler?"

"What an excellent idea Miss Sherborne."

And so she did.

Paddy collected David soon after midday, driving the first few hundred yards in silence. Unable to restrain himself further he said, all much too casually, "Did you have a good evening Sir?"

"You know bloody well I must have done you nosey s…s…s…sergeant. All I will tell you, since I am a gentleman, is that if I complete one of those five miles tomorrow morning it will be an absolute miracle, a triumph of mind over body. I will say no more."

"You don't have to Sir, its written deep in the bags under your eyes, so it is."

As this, David grabbed the rear mirror turning it to him. There was, of course, no such evidence, Paddy laughing his head off as he readjusted the mirror.

There were, in fact, no more runs. On the Monday they spent the day being suspended six feet off the ground in parachute harness, being swung backwards, forwards, sideways and in circles, then being released at any point, falling to the mat to instinctively know which way to roll over. They all suffered bumps and bruises, one member of the stick being unfortunate enough to break a wrist, which reduced them to nine. The next day they practised exits from the hole in the floor of a mocked-up Witley. At first they did this without parachute packs on, but after the midday break they were issued with dummy packs. Wearing these they found exiting to be a very different kettle of fish.

The problems involved in exiting through a hole in the floor of the aircraft are these. Firstly the hole is only just big enough to allow the passage of a biggish paratrooper, such as David or Paddy, complete with a large parachute pack weighing something like thirty pounds, protruding some 10-12 inches at the back. Secondly it is necessary to sit in the hole before jumping as there is no headroom to enable the person jumping to stand up and 'feet first' through it. The procedure therefore is as follows. You climb into the fuselage and sit on the floor of the aircraft. You then shuffle along on your backside until you come to the hole. When you come to the hole you swing your legs into space and sit very upright. On the command 'Go' you push yourself upwards and forwards and immediately adopt the soldiers position of 'attention' – that is, head up, chin in, hands clasped firmly to the seams of the trousers, body completely rigid. Now what happens if you fail to adopt this course of action? If you fail to push upwards and outwards enough, the bottom of the parachute pack catches on the side of the hole, tilts you forward, as a result your nose makes unwelcome and very painful contact with the other side of the hole. This is known in the trade as 'Ringing the bell,' and was the reason for many early paratroopers before the days of walking out of doors, ending their parachuting course looking like prizefighters. Assuming you pushed upwards and outwards correctly, but gave too much push, you again, because of the lack of space, rang the bell. If you pushed harder with one hand than the other and exited successfully you could well be in trouble because you had started yourself spinning which would be magnified a hundred times the second you hit the slip stream from the engines. The rigging lines of the parachute would get entangled giving you a much faster rate of descent than normal and a much heavier landing. In the worst scenario the chute would not open properly at all, leaving you to be scraped up and taken away. This latter event was known as a Roman Candle.

After a number of near misses to their respective nasal organs, David and Paddy were making very creditable exits. The instructor came over to them as they stood watching others in the stick.

"Enjoying it now Sir, are we?" he asked.

"Flight, I've been a service man long enough to know that when an instructor comes up to you with an angelic look and asks a simple question like that you can guess he's got something pretty bloody diabolical lined up to take the smile off your face. Am I right or am I right?"

"Oh I wouldn't exactly say that Sir. I just thought you might like to know that tomorrow morning you're on the fan."

"This is where I begin to wish I'd never heard of such a stupid pursuit as jumping out of airplanes."

"Me too Sir," agreed Paddy, and added to the world in general one of the soldiers prayers, "Mother – sell the pig and buy me out."

The instructor wandered off leaving the two riflemen staring after him.

"Have you noticed that he always comes and tells us all the bad news, not the others? When he relishes in the gory bits it's usually to us," David ruminated.

"Well Sir, what it is, is this. Tonight he'll be able to go into the sergeant's mess and tell his mates he put the shits up that officer today. If he went in and told them he'd put the shits up a lance corporal there would be no kudos in that, but putting the shits up a captain puts him in division one."

"He didn't put the shits up me," protested David.

"Well you surprise me there Sir. I had to move round to the windward side of you after he told you, that I do know."

"Cheeky bugger."

Their conversation was interrupted by the instructor bellowing that was all for today, with an instruction to report to Hangar 5 in the morning, to experience the delights of 'the fan.'

"Look, the sadistic bugger's drooling all down his chops," Paddy observed.

As he made the remark to David the subject of his none too complimentary remark came towards them spouting cheerily, "See you in the morning then Sir, have a good night's sleep."

David did, in fact, have a good night's sleep, partially due it must be said to his not having fully overcome the lassitude attributable to his nocturnal activities over the weekend. He woke up to a realization that today was the day upon which he could very well disgrace himself. He knew he would do what he had to do even if it killed him, but whether he would be socially acceptable in a crowd afterwards he had considerable doubts. The problem was compounded by the fact that they had not yet actually seen the fan. They knew its reputation, that it was more horrific than actually jumping out of a Witley, but not having actually seen the bastard gave it added dread. Comforting himself with the thought that by this time tomorrow it would all be over he went downstairs for breakfast.

As they were driving to Ringway, Lance corporal Dudley, the young A.T.S. driver allocated to them, looked across to David and asked, "Sir, is that right you're on the fan today?"

"By God, bad news travels fast – but yes, we are."

"Sir, did you leave me anything in your will?"

"Paddy, will you deal with this young lady – when she's not driving of course."

"Well Sir, seeing as how I'm spoken for you might say, I don't think I can help you there. On the other hand there must be other people we know who have had good practice at it lately."

"I'll ignore that remark. Anyway," (to the lance corporal) "I don't know what all the fuss is about. If those lunatic instructors can do it, certainly two of His Majesty's riflemen can – probably twice as well."

"Well, all I can do is wish you the both the best of luck Sir, and will hopefully collect you at four o'clock. If you're not around by 4.30 I'll come on over to the Sale Military Hospital, they take all the casualties there."

"What's your first name corporal?"

"Amanda, Sir."

"Lance Corporal Amanda Dudley, be advised, you are on my payback list immediately behind that sadistic blasted instructor."

"I shall wonder all day what my punishment could possibly be," she said cheerily, as she delivered them to Hangar Five.

They joined the remainder of their stick already assembled, and waited for their instructor to arrive. David noticed that there was very little backchat going on, everyone was obviously feeling a certain dread at the forthcoming final stage of his ground training, each probably wondering why the hell he had volunteered in the first place, even the stick joker – there is one in every stick – was strangely quiet.

"No one deserted," came a far too cheery voice from their mentor as he appeared through the nearby side door. Each gave a sheepish grin.

Paddy whispered to David, "If I meet him out one night he'll laugh the other side of his kisser, he will."

They were taken to the far end of the hangar where they got their first sight of the monster they had been led to fear – except that it did not look particularly fearful. It comprised a wooden builder's type ladder fixed to the end wall running up for around fifty feet David calculated, into the apex of the roof. A platform probably about twelve feet square had been constructed at that point which, in addition to giving space for those about to use this instrument of torture along with the demon instructor, also housed what looked like a large centrifugal fan from which a wire ran over a pulley at high level back to the platform. At the end of this wire was a parachute harness.

The suffering therefore was threefold. Firstly you had to climb vertically up a ladder, which was fitted with no safety loops whatsoever, for fifty feet. You then had to step off the ladder on to the platform. Finally you had to put the harness on and step off into thin air fifty feet from the hanger floor and rely on the belief that as you fell faster and faster the fan would act as an air brake and slow you up before you hit that little tiny mat you could just discern from the platform before you jumped.

David had always maintained that standing on a chair to put a light bulb in gave him vertigo. He was now being faced with a fifty feet climb up a ladder! The coming down in the harness held no great worries for him, trusting as he did in the fact that it must work; so many people had done it before him. But the climbing up was a personal thing, it gave him a cold sweat to think he might get half way and be stuck – unable to go up or down – what the hell would they do then, and how would he explain to everybody he had failed his course because he was unable to climb a bloody ladder? He didn't know it, but it had happened a number of times in the past, once to the extent of having to get the R.A.F. fire brigade people to literally rescue a would be paratrooper so paralysed with fright half way up he had to be put into a bosun's chair arrangement and lowered to the ground.

"I reckon this alone should earn us our wings, Sir, so I do," came Paddy's voice at his elbow.

"All I can say is you'd better start standing on the windward side again pretty sharpish," replied David.

"Now, gather round," called their tormentor. "I am going to go up to the platform, put on the harness and jump. There are two good reasons that you are able to do this. One, when you get up in the balloon in the next day or so for your first proper jump, you will look down from a far greater height than you will in here, but it won't feel any different to jumping in here. Secondly, and most important, this jump from the fan will teach you to have implicit faith in the equipment. You are to jump into thin air with only a wire attached to you, but because you have absolute trust in your instructors and the people who make the equipment you use, you will KNOW that you will land safely. Provided you keep your?"

"Feet and knees together," they all shouted.

"Louder."

"Feet and knees together," they yelled.

The little homily and the bellowed chorus did what it was intended to do. It reduced, even if it did not totally dispel, the tension, and it got the would-be paratroopers laughing where before they were definitely po-faced, as David's friend Charlie Crew would have described them.

The flight sergeant turned and faced the ladder. "When you go up, take it steadily, and follow the sailor's maxim of one hand for you and one for the ship. In other words don't try and rush it." With that he scaled the ladder to the platform, buckled on the harness, stepped off at attention into thin air, hurtled to the ground for the first twenty five feet than rapidly having the speed of his descent retarded by the air brake, he hit the mat and rolled over.

"There you are – nothing to it. You going to be first Sir?"

David had known all along this would happen. There was no way this deranged inquisitor, this moronic torturer, this, this, this bloody R.A.F. wallah would forgo the extreme pleasure of seeing an officer with the wind up, a pleasure he had been anticipating for the past couple of days. When I go he'll have a blooming orgasm thought David. Nevertheless he replied, "I am so glad you asked me, flight, I was so hoping you would."

The flight sergeant re-climbed the ladder to the platform, David following him. During the whole of the ascent he stared steadfastly at the brickwork of the wall in front of him, looking neither up nor down until he found his head and shoulders level with the platform.

"Keep climbing Sir, until you can step off easily," which David did, noticing that the instructor kept a firm grip on his arm as he did so.

"He doesn't want me to go arse over tip after all," David thought. Swiftly the harness was strapped on.

"When I say, 'Go' you step off at attention and then get ready for landing Sir – right?"

"Right flight."

David looked down. Fifty feet was a long drop. He saw the upturned faces of his fellow trainees with Paddy holding his arm up and giving the 'thumbs up' to him. He saw that tiny square of matting upon which he was supposed to land and roll over. Then he heard the explosive command 'Go.' He stepped forward, plummeted like a stone, felt a restraining pull on his harness, looked for the mat, saw it hurtling up at him, hit it, did an extremely professional forward right roll, and it was all over. Paddy ran forward to unfasten the harness; David got to his feet, dramatically dusted himself down, looked at the stick and said,

"Piece of cake, gentlemen, piece of cake."

The fact that his knees were still trembling was not, fortunately, noticeable to his audience.

They each had a second go during the morning. Before they broke for the midday meal they were told they would be taken for a ride in a Witley bomber the next morning, just to get them used to the noise and being buffeted about. After lunch today they would be given a tour to watch the 'Waafs' packing parachutes. "And I warn you don't make licentious remarks to them or you may find a pile of dirty laundry in your parachute pack when you jump," the flight sergeant added.

One member of the stick was heard to ask, "What does licentious mean?"

The flight the next day was uneventful. For most of them it was the first time they had been airborne. It was noisy, bumpy (purposefully so David thought, so that the instructor would know who, if any, would be prone to airsickness), and totally blind for most of them - only the ones nearest to the hole in the floor could see anything, there were no windows in the fuselage. David was reminded of his two flights in the Lysander, which led to his thinking of 'Sophie' with whom he was flown out of France. He smiled to himself as he remembered she was airsick all over his trousers. I wonder where Sophie is now he asked himself.

They landed with a bit of a bump, at which they bounced a little, sitting, as they were, unsecured on the floor of the plane. The instructor gathered them together remarking that would probably be the only time they would land in an aeroplane and secondly they could have the rest of the day free, the weather looked good for tomorrow so with a bit of luck they might get one or two balloon jumps in.

That evening David telephoned Maria Schultz. Maria was the sister of one of David's comrades at Calais who sadly was killed in the vicious battle for that city. They had been out together during David's previous leaves and he was very fond of her. When he left to come to Ringway she had given him a small golliwog, from which, as a child, she would never be parted, as a good luck charm to carry whenever he jumped. Its efficacy was to be tested on the morrow most likely. When he was eventually connected Mister Schultz excitedly answered the telephone.

"David, how wonderful to hear from you. Now tell me how is your jumping course going? You have not had any injuries or accidents or anything. You are quite well I hope. We have talked about you every day, wondering what you were doing; or rather what they were making you do." David let him go on. Mr and Mrs Schultz had been so grateful to him for helping them over the loss of Cedric, their son, that they would have raised a statue to David Chandler had they been allowed. Eventually his spate of words slowed until he concluded, "But you will want to speak to Maria – she's almost pulling the receiver out of my hand as it is!"

"Thank you Mr Schultz, and please give my kindest regards to Mrs Schultz." There was a short delay.

"David, how lovely of you to telephone. I've been wondering how you've been getting on." At hearing her voice, David had a surge of affection for this serene, charming, graceful girl. She had made it obvious to all at Sandbury that she was 'very taken by our David,' as Ruth had expressed it to Jack Hooper along with the rest of the Chandler family after her visit to them during David's leave.

"Well, the news thus far is that purgatory is without doubt an easier place to endure than Ringway. Our instructor is a rival to Old Nick himself, and the bumps and bruises all over my anatomy are testament to his pathological ability to get the utmost pleasure from other people's suffering. Apart from that I'm absolutely fine."

Maria laughed and laughed. David continued, "However, weather permitting, tomorrow is the first day that my talisman will be put to the test."

"You are jumping tomorrow?"

"Yes, twice probably if the weather holds."

There was a pause. A concerned voice continued with, "You will take care won't you David, dear David."

"You can count on it. Now, I haven't got a name for my golly, and it occurred to me that if the intrepid chap is going to jump he ought at least to have a name. Any suggestions?"

"I just called him Golly – I suppose most children do. Could I call him Cedric, or do you think that might not be right?"

"Cedric would have been fully in agreement with that, so Cedric he is. Tomorrow I will get identity discs stamped out to put under his jacket, and sometime tomorrow Cedric and I will take to the air." He said all this light heartedly though the saying of it brought the collywobbles back into the pit of his stomach at the thought of launching himself into space.

"David, dear, will you telephone me again tomorrow to let me know how it went?" The fearful note had crept back into her voice again, "Or I will telephone you if that is more convenient."

"No, I will ring you – and don't worry – everyone tells me it's a piece of cake!" He rang off, saying to himself, "I wish I could believe the blighters though!"

Friday morning dawned fine and a little misty, but soon cleared to provide a beautiful, calm autumn day. The stick, along with two others, was bundled on to a three-tonner to be taken out to Tatton Park on the road to Chester to where the captive balloon with its suspended basket was awaiting them.

The flight sergeant gathered them together, supervised the fitting of their parachutes so that they were as comfortable as was possible, and in particular the straps did not impede the free movement of your wedding tackle. "You don't want to get that crushed, you may need it sometime," said the flight sergeant. He continued, "Now, you are going to experience the second greatest thrill of a man's life – good luck to all of you." He turned to David.

"As you were first on the fan you will be last to jump," the instructor told David. Why is it, David thought, I can't believe he is doing me a favour? The instructor continued, "So I reckon your sergeant can show them the way down, don't you?"

The jumping platform was a box arrangement with sides some four feet high, the floor having a hole in it the exact size of the Witley exit. Five men and the instructor piled into it standing round the edges of the hole, hanging on to the sides. Gradually the balloon was released. There was a little breeze at about two hundred feet, which drifted it away from its operating vehicle causing it to sway a fraction. The faces of the men in it showed the different feelings they were experiencing at a point in their lives where there was no going back. One tight-lipped, another smiling excitedly, another seemingly more interested in the view than what he was about to accomplish, yet another looking decidedly unhappy with his present situation, and regarding them all the instructor watching each one carefully so as to accurately describe their reactions in his report which would follow them to whichever unit they would be posted.

After reaching seven hundred feet their ascent halted. With the balloon swaying gently, the instructor said to Paddy, "Now remember all you've been taught Paddy, let me hook you up." This he did with Paddy thinking, 'who the bloody hell said he can call me Paddy?' "Right now, sit in the hole." Paddy did as instructed. "Now when I say go, you go - OK?"

"Yes flight."

"Right, GO."

Paddy made a textbook exit, the chute opened; he hung on to his harness and executed a creditable backward landing some four hundred yards from the point where David and the remainder were standing. In turn numbers two, three, and four, jumped and joined him. There then seemed to be a delay before number five should have emerged through the hole. At last the instructor leaned over the side of the box and yelled "Winch her down" – number five had jibbed, despite all his training, the simulation of jumping, and particularly the frightfulness of 'the fan' he had jibbed when the moment of truth arrived. As soon as the box reached ground level he was whisked away – there was obviously a long standing drill to cater for this emergency – the stick never saw him again. The stick was now down to eight.

"Right in you get," the instructor ordered. They piled in, a couple of them looking a little strained at knowing one of their number had refused to jump. They noted that the instructor himself had strapped a parachute on and would be jumping with them.

"How many jumps have you done flight?" one of the young squaddies asked.

"This will be one hundred and fifteen my son," the instructor replied, "so you can see there's nothing to it." David could not quite follow the logic of that remark, except that it was meant to reassure the would-be paratroopers after their witnessing a refusal.

They reached seven hundred feet and the balloon swayed a little in the breeze. "Who's going first?" asked the flight sergeant. One young soldier immediately volunteered, his action being immediately noted in the instructor's mind for inclusion in his report. The first three made their exits leaving just David and the instructor.

"Right Sir, you OK?"

"Yes, ready to go." David then had the surprise of his life. Before he could move the flight sergeant said, "You know the drill – see you down there," and with that just stepped through the hole, leaving David speechless and terribly alone in a swaying balloon seven hundred feet above Tatton Park. He quickly gathered his wits, sat on the edge of the hole, did everything he had been taught in casting himself into space and found himself falling and falling. It is only around three seconds before the parachute opens, but it feels like a lifetime. Eventually the chute billowed above him. He felt a great surge of exhilaration, immediately studied the ground below, particularly the smoke generator which showed him which way the wind was blowing, landing with a thump that momentarily knocked the breath out of him. The flight sergeant ran over. "We do that to all the officers," he said, grinning widely.

"One day one will forget King's Regulations and knock your bloody block off," was David's reply.

"He'd have to be good," came the laughing response, "I got a bronze medal in the British boxing team in the '36 Olympics."

David gathered his parachute up thinking 'what do you have to do to put one over on these sods!' He smiled back with good grace.

"Tell me Sir, all these bods here are Parachute Regiment draftees. What are you and Paddy here for may I ask?"

"You can ask, flight, but I'm afraid I can't give you an answer."

"I thought so. Well bloody good luck to the pair of you whatever you're up to."

"Thanks – I'll pass that on to Paddy."

They got their second jump in that afternoon, again from the balloon. The wind had freshened somewhat, which made the landing heavier, but it was astonishing how they all took it in their strides, rolling over like seasoned paratroopers, proving the benefit of all those bumps and bruises acquired in the hangars.

At the end of the day the flight sergeant told them that again, weather permitting, they would do another balloon drop on Monday, a night jump from the balloon on Monday night, and then four jumps from the Witley during the week. If the weather held they would all be fully fledged paratroopers by next weekend, would be presented with their wings, and be sent on leave. They all kept their fingers crossed for fine weather over the next week, but it was not to work out quite as they had hoped.

Chapter Eight

Time passed fairly quickly for Harry during the next few weeks despite the fact that most of it was spent in his office. Major Deveson had managed to get his second in command promoted sideways on to divisional staff where, as he confided to Harry, "He'll be as useless as all the others there." He was replaced by a young, energetic, newly promoted captain, who just loved dashing around the countryside, thereby leaving Harry to carry out the serious work of running the unit. One of their lorries was stolen. The driver had stopped to have a quick pee, left the engine running and seconds later when he came back, there it was – gone.

"How the hell can they steal a lorry and get away with it on a small island like Singapore?" Harry asked the police inspector from Bukit Timah station. The permanent road block at the Johore Causeway had been notified so that it would be unlikely to get on to the mainland, particularly as it would be driven by a civilian – "Unless they paid a squaddie to do it," suggested the Inspector, "Then they might get away with it." He continued by saying that in his opinion the superstructure would all by now be stripped and a new shape of body, radiator cover and front bumper fitted so that it would take very close examination to establish its origin, and even then with every single identifying number removed or filed off it would be impossible to trace it back to Harry's company.

"If you only knew the paperwork this is going to give me," he complained to a totally unsympathetic Inspector. "I've got a court of inquiry to prepare and the adjutant has dumped the court martial papers for the driver on to me. I've got to indent for a new vehicle and that requires half a ream of foolscap forms."

"I tell you what we'll do," was the reply. "I'll get all my paperwork, and you bundle up your paperwork, and we'll have a nice bonfire out on the parade ground. After all, you are never going to see that bloody truck again so that seems the neatest way to finalise the matter. Oh, and by the way, do I get an invite to the execution of the driver – I presume he will be executed after all the trouble he's caused us – why couldn't he have peed up against the offside rear wheel like all civilised drivers instead of going into the bushes, then none of this would have happened?"

"If he had been a Jap driver that's probably what would happen to him," suggested Harry.

"You sound as though you think we might get to know more about the Japs in the not too distant future."

"Well, you've been here more years that I have," Harry seriously replied, "and I've no doubt you hear things that I don't. It is now the beginning of November. There is no doubt in my mind that when they are ready, they will come, and frankly I'll bet my next month's pay they are ready now."

The inspector looked at him quizzically.

"I doubt if there are more than half a dozen people in the top echelons of government, army, navy or police, who would give a ha'porth of credence to what you have just said."

"And what about you?"

"I and a number of people in the middle strata of control and authority here believe exactly as you do and are doing all we can to prepare. The top brass have all got their heads so far into the sand that you can look straight up their backsides. Anyway, I'll be off. By the way, how are you fixed tonight? We've got a little party on, not just police, civilians and a couple of navy chaps as well – like to come along? I think you might find it interesting."

Harry immediately accepted the kind invitation and having established the time and whereabouts of the get-together, shook hands with the inspector and saw him to his car, driven, he noticed, by an immaculately turned out Malay constable.

As he put on his fourth clean tunic of the day he reflected on the fact that sometimes you meet someone, male or female, with whom you immediately strike an accord (like with Megan he thought, only that was not striking an accord, that was like being hammered in the guts with a piece of four by two. He grinned to himself at the memory of his first seeing her when he had visited young David in hospital). The inspector epitomised the vast majority of decent British officials who carried the burden of administering and policing the colonies efficiently and fairly without thought of vast rewards. He looked as though he could handle himself if he was in bother, too, Harry judged.

Arriving at the police sports pavilion on the outskirts of Singapore city, he gave his name to the Chinese sergeant at the door and was immediately ushered in to be greeted by Robbie Stewart, the inspector, and taken to a tall distinguished looking man, mid forties, Harry guessed, in civilian clothes.

"Harry, this is Superintendent Hollis."

After the usual introductory small talk, the superintendent gave Harry a penetrating look, followed by, "I've heard about you, you saved the life of young James Coates I believe?" Harry looked at him in total astonishment. "It's alright, Judge Coates and I are very old friends, in fact he and I were after the same girl at one time, but neither of us got her I'm sad to say."

"Sir," Harry began.

"No Sirs here Harry, you'll find out why in a short while. My name is Clive. I'm the nominal boss if you like, but that's as far as it goes."

A trifle mystified by this reply, Harry kept his own counsel concluding all would, in due course, be revealed. He had not long to wait. Robbie called for silence and proceeded to address the fifteen or so men present, most in their early to late twenties Harry guessed. He started by saying the super wished to say a few words. There was instant attention from all.

"I want to introduce Harry Chandler to you. He was decorated for his bravery before Dunkirk. I had a strong recommendation from on high that he would be exactly the type we would want, he has had first hand experience of killing Germans, in particular he has had experience in the demolition of bridges, an accomplishment which we lack. I recommend him to you."

Robbie continued with, "May we have your approval?" Immediately every listener raised an arm. He turned to Harry indicating he should follow him and the super to a side room, whilst two Royal Navy people, a sub-lieutenant and a chief petty officer started to unpack a largish plywood case. The meeting in the side room was brief and to the point.

The Super said, "The Japs will be attacking us soon. We know only too well the disgraceful state of the defences in Malaya generally. Unlike the government and service chiefs here we are convinced there is no possibility of our being able to contain them. As a result, six groups like us have prepared positions in the jungle at intervals along the mountain range that runs more or less down the spine of the country. Only Robbie and I know, other than the Chinese, who are already there, where our camp is and we do not know where the other camps are. The purpose of these camps will be to operate guerrilla warfare against the occupation forces. As a soldier you will have to obey your superiors, as I know you would, until such time as you are surrendered. You will then do everything in your power, with our help, to get to the camp. If you decide you do not want to take part you may say so now and no ill will will be thought of you."

The seriousness of all this preparation, the brutal manner in which the military situation had been put to him, the calibre of the people he had met who were endeavouring to think further ahead than the block-heads in Fort Canning, all induced him to answer without irresolution of any description – "Count me in." Later the problems he could envisage in deciding when it would be right for him to forsake his unit and join the new force presented him with a deal of heart-searching. 'It will have to be played by ear,' he told himself, which is the age old phrase with which people assure themselves when they have no idea whatsoever of what to do anyway.

They returned to the main room to see the contents from the plywood case being removed. It was a bicycle frame, no wheels, fitted with a stabilising support on each side to enable a pedalist, if there is such a word, to turn a large pulley, which in turn operated a generator, which again in turn gave power to a wireless receiver/transmitter. They were told that C.P.O. Martin and Mr Rogers had designed and built the equipment in secrecy in an annex to the wireless telegraphy hut at the naval dockyard, and was to be taken to the camp at the weekend. Harry reflected that these people certainly knew what they were doing and what a disgrace it was that the powers that be in the government in London and the colonial blockheads in the peninsula itself had not got a fraction of their foresight. The trouble was that for two hundred years Malaya had slipped into a lethargy that could not contemplate, let alone act on, the possibility of war. Next to India it was the cream of postings for government and service people of all ranks, an opportunity to live in the kind of luxury they would never be able to enjoy elsewhere or at home, and which they could not envisage could ever be disturbed. This was despite the fact that General Dobbie, G.O.C. Malaya in 1938 and 1939 after carrying out exercises on the peninsula had not only reported that contrary to general belief, the Japanese, if they attacked, would attack Singapore, since they would be unable to get through the Malayan jungle, could in fact land on the eastern seaboard at the frontier with Siam. A further point he made was that this would be particularly possible during the monsoon of October to March when air reconnaissance would be difficult on the R.A.F.'s part because of poor visibility. He even pinpointed the exact spots where the Japs could land and where eventually they did make their landings! No notice was taken, the government spent £60,000 on building more machine gun emplacements on the south side of Singapore Island and that was that. The situation then in November 1941 was that the governor and service chiefs had been given clear warnings of what could happen to them as far back as 1938 and were still carrying on a peace time routine of wearing collars and ties at their offices and dressing for dinner in the evenings, living literally in a fool's paradise.

Harry drove back to his quarters that night, his head full of the events that had occurred since he had awakened that morning. His thoughts darted from one set of circumstances to another, the culmination of which caused him to say out loud, "What the bloody hell have I let myself in for?" Perhaps they could all be wrong about the Japs. Perhaps they would think twice about attacking the British Empire. On balance, he considered the latter to be wishful thinking.

He met the group three more times before the balloon went up. On the 2nd of December he went into Singapore town to see the mighty battleship 'Prince of Wales' and battle-cruiser 'Repulse,' lying in the roads. An aircraft carrier, which should have joined them, had run aground in Jamaica and was under repair. This absence proved fatal, capital ships without air cover are sitting ducks.

Whilst in Singapore, Harry posted a letter by airmail to his father, but instead of addressing it to Chandlers Lodge, he sent it to the factory, marked 'Strictly Private.' He had thought hard about sending it, coming to the conclusion should hostilities not commence, no harm would be done, on the other hand if war broke out and he survived fighting the Japs, managing to get away to the camp, his family would hear nothing of him perhaps for a very long time. He wrote:-

Dear Dad

This is a bit of a cryptic letter, but I know you can read between the lines. If hostilities break out here you may not hear from me for some considerable time. Assure the family no news is good news and when I am able, I will contact you. I shall be doing a sort of 'David.'

Yours
Harry

He took the airmail letter into the main post office asking an extraordinarily pretty Chinese girl when it would be despatched, receiving the answer, "You're just in time, the mail will go to the flying boat in about an hour." He was very lucky; only one more flight left Singapore before the Japs struck.

And strike they did. There was no declaration of war. In the early hours of the eighth of December 1941, they landed at the three beaches at which General Dobbie had prophesised they would, two in Siam and one in Malaya, at Khota Bharu. Simultaneously their forces struck Pearl Harbour and against the American land forces in the Philippines, despite the fact their diplomats were still negotiating in Washington about oil sanctions and other matters. They met strong resistance at

Khota Bharu from British and Indian troops and were held on the beaches. General Percival telephoned the governor, Sir Shenton Thomas, giving him the information regarding the Khota Bharu landings. Sir Shenton's reply was, "Well, I suppose you'll shove the little men off."

At 3am the duty officer burst into Harry's room shouting, "It's started, they've landed up north." Harry jumped out of bed, pulled his trousers on, stuck his feet into his boots and ran to the bugler's room.
"Sound the general alarm," he ordered.
There was then the incongruous figure of a six foot tall soldier of the Royal Army Service Corps clad only in a vest, which barely reached his navel, blowing the age old army call to arms.
"Da da da da da da daaaa" interpreted by the rank and file as, "Bang your balls against the wall."

After a few minutes fully clad and carrying personal weapons, over two hundred men had assembled on the parade ground. Harry reported to the major there were a few absentees and suggested they disperse the vehicles, at present drawn up in neat lines – a gift of a target for enemy bombers when it got light. Major Deveson told him to go ahead. Harry immediately detailed the vehicle maintenance section to cut four large holes in the wire fence which separated them from a small, neighbouring rubber plantation, then asking the junior officers to disperse their sections at certain points in the plantation, was satisfied the company presented a great deal less of a target than it had before. He reported back to the major.

At 4am Major Deveson was called to divisional headquarters. It was still dark but as he drove towards Singapore City he was astonished to see all the street lamps on, advertising signs lit up, and public buildings, hospitals etc, not blacked out. His surprise turned to anger at the stupidity of the authorities as over the sound of the engine of the P.U. in which he was being driven, he heard the throb, throb, throb, of heavy aircraft engines overhead and seconds after the scream of bombs. Most of the bombs fell in the Chinese quarter a couple of miles ahead, the major and his driver taking cover in a monsoon ditch – not the nicest place to be as you never know what sort of reptilian company with which you are going to come into contact. There were two hundred casualties in this first raid, mainly Chinese – there would be many more to come.

Harry heard the aircraft and immediately got his company

headquarters staff digging trenches – no such things as air raid shelters had been considered necessary. All around the camp the officers were doing the same thing. At least they had plenty of tools. Each vehicle carried its own shovel designed to dig it out should it get stuck at any time.

"When in doubt, brew up," Harry said to no one in particular just as it got light, then called to the Company clerk to do exactly that. He switched the radio on to try and glean the up-to-date news, when to his astonishment, his office door burst open and a large, red faced civilian almost ran in.

"Who the hell are you?" Harry roared. "Ransomes, what's this civilian doing here?" The clerk came running in.

"I tried to stop him Sir, but he just pushed me over." Ransomes was rubbing his ribs, which had obviously made contact with some immoveable object.

"I own the plantation next door. What the bloody hell do you mean by parking your lorries there – you could damage the trees. In fact I saw a couple had been damaged, and you'll have to pay you know – I'll see to that."

Harry looked at him with a mixture of contained fury and total disbelief. He remained silent for a short while.

"Well? What have you got to say?"

"What I have to say, you gormless slob, is that very soon you are going to have to fight for that plantation, if it's not bombed to bits that is beforehand. So sod off out of my sight or I'll have you put in the guardroom until the police get here. You and your property will be under military orders from now on and those vehicles will stay there under cover until I get orders to move them into action."

The planter started to bluster until Harry, in a voice of thunder, shouted, "Sod off." He turned and went.

Harry heard him saying, "I'll talk to the general about this." What Harry said in reply could not be found in a lexicon of polite conversation. Reflecting afterwards he could see it was symptomatic of the ingrained attitude of the planters and business people toward the soldiery. Apart from the governor they were the aristocrats of the society, they were the people who produced the wealth of the country, rubber and tin, as a result they expected to be deferred to, particularly by the military.

At nine o'clock major Deveson returned, grim faced.

"I have never been to a military order group in all my army career," he began, "to compare with the shambles I have just witnessed. What it all boils down to is that this company has to be split. One half to join 11th Div at Ipoh, the other half to be attached to the 8th Australian division. Headquarters will remain here. Get the "O" group in will you Mr Chandler."

The officers assembled and were given their tasks, being told to be ready to move in twenty four hours. When they had gone to organise their men and vehicles, Harry asked the major, "Sir, I've not seen or heard of where our tanks are."

"The simple reason for that Mr Chandler is that apparently there is not a single bloody British tank in the whole of Malaya. The Japs are landing with tanks and not only do we not have one miserable armoured vehicle to fight them with, but we have no bomber planes to bomb them with, and the Brewster Buffalo aircraft we have are so inferior to the Jap Zero that they will be lucky to last a week. One other piece of cheerful information I gleaned is that we have hardly any anti-tank guns, and the machine gun units are only a third up to strength. Apart from that, all would appear to be absolutely one hundred per cent." He sank back in his chair and mopped his brow. "I tell you this, sergeant major, someone should be hung, drawn and quartered if the small amount I have learnt this morning is true, and I'm pretty sure I don't know a tenth of it."

He was right. The nine-tenths he knew nothing of included such items as:- all the navy planes were being flown out to Java and on to Australia. The complete navy base was to be evacuated. The main trunk road from the invasion point to Singapore 250 miles long, which the Japs must use as the axis of their advance, contained some 250 bridges, each of which was a potential defence point. Not one had been prepared for demolition. There were no defences whatsoever on the causeway side of Singapore Island. Six of the thirteen British battalions Percival had to fight the Japs, had come straight off the ships and were virtually all young untrained recruits.

And so the list continues. Percival's boss was an R.A.F. man – Brooke-Popham. What did he know about land warfare? Yet he was in charge. We had been at war for two years against Germany and Italy – the government and the general staff had obviously learnt absolutely nothing. Their combined ineptitude beggars belief.

The next two days were frenetic for Harry, getting the trucks checked out; armament issued to the men and, in particular, to the anti aircraft vehicles, which would travel with the convoys. Sorting out the sick, lame and lazy, although to be fair, they were few in number, it was a good company with a fair proportion of regulars in it, but in any unit there were always a few dodgers. The problem was, when you were going to confront unknown perils, whether it was best to let the dodgers dodge, or to force them to face the dangers with all the others. Harry had no doubts. 'Medicine and Duty' was hinted to the M.O., who conveniently obliged, followed by a word in the ear of their respective sergeants or corporals to keep a very strict eye on them.

And so on 10th December the company split up, never again to be a unit. With virtually all the vehicles gone, the place was strangely quiet, unless you could accept the continual bombing of the city ten miles away. They did not bomb the naval base – they would want to use that.

That afternoon Harry decided to visit Robbie at Bukit Timah, having to shelter twice during the short journey. Robbie was very pleased to see him and was able to give him a piece of vital information. "Your rendezvous permit is the 96 milestone near Sulong, south east of Muar. Opposite the milestone there is a small track, running alongside the river. Two miles along there you will be met."

"How will whoever is meeting me know when, and for that matter if, I am coming?" asked a mystified Harry.

"There will be sentries there at all times, they will know who you are."

Harry was a long time getting to sleep that night. It was two weeks to Christmas. He wondered, if he saw this Christmas, whether he would see any after that. He cheered himself with the thought that when he first arrived he had gone to Robinson's in the city and purchased Christmas presents for all the family along with a case of tinned pineapples and another of peaches. The assistant who dealt with him had taken his cheque on his English bank without demur, calculating the pound equivalent for him. When Harry asked him whether he required identification he had almost thrown up his hands in horror at the thought of insulting a customer in that manner. Thinking about it later, Harry concluded they wouldn't be so daft as to put the goods on a ship without clearing the cheque at the local branch first, ending his thoughts on the matter with 'and neither would I!!'

And so he went to sleep while the Japs continued to pour down the main trunk road and the western coastal roads. They did not have it all their own way, but in the main, the first few days showed a degree of disorganisation on the part of the commanding generals it would be impossible to comprehend. This communicated itself very speedily to the troops and this, combined with the drenching monsoon rain hour after hour, their inability to find a place to stop and set up a proper defence, all reduced morale to zero. An army in retreat soon becomes a rabble; this army was rapidly assuming that description.

Chapter Nine

When they awoke on the Monday after the week in which they had made their first two balloon jumps, David and Paddy were seized with exactly the same conclusion – there would be no jumping today. In fact Paddy, sleeping up in the attic, had been forewarned by being awakened by the furious slapping of a tree branch on the roof nearby indicating 'a fair old blow' as he put it to David later. Needless to say, like all old soldiers, having identified the cause of the interruption to his slumbers, he promptly turned over and went back to sleep again. Nevertheless, they journeyed to Ringway to be met by the flight sergeant who reluctantly had to tell them the 'Met' people had informed unit HQ that the storm currently raging would, in fact, increase in intensity over the next few days and that winds were expected in excess of 50 mph or more.

"My experience is that even if those winds terminate in the next four days or so it usually takes another couple of days for things to settle sufficiently to be able to jump, so I can't see you getting airborne again this week."

The instructor's fears were not only well founded, the winds along with torrential rain stretched into the second week so that it was the second week in October before, once again, they were driven out to Tatton Park to do their third balloon jump in daylight, followed at eight o'clock with their first experience of jumping in the dark. During the enforced idleness caused by the foul weather, they had all been kept in trim by the P.T. staff, rehearsing over and over landing from the chutes etc, as well as exiting from the Witley mock-ups. In between, the future 'Para' boys had picked up some of the new regiment's songs, the first of which David was to hear on the 3-tonner going out to Tatton Park, sung roughly to the tune of 'Knees up Mother Brown.'

When first I came to Ringway, my Colonel he advised,
Take lots and lots of underwear. You'll need it I surmise,
But I replied by Gad Sir, whatever may befall
I'll always keep my trousers clean when jumping through the hole.

There were many verses. David asked the instructor whether he knew who composed these songs, to which he replied that no one seemed to know – they sort of evolved.

Another, to the tune of John Brown's Body had innumerable verses, including:-

> I'd like to find the Sergeant who forgot to hook me up,
> I'd like to find the Sergeant who forgot to hook me up,
> I'd like to find the Sergeant who forgot to hook me up,
> 'Cos I ain't going to jump no more.
>
> Glory, glory what a helleva way to die,
> Glory, glory what a helleva way to die,
> Glory, glory what a helleva way to die,
> 'Cos I ain't going to jump no more.

They scraped me off the tarmac like a lump of strawberry jam.
And so on, to 'Glory, glory.'

Other verses about Waafs putting their 'knickers in my chute,' and so on, all ending with 'Glory, glory' bolstered up the esprit de corps, fired up the feeling of being 'special,' and was greatly encouraged by all the training staff. Other songs, too lewd to print, included one about a father who 'kept a shotgun for a paratrooper far far away,' another about 'eagles flying high in Mobile,' it was all great fun, shortening the time when you had to face the serious business of hurling yourself into space.

David's day balloon jump was uneventful. He had a little chat with Cedric before he tucked him inside his Dennison smock, the camouflaged garment the paratroopers wore over their uniforms. When they were first issued considerable amusement was generated by the fact that it had a tail piece, which hung down and was then pulled between the legs to be studded into fixings at the front. "Like bleeding cami-knickers," was one opinion.

The night drop was altogether different. David went last of four, the instructor staying with him on this occasion. For some reason the wind started to gust up as they were being winched up, at seven hundred feet it was decidedly bumpy and what was even more upsetting, seemed to be changing direction every minute. It was a dark night with more than a hint of rain in the air, when the first two went. The third man sat in the hole was told to go but refused to budge.

"Come on son," the instructor spoke in a quiet, persuasive voice, "just give yourself a shove, you'll be alright." The lad still did not move. "Right then, up you come, you're not the first, and I don't suppose you'll be the last."

When the lad, for that was all he was, still in his late teens, climbed back on to the platform, his eyes streaming with tears, all he could say was "I've let you down, I've let you down."

The instructor cut him short with, "Into the hole Sir." David duly sat in the hole. "Go," and away he went, knowing there was the long drop before the welcoming sight of that beautiful canopy would open above him. Open it did. 'Now, where's the ground?' he said to himself, wondering which way the wind was blowing until he faintly saw the smoke bomb, then wondered at which point of his swing he would hit the ground. It was terribly dark, and while he was inwardly complaining about how dark it was he hit the ground with such a wallop, with no semblance of a neatly controlled roll over, which so totally knocked all the breath out of him, that he lay there for several seconds gasping for air.

As soon as he got body and soul together he scrambled up, noting in the process that his limbs all seemed to be in working order, ran around to gather his parachute, which was being blown about quite severely by the increasing wind, to be greeted by a breathless Paddy saying, "Bloody hell Sir, we thought you were being blown to Chester." It was one of those freak gusts which had caught him and which had taken him a fair distance away from where the others had landed. However this had, at least, concealed from all, including the instructor, the absolute balls-up he had made of the landing itself, so 'all's well that ends well' he recited to himself, or so he thought. When he rejoined the stick, the balloon by now having been winched down, the flight sergeant joined him.

"I've seen some unusual landings in my time Sir, but that one was the most bizarre, the most extraordinary, the most theatrical one I've ever known. Yet you got away with it. You land on one cheek of your arse, with one leg in the air and your elbows ploughing the ground up, yet you're still in one piece. How did you do it?"

"In the first place, flight, how the hell did you see all that in the dark?" The flight sergeant held up a pair of binoculars which he must have had tucked away in his smock.

"You would be surprised how much you can see in the dark with these," he said.

"I assure you I wouldn't" David replied, having himself found that out by practical experience. He continued, "All I can say is the devil looks after his own."

The flight sergeant grinned. "The good thing is you didn't panic, you gathered your chute before it could drag you away, lots of people making bad landings forget that and get further injuries being dragged in high winds."

David rejoined the stick, and meeting Paddy said, "We still haven't scored one point over that sod," but said with a marked degree of admiration in his voice.

The stick was now down to seven as on the next day they filed out on to the tarmac in front of the Nissen huts and hangar of the main building, to emplane on to the real live Witley for their first aircraft jump. The fuselage, they knew, would not allow them to stand up, but they shuffled along on their backsides, four on one side, and three on the other side of the hole in the floor through which they would soon be ejecting themselves, trusting to providence, and to the hope that the Waafs who had packed their chutes had been in a good mood, not overhung, had no sex problems, conversely had not had too much sex, and in general would have done the packing job properly. Most of those jumping were talking nineteen to the dozen showing they were strung up, while the instructor kept a watchful eye to see if there were any that were appearing particularly fearful. The seven left in the stick were all pretty solid chaps, but past experience had shown that you could never tell who was going to jib, or when. It was not unknown for a man to pass the course with flying colours, only to get to his battalion and jib on a training exercise.

David had a few words with Cedric before emplaning. He was to go number one, Paddy number two, so as the plane's engines revved up and they coasted to the end of the runway, they sat opposite each other on either side of the hole. The aircraft turned, revved more until the whole contraption seemed it would shake itself to pieces and off it went, lumbering along, gaining speed, hitting bumps in the runway here and there, until what seemed an interminable time it gradually lifted. Through the hole in the floor David and Paddy could see the airfield perimeter, the green fields of Cheshire, occasional cottages, then following a 180° turn they flew over the sleepy town of Wilmslow where people were so used to low flying Witley bombers overhead that they rarely bothered to look up. There was a farm it seemed every few hundred yards – they've got a lot of farms in Cheshire – their sightseeing suddenly being interrupted by the stentorian voice of the instructor – "Hook up!!" The seven hooked the end of their static lines on to the secure wire running along the floor beside them; the instructor scrambled past each man to check it had been done properly then returned to the hole, indicating to David to sit in, in readiness to jump. After two or three minutes a red light shone on the instrument panel. "Wait for the green light," the instructor yelled, and on the instant the green went on, David lifted up and forward, immediately adopted the attention position and found himself being buffeted by the two mighty engines as they firstly blew him to a horizontal position one way, only to be immediately jerked back the other way by the almost instantaneous cracking open of his canopy, leaving him swinging around in mid air in a strange silence after the deafening noise of the flight and the momentary thunder of the exit. He gathered his wits, spotted the smoke and as he saw the ground hurtling up at him, made a very creditable landing. He was as excited as a child at the success of his first 'proper' jump, and looking toward the place where Paddy should have landed saw the big Irishman doing a little jig, and spotting David giving the 'thumbs up' with both hands.

By Friday they had completed their jumps without further incident. On returning to Ringway the instructor told them they were to parade in best battle dress the next morning to receive their wings from the station commander, after which they would be sent on leave. "This, of course," he added, "does not apply to the officer and the sergeant."

"Jesus Christ", whispered Paddy to David, "he's still bloody scoring points."

They paraded the next morning along with two other sticks and were handed their wings by the group captain. David and Paddy had been positioned a pace away from the para lads. When the 'Groupie' came to them, he shook hands with both of them saying just, "Good luck, you two, wherever you're going."

Lance corporal Amanda Dudley was waiting for them as they left the small parade ground.

"I've to take you to the commandant," she said.

"Don't tell me he works on Saturday afternoons?" queried David.

"He probably gets time and a half, being a civilian," Paddy concluded, "though I don't suppose he wants me, does he?" – to Amanda.

"He said both of you. I think he's got your course reports so he's sending you back to your unit."

"What can we do to deal satisfactorily with this lance corporal do you think Paddy?"

"Well Sir, she's a bit cheeky now 'cos she knows we're not going to have to put up with her much longer."

"The day is suddenly getting brighter at that prospect. No, I'll take that back. Whatever the headmaster has decided for us I will tell you now, Lance Corporal Amanda Dudley, that one of the few pleasures we have had in this military purgatory, has been the sight of your smiling face at the end of each day. Conversely of course, that didn't obtain when we met you each morning when you were laughing your pretty head off at the thought of the torture to which you were taking us. By the way, do you know our late flight sergeant Instructor Smilie?"

"Yes, we're getting engaged at Christmas."

David and Paddy looked at each other with eyebrows raised.

"She's a dark horse isn't she?"

"She is that Sir. You know, Amanda, he never stops scoring points. You can never win. It's born in him."

"I'll soon have him trained don't you worry," laughed Amanda, "he's a very caring, loving sort of chap when you get to know him."

"Amanda dear, be advised," continued David, "there really is no such thing as a loving, caring R.A.F. flight sergeant. You might get a loving, caring R.A.F. corporal, though that's to be doubted, but flight sergeants have to be drained of the milk of human kindness as part and parcel of being weighed down with all those stripes on each arm and the crowns on top."

Their banter was interrupted by the approach of none other than Flight Sergeant Alistair Smilie.

"I believe congratulations are in order flight," David enquired.

"Don't believe everything she tells you Sir," the flight sergeant joked back. "I've had several other very good offers."

"Well now," Paddy interjected, "I reckon you're treading on eggshells there, firstly Amanda said she had three first reserves in case she changes her mind and second she asked whether I was spoken for. Now I wouldn't like to tread on your toes, seeing as how kind and gentle you've been with us, but I did mention to her my family were landed gentry in Ireland and worth a bob or two."

"In that case we shall be engaged at Christmas and married at Easter, and you're both invited to the wedding." There was a silence for a moment, David looked at Paddy, Paddy looked at David. David replied, the banter gone.

"I think we shall be otherwise engaged by then, but many thanks for the invitation and the very best of luck to both of you."

When they arrived back at Wilmslow that afternoon, the duty sergeant told them that the commandant wished to see them. In brief, he congratulated them on an excellent course report, told Paddy he could go on seven days leave as from the morrow, but that David would have to forgo leave for a while and have it made up at Christmas time.

"If you come in at 10 o'clock tomorrow morning I will make it all plain to you," he told David.

After the meeting with Robin, they headed for the two phone booths, Paddy to phone his Mary, and David to call firstly Chandlers Lodge and then Maria at Chingford. To his annoyance there was an hour's delay. It would be tempting the fates, for obvious reasons, to book both calls at the same time, so he booked the call to Sandbury, went off to his room to smarten up a bit for the evening meal – they had just a buffet style supper on Saturdays and Sundays – and half an hour later booked his Chingford number. Everyone at Sandbury wanted to speak to him and congratulate him on his getting his wings. Anni and Ernie were there, Ernie telling him he could 'drop in' on them at any time. As time was moving on he had to ask his mother, who had let the others go first, whether he could ring her back on Sunday.

Ruth, in her usual understanding way replied, "of course dear, and give Maria my love," ending with, "I presume it is Maria?"

David laughed. "Yes, it is, oh, and Mum, why don't you try and get a commission in the Intelligence Corps – they could do with people with your perspicacity."

"If I knew what perspicacity meant perhaps I would." They were both laughing as David replaced the receiver.

He had barely returned to the dining room when a mess waiter came up to him. "Telephone for you Sir, booth two."

"Thank you very much."

"Why aren't you down at the Palais, its Saturday night you know," were his first words.

"You are speaking to the wrong person," came the guttural reply. "I'm afraid my nights at the Palais are long gone. You see I answered the telephone and thought I would just say hello, and ask if you have finished your jumping."

"How nice to speak to you Mr Schultz. To answer your question yes, I have finished my jumping course, but I fear that I have far from finished my jumping."

"Well, God bless you David. I had better give the telephone to Maria now or she will wrap the cord round my neck – nein?"

"Bye bye, Mr Schultz."

There was a momentary break. "David, have you got your wings?" It was a breathless Maria who had been champing at the bit for all the interminable seconds her father had been hogging the call.

"Yes, we've all got our wings, Paddy me and Cedric. Now the only problem is that Cedric's wings are much too big for him, so I don't quite know what to do about that."

"Can you send them to me and I will make a miniature pair for him and put them on when you come on leave."

"Now that's the bad news. I shan't be on leave until Christmas time, something has blown up."

Instantly he sensed the apprehension in her voice. "You're not going away again?"

"Not as far as I know – I shall know more tomorrow."

"Please David; please let me know tomorrow, if you are able of course."

At ten a.m. precisely, David presented himself again in the 'headmaster's' office. Robin was accompanied by a slight, dapper, scholarly looking man, who he introduced as Professor Fielding, David thinking 'and I bet a pound that's not his real name.' Robin went on to say that the professor was only with him for one month. As the jumping course had overrun its estimated time span to the extent it had, there would not be time for him to take leave. It was most essential he spent the whole month closeted with the professor. He apologised about the leave.

"No problem, Robin, However, I would be interested to know what the subject matter is that I shall be digesting."

Robin continued by informing David that the professor was an expert on Switzerland, having served there for many years. He omitted saying in which way he had served, which David quickly noted.

"You will be based at first in Berne. It is essential therefore that you know the city inside out, basic details of routes to and from, the local accent, local history, Swiss political parties, all, in fact, there is to know about Berne and the Canton it is in. Next, Switzerland is the very hub of espionage groups, literally from all over the world including particularly Russia, United States and, most importantly, Germany. Professor Fielding will be filling you in, conversing with you all the time in Swiss-German, with all the basic details you must know to live safely and eventually to have built up a solid background of having lived in Berne, when you move on to your final operation. The Professor knows nothing of your operation and will not know. He is here purely to prepare you. Any questions?"

When do we start?"

"Tomorrow. Six days a week for four weeks. Eight till Twelve. Two till six."

"What do I do in my spare time?"

They all grinned.

And so, on Monday 27th October 1941 at eight o'clock in the morning, David presented himself in Room 8, a small room, probably originally a breakfast room at the rear of the house overlooking a different aspect of the same garden you could see from Robin's office. The professor, although a small man, had a deep, resonant voice. Interesting, David thought, he's got an interesting voice, though quite what he meant by the description he would find difficult to elucidate.

David was a little slow in his German at first. After the first day, he began to feel his feet, until by the end of the week he was thinking in German, although as the professor continually chided him, his accent was not yet up to scratch.

Gradually he began to know Berne better than he knew London or Manchester. As he had learnt so thoroughly in his preparation for his Le Mans operation, it was attention to detail that could save his life in the event that he should be suffering a grilling by the Gestapo. Having a Swiss passport would give him a considerable amount of protection, but that would rapidly disappear if the answers he gave them to basic questions were vague or incorrect.

"When you leave the main library, which way do you turn to get to the station?"

"You turn left, and left again and it's on your right."

"Excellent, but remember, think in metres so that you are not tempted to use yards. Remember when you cross the road to look first to your left, not to your right as you do here – a little thing like that can give you away to someone observing you."

And so it went on.

On Sunday 2nd November he had a long lie-in. The continual absorption of the mass of information fed to him by the professor had worn him out mentally and physically. The fact that he would probably never need to use any of it was a bit galling; conversely the knowledge of one little factor could be the difference between life and death.

Late that afternoon he telephoned home to hear the news that his old unit at City Rifles was going on leave preparatory to going overseas, and that Charlie Crew and Mark Laurenson would be visiting Chandlers Lodge the following weekend. His mother asked could he get away to join them. He knew that would not be possible, so sadly asked his mother to give the visitors his best wishes and to tell that idiot Charlie to write to him and 'keep his head down.'

The following Sunday, the 9th, he was late in telephoning, and was greeted with the news that Rose and Mark were engaged. He was thrilled and delighted with the knowledge that his sister was to be happily married again, he had the highest regard for Mark Laurenson both as a man and as a soldier. As he had said to himself in the past – she could do a lot worse. As these thoughts ran through his mind, he heard his mother saying, "And the wedding is hopefully on the 22nd of this month – God and Cannon Rosser willing – and you must be here. Mark wants you to be best man."

David, having given Maria all the news and asking her if she would like to keep that weekend free in the hope that he could lean on his commandant to give him the time off, wandered off to his room. As he lay on his bed reflecting on the happenings of the past two years, his marriage, Rose's marriage, Jeremy's death and then Pat's death, he was overwhelmed with such a great sadness that he had to bury his face in the pillow to muffle the sobs that welled up from the very depths of his being. It was not often that this despondency hit him, but when it did, it hit him very hard. Gradually he calmed and went into a sort of twilight of wakefulness, eventually to recover his normal stability and get himself to bed.

At breakfast on Monday morning he buttonholed Robin. "Could you spare me five minutes before I start with the professor please?"
"Yes of course – anything I can do now?"
"My widowed sister is marrying my ex-company commander on the 22nd of this month. My old unit is on an overseas posting. Do you think I could have that weekend?"
"Of course. Finish up on the Thursday and have seven days – from what I've heard from the professor you've more than deserved it."

That evening, despite infuriating delays, David spent time glued to the telephone. First to Maria asking her to stay over at the Angel and go to work on Monday morning from Sandbury, then his mother and Rose, asking his mother to arrange for Maria to stay at the Angel from Friday night until Monday morning. Finally he managed to get Charlie and Mark at the R.A.F. mess at Highmere – "A very comfortable billet, we shall dream about in the months to come I fancy" as Mark had remarked with a degree of prescience worthy of a prophet.

Thursday 20th November came. David said goodbye to the professor who was also leaving that day, although he failed to mention to David where he was going. Par for the course David thought. Paddy had his dress uniform packed in so much tissue, which he had purchased in Wilmslow, that it took up twice its normal space in his valise. His tunic and battle dress blouses now sported the pale blue wings of the parachutist, which would, and did, occasion much comment in Sandbury.

It was nice to be going home.

Chapter Ten

When David arrived at Sandbury station he was astonished to see none other than Charlie Crew standing on the platform, complete with a porter and trolley.

"Charlie – how the devil did you know I would be on this train?"

"Reconnaissance dear old sport, reconnaissance. I did a quick recce of Bradshaws from Manchester, time taken to get from Euston to Victoria and with this information pinned you down to this one or the next. Before you start complaining I am sharing a room with you at Chandlers Lodge, so I do hope your nasal organ is in better tune than it was when we last shared a room."

"You haven't changed a bit you blighter."

"Ah, but you have. The weight of those wings on your right arm makes your shoulders lop sided. Why didn't they put them on your chest?"

"I understand the R.A.F. top brass objected. They insisted they should be the only ones allowed to wear wings on the manly breast."

"You're joking."

"No, God's Honour. I got that from a very high authority."

"You mean a lance-corporal in the orderly room?"

"None other. Actually she was a full corporal."

"I'll say no more."

They arrived at Chandlers Lodge to an ecstatic welcome from the family, Ruth, Megan, Anni and little David, and of course Rose and little Jeremy. He held Rose tightly and said in a very low voice, "I am so happy for you, you couldn't have chosen a better man." Rose just smiled, not far from tears; she was still suffering from a mixture of feelings and would do for a long while yet.

At five o'clock, the two new Canadians arrived and were introduced, and shortly afterwards Fred came bustling in with none other than Tim, Alec and Jim who he had met at the gate, he on his bicycle, they in the staff car. It was bedlam for a while, lubricated by copious drafts of the Whitbread's Light Ale from under the stairs. Everyone wanted to know what it was like to jump out of an aeroplane, along with the usual remarks such as "Are you issued with special underwear?"

"Is it true that if you don't do your leg straps up properly you end up a eunuch?" And so on.

At last Ruth broke up the gathering by announcing dinner, Tim,

Alec and Jim climbing back into the staff car to go back to camp. After dinner Karl, Ernie and Jack Hooper arrived to again quiz David, along with assisting in further reducing the nectar stocks from under the stairway.

David was up early on Friday morning, had a light breakfast and then told his mother he was going to see Pat. Ruth reflected 'he never says I'm going to the churchyard, as to visit Pat's grave, he always says I'm going to see Pat.' She did not attempt to analyse this fact further other than to surmise that being so close to her perhaps he could see her as clearly as when she was alive.

Whilst they were having breakfast, Ruth had told David she was sorry she had not been able to get Maria put up at the Angel. All the rooms had been taken with Mark's family all coming for the weekend. Fred's friend at Rotary, Johnny Quirke, who owned 'The Three Bells' at the other end of the High Street had three rooms which he let mainly to 'commercials,' so they had booked her and Cecely in there. Johnny was a lovely man, the rooms were comfortable, he and his wife would see that they were well looked after. She added, rather casually, "Are you getting close to Maria David?"

David replied quite seriously "I think you can say we are in the category of being best friends. I wouldn't go further than that at the moment. I don't know anyone, other than family, who I like more." He paused for a moment or two. "We shall see," he concluded, though exactly what he meant with those three words left Ruth guessing.

The wedding day dawned cold and blustery, but at least it was dry. Rose had elected to wear a figure hugging baratheia suit in a delicate shade of dove grey, superbly cut and made by the same lady, Mrs Abbott, who had made her first wedding dress. The revers were in a slightly darker shade, this part of the outfit having caused some problems in finding the right material. By sheer good fortune in rummaging around in the 'Country Style's' stockroom, they found some swatches of pre-war cloths. Swatches in the 1930's were of a substantial size, not the postage stamp size of the current period, to disappear altogether in a few months until long after the war. Two of the swatches therefore produced a rever each and solved the problem, leaving enough to cover the buttons giving the whole outfit the elegant finished appearance of a classic English tailored garment.

David was best man. Mark was, of course, also in uniform. Whilst talking to Fred on the telephone the previous weekend, he asked him if he too could wear his Home Guard uniform. Fred's immediate reaction was that his battle dress, the standard uniform for the Home Guard, would look poverty stricken along side the service dress uniform and Sam Browne belts of David and Mark.

"If I know Mrs Chandler," Mark had replied, "it will be as immaculate as a field marshal's." With persuasion from both Ruth and particularly Rose, he eventually agreed to wear it, and as Mark had prophesised, it was as spruce as any there. With his two rows of medal ribbons from India, South Africa, and the Great War he was the epitome of the old soldier, still serving his country in its hour of need.

As Rose stood on almost the same spot at the step of the chancel as she had such a short time ago stood with her beloved Jeremy, she had a momentary feeling of panic seize her. Mark had reasoned that this could be the most difficult part of the day's proceedings for her and without making it obvious, clasped her hand firmly to show her he understood. Cannon Rosser conducted a cheerful, light-hearted service. Along with the official photographer outside the church, there were representatives of not only the local press, but also the county press, the county upmarket glossies, and as Mark would find to his cost later, The Tatler and Bystander, appearing in which damaged his monthly pay cheque to a very considerable degree when he returned to the Mess.

The reception at the Angel was as well provisioned, as it was possible to provide under the exigencies of war time rationing. David and Charlie were introduced to Mark's mother and father, telling them with due solemnity that they had been instructed with draconian severity not to tell tales about Mark unless they wished to be demoted to lance corporals. Mrs Treharne, who lived in David's bungalow since losing her daughter and son-in-law in an air raid at Hampstead, found herself with Cecely, from Malaya, which long conversation sparked off events of significance to occur in the very near future.

The newly-weds went off at 8.30, little Jeremy with his new nanny having been despatched soon after the wedding ceremony. Arriving at Berners Hotel they went in to see the baby was sleeping soundly, said goodnight to nanny and retired to their apartment. Both had had previous misgivings about this first period of married life they were to face together. In normal courtship a couple gradually, sometimes precipitately, reaches a degree of intimacy, which automatically gives them a direct passport to full union without self-consciousness. Rose appreciated that if she appeared hesitant, Mark being the gentleman he undoubtedly was, would not attempt to force the issue, she had therefore decided that as soon as they were alone, she would make it plain that she needed him. She, therefore, took the 'Do Not Disturb' label from the inside door knob, firmly placed it on the outside, closed the door and locked it. Turning to Mark, who was watching her with amusement, she said, "It looks at though I am at your mercy," and flew into his arms.

After the reception, a number of guests drifted back to Chandlers Lodge. Cecely was a main attraction in that everyone who had not met her before wanted to know how Harry was faring, and was it true that her brother-in-law was one of the people Harry had saved. She had hoped that James, her brother-in-law, would be able to be there, but he was stationed with the D.L.I. in Iceland at the moment, although they were hoping to be sent back to the U.K. soon, and could not get leave.

When Ruth and Fred eventually got to bed in the early hours of Sunday morning, despite the fact it had been a long day, they both found it difficult to get to sleep. Feeling Ruth fidgeting, Fred asked the obvious, "Can't you get to sleep?"

"No, I don't know why, I really am very tired."

He put his arm beneath her and pulled her towards him. "Don't worry unnecessarily. I know you're afraid of what could happen, but the old army saying 'it may never happen' is very true."

"Yes, but even that reassuring saying only says 'may'."

He was hoist on his own petard there, so wisely kept quiet. They, and many others in that congregation today, knew that major Mark Laurenson had a lot of fighting to do before this war ended. A stray bullet could widow Rose for the second time – how could she possibly survive that?"

David collected Maria on Sunday morning from the Three Bells, to which hostelry he had escorted her late the previous evening. They were all going to church on Sunday morning and then back to Chandlers Lodge for lunch. Ruth had been saving her meat coupons, using such items of non rationed goods as she could do so that they could have a sizeable leg of lamb for their main meal. David and Charlie had, of course, brought their ration cards with which the army issued them when they came on leave, so with a little prudent juggling, Ruth not only had reasonable portions for lunch but also enough left to make s shepherds pie on the morrow. All over Britain, careful housewives were doing the same thing, with the exception, of course, of those who had connections with the black market, which despite having its members occasionally being caught and prosecuted, was still very much alive and kicking.

In the afternoon Jack, along with Buffy and Rita, Jack's wife Moira still being in America, came to them from the Hollies. Anni, Ernie, Karl and baby David joined them, Cecely and Mrs Treherne having had lunch with the family. They were all interested to meet Mark's parents again. Introductions had, of course, been made at the wedding or at the reception, but as is usually the case, there had not been any opportunity for a prolonged discussion. Charlie answered the door when they arrived, taking their coats, as a result being ribbed by David, "You'll make a good butler after the war."

"Not at all old boy" came Charlie's inevitable riposte. "Mr & Mrs Laurenson are my boss's parents. Therefore my courtliness will undoubtedly be mentioned to him in due course, to my ultimate benefit."

Ruth and Fred had by now come into the hall to greet the guests. Fred saying, "Take no notice of these two."

This produced the reply from Mr Laurenson, "We've been forewarned about young Charlie here, but I understand that David has deserted them to go jumping out of aeroplanes for some peculiar purpose or other. Have you had his head examined yet Mr Chandler? – as a lawyer I would think you could get him medically discharged – there must be something not quite right with someone who does things like that."

With general amusement they joined the others in the main sitting room. "Ladies and gentlemen," Fred began, "may I introduce Mr & Mrs Laurenson, although I believe some of you may have already had a few words with them." There were the usual polite hellos, to which Mr Laurenson replied,

"Well ladies and gentlemen, as you will all undoubtedly be on Christian name terms with each other, we are Hector and Naomi. We live in Shrewsbury, which as you will already know, is the most beautiful town in the West Midlands, that is when it's not being flooded by the River Severn. We are both very pleased to meet you all."

There was a moment's silence, interrupted by Naomi taking his arm and adding, "He loves making little speeches you know. I suppose it's because he comes from a long line of lawyers."

Ruth had organised a buffet supper, with help from Anni, Megan and Maria. David was in charge of the bar, Charlie cheerfully announcing to all and sundry he was the potman, and would doubtless be press-ganged into the washing up in due course. David noticed the Laurenson's having quite a deep conversation with Maria at one stage. After a reasonable interval he joined them.

"Maria has been telling us of how you knew her brother at Calais," Hector commenced. "Mark has, of course, told us of your exploits."

"Cedric was one of the bravest people I have ever had the privilege of knowing," David replied, "he was totally fearless." He slipped his arm around Maria's waist as he spoke, to help her, if possible, in the event of her becoming upset. David was pleased to see that she now thought of her brother with a feeling of pride instead of sorrow, and at this perception, tightened his hold upon her, being rewarded by her looking up at him with a look of such tenderness that, despite the presence of so many, made him fleetingly brush his lips against her hair. It was a moment that stayed with them always, but it did not go unnoticed elsewhere. Ruth and Fred saw it, looked at each other and found themselves with mutually raised eyebrows. Charlie saw it and catalogued it for later use – ribbing of one, David Chandler.

Hector and Naomi of course saw it at first hand, causing Naomi to say to Ruth later "Do you think you may have another wedding in the family soon?" Megan noticed it and suffered a little pain at not being able to receive such tenderness from her Harry, so many miles away. The one person who would have noticed it – David did not christen her Hawkeye for nothing – was enjoying the first full day of her honeymoon, despite the fact that baby Jeremy had already been described by one bejewelled lady living at the hotel as 'the image of his daddy.'

So the weekend passed, the guests departed, life got back to normal. David saw Maria off to London on the eight o'clock from Sandbury arranging to meet her from work on Tuesday. He was surprised to get a telephone call from her during her lunch hour, apparently she had telephoned home and her mother had suggested, so that they could see David, they should go to Chingford on Tuesday and David should stay over and go back to London with Maria on Wednesday morning. David immediately fell in with this arrangement, the announcement of which to his mother received her blessing, and her further announcement of the arrangement to Fred receiving a repetition of the raised eyebrow syndrome of Sunday night.

It was a long goodbye to Maria at Marble Arch station on Wednesday morning. Despite the sadness of parting, Maria went to work with such gladness in her heart. She knew she was deeply in love with David, she was certain, although he had not as yet expressed it to her, that David was, if not as deeply in love as she was, he was very affectionate towards her. His final words to her had been 'I don't know how I am going to manage to be without you until Christmas.' Her heart had leapt. He had not mentioned any further leave until now, she had, in fact, been filled with the dreaded thought that he might just disappear again as he had before. Similarly she fully appreciated the loyalty to his beloved Pat, which would inevitably be struggling inside him with his feelings for her. Maria was a highly intelligent, sensitive young woman; she knew this was a situation, which could not be rushed. Her parents knew this as well, they lived in the hope that all would turn out well for them both.

"I don't know how I am going to manage to be without you until Christmas."

"Shall I see you at Christmas?"

"I'm fairly certain I shall be home."

Maria did a little jig on the Oxford Street pavement to the amusement, not only of David, but also several passers-by including a pair of lance-corporals from City Rifles. As they smartly saluted the officer – David had worn his service dress for the visit to Chingford – one cheekily said, "Don't believe a word he says Miss." They were gone before David could think of a suitable reply.

"I will telephone you as soon as I know," and with that they kissed lightly again – it would not be done for an officer to be seen indulging in prolonged snogging in Oxford Street at 8.30 in the morning!

David decided to walk to Victoria, and then wished he had decided otherwise. A constant stream of soldiers on leave saluted him, particularly if they saw his medal ribbons and decided he deserved to be saluted. David returned each salute correctly, accompanied by 'Good morning,' which surprised a number of them who considered civility and commissioned rank did not exactly go together. There were the inevitable few bolshie ones who decided that saluting officers whilst they were on leave was against their religion, so conveniently looked into a shop window. On one occasion it amused David mightily to notice the squaddie was intently studying the latest in ladies' corsets – large ladies' corsets at that!

David returned to Wilmslow the next day, Charlie travelled with him to London and having said goodbye, made his way to his grandfather's estate in Worcestershire. After the turmoil of the weekend, the house seemed strangely quiet, although as Ruth commented that evening 'With Christmas almost on us, I've really got to get cracking.' First of all on the list was to establish who would be there, and when. Second on the list was how to feed them. The food was a perennial problem. The basic rations were extremely basic, on the other hand vegetables, bread, flour, milk and offal were plentiful, so a competent housewife could always make something. Considerable help in the form of recipes using what was generally in the shops were issued by the Ministry of Food, the general opinion being 'what doesn't fatten will fill.' Despite the shortages and the substitutes, it was generally assessed by experts after the war that the health of the nation during the rationing period was as good as, if not better than, the days of plenty.

On Monday 1st December a large parcel arrived, delivered by Carter Patterson, clearly marked 'Opened by Customs.' It was from Harry, or at least from Robinson's of Singapore. It contained Christmas presents for all the family; the whole marked 'Unsolicited Gifts from Service Personnel.' Provided these were not wildly extravagant they attracted no duty. Ruth asked the carrier to put the heavy box in the hall, and rewarded him with the customary shilling. The next day the Carter Patterson man returned with yet another heavy wooden box, again from Robinson's, which the bill of lading described as tinned fruit. Another shilling changed hands. On Wednesday the same man returned with yet another box, which in this case contained tinned meat and fish. Up until now, except to say thank you for his shilling (as Fred remarked "He makes more in a day in tips than I did working on the land for a week," to which Ruth replied, "And what is the comparison now?" – no answer) the carrier had said nothing. Today he just said, "It looks as though you won't starve over Christmas." Neither of them could have envisaged that in a few short hours this Aladdin's cave of goodies in Singapore would be no more for long, long terrible years, and that starvation for many in that land of plenty would be the norm.

The final box having been delivered, Ruth telephoned Megan. They had known the crates would be arriving. Harry had had them despatched to Chandlers Lodge since it was feasible that Megan would either be in hospital, or waiting to go in to have her new baby. Megan answered the phone on the instant saying she was about to telephone Ruth. She had not been well all night, as a result the matron at Sandbury Hospital had told her to come in and be looked after. Megan was a sister at the hospital and very highly regarded. The whole hospital staff considered the baby would belong to them as much as it did to the Chandler family – it would be receiving very special attention on its entry into the world. Ruth immediately offered to get Fred to bring the Rover round to take her – he'd just got his new petrol ration – but Megan said that matron was sending the hospital ambulance. "My God," exclaimed Ruth, "you are important, only royalty would normally get that privilege." Further evidence of her importance was observed by her being accommodated in a private side-ward, in being allowed more than two visitors at a time and being allowed visitors from one o'clock through to eight o'clock, way outside normal visiting hours. On 6th December she seemed rather tired, at this point the matron, putting her foot down and cutting back the visiting time. She went into labour the following day, and shortly after midnight on 8th December she gave birth to a beautiful daughter, to be named Ceri Rose.

The significance of this timing was not immediately realised. At that very moment Japanese bombs began to fall on Pearl Harbour, Hong Kong was attacked, landings were made in the Philippines, and of most concern to the Chandler family, the peninsula of Malaya was invaded by the most evil hordes since those of Ghengis Khan. The jubilation therefore of the family and the host of friends and colleagues of Megan and Harry swiftly turned to alarm and apprehension that Harry was once again in a theatre of war. The first that Megan heard of it was when a probationer blurted out to the sister attending her, "The Japs have invaded Malaya and bombed Singapore – it's just been on the wireless."

Megan went pale, saying to the sister, "Is this true, my Harry is there." The sister immediately sent the probationer to get matron. Matron Duffy was not only Megan's boss, but also a very good friend. She came into the side ward, took Megan's hand and told her she had been listening to the news bulletin, which so far had not been over informative.

"Don't worry Megan dear, they'll soon push them back into the sea, Harry will be alright. Now let me see this beautiful little daughter of yours. Have you cabled Harry yet?"

"Yes. My father-in-law sent out all the telegrams and the cables to Harry and Moira from his office this morning. Oh, why couldn't I have had my baby in peace?" She began to cry softly.

Matron Duffy cradled her up. "Now, now, you're bound to be a bit low for a few days – you've seen enough new mothers to know that – but be brave, if anyone can look after himself better than Harry Chandler I've yet to meet him."

But even Matron Duffy could have absolutely no conception whatsoever of how Harry Chandler was going to have to look after himself over the next few weeks, months and eventually years.

Chapter Eleven

When Harry awoke early on the morning of Thursday 11th December, he turned on the radio for the six o'clock news. In total disbelief he heard an excited announcer stating that on the previous day the mighty battleship 'The Prince of Wales' and the battle cruiser 'Repulse' had been sunk by 80 Japanese torpedo carrying aircraft as the ships, with their attendant destroyers, were sailing to oppose the Japanese landings. It was one of the blackest days in British naval history. Combined with the sinking or disabling of nineteen warships at Pearl Harbour it meant that the whole of the Pacific Ocean was almost exclusively Japanese territory. When Hitler was told of these successes at Rastenburg, his operational headquarters in East Prussia, he told his staff, "It is impossible now for us to lose the war, the Japanese have not been vanquished for three thousand years." It would take a long time for it to happen but that was another mistake he made.

Harry got dressed quickly and hurried into his office. Major Deveson was already there. With the vehicles all gone, except for a handful in the workshops and those attached to headquarters, there was little for them to do.

"Have you heard how they are doing up north Sir?" asked Harry.

"Not yet, but I can tell you exactly what the first communiqué will say." He continued. "Our troops on the northern frontier are inflicting heavy casualties on the Japanese forces and retreating in good order to take up prepared defensive positions."

The seven o'clock news announced the situation in terms almost word for word as the major had promulgated. They looked at each other.

"You're in the wrong job Sir."

"I wouldn't be surprised if we're both out of a job soon Mr Chandler," replied the major despondently.

That evening they received some excellent news. Although it would not directly affect their theatre of operations, a bulletin announced Germany had declared war on the United States. This momentous event meant that American muscle and American industrial power would now augment the British and Russian war machines to defeat Germany and when this was done their full might could be directed against Japan. There was a flicker of light on the horizon.

Early next morning Fred's cable arrived.

"DAUGHTER BORN 8 DECEMBER. BOTH VERY WELL. LETTER FOLLOWS. DAD."

As he read it the major arrived.

"Do you drink whisky at eight in the morning Sir," asked Harry, smiling like a Cheshire cat.

"God, don't tell me we've won the war already," quipped the major, as he took the cable being handed to him, and having read it replied, "This is undoubtedly such an occasion."

Harry dived into his desk drawer and brought out a bottle of Teachers and two tumblers, filling each one half full.

"What's the baby's name?"

"I don't know Sir, nobody ever tells me anything."

"I know the feeling. Well, anyway, here's to little miss unnamed Chandler far away. May she live a long and happy life."

"Hear, hear."

As they raised their glasses the door opened and in walked Robbie Stewart.

"What's all this?" he cried, "boozing at eight o'clock in the morning."

Harry swiftly found another glass, added a copious quantity of amber liquid to it and handed it to Robbie along with the cable. Robbie raised his glass, "To the little one," he said, "not forgetting her very clever mum."

As they toasted the new arrival they heard the throbbing of heavy aircraft approaching and shortly afterwards the scream of the bombs descending again on Singapore town. It was a very light raid this time, the main bomber force being used against the naval base at Penang in the north-west where six hundred civilians were killed.

Robbie had called to say that they had found the stolen 3-tonner. Harry looked at Major Deveson in dismay. "I have to tell you it is more or less unrecognisable as a military vehicle," Robbie continued, "but it is definitely yours- they failed to scratch out all the identification numbers."

There was silence for a moment or two, broken by Harry asking, "Is there any way you can push it over the harbour wall into fifty feet of water anywhere? I explained to you the number and variety of forms I had to complete to get the bloody thing written off and replaced. Now I have even more forms, some of which I've never seen or heard of before. I wouldn't mind betting, to get the blasted thing back, get it refurbished, return its replacement to ordnance, get a replacement driver", he paused, "I really don't deserve this."

The other two grinned at him. The major offered the view that in a few weeks time he may wish he was pushing his pen in his comfortable office at Nee Soon. Robbie suggested that the reason C.S.M.'s were paid at super-tax rates was so that they could carry out such dangerous and unrewarding tasks as this present one. As he finished they heard the approach of a low flying aircraft, the scream of a bomb, which obviously had failed to clear its bomb rack over Singapore town and had now decided to release itself, followed by an enormous explosion, which blew in the windows surrounding them. No one was hurt; they had all, on hearing the first screaming of the descending bomb, dived under the office desks. When the dust settled, they picked themselves up. Harry looking out of the now glass-less window across the parade ground, started laughing until he was almost in hysterics. Mystified the other two looked at each other.

"One bomb, and he's bomb-happy by the look of things," suggested Robbie. Harry turned to them.

"It's fallen in the middle of the plantation," he told them. "The other morning the owner came over here shouting and swearing because I had parked all our vehicles under his trees. His last words when I threatened to throw him out were, 'You'll have to pay for any damage.' I wonder how much he'll charge the Japs?" He paused for a minute and continued, "Still doesn't solve our stolen truck problem though does it? I'll get a driver to come over and pick it up this afternoon – will that be O.K.?"

The strange thing about this truck was that it was eventually parked behind the workshops – there was no one spare to work on its refurbishment. When eventually Singapore fell, the Japs used it in its garish state (the Chinese love making their vehicles, even stolen ones, things of beauty) and continued to use it all through the occupation. No maintenance, other than the provision of oil, grease and water, was carried out on it, and in 1945 it was still going strong, a triumph of Bedford quality!

On December 16th having pushed down from the northern town of Alor Star, the Japanese captured Penang island. European citizens had been evacuated, but no one in authority had thought of destroying the boats. Powered launches, all manner of craft, were there for the taking. All it needed was an axe through the bottom of each one to render it useless, but nobody thought to order it. As a result, the Japanese formed a complete seaborne invasion force, which was able to outflank the land forces as they retreated down the mainland trunk road. Time and again when the land forces found themselves in a reasonable defensive position, they were outflanked from the sea. There were no aircraft to attack this flotilla, half the Buffaloes had been destroyed on the ground, and when a few Hurricanes arrived they proved no match for the Zero.

Later that day another cable arrived for Harry. This was also dated 8th December, so had been considerably delayed.

"MEGAN AND BABY WELL. BABY NAMED CERI ROSE. LETTER FOLLOWS. DAD."

The major came into Harry's office as Harry was studying the cable, looked at Harry with raised, questioning eyebrows, in reply to which Harry handed him the paper.

"That's an unusual name. How do you pronounce it?" the major queried.

"I only know because Megan has an aunt of that name. It's pure Welsh and pronounced Kerry. Rose of course is my sister."

"You have a very diplomatic wife sergeant major. Embraces both sides of the family, keeps everyone happy, very clever."

Harry grinned. "Ceri – Ceri – I like it. One thing's for sure, there won't be many Ceri's in Sandbury, or Kent for that matter."

"Right now, back to business. I have to go up to Malacca tomorrow to the corps HQ. I'd like you to come, so if you will organise the Dodge, driver, and relief driver we'll leave about 6.30. We'll go by the coast road to Batu Pahat and Muar; it should be quieter that way rather than on the trunk road. We'll take small arms with us, you and I tommy-guns, the other two their rifles. Oh! And food for three days, although we may be able to scrounge a crust from the Aussies there if they're in a good mood."

"Right Sir, consider it done." Harry was more than pleased to get off his backside again, and rather looked forward to meeting some of these antipodean warriors he had heard so much about from his father who had served with them at one time in the Great War. That is not to say he had not heard about them in the present conflict. When they first arrived in Singapore they had more or less torn the place apart until the combined British/Australian redcaps had thoroughly sorted them out. The general opinion was they were loud, undisciplined, too fond of the booze, and in Harry's opinion didn't like losing at cricket, the latter being by far their major fault. Harold Larwood sorted the buggers out though – Harry grinned at the thought.

At 6.30 prompt the Dodge nosed its way out of the almost

deserted depot towards the Bukit Timah road and then made its way north over the Johore Causeway. They travelled up the trunk road for about twelve miles before turning westerly at Skudai towards the coast. The road running sometimes alongside beautiful beaches, sometimes through primeval mangrove swamps, was well metalled, as a result they made good time to their first stop at the rest house at Batu Pahat. Over the ferry and then on towards Muar they enjoyed the most beautiful scenery Malaya had to offer. Miles and miles of silvery beaches overhung with coconut trees, gentle waves from the Malacca Strait breaking enticingly on the smooth shore, gorgeous sunshine not yet blasting down as it would in an hour or two, flying fishes by the score – it seemed impossible that only a couple of hundred miles away people were killing, people were dying, a whole way of life was being destroyed, never to return.

They arrived at Muar at lunch time having made very good time. Harry asked if they could call in at Nigel Coates house, to which the major gladly agreed. Haji Mahomed answered the door. He was most excited at seeing Harry again but had to tell him that the Tuan was in K.L. for two or three days, "But we have been told that Mrs Coates has been made very welcome by your family in England," he added.

Saying their goodbyes they returned to the Dodge just as Ah Chin appeared from his quarters at the rear of their building. Harry called, "Ah Chin – how are you?" At that the cook turned and recognising Harry, approached him with a series of wide smiles, a series of mini-bows and a torrent of words of which neither Harry nor his major understood one syllable.

"This man is the greatest chef in Malaya," exclaimed Harry, shaking hands firmly with Ah Chin. With the commotion produced, the family of Ah Chin, including what seemed to be a disproportionate number of children, came out to see what the fuss was all about, soon crowding around both the major and Harry, as well as climbing on the Dodge and making friends with the two drivers. One sounded the hooter, then they all wanted to have a go! Eventually Ah Chin bellowed something – it was extraordinary how commanding a voice he had for such a small man – the children immediately jumping down to stand behind him. "Can you imagine kids in England taking notice like that?" one of the drivers asked.

As they drove towards the gates on to the road to the ferry, the children all ran alongside, Harry turned to wave goodbye to Ah Chin, who by now had been joined by his wife and probably his two daughters, Harry guessed. They returned his waving, Harry thinking, 'I wonder if I shall ever see them again?' He would see them again, the circumstances for all of them would, however, be different beyond belief.

Taking the ferry across the River Muar, they had a further forty miles or so of coast road to cover to get to Malacca with again mainly silvery beaches to the west, but in this sector miles of paddy fields and other cultivation stretching as far as the eye could see to the east. A military policeman directing traffic at the outskirts of the ancient town directed them to corps HQ, housed in a compound of four large civilian dwellings taken over at the outbreak of hostilities. The major jumped down and went into one of the buildings whilst Harry and the drivers stretched their legs. He was not away for more than ten minutes. Harry joked, "Didn't take them long to make you a general Sir?"

Major Deveson grinned. "I apparently have to see the GSO!" he replied, "he's a full colonel, but he's on his way back from up-country and won't be here until late. I've to come back in the morning."

"Any idea what it's all about Sir?"

"Not a clue. Mind you, the way things are with the top brass he probably doesn't know either." Hearing this exchange the two drivers exchanged grins.

"And you two can forget I ever said that," he said with mock severity.

They returned at eight o'clock the next morning, the two drivers showing signs of being a little hung over, their comments to Harry including the opinion that, 'these corps HQ people know how to look after themselves.' At 8.45 the major reappeared beckoning Harry to join him at the doorway of the GSO building. "He wants a word with you sergeant major." Utterly mystified at what a full colonel would want with the likes of him, Harry gave his tunic and belt a quick check and followed the major back into the building, to a large office overlooking the rear garden. Seated at the desk was a fairly elderly Great War veteran, covered in medal ribbons and red tabs, a captain from what Harry instantly recognised as the Royal West Kents standing at his right elbow. They both saluted.

"I'll be brief Mr Chandler. I have offered Major Deveson a GSO2 job at corps HQ that will be moving from here shortly. He would like you to be his staff warrant officer. I couldn't agree it without seeing you. How do you feel about it?"

Harry had never been one to be lost for words. Even with the brigadier, the general and Colonel Tim back at Sandbury, he had always been able to converse with them without the slightest familiarity, which experience stood him in good stead now.

"I would consider it a privilege to be able to continue working for the major Sir."

"That's settled then. God, I do wish everything I have to do at present could be settled as easily. Incidentally the major, as you call him, as GSO2 is now a lieutenant-colonel, and your staff position carries W.O.I. rank, both as from today. Colonel Deveson has all the further details. We've given you seven days to get your present company handed over so you haven't a lot of time. I'll see you again in a week or so." With that he stood up, all six feet three of him, shook hands with the colonel and with the now regimental sergeant major, and concluded "As they say in what they quaintly call the Senior Service, welcome aboard." They both smiled, took a pace back, saluted and marched out.

They travelled back on the main trunk road but made such poor time that by night fall they had only reached Ayer Hitam. There was no room at the Rest House, cluttered as it was by refugees fleeing from the north, hopefully to reach the safe haven of fortress Singapore. Rather than drive with reduced lights on a road full of every conceivable vehicle from rickshaws and trishaws to three ton lorries, to say nothing of hand carts and what appeared to be self propelled bundles of all manner of goods, underneath which one could, with careful scrutiny discern a Chinese man, woman or child providing the motive power, the colonel, as he now was, decided they would snooze in the truck until first light and then push on. Whilst it was a sensible decision it was not a very happy one. They were plagued by mosquitoes, the jungle noises from the beluka – secondary jungle – beside which they had parked varied from noisy to alarming. All in all they were glad at first light to throw off their blankets and brew up before joining what was now probably the most motley queue ever seen on a main road. Twenty miles from Johore Bahru they pulled out to pass a broken down Ford V8 pilot. As they came level, a white lady waved them down. The colonel told the driver to stop. The car contained two other women and no fewer than five children, all looking as if they had been without a wash for several days and in considerable distress.

"Have you any petrol please. We've run out and have not been able to buy any anywhere."

"Where are you from?" asked the colonel.

"Ipoh, we were bombed out a week ago."

"We can't give you petrol. Davies" – to one of the drivers – "fix a tow rope." Davies jumped from the back of the truck and speedily did as he was commanded. "We'll tow you to Nee Soon and then see about getting petrol."

It was a bit of a jerky start – the lady driver forgot to take the hand brake off. However, they soon got under way and steadily nosed on through the traffic towards the causeway. Theirs was not the only tow. At one stage a beautifully decorated Chinese owned lorry was pulling no fewer than three cars all crammed full of people until it apparently had to give up the ghost having itself run out of fuel.

Dusk came and in twenty minutes it was dark as they made the last few miles over the causeway on to the Bukit Timah Road and then to Nee Soon. Pulling up outside the company office, the major alighted and went back to the exhausted occupants of the Pilot.

"Where are you heading for in Singapore?" he asked.

"Alexandra married quarters. We have friends there who will put us up until our ship leaves on Monday."

"So you are army people?"

"Yes, our husbands are both majors in the Argylls."

"Well you had better stay here overnight. With our people being up country there's ample room in that block there. I'll get you some food organised for say an hour's time – give you a chance to shower etcetera. Then in the morning we'll find you some petrol to get you into town."

"Major, you are so kind. Thank you very much."

"Not at all, we must look after our own."

The meal was, although somewhat spartan, a lively affair, as any meal would be with five children present newly released from days of the confines of a crowded car. They had experienced several frightening incidents, firstly from people, seeing only women and children in the vehicle, endeavouring to either seize a lift, or on two occasions attempting to remove them and take the car. In addition as they came through Trolak and K.L. the road was machine gunned by Zeros. They were frightened to stay in the car; they were even more frightened to hide in the roadside monsoon ditch in case the car containing all their possessions was stolen from them. There was the constant fear of getting a puncture, or breaking down, and finally when they found they could get no petrol and had used their two gallon spare can, they began to get really alarmed. What money and jewellery the two ladies owned they were carrying with them, to say nothing of their passports, shipping documents and so on.

"Well, provided Mr Tojo doesn't send his horrible men over tonight, you can get a good night's sleep and we'll see you for breakfast at eight o'clock."

They thanked the colonel and Harry profusely for all their kindness and asked if they could take their names and home numbers so that they could contact their wives when they reached England. This duly carried out; they all went off to bed. There is no happy ending to this incident. The ship they were on was bombed in the Banka Strait after it had left Keppel Harbour. Just two of the children survived the bombing, spending the next three and a half years in the care of others in a particularly evil Sumatran camp. The Banka Strait became a graveyard of refugee ships, the Sumatran camps, the graveyard of more than half of those thousands who survived the drowning of their companions.

On Christmas Day Harry and the colonel handed over the company to a major who had landed as a reinforcement for India only the day before. On Boxing Day they put their goods into the Dodge and with their driver and two batmen – Harry as an RSM now merited a batman – they made their way north to Malacca, where they were immediately redirected further north to Kuala Lumpur.

"Oh well," Harry said, "Was it Shakespeare who said, 'it's better to travel hopefully than to arrive'?"

"Robert Louis Stevenson I think," replied the colonel, "however, Shakespeare said in As You Like It, 'When I was at home I was in a better place,' and he wasn't far wrong I must say."

They arrived at K.L. on the 28th after a very slow journey during which the stream of traffic was twice attacked by Zeros.

But this was not the end of their travel by any means.

Chapter Twelve

Arriving back at Wilmslow, David reported to Robin and was asked if he would mind waiting for half an hour. He retired to the reading room, which was occupied by one other person, a captain in the Royal Engineers he had not previously met. They introduced themselves, the sapper asking David if he too had just arrived. David's training thus far had been so intense that he automatically found himself answering his questions without actually telling him anything, until Robin appeared, apologising for keeping him waiting, asking him to come into his office. David opened the interview.

"Robin, I realise one doesn't ask questions but do you think I could break the rule on this occasion since I feel it may affect me?"

"Fire away, but you know as well as I do you may not get an answer – we'll all make excellent politicians after the war," he added with a smile.

"Hilary Jarvis. I understood we might be travelling together at some time, but I haven't seen her since I first came here. Is she alright?"

Robin sat silent for a few moments.

"I have to tell you that, no, she isn't alright."

David's heart sank. He had already lost his first secret mentor, Jessica, who had been shot by the Gestapo.

"Don't tell me we have another Jessica situation."

"No, no, it hasn't come to that – at least not as far as we know. We have just lost touch that's all. There could be many reasons for this as you will know."

"How long before you assume the worst?"

"David, I have to tell you, we are passing that stage at this very moment."

David sat silent. He had seen his comrades killed around him at Calais. Although this saddened him greatly, particularly the loss of his greatest friend and brother-in-law Jeremy, it did not seem as evil as the killing of these two beautiful girls. He pulled his thoughts together – they did not know Hilary was dead, she could be secreted away somewhere for her own safety and in due course would be able to emerge. He looked at Robin.

"This means she will not be coming with me."

"I'm afraid so. Now down to business. We are sending you down to Beaulieu up until 21st December when you can go home and return here on Sunday 4th Jan. This is to give you an introduction to cipher work. It may be that you will have to return there if we think you need to be more proficient, otherwise I am hoping we can get you away by the middle of January. Where to and for how long we shall let you know in due course."

"The day before I go, I bet," David joked. Robin replied with a grin.

The next day, after a somewhat disturbed night worrying about Hilary, David made his way down to Hampshire.

He soon settled in, finding the intensive brain work required to understand cipher work very taxing. With his usual tenacity he stuck at it, but had to admit that unlike some there, he was not a natural. To become anything like proficient he was going to have to pull out all the stops. It was late on December 8th when he heard the news about Malaya. He had become friendly with a man, he judged to be forty or thereabouts, a refugee from Austria named Jacob Ribritz. With him he was able to continue practising his Swiss-German, as Jacob had apparently spent a number of years in Switzerland. Most of this took place at meal times and during the late evening – they worked until eight o'clock each day – it was the Austrian who told him the news when he met him after dinner. David was obviously troubled by the information, leading Jacob to enquire whether he had relatives there. When David said his brother was in Singapore his new colleague re-assured him that the Japanese had landed in the north, they would find it very difficult indeed to fight their way through the jungles of Malaya, and even if they did, Singapore was known to be an impregnable fortress.

"I just hope this won't be another Dunkirk for him," David concluded, and afterwards thought, at Dunkirk they had England to make for, and hundreds of little boats to help get them there. What have they got at Singapore, and come to that, where could they safely go to? He got an atlas from the library but after considerable examination of that part of the world, of which he admitted to himself he knew practically nothing, he could not find the answer to that last question. Java lay to the south, it would obviously be next on the Japanese shopping list if they were successful in Malaya and Singapore, then what seemed thousands of miles away was Australia, it would take more than a small boat to get there. He suddenly got a grip on himself, 'What the hell am I thinking like this for? The army will stop them and drive them back into the sea. With the help of the R.A.F. and the Far Eastern Fleet of the Royal Navy, they will give the nasty four-eyed little bastards what they deserve.' He was not to know, of course, that the R.A.F. was barely a token force, equipped with sub-standard aircraft, the 'Far Eastern Fleet' comprised two huge battleships, which would both be sunk on the same day, and a half dozen ageing destroyers. He finally consoled himself that if anyone could look after himself it was Harry. What was odd was that everyone who knew Harry said the same thing. It is strange how often a person can get a reputation for doing something, being something or capable of achieving something without any really positive evidence. In Harry's case, everyone who knew him had the feeling he was someone who could be relied on absolutely, though they had no unequivocal grounds for arriving at the decision.

On Sunday 14th December David borrowed a motorcycle and made his way over to Romsey for the day. It was only half an hour away. Buffy and Rita were delighted to see him; they had not had much opportunity to talk at the wedding. With so many people to talk to and of course you were what one might describe as being somewhat occupied, Rita pertly put it. Buffy grinned.

"I had quite a chat to Maria – it is Maria isn't it?"

"You know jolly well its Maria – you were asking her name the minute you set eyes on her," teased Rita.

"She's a jolly nice girl. Somehow or other we got to talking about literature. Oh, I know, I asked her what she did in her spare time thinking she would say she went to the flicks or to the Palais or somewhere, and she said she went to evening classes twice a week. Again I thought she's probably learning cake making or something, only to be told she is studying English literature – not for examination purposes but because she hoped that one day she could become a writer." He paused for a moment, then continued with, "Do you know, I've just done a terrible thing. She seemed a trifle embarrassed that she had let slip she thought she could become a writer, and asked me, please, not to say anything to anyone else. I naturally gave her my word that not a syllable would pass my lips." He paused again before going on, "But then it doesn't really matter because you probably know all this anyway David."

David thought for a moment or two. "No, I didn't know. On the other hand I can understand why she hasn't said anything to me. She is essentially a very modest person, that's one of the reasons I like her so much." Buffy and Rita's eyebrows raised in unison at this last expression.

Buffy thought he had better jolly his way out of the situation he had put them in. "I don't think it's that at all. I think she probably doesn't want to appear an egghead in the company of the licentious soldiery."

"Me – licentious?"

"Well you're in the Rifles aren't you? Now if you had been in the Hampshires, such a thought would not have crossed her mind."

125

They had a pleasant day together, David saying he had better start back before dark, as he was somewhat unsure of the way. All signposts had been removed during the invasion scare and it would be a long time before they were replaced. He had an Ordnance Survey map, but riding a motorbike on a day which had been blowing snow on and off all day, wearing a pair of thick gauntlets which he would have been reluctant to remove to study a map, decided to 'follow his nose.' Unfortunately his nose let him down, he got thoroughly lost in the middle of the New Forest with not a soul to ask directions, until eventually he was lucky in spotting an army truck approaching which he waved down and was put on the right road. The half hour journey had taken well over an hour.

Having divested himself of virtually every piece of warm clothing he possessed – as he had told himself 'it's going to be proper brass monkey weather on that motorbike' – he warmed himself in front of the enormous log fire in the walk-in fireplace in the main sitting room. Paddy had stayed behind at Wilmslow at Robin's request to meet a 'visitor' he would like Paddy to have a few days with, after which he too would go on Christmas leave; as a result, David shared a temporary A.T.S. batman. As he gradually thawed out he saw this young lady beckoning him from the doorway. He walked over, to be told, "Lady for you Sir on Number Four." It was his mother.

"I'm just trying to firm up the Christmas arrangements," she told him, "have you made your plans yet?" She knew he would be coming on leave on Sunday 21st.

Christmas plans are more difficult than organising a full scale continental invasion, David thought. Not that he would ever be likely to be called upon to carry out such an exercise, but there was always the problem at Christmas time of how to divide yourself up to keep everybody happy. That's one of the penalties of being so popular I suppose, he modestly told himself.

"There's a slight alteration Mum. I understand we shall get away after lunch on Saturday 20th, so I should be home on Saturday evening sometime."

"That's no problem. What I wanted more particularly to know was will Maria be with us over the Christmas period at all, or will you be going there? We thought of having a bit of a party on Boxing Day, particularly as we have heard that Moira will be back on or about the 20th."

"That's great news. Uncle Jack will be pleased, although if she is back on the 20th do you think he'll be fit enough for a party by the 26th?"

"David – behave yourself. Anyway, phone me back when you

have spoken to Maria."

David spent a few minutes telling his mother of his visit to Romsey at the end of which he booked a call to Chingford. It was answered by Mr Schultz in a very short while, who immediately broached the subject of Christmas. "David my boy, I am sure you will want to spent Christmas with your family. Therefore if you should want to invite Maria please do. Do not consider us, we see her all the time. You know, my talking to you like this, she will kill me for, nein? I don't mind. None of us know where we shall be next Christmas. Mrs Schultz and I will be quite happy here on our own – you tell Maria if she argues with you."

"Civilians are not allowed to argue with the military Mr Schultz – are they?"

"No, definitely not."

"Good, if she argues I'll tell her you said so, and you are an authority on the subject." They both laughed as Maria took the telephone from her father.

"I've just come in – what has my father been saying to you?"

"He's been telling me about that sixteen stone stoker you've been going around with again."

"He's put on weight – he's seventeen stones now."

"Is that with or without clothes?"

"David Chandler, that is a very naughty thing to say," she was trying to suppress her giggles as she spoke. Up until now David had always been perfectly proper in his approach to her. Whilst that last remark could not be construed as anything approaching salaciousness it did indicate a movement of familiarity between them which each mentally noted and felt pleased about.

"My purpose in telephoning you, apart from the pleasure of hearing your beautiful voice, is to ask you to come to Chandlers Lodge for Christmas. Mum and Dad are throwing a party on Boxing Day. Can you do that or will you be working?" He hurried on. "Your father and mother assure me that they will be quite happy on their own, since they see you every day." He paused for a moment. "In fact, they suggested they would be grateful for the peace and quiet."

"That's one I owe you David Chandler. The answer is I would love to come. The second answer is that I shall not be working as I have to leave next Wednesday – I am being called up in January."

"You're what?" David almost bellowed into the mouthpiece.

"I'm being called up. I have to go to a tribunal on January 14th."

"Isn't there any way of getting out of it?"

"Would you?"

With those two words David knew he had no argument. His mind in a turmoil, he hardly knew what to say.

"But you have to mix with a lot of unpleasant people in the forces."

"You mean like you and Paddy and Charlie?" He was definitely not winning this argument.

"David darling" – it was the very first time she had used that term of endearment to him, whatever she said next would not remain in his memory as that did.

"David darling, every day I meet a lot of nice people. I also meet quite a few very nasty men, and women for that matter. The men can and do use all sorts of language to me, I have vulgarity used to me, all sorts of licentious suggestions made to me, I think it would be most unlikely if men in the forces even began to compare with what is considered a fair game between some men and the girl who is having to wait on them."

There was a long pause broken by David.

"And am I really your darling?"

"From the minute I first saw you."

"And you are mine too."

It was a long week that followed until on Saturday 20th, David hauled his kit and himself into the back of a fifteen hundred weight truck to be taken to Southampton station. Although he, of course, had first class travel warrants, the first class section of the train was full to the brim, mainly with naval officers. As a result he had to stand in the corridor all the way to Waterloo, and with not a spare porter in sight had to carry his kit to the waiting taxi queue. Over thirty minutes standing there in the bitter cold produced the thought that he must be getting soft. All that sitting around in classrooms was turning him into a chair-borne warrior. When he was installing coastal defences up at Colchester a few years back – a few years? It was only two years ago, it seemed a lifetime – a bit of cold, discomfort and waiting around would have been shrugged off as the norm. And then he thought of Harry, sweating it out only a few miles from the equator, and consoled himself with the fact that Harry would not get his balls frozen off as they did up on the east coast.

Having telephoned home from Victoria, he was greeted by the welcome sight of his father along with the equally welcome sight of the Rover into which they dumped his kit. "I'm damned glad I didn't have to take all my kit with me to Beaulieu, I would never have been able to lug that lot across London."

His father grinned. "You're getting soft in your old age."

The family, including Karl, Anni, Ernie and baby David, were all there, with Cecely and her two children who had come up to Chandlers Lodge for the weekend, the two children being on their Christmas holidays. Swiftly his mother whisked David away to the kitchen. "You must be starving if you have had nothing since lunch time. I suppose there was nothing on the train."

"The days are long gone when you can get food on a train, always assuming you can move up and down the corridors, which mostly you can't," replied David. "They do stop for short breaks at main line stations like Crewe or York so that you can get out and buy a sandwich or something from the various mobile canteens like the Salvation Army or W.V.S.," and then the thought of the Rotary canteen flashed across his mind, and his beloved Pat, which led to a feeling of guilt that he had not thought of her all day.

Immediately his mother realised the thought, which had halted his conversation, knowing that the word canteen was synonymous with Pat, and always would be. Quickly she interjected, "Well, eat that up now and I have some apple pie keeping warm in the Aga."

As he sat eating, his mother watched him closely. "Is there something wrong?" she asked.

"I've always said you would be a great asset to the Intelligence Corps. What makes you think there is something wrong?"

"I know you, David Chandler. When you had been up to something as a lad, and later when you had something troubling you or not quite right, you had two little pleats between your eyebrows. You've got them now on and off. So what's on your mind? Always assuming, of course, it's a fitting problem to tell me about."

"Maria has told me she's got to go to a tribunal to be called up."

"And you don't like that idea? After all, she would be helping in the war effort."

"It's the idea that she might have to mix with all sorts – she might even find someone else."

"If it comes to that – so might you – you mix with all sorts." David winced at the thought of his olympian night with Pamela. "Anyway, would it worry you that much if she found someone else?" The mischief in this question escaped David completely.

"Yes it would," he replied vehemently. Realising immediately he had been caught out, he added, "You crafty blighter – you tricked me into that."

"No I didn't – I've known it for ages, and I am very pleased about it, she's a lovely girl."

On Monday David had to race around Sandbury to buy Christmas presents for all the family, increased now by the presence of Cecely, Greta, Oliver and Mrs Treharne. In the course of going from shop to shop he called in to Country Style of which he was, of course, the owner since Pat's death. Mrs Draper was most pleased to see him; he in turn, told her how grateful he was to her for all she was doing. There was, however, a small problem. The young assistant who had been with her for the past year, and who was doing really well, was going to be called up in the new year. "So I shall advertise again. I don't know as soon as you train a girl up they come and snatch them away. Other shops are having the same problem;" Mrs Draper went on, "one girl in the jewellery shop across the road was called up to industry and was set to work in a milk bottle factory. Just imagine it, diamonds one day and milk bottles the next. Still, I suppose it's happening everywhere."

David's major problem was what to buy for the babies. He had visited Megan over the weekend to be told he was to be a godfather again. He pointed out he might not be here whenever the christening was to be, to be told he would have to appoint a 'stand in.' However, Megan was able to guide him on suitable purchases for the very young, he had already decided on Conway Stewart pens for Oliver and Greta.

On Tuesday 23rd he travelled up to Marble Arch to meet Maria from work. Waiting just inside the entrance doors – the corner of Oxford Street and Cumberland Place was a cold bleak place in the blackout at 5 o'clock on a late December afternoon upon which to wait outside – he spotted the immaculately turned out figure of Mr Stratton coming towards him. "Captain Chandler – how great to see you. Miss Schultz told me you would be meeting her from work so I thought I must come and say hello. You know we are losing her tomorrow?"

They talked on for some ten minutes, David asking after his family to be told how deeply they still felt the loss of his little granddaughter who was killed in an air raid. He was sad at losing Maria. Not only was she superbly efficient at her job – it was plain that no higher accolade could ever be awarded any person than this in Mr Stratton's books – but she was such a thoroughly nice person. "If you both should be passing this way at any time in the future, please call in Captain Chandler, I would be so pleased to see you."

"You can count on it Mr Stratton, you can definitely count on it."

They had a pleasant evening in the Cumberland until David took Maria to Marble Arch to catch her last train to Chingford. Having arranged that he would meet her from work the following day to help her with her suitcase she told David that Mr Stratton had arranged she could leave at midday to avoid the Christmas Eve rush.

On Christmas Eve therefore, David duly presented himself again at Lyons Corner House, collected Maria and suitcase, shook hands with Mr Stratton and on leaving was lucky enough to wave down a passing cab to take them to Victoria. Once in the cab he gave Maria a long, welcoming kiss, which fairly took her breath away. Although the driver had a clear view of them in his mirror, he took no notice. He had seen it all, up to and including full scale copulation on that back seat. In the small taxi drivers' coffee hut in Leicester Square he told the story of how he arrived at Paddington one evening to be asked to hang on for a couple of minutes – they hadn't finished! Still, he concluded, he got a good tip. He used to meet two respectable suburban ladies at Waterloo each day for some months who arrived on the 1.50 Getting into the cab they undressed and changed from their two piece suits into short skirts and low topped blouses, putting the decorous clothing into a suitcase which they left by the driver on the cab luggage rack. The cabbie then took them to Golden Square where they plied their trade all the afternoon, after which he collected them at 6.30 to take them back to Waterloo, changing into their Wimbledon clothes on the way. It was a 'good earner' until inevitably they 'got nicked' and the husbands found out."

Christmas Day was still a day of plenty in the Chandler household. The contrast to what was happening elsewhere in the world was unbelievable. The Germans had set up a prisoner of war camp at Hola in Poland. Over 100,000 Russian soldiers were incarcerated there in mid-December in an open field surrounded by barbed wire. In freezing temperatures, and given no food, by the end of December they had all died. Polish civilians who tried to give them food were summarily shot. There was not one survivor. Altogether some four million Russian P.O.W.'s were to die in German hands.

On Christmas Day in Hong Kong the British forces surrendered, having put up a spirited defence against overwhelming odds. On Christmas Eve over fifty British and Canadian prisoners had been tied up and bayoneted to death, similar occurrences taking place on Christmas Day to both soldiers and nurses.

On Christmas Day in Leningrad nearly 4000 people died of starvation. It was so cold and the enemy shelling so persistent they could not be buried.

On Christmas Day in Malaya the retreat, if it could be called that, continued unrelentingly southwards towards Kuala Lumpur, the capital of Selangor and the most important town on the mainland. Harry's stay in his new headquarters was to last for just a week.

On Christmas Day in the White House at a conference of the Allied chiefs of staff, General Sir Archibold Wavell was appointed commander-in-chief Far East. A brilliant soldier, he succinctly put it, "I have heard of men having to hold the baby – but this is twins." Neither his gallantry nor his competence would be enough to combat years of neglect and lack of vision by British Governments, up to and including that of Churchill himself.

None of this horror was known at Chandlers Lodge. On Boxing Day evening they held the party, additional lubricants being provided by Colonel Tim, Alec and Jim from their Canadian Naafi ration. It was a great evening particularly since Maria, Cecely and her children were able to thoroughly mingle with people they had not met, or had only been briefly introduced to before. Late in the evening Fred called all present to order.

"I give you a toast ladies and gentlemen. To absent friends – particularly Nigel and Harry – and good luck to all here during the coming year." The toast was drunk. In that coming year a number of them were to need that luck. Tim, Alec and Jim on the combined ops raid on Dieppe, Mark Laurenson and Charlie on the battlefields of the Western Desert, David going he knew not where and on the other side of the world, Harry facing horror and privations the folks at home could not even dream about. How many would still be alive in one years' time?

Chapter Thirteen

It was October 3rd 1941. Dieter von Hassellbek stood on the top of his stationary tank facing towards Moscow. It was a dull, miserable day, raining from time to time, the wind giving an indication of the icy blasts to come. His regiment was in reserve, which makes a change he had said to himself. On the Moscow front that day the Wehrmacht had amassed some 2000 tanks. Hitler had said, 'Today begins the last, great, decisive battle of the war. Operation Typhoon would soon wrest three of their greatest industrial districts from the hands of the Soviets.'

As Dieter stood there, listening to the dull thunder of the guns some four or five miles ahead, watching the Stukas and medium bombers flying above him, giving a cheery wave to passing infantry men as they moved through to mop up after the tank battle, he suddenly wondered how his friend David was faring back in England. It was his fervent hope, along with many others of his comrades, that this war against the Ivans would be quickly finished and they could then make an honourable peace with England. In the meantime the barbarians must be crushed. Neither he nor his comrades had the faintest notion of the barbarity of their own einsatzgruppen working behind the lines killing daily tens of thousands of innocent Jews, Gypsies, racially and mentally inferior elements and others. In one ravine at Babi Yar near Kiev, 35,782 men, women and children were marshalled together and machine-gunned to death from the high points on either side. It is a staggering indictment of the German psyche that they were able to give an exact number, 35,782, of human beings killed on that day. They had actually detailed people to count the victims. Why? It was a massacre, why bother to know how many were sacrificed? But they did. All of these massacres were methodically enumerated and the totals transmitted to their control. It was efficiency at its most devilish.

The forward troops of course had no mercy for the commissars they took captive. Once discovered they were immediately executed, in fact it would be fair to say that the Russian soldiers themselves would probably have volunteered as the firing party. Dieter and his fellows felt quite indifferent to the sight of a Bolshevik fanatic having his brains blown out – they were the immediate and visible manifestation of the corrupt and evil system of communism against which they were here to free the world. And when that happens the English, the Americans, and most of the rest of the world will owe a debt of gratitude to the German Wehrmacht.

Since Dieter had crossed the Russian frontier in General von Bock's army on 22 June he had twice distinguished himself, had received his Iron Cross First Class to complement his Second Class won in the Polish campaign, and had been promoted to captain. In the middle of September his unit had received a nasty shock when it ran up against the new Soviet T34 tank. They found to their surprise and alarm that not only did this tank outgun them, it was so well armoured that the Mark IV panzers main 73mm gun would not penetrate the front armour of the T34 until it was ranged at around 100 metres, which was suicidal. Dieter had won his decoration for doing precisely that thus preventing a breakthrough to the rear of their thinly held position. A new German tank was being built to combat the T34, but it would not be available until the new year. Similarly the T34's were, as yet, in small numbers, what there were being despatched to the Moscow front to ensure the capital was held.

And so on October 3rd Dieter was again awaiting the order to advance. The days were getting shorter now. There were flakes of snow in the air; the warm days of chasing over the firm Russian steppes were to be exchanged for the quagmires producing the autumn rains, to be followed by the dreaded Russian winter. As he stood there he could see lines of foot soldiers streaming towards him. Lifting his binoculars he saw they were prisoners – thousands of them. They must have been encircled, disarmed, and told to walk westwards towards Smolensk. As they got nearer Dieter could see they were badly clothed, badly shod, even worse than he had seen them in the past. What is more, they were obviously so demoralised their captors had not even provided guards, just told them the direction in which to go. 'Who the devil is going to marshall and feed that lot?' Dieter asked himself. The answer was 'probably nobody.'

A tug came on his trouser leg from the wireless operator seated below him. He was handed a message form. 'Move line 82 degrees 5 kilometres then 2 kilometres 92 degrees. Wait further orders.' He sent a signal to his squadron to follow and set off as ordered. As he got underway, a flight of Stukas flew over at about 1000 metres. In a short while they increased height a little, circled, picked out their targets, and commenced their screaming dive. Dieter enjoyed considerable satisfaction from watching this. He had been instrumental in getting the army to cooperate with the Luftwaffe – not an easy thing to do on either side at any time – in providing close support to forward armour. As a result of his suggestion, put to the famous General Guderian, probably the greatest of all tank generals, a special control vehicle manned by Luftwaffe forward observation officers in direct radio contact with a close support airfield, was able to call on accurate fire power as and when required. A Mark IV panzer might find a T34 difficult to handle, but an accurate attack by a Stuka would blow one out of the ground, as well as scaring the daylights out of the supporting infantry.

The squadron moved steadily on, accompanied from time to time by shells incoming from the Russian heavies. The tanks were well spread out; a hit would be most unlikely. They reached the seven kilometre point, radioed 'in position' and waited. It was getting dark when the order came 'Harbour. Prepare to move 0600.' They adopted standard all round protection, at the completion of which Dieter made a thorough inspection to ensure they could not be surprised during the night neither by Russian troops nor partisans who they knew by experience were very active on the approaches to Moscow. When he returned to his tank, a message awaited him from his colonel to report to regimental headquarters. Scrambling into the sidecar of a motorcycle combination sent for him, he made his way some three kilometres back to a tented area beneath a small thicket of birch trees.

The colonel was a short, stocky Prussian who had a fearsome reputation as a disciplinarian but was, nevertheless, highly regarded as being absolutely and totally fearless. On more than one occasion he had been seen in his little Kuppelwagen right up at the front with the leading tanks in set piece battles with the Soviets, and despite this rather dangerous habit it was said he never had problems with getting volunteer drivers!

Dieter saluted. "Von Hassellbek, this is Hauptmann Fischer, he is to take over your squadron, and before you argue this is an order from General Guderian. You are to go back to Frankfurt-am-Oder to take part in a symposium being arranged by army command; I know nothing more than that. Hand over to Fischer this evening and be back here ready to leave for the railhead at 0900 tomorrow. That is all." The two officers saluted and left, as Dieter left the tent doorway the colonel called after him, "I believe there is quite a reliable train service between Frankfurt and Munich, von Hassellbek." It was the first unmilitary sentence Dieter had ever heard him express – and how did he know my Rosa was in Munich, he wondered? At the thought of the opportunity of seeing his wife again after so long, his heart leapt.

The journey to the railhead was interminable. The roads were literally falling to pieces. The further west they drove the more it rained. Time and again they witnessed lorries and tanks stuck in the morass. 'What the hell is it going to be like when it really rains?' Dieter pondered. They arrived at Smolensk. Again he thought 'How the hell will those prisoners make it this far on foot?' The answer, of course, was, in most cases, they didn't.

Arriving at the railhead he was directed to a platform almost on the northern edge of the station. The other track – the furthest north – was packed full of civilians, men, women and children. They were surrounded by SS troops, many with ferocious Alsatian dogs. Although there were many hundreds of them they were strangely quiet. One child, probably ten or so, dropped a ball it was carrying which rolled towards Dieter. As she ran to retrieve it, a guard swung a heavy stick hitting her across the upper arm sending her sprawling at Dieter's feet. As he bent to pick her up the guard raised the stick again. Dieter grabbed his arm and wrested the stick from him.

"What sort of man are you to beat a young child?" he demanded.

"She's a Jew," replied the guard.

"First of all, you ignorant lout, you stand to attention when you speak to me, secondly you call me Herr Hauptmann. Do you understand?"

The child, in the meantime, had picked itself up, retrieved its ball and disappeared into the anonymity of the crowd. The guard replied, "We're not answerable to you." Dieter looked around to see if there were any military police on the platform, seeing one, beckoned him. The policeman saluted smartly.

At the same time a tall, thin bespectacled S.S. Lieutenant appeared. He saluted Dieter, "What is the trouble Herr Hauptmann?" he queried.

"This man attempted to beat a child, and when I interfered was offensive. He said he was not answerable to army officers."

"Strictly speaking Herr Hauptmann, that is true. We are answerable only to Reichsminister Himmler. However, I shall charge and punish him you may be sure." Dieter decided he had to leave it at that. As he walked away, accompanied by the M.P. he asked who the people were.

"Oh, that's another consignment of Jews for Sobibor" he was told.

"What happens at Sobibor?" he asked, almost flippantly.

"You don't know Sir?" the M.P. enquired.

"No – I've been up at the front for the past few months."

"Sobibor is a big industrial centre. The Jews are taken there. Those who can work are put to work, the others are gassed. Those who work are worked to death. Most of those S.S. people are ex-convicts released from gaol to do that dirty work."

"You mean the children and old people are gassed?"

"Yes Sir, but I think I've said too much."
"Not at all sergeant, it will go no further."

But the memory of that little girl and the fact that within days she would be ending her days in a gas chamber was the first stirring within him of the appreciation of the evil these Nazis were perpetrating. This small incident more than anything else, led him to question what the German nation was doing. His mind was in turmoil as he sat in his first class compartment watching through the window the hundreds of condemned civilians passing him as the long, heavily laden train slowly drew out for Warsaw and then Frankfurt-am-Oder. He had no doubt whatsoever of the German correctness of invading Russia. If other European countries were in Germany's position they would have done the same. You can't live forever with the thought of ten million soldiers under arms within striking distance of your frontier without doing something about it, particularly since those same people had declared indisputably that they intended to impose communism throughout the world. And the S.S. He had met the Waffen S.S. in action on several occasions. They were not a rabble, their bravery and discipline was fast becoming a legend. Like most other units they went beyond the normally acceptable practices of war from time to time, particularly where partisans, and villagers suspected of aiding and abetting partisans were concerned, but he was sure they would not want to be part of the gassing of innocent women and children. Then the terrible thought struck him. INGE. What if his sister was part of this. He knew she had a senior position in the concentration camp system in Germany, but concentration camps in the Reich, as far as he knew, and that applied he judged to most Germans, were essential in containing communists and others who would sabotage the war effort. His thoughts in a turmoil, he dozed off, uncomfortable though he was. When he awoke an hour later, it was dark.

There were no incidents that night. 'Incidents' usually meant being fired on by partisans from out of the darkness. However, the einsatzgruppen had made a top priority of clearing a wide corridor through which the railway passed by the simple means of burning to the ground all possible shelters, farms, houses etc and exterminating any peasants who attempted to return to re-establish them. Once they reached the old Polish border they felt reasonably secure, there was little resistance at this time from the Poles.

For two long days, Dieter suffered this journey, living on the rations he had brought with him, and hot soup always available for the train passengers at the larger stopping points. At six o'clock on a dark, miserable, cold, wet morning they crawled into Frankfurt, on the west bank of the River Oder. 'Where do I go from here?' he asked himself as he, and a few others, alighted from the train, the majority of the passengers would be going on to Berlin.

He looked along the platform and saw a sergeant along with a private soldier coming towards him. The sergeant saluted smartly. "Hauptmann von Hassellbek Sir?" he asked.

"Yes sergeant, and am I pleased to see you. Firstly, my arse has gone to sleep through sitting on that blasted train all those hours and secondly, if I don't soon get a bath they will have to fumigate me." The sergeant smiled at the jocularity. He recognised the sort of camaraderie that existed between officers and N.C.O.s under active service conditions and which he missed so much in his safe job back at base. Even though that was compensated for by the knowledge that he had a comfortable bed to sleep in at nights instead of some slit trench somewhere out in the wilds, the overbearing manner of the base dodgers was, to say the least, very irksome. Well, he concluded, he was graded since he was stupid enough to get himself wounded in the Polish campaign, so there was nothing he could do about it. The day would come when, if you even had only one leg, you would have to do something, but that would be a couple of years away.

The private took his kit on a small handcart and introduced himself as Gefreiter Muller, who would be his servant during his stay at Headquarters. He was taken to a hutted camp where a forbidding looking, extremely rotund lady (she doesn't live on army rations I bet, was Dieter's immediate judgement), booked him in, telling him his room was along the corridor to the right. The feldwebel took his leave saying that he would be there to collect Herr Hauptmann at 7.30 the next morning; he could in the meantime 'learn how to smell nice again.' Dieter laughed and thanked him.

The next morning he was driven from the dormitory to about twenty kilometres out of Frankfurt. They were stopped by military police at the gateway to a long drive leading up to an impressive, porticoed building situated on a mound with extensive views overlooking the sweep of the River Oder. "This used to belong to Julius Goldstein, the financier," volunteered the feldwebel.

"What happened to him?" asked Dieter in all innocence.

"I don't suppose we shall ever know," the sergeant replied, "but then it doesn't do to ask Sir, does it?" Another good man who may have to be with them but is not necessarily for them Dieter concluded.

"I'll collect you at six Sir, unless they telephone me to the contrary."

Dieter made his way up the long, broad flight of steps, through the enormous double doors into the first large hallway, from which he could see several smaller hallways branching off. The building was immaculately maintained, superbly fitted, it was a palace. He approached the central desk, manned by a donnish looking sergeant major – and that's a contradiction in terms if ever there was one he mused.

"Ah Hauptmann von Hassellbek, you are expected."

After two and a half days in that bloody train I'm glad to hear it, he thought.

"If you will be so kind as to take a seat I will get a guide to take you to the meeting room." Dieter saw him suddenly stiffen to attention and looking round, saw the impeccably uniformed, tall, blonde, blue-eyed, incredibly handsome figure of General Reinhard Heydrich.

Dieter gave a flawless military salute, which was answered, by a brief wave upwards of the general's right hand. He said "Heil Hitler," accompanied by a luminous smile and the statement, "You've been busy," pointing at the Iron Cross on his tunic. Dieter smiled in return. He considered later the total contradiction of his bifurcated attitude towards people like Heydrich. Here was a man who would, as he could readily admit, attain instant loyalty from him as a result of the force of his personal magnetism, yet he was one of the leaders of this National Socialist gang, so many of whom were thugs and morons.

The stranger thing was the difference in the two Reinhard Heydrichs. The gentle, fastidious, artistic, Mozart loving family man on the one side, and the womanising planner of the killing of six million Jews on the other. Sigmund Freud would have had a field day.

Dieter's guide arrived, asking him if he would kindly follow him to the conference room. The room was an ornate affair, gold stucco everywhere, two crystal chandeliers as big as hayricks, the polished wooden floor so burnished you could see to shave in it. He had the quick thought that since this was probably the ballroom in its heyday, you would have been able to see whether your dancing partner had any knickers on or not.

His guide took him to the chairman of the meeting. "Herr General, Hauptmann von Hassellbek."

"Yes, we know each other." It was Guderian.

Dieter produced another of his exemplary salutes at which the General held out his hand.

"We meet in very different places do we not von Hassellbek? I've asked you to come here," asked me thought Dieter – since when did generals ask captains. "I've asked you to come here to give the views of the actual user of the tank under all sorts and conditions of service. It will all be explained to you in the preamble. However, despite the fact you are the most junior officer here, I felt that what I know of you and your enquiring mind I could ensure that you would put straightforward views to the staff officers and manufacturers present without fear of being intimidated by their rank."

Dieter grinned. "And which military prison do I end up in if I promote the unpopular view?" he asked.

"That's what we're looking for. You see von Hassellbek," he drew Dieter a little aside. "Everyone here has a vested interest. Some want a cheap job quickly. Others want an expensive job we cannot afford and would take too long to make. Others want a bigger share of the budget at the expense of planes, submarines, or something else. What you have to do is to tell them what needs improving in our exiting panzer set up from the point of view of the man pointing the tank at the Ivans. If it means to do this properly we have to have a bigger share of the cake, so they will have to be told."

Leaving Dieter, the general took his seat at the head of the table, asking the some fifteen to twenty Wehrmacht and civilians to be seated.

Like all meetings it was a mixture of pointless argument, well practised rhetoric, intelligent suggestion, views promulgated with the benefit of sound experience, views promulgated with the sole benefit of self interest, all of which being deftly dealt with by General Guderian allowing no one, high ministry man, senior Krupps man nor senior Wehrmacht man to hog the floor. They broke for lunch. Several people buttonholed Dieter to ask him about the fighting at the front, and when would they be in Moscow. He had to tell them he was only a very small cog in an enormous wheel, and jokingly added that Field Marshall von Bock rarely consulted him on advanced strategy.

He had still not been called upon to speak by the end of the afternoon session. At five o'clock, General Guderian called the meeting to a close for the day, saying that he would summarise the next morning, continuing all day, and all night if necessary, as they could not go on into Friday. Dieter suspected this was because they all wanted to get home for the weekend; in fact it was because the Fuhrer himself required to see the principles at his East Prussian headquarters, 'The

Wolf's Lair' at Rastenburg on Sunday.

When Dieter arrived back at his quarters, his servant told him there was a message waiting for him at the reception desk. He had asked the sergeant major to endeavour to find out the whereabouts of his wife, at the university at Munich where she was on a final year of a medical degree, at some hospital at which she may be working, or even at home with her mother in the city itself. The message read 'Am at mummy's flat. Please telephone. Lots of love Rosa.'

There was a delay in getting through to Munich, but at last he heard the voice of his darling Rosa, to whom he had not been able to speak for over three months, and had not seen since January. He had to tell her he had no idea at all whether he would be able to get leave to see her, he was back temporarily in Germany but that was as much as he could tell her, he would know more on the morrow.

The next day Dieter was called upon to give the view of the fighting man as to what was required in a tank to fight on the Eastern Front. He started by saying the MK IV was a first class weapon, regarded with great affection by the panzer men. It was fast, reliable, and did not burn easily when hit. However, as is the case with all machines, it gradually becomes outdated, in this case by the T34. "My crew knocked out three T34's in one morning so they are far from invincible. We took prisoner the commander of one of the tanks, ordering him to ride on our tank until we were put in reserve later in the afternoon. I then interrogated him. He was a Colonel Petrov, had been responsible for the initial testing of the T34 in the Ural's. He told me a great deal about the design of the tank, its strengths and weaknesses. He himself, whilst a patriot, hated the Bolshevik clique. Two of his uncles were senior army officers who were eliminated by Stalin in the 1936 purges. He hoped that Germany would soon win the war so that Russia and the Reich could join in an honourable peace and push international communism from the face of the earth.

The advantages of the T34 are as follows. Firstly it has a 75 millimetre high velocity main armament, which means it has a greater range than our standard armament. It can, therefore, hit us before we can hit it. Secondly the engine is designed to be replaced very quickly, which means it can be stressed to a greater extent than our power units. Thirdly the body armour, especially at the front, is thicker and where possible, slants against the horizontal inducing solid shots in particular to be more likely to ricochet from the surface. Probably its greatest advantage however as we shall undoubtedly experience soon, is that its tracks are wider than the MK IV, therefore will make the T34 much more manoeuvrable in the mud, and then the snow."

"If I may interrupt my report Herr general, I would be most grateful if it could be known that forward troops still do not have any winter clothing and when I left the Moscow Front it was already beginning to snow. Combined with the chill factor of the wind blowing out from Siberia, it is getting very cold indeed." A number of the senior army people looked at each other with some concern.

Dieter continued saying he had had long and comprehensive talks on the T34 design and performance factors, rate of fire and so on which he had written out in full and passed to his commanding officer, who in turn had forwarded them to divisional intelligence. "In fact we sat up most of the night," he said. The colonel was then sent on to division and that was the last he saw of him.

"To conclude therefore, gentlemen, if it were possible, we should have a tank with more frontal armour, wider tracks for combating the ground conditions, if possible mounted with our superb 88 millimetre gun and finally a means of transporting it. At the moment virtually all the mileage of our average tank is taken up by its moving from one sphere of operations to another. Its engine life is very limited as a result of the enormous amount of low gear work it has to do. The ideal would be to have tank transporters on call from suitable bases to move units from reserve positions to operation points. These could also be used to remove to workshops tanks that have been knocked out but which would be repairable. Thank you gentlemen."

The general rose. "Are there any questions you would like to ask Hauptmann von Hassellbek?"

A Luftwaffe senior officer raised his hand. "How did you converse with this Petrov over such a long period?"

"Sir, I speak fluent Russian."

Guderian interjected "Yes and French and English I recall – is that not so?"

"Yes Herr general."

A general from the quartermasters department raised his hand. "I am concerned you have no winter clothing. May I speak to von Hassellbek afterwards on this matter general?"

"Yes, of course, I am as surprised as you are. If this is the case on my front, someone is going to get a very well placed kick up the arse I can tell you.

A man from Porsche, one of the biggest of German panzer builders raised his hand. "It would not be possible to put an 88 millimetre gun on to a MK IV chassis, but we are at the moment looking at plans to fit the long barrelled version of the 75mm which will be a match for any Russian gun. We shall give very serious thought to everything the Hauptmann has suggested, Herr general," he added, smiling at Dieter.

"I'm pleased about that; he and his comrades are the ones who suffer if our development lags behind."

And so the conference drew to its close. As he was gathering his papers and preparing to leave for his quarters, where he assumed his further movement orders would be ready for him, General Guderian called him over.

"Von Hassellbek, there are one or two things I need to speak to you about. Firstly I understand you have had no leave since well before the beginning of the campaign. You will, therefore, proceed on leave for ten days from tomorrow, returning here, from which base you will be redirected. You will not be returning to your old regiment, you are promoted to major as from today and will take over the deputy command of a regiment in a new division being moved up to the Moscow area. It will be hard work knocking them into shape that is why we need people with your experience for the job. Is that all clear?"

"Yes Herr general, thank you very much. You may rest assured I shall not let you down."

"That, my dear boy, I knew already."

Dieter saluted and left for his quarters, where the extremely rotund receptionist had his papers made out ready for him, with the exception of the section indicating the destination of his leave pass – Ulm via Munich as he quickly informed her. She had, in addition, two sets of his major's insignia. "The gefreiter will fix these on before you go Herr major," she said affably – "and congratulations. We have so many majors and obersts back here who don't really deserve the ranks they hold, as you do."

A surprised Dieter thanked her courteously; rethinking that perhaps she did live on army rations, but possibly had a problem with her metabolism.

Although he would have to sit up all night (couchettes were for colonels and above) Dieter decided to take the night train to Munich, firstly because that way it would not cut in to his leave time, and secondly he would have found difficulty in sleeping in his quarters anyway at the thought of being with his darling Rosa again. The train covered the three hundred or so miles without incident pulling into the giant Hauptbahnhof station shortly after six o'clock on a dark, cold, wet morning. A horse cab took him to Rosa's mothers flat in Goethe

Strasse. He gave the door a vigorous knock, answered after a seemingly endless wait by Mrs Reuter – Rosa's mother – calling out for the whole street to hear, "Rosa – it's Dieter." There was a patter of bare feet on the hallway floor as Rosa rushed and threw herself into Dieter's arms, whilst the old coachman and the mother smilingly looked on. Eventually composure reigned, Dieter paid the cabbie an old Great War veteran who gave him a smart salute as he took up his seat on the cab again, and the three went into the flat.

The leave passed quickly as all leaves do. After three days in Munich they travelled to Ulm to Dieter's home, spending the rest of the time with his parents. They were all very proud of his promotion at such a young age. On several occasions they wondered how David and Pat and the Chandler family in general were faring, whether they had survived the merciless bombing of the Luftwaffe and the starvation brought about by the U-boat campaign. Because of the war situation the University Medical School had reduced the length of the course by a year. As a result, Rosa had now qualified as a doctor, but for her first year of practice had to serve in the prison system. She had been posted to Mauthausen, about 130 miles from Munich, near Linz in Austria. Although she had no direct contact with the prisoners, her duties being in the hospital set aside for the guards and civilian staff, she nevertheless could see part of the huge arrangement of barrack blocks housing thousands of inmates. She had said nothing of this to Dieter until one frosty morning as they walked along the bank of the Danube she said, "This water will flow past my hospital in a few hours or days or whatever. I wonder how many more will die."

Dieter looked at her with concern. "What do you mean?" he questioned. "Do you have an epidemic there or something?"

"Just an epidemic of killing. That is all," and she poured out the whole story. She had asked the housekeeper at the doctor's quarters, where the prisoners' doctors were domiciled.

A strange look from the rather severe, middle-aged, committed Nazi lady was accompanied by, "The prisoners need no doctors."

"So what happens if they become ill?"

"They either survive or die. They should not be there in the first place. They should not have conspired against what our Fuhrer is doing to restore our country's greatness."

Rosa went on to say that she had a sudden feeling that this woman was a Gestapo informant at the least, if not a member of that organisation herself. Quickly therefore she had replied, "I quite agree with you, my sister-in-law is a senior officer in the administration of these camps, a close associate of Herr Himmler." The woman was immediately impressed with this name dropping, and offered to arrange for Rosa to be shown the camp should she so desire. This confirmed her opinion that this 'housekeeper' had more influence than one would expect from a person in that capacity. Rosa had accepted the offer and the following day was collected by a young S.S. officer in a Kuppelwagen. They drove through line after line of barrack huts, until Rosa asked whether she could see inside one. The young second lieutenant hesitated for a moment, replying that he had been told that as a relative of Reichsminister Himmler he had been ordered to do anything the Frau Doktor asked, but the insides of the buildings were very unhealthy places and he would not like to risk her safety. "I am a doctor," she replied, "so can very speedily assess whether I am in danger or not."

They stopped therefore at the next barrack block. Descending from the Kuppelwagen, Rosa noticed that the officer unbuttoned the leather cover on his Luger holster, whilst the two guards prepared their Schmeisser sub-machine guns for use. The officer indicated to one of the guards to throw the door open. It was August and very hot. As the door flew open inwards they were engulfed by the most appalling stench that made each of them take a pace back, and Rosa to almost vomit. She overcame her revulsion and took several paces into the hut. As far as the eye could see there were wooden bunks, four high, down each side wall and in two tiers down the centre of the building. A little way down she saw people sleeping on three of the bunks. Approaching them she quickly established they were dead.

"These are dead Herr lieutenant," she said through the handkerchief covering her nose and mouth.

"Yes, the Kapos will remove them tonight," he said. She noticed he said this completely without any feeling of any description in his voice. She was more than glad to get out into the fresh air. They journeyed on in silence until rounding a bend in the rough road they came to the face of a huge stone quarry where it appeared tens of thousands of men and women were breaking stones and loading them into small railway wagons, others were pushing the wagons to a central point where they were tipped into large wagons on a normal gauge track. The scene would have been biblical in its presentation had it not been for the guards with Alsatians snapping at the heels of the wagon pushers, other guards with whips not reluctant to use them on the stone breakers, and over all the haze of dust with shafts of sunlight piercing through. Again there were bodies lying at the side of the workings, at least twenty or thirty in the nearest pile Rosa calculated. She pointed to them. The young S.S. man repeated his previous pronouncement. "The

Kapos will take them away tonight."

With some irony in her voice Rosa said, "You must keep the Kapos busy?"

His reply to this was, "They are all Jews, they work till they die, that is the way it is."

As they spoke, a long burst of machine gun fire could be heard from the other side of a low hill away towards the camp.

"What is that?" she asked the young officer.

"We have a rifle range where another unit trains its new recruits," he replied.

"That was not rifle fire, even I know that."

"They fire machine guns as well of course."

"I see. Can I see that?"

"I'm afraid not Frau Doktor. It is a different unit. I have no authority there. You would have to get fresh authority from the Einsatzgruppen Office at Reichsminister Himmler's H.Q. Nobody is allowed in there."

"And so my visit ended," she went on. "I found out afterwards from a friendly porter, that the people in the area where I heard firing were, in fact, Russian prisoners and that they were being systematically liquidated." There was a silence between them for a little while, broken by Rosa confiding to Dieter that in the final session of her years at the university she had been approached by a group of students who had formed an anti-nazi, anti-war organisation, with affiliations they said all over the greater Reich. Their objectives were to stop the war and bring about a democratic Germany. Dieter stopped abruptly.

"Rosa darling, you must not get involved with people like that. Even to be known by them would result in your being put into a camp. They talk of democracy but basically they are communists, they have no more intention of seeing a democratic Germany than have the Nazis. Please Rosa, promise me you will have absolutely nothing to do with them. Please!"

"I promise. But how do I sleep at night knowing what is going on a few hundred metres from where I am enjoying good food and a comfortable bed?"

"This is the great tragedy of people like us – the vast majority of the people have no knowledge of what is going on – we have some knowledge, and we must live with it in the hope and belief that someone, somehow will be punished for it someday."

The tragedy was that eventually politics determined millions of innocent Germans suffered whereas only a handful of the guilty were punished.

Chapter Fourteen

Lieutenant Colonel Deveson, W.O.I. Harry Chandler, and their three men arrived at K.L. on 28th December after a difficult journey from Nee Soon. The road heading south was a succession of slowly moving traffic interspersed with broken down vehicles. Where the car or truck had failed mechanically the owners or drivers could be seen siphoning out any remaining petrol to use as a bargaining factor to get a lift on a vehicle running out of that precious fluid. The side of the road running north upon which they were travelling, whilst not so crowded, had mainly military vehicles carrying supplies to dumps closer to the fighting, and military and civil police doing everything possible to prevent a total log jam. The Chinese in particular were most reluctant to have their cars, vans or lorries pushed off the road into the ditch when they had broken down. In many cases that vehicle and often its contents, was their only source of income, the last thing they wanted was to lose it altogether. Both the military and civil police however were at the stage where they could no longer brook any argument. If a vehicle was blocking the road into the ditch it went, despite the protestations of the men and the wailing of the women.

The new arrivals were allocated their quarters, it would be the most comfortable accommodation along with the most enjoyable food they would enjoy for some years to come, those, that is, who survived. The colonel's main job, with the assistance of three staff officers, and Harry in charge of the office staff, was to receive the train and convoy loads of supplies and then break them down into the correct loads to be redirected to divisions and other smaller units. Their main problems were two-fold. Firstly, they rarely knew the current whereabouts of the unit to which the supplies were to be directed, secondly, the information about unit strengths was rarely up to date. They worked closely with the Royal Army Ordnance Corps – R.A.O.C. – for whom they also had to carry ammunition and other supplies, it was a very complex business made even more difficult – sometimes impossible – by the incredibly fluid state of the battle.

They worked sixteen hour days in an endeavour to keep all supplies moving. On New Year's Day they were at their desks at 7 a.m. when shortly afterwards the colonel burst in. "The Japs have made a seaborne landing above the Slim River," he said, "we've got to get all the stores we can back from forward dumps to K.L. and then back to Tampin near Malacca. In the meantime the new troop arrivals arriving by rail at 10 o'clock have to be lorried forward to reinforce General Heath's men at Trolak, just north of Slim River. Will you organise that Colonel Deveson?" His 'boss' looked at Harry – Harry knew what was coming.

"Mr Chandler, this has got to be a hands-on job. When you get to the railhead, get these new arrivals on all the trucks you can muster. Go with them to Div Rear HQ wherever that might be, and bring the trucks back straight away. If we don't have someone there to turn them around they will either hang about, or worse than that, get pinched by anyone who can lay hands on them."

"Right Sir, I'll take a motorbike, I shall be more mobile on that than in the Dodge."

Harry went to div pool and requisitioned a Matchless, went on to the lorry park and explained his orders to the captain in charge there. He had taken the precaution of getting a reasonably impressive authority typed out and signed with a flourish by the colonel. "Pieces of paper work miracles," he had said to Colonel Deveson. In the space of less than an hour he had got a hundred odd three tonners lined up telling the warrant officers and N.C.O.'s to follow him and simply get the men off the train, on to the lorries and then up to Trolak, or regions adjacent, a distance of some sixty odd miles. After a quick reconnaissance at the station, he arranged for the train to stop so that the first carriage was by the main goods exit, normally the guards van would stop in line with this. This would leave five coaches short of the platform, but when the first five coaches had dismounted, the train would be moved forward so that the remainder could alight. Despite his extempore calculations being reasonably close, in the event he found he still had almost a hundred sepoys he could not get on to the trucks. He walked across to the station masters office, asking for the motor traffic manager. All large stations in Malaya, he reasoned, would have a substantial quota of lorries to deliver out to plantations, mines and so on. A Malay, dressed impeccably, and by his demeanour and presence a senior manager politely asked how he could help.

"I have to requisition five of your lorries for a day," said Harry, waving his piece of paper. "This is very urgent." To his surprise, the Malay turned to an underling and in a controlled voice ordered him in Malay to have five Crossleys out at the front with drivers immediately. Harry shook hands with the manager, saluted him smartly, which courtesy put him high up in the estimation of his clerks who were keenly watching.

As a result, within an hour and a half of the train arriving, a battalion of the Punjab Regiment with sundry ancillary troops were clear of the station and on their way to the Slim River. There was a downside to this well carried out movement. Harry and one or two senior sergeant majors who were supervising the loading of the men on to the trucks had serious doubts about the quality of many of the soldiers being sent forward to meet Japan's finest troops. Many of them were very young, unseasoned and under-trained. They had just landed from, what for virtually all of them, was their first sea voyage, they were all wearing uniforms designed for desert warfare, the Middle East having been their proposed destination initially, they were under-equipped and as it was eventually to prove, often poorly led.

The sixty odd miles at convoy speed took until late afternoon before they reached the M.P.'s at the marshalling area. Ahead of them they could clearly hear the battle raging. For once, the retreating troops had found themselves in a defensible position and were able to beat off sustained attacks by the cream of Japanese infantry. At one point on the front, a feature called Thompson's Ridge; the Japanese did break through, until a company of Sikhs led by their British officers carried out a bayonet charge in the old traditional style and cleared the ridge. It was the first evidence that trained troops properly led were more than a match for the Japanese.

Turning one hundred odd vehicles around in the dark and moving them back sixty miles was no easy task, but shortly after midnight Harry got the convoy back to base.

"You can have the rest of the day off," he joked to the C.S.M.'s and sergeants as he thanked them, asking them to say 'well done' to the drivers. He himself thanked the Crossley drivers and waved them away from the park to their homes in the town, to wives or mothers who had wondered what the devil had happened to them.

The next few days were spent moving dumps of various kinds ever southwards. The battle raged at Slim River, the Japs far from getting all their own way. The Rajputs, the Hyderabads, the Argylls, all performed heroically, but the Japs had tanks, dozens of them, and used them well to outflank and encircle. None of the new arrivals had ever seen a tank – they were totally demoralised by them – even more demoralised by the fact that their King Emperor had not provided them with a single tank to pit against this enemy, and precious few anti-tank guns to combat them. By January 5th it was obvious that Kuala Lumpur itself would soon be under ground attack. All HQ staff were removed sixty miles south to Tampin. "The Australians are there and thereabouts," Colonel Deveson told Harry, "they should hold them."

"If they fight as good a war as they talk they will," Harry replied, a doubtful tone in his voice. The sad thing about the Australian troops in Malaya, from their General Gordon Bennett downwards was that they did not. With the example of Australian courage in 1914-18 in France and Gallipoli, and in the Western Desert in 1940 and 41 undeniably proven and written into the records, it was expected they would be the backbone of the Empire forces in the defence of Malaya and Singapore. With one or two notable exceptions they were poorly led at the top and ultimately provided some four thousand deserters who flooded back into Singapore Town, causing the inhabitants and refugees in that city to be more afraid of them than was their fear of the Japanese.

In the chaos of the move to Tampin, Harry lost touch with major Deveson. When he reached Tampin, the GSO1 told him to go to Malacca and remove whatever he could from there to Ayer Hitam, literally the last stop before Johore Causeway and Singapore Island. On arrival at Malacca, he met a patrol of Australian Bren gun carriers, the lieutenant in charge suggesting he took his lorries and buggered off, the Japs were dug in about ten miles up the coast road, and unless they were waiting for something to happen inland, could be here by tomorrow. Harry therefore told the lorries to turn and make their way back on to the trunk road to Ayer Hitam.

"Can you help me to destroy a couple of dumps here?" Harry asked. "There are two petrol dumps and a large rubber godown, a vehicle workshop and a base stores. A few well placed two inch phosphorous bombs from your mortars will do the job quicker than I can."

"Lead on mate, these sods haven't fired a bloody shot yet of any kind, it will give them a bit of practice."

Harry led them to the map references he had been given, having told the truck drivers to turn and make for Muar – he would catch them up on his motorbike later. His first stop was a dump of cans of petrol. He pulled the three carriers up about 150 yards short.

"Can you reach that?" he asked.

"Sure thing, but can't we go closer?"

"When that lot goes up you will find you may already be too close. Now – right in the middle – right?"

The mortarman took aim, overshot by a mile. A second bomb landed in the stack.

"Now can you put an H.E. on it?" asked Harry. The squaddie

selected a high explosive bomb and did just that. The resultant fire ball only lasted seconds but it was like every bonfire night Harry had ever seen rolled into one. It went upwards at an incredible speed getting bigger and bigger in circumference until suddenly the vapours all burnt out leaving the dump a mass of flame so hot the watchers were almost singed by it. They swiftly got into their carriers and moved back, accompanied by exclamations as original and unrefined as even Harry had ever heard. They repeated this on the second dump, the rubber godown was an easy job, but the vehicle workshop and the base stores were a little more difficult until one Aussie had the bright idea of puncturing a 45 gallon petrol drum and letting it flood the floor of the workshop, followed by throwing a hand grenade into the middle of it from behind the safety of a brick wall. As it was, the resultant heat blast nearly blew him off his feet, but it did the trick.

"We'd better make tracks for the ferry at Muar" Harry suggested, "that's if it's still running."

"Lead on MacDuff," replied the lieutenant, "but not too bloody fast on that thing." They set off and had covered some ten miles, when they came to a left hand curve in the road with a big thicket of bamboo on the inside curve obscuring the view towards Muar. As he rounded it he was, to say the least, surprised to see a patrol of some fifty or more Japanese infantrymen on bicycles no more than two hundred yards away. It sounds ridiculous to state that the bicycle was the secret weapon of the Japanese in Malaya. Their riders were provided with carefully prepared maps compiled over the years by so called Japanese tourists, Japanese mine owners and planters, of secondary roads, plantation walkways, even game trails, which enabled them to cover some twenty miles in a day carrying anything up to a sixty pound load. In this manner, they were able to outflank positions, set up road blocks, or attack reserve troops particularly at night, causing vastly more alarm and consternation than their numbers warranted. This unit had emerged on to the main road from a bund running across an enormous stretch of paddy fields. No other form of transport could have made use of that approach.

Harry put all his brakes on. He wondered why the Japs had not heard the clatter of the Bren gun carrier tracks. Still partially screened by the bamboo, he swung the bike round and raced back to the first carrier, who seeing Harry stop, had halted himself and the two following.

"Japs, about fifty of them," he said.

The lieutenant gave the hand signal to his other units – carriers rarely had the luxury of radio contact – telling them 'enemy ahead in numbers,' at which they prepared their Bren guns for firing. He then gave the universal 'onward' wave, and charged off round the bamboo clump to meet at one hundred yards fifty odd somewhat startled Japanese infantrymen. These same infantrymen had, of course, clearly heard the clatter of the carrier tracks, but knowing as they had been told that the British had no tanks in Malaya, confidently assumed they were their own tanks. Carriers of course, although tracked vehicles, and armoured against rifle and machine gun fire, are not tanks, being open topped and having no main armament other than the Bren light machine gun.

Harry, following very close behind the rear carrier, suddenly found himself in the middle of a pitched battle. The front two carriers had halted and were firing straight down the road causing absolute carnage. In the meantime, the Japs that were near the edges of the road had hurled themselves off their bicycles and got such cover as they could from the steep sides of the embankment before they started to return the fire. It became obvious to their officer that the only way they would be able to eliminate the Bren guns firing down on them would be to bomb them out. He shouted for smoke bombs to be thrown, but to throw a smoke grenade, or any other grenade any distance, you have to at least partially stand up. The men throwing the bombs were cut down as soon as they raised themselves, but by good fortune on their part, the bombs had been activated and with the breeze blowing from the Japs towards the carriers, the whole area was soon thick with smoke. The carrier commander shouted to the rear carrier to go back fifty yards, at which the driver revved hard, locked his right track, swung round one hundred and eighty degrees (nearly knocking Harry over in the process) and did as he had been ordered. Harry, in the meantime, had put his Matchless on its rest, removed his tommy gun from one of the panniers and sought the cover of the rear of one of the carriers.

In a situation like this, friend and foe are usually thinking the same thing – what the bloody hell shall I do next? The Aussie commander decided to dash through the smoke two abreast, firing over the sides of each carrier at the Japs down in the paddy, then clear of the smoke, turn and come back. Any enemy emerging from the smoke would be cut down by the third carrier. The danger in this was the Japs only had to lob grenades for a lucky one to land inside the open topped carrier and R.I.P. for the occupants thereof. "Shit or bust," he shouted and waved them both forward. A shower of grenades followed them, a number hitting the armoured sides of the carriers and bouncing off, and one was actually falling into one of the carriers but was deftly caught by the

Bren gunners' number two and thrown back. "Howzat," he yelled, laughing his head off.

One drawback to the commander's extempore plan was that Harry suddenly found himself all alone in the middle of a smoke screen, standing in the middle of the road, with one carrier fifty yards away in one direction and the other two a hundred yards away through the smoke in the other. He was singularly unhappy about this so decided to slide down the embankment to get some cover of a sort. As he moved towards effecting this enterprise, out of the smoke charged the Japanese officer waving a sword, which seemed to Harry, in the split second he had to observe this, to be almost as big as the man himself, and very lethal looking too. From a distance of no more than three or four yards Harry fired his tommy gun. It was so close, and the .45 round headed bullets so heavy, that the prolonged burst almost cut the officer in two. Even so, the impetus of his original charge, with his sword raised, brought the razor sharp weapon down only inches from Harry's shoulder, clattering on to the tarmac in a shower of sparks. Immediately he jumped down on to the embankment as another Jap arrived with the standard rifle fitted with the extraordinarily long bayonet favoured by the Japanese, appeared out of the smoke. He despatched this one without difficulty. By now the smoke was clearing, but shots were being fired out from the thicket of bamboo into which an unknown number of the Japs had fled. The carriers all swung round to face this fresh target.

"Fire three magazines at low level into the bamboo, then follow me," he yelled.

"Fire!!!" The noise of three Bren guns firing bursts into the timber will be heard all over Malaya, Harry thought.

He started his bike up and swung round to speak to the officer. "Any casualties Sir?" he yelled.

"One bloke got a bit of a grenade in his head," replied the Aussie cheerfully, "he's Irish so it didn't do any damage. Lead on to Muar – I reckon we'll have company soon."

Harry picked his way through dead Japs and discarded bicycles. At a quick count he reckoned there were thirty odd bodies on or at the roadside, caught in the first deadly attack by the carriers, plus a number lying face down in the water in the paddy either side of the road who had found to their cost they had nowhere to run. There wouldn't have been many in the bamboo at that rate he calculated, and those nine magazines of which they had had the discomfort of taking delivery would doubtless further reduce their numbers. A good afternoon's work he concluded, as the carriers turned to follow him, riding roughshod over bodies and bicycles alike.

As they approached Muar, at the bridge over the small Kesang River, they were met by a burst of fire from prepared positions on the river bank. Harry needed little persuasion to brake, turn and hasten back to the comparative safety of the rear of one of the carriers, which in the meantime had pulled in to the side of the road. As they peered down the road to see what the hell was going on, the officer through his binocular caught sight of a turban.

"They're ours," he yelled.

"Yeh, but do the bastards know we're theirs?" came the unambiguous reply from one of the gunners.

Apparently they did. A white officer appeared in the middle of the bridge waving his arms presumably indicating they were welcome.

"I'll ride down and have a shufti, Sir," Harry called out, and slowly made his way two hundred yards or so until he could clearly see it was a British officer. He speeded up, stopped, saluted the officer, a lieutenant saying, 'Three Australian carriers Sir.'

"Holy Moses," came the reply, "you frightened the life out of my chaps. They've never seen a tank before and thought their number was up."

"Well, they're not tanks Sir, you know."

"Yes, I know that and you know that, but unfortunately they don't. We only came off the boat a week ago, this is the first time we've been committed."

"Which regiment are you Sir?"

"Rajputana Rifles."

The Rajputana Rifles would soon be committed to the extent that few who came off the boat would ever see their native country again. They were heavily shelled for four days before the Imperial Guards Division under General Nishimura eventually overran them driving them back on to the northern bank of the River Muar, that dark, filthy, snake infested river over which Harry had looked on the day he met Nigel Coates, and across which few would make their escape.

"We have to get over the ferry to rejoin our units," the Australian lieutenant told the rifleman.

"I don't know if it is still working – it was bombed yesterday," the Rajput replied. As they spoke, the first salvo of shells arrived, falling well short of the Indian positions. "Anyway, good luck."

You're the one who's going to need the good luck pretty soon Harry thought, but kick-started his bike to lead the carriers to the ferry. It was beginning to get dark, he wondered whether the ferry could operate in the dark; he was soon to find out. Their first sight of the ferry in the last of the light before the tropical night swiftly descended on them was of a vessel sitting neatly on the bed of the river half full of water.

"That's not going far Sir," Harry called to the Aussie officer.

"Now what do we do for Christ's sake?"

"We'll have to go back towards Kesang and take the road out through the mangroves to Tangyat," Harry replied, looking at his map.

"Right, we'll brew up and start at first light," the Aussie replied, "but there is one small, tiny, little problem. What are we going to use for petrol?"

"Line of my arm, 2000 yards, there should be a couple of thousand gallons," said Harry, pointing across the broad river towards the dump he had established a couple of months before.

"Sergeant major, you're a bloody genius. Right you lot, all out and find a bloody boat, then the R.S.M. will wave his magic bloody wand and get us tanked up again. Are they four gallon cans?" he asked Harry. Harry nodded in assent. "Right we're about a quarter full, that means we need fifteen gallons each plus a cup full for the R.S.M.'s motorbike. So it's got to be a biggish boat or you'll be all night rowing backwards and forwards." They not only found a boat, they found four Malays who would row it for them – for money of course. So Harry and four Aussie squaddies began the journey across the, fortunately, sluggish river. It would be just my luck for the current to sweep us out to sea Harry thought to himself, then reassured himself that these boatmen had made this crossing many times, so all would be well.

They hit the bank on the other side a little west of the Coates house. Harry led the Aussies to the now depleted dump, which was still guarded by a Ghurkha picquet. Harry waved his magic paper to the havildar in charge and the four men took a can each to the boat, three of them returning for another can. Harry was playing safe by leaving a man with the boat, the last thing he would want would be for the Malays to push off with a nice little earner of petrol and leave them on the wrong side of the river!

It was ten o'clock before the vehicles were all fuelled up. They brewed up, had some bully and biscuits and got themselves as comfortable as they could tucked away in the various compartments of the three carriers. Not that it was an uneventful night. The mosquitoes at Muar resembled Stukas in their size and ferocity, they were more than pleased when the morning light began to filter over the horizon telling the mozzies it was time to piss off to wherever it was they hid themselves during the day.

After a quick brew and some biscuits and jam they moved off

back towards Kesang, after a couple of miles striking inland through the stinking mangrove and then skirting agricultural land around Mount Orphir. It would be some eighty miles to the trunk road – always assuming the Japs had not made another right hook through the several minor roads there were between the mountain and the trunk road and blocked them off. Harry's fears, which he had discussed with the Australian lieutenant increased as the normal rumble of guns they had been hearing for the past two days was getting decidedly closer. They had reached the small town of Sagil, about half way to the trunk road, when they saw a body of troops straggling towards them. They were Indian, led by a British captain. Harry speeded up, turned his bike and shouted, "What's happened Sir?"

"The Japs have cut in behind Mount Orphir and cut off this part of the country from the trunk road. We've to set up a road block at the edge of the mangrove to stop them getting to Muar."

"They are already on the coast road from Malacca to Muar Sir, we met their forward units yesterday. The Rajputana Rifles are down there."

"In that case we'll put up a barrier where the mangrove starts. They won't be able to outflank us there through the swamp.

By this time the Australian lieutenant had dismounted and joined them. Harry briefly put the situation to him.

"The best thing we can do is to go back and help the Rajputs," said the Aussie, "that'll secure your rear hopefully, and give you somewhere to withdraw to if need be." Afterwards he added to Harry, "We'll probably have to ditch the carriers eventually and get over that stinking bloody river – I can't see this lot or the Rajputs stopping the Jap tanks."

They turned to cover the thirty odd miles to the Malacca-Muar coast road. Very soon they heard the continued rumble of artillery, the troops at Kesang were taking a real pasting. As they approached the coast road junction they found it was not only the Rajputs at Kesang who were suffering. A furious artillery bombardment of Muar itself was taking place. They turned toward the Rajput positions and were met by the same lieutenant they had spoken to the previous day.

"We're not under attack yet," he told them, "but we had a proper stonking this morning with several casualties. It's lifted now and plastering the country on this side of the river. I'm expecting the infantry to move at any time."

But they didn't. For some reason the artillery bombardment continued – probably the worst of the whole campaign, and it was three days later when the nerves of all the dug in sepoys, and Harry and the Aussies for that matter, were strained to breaking point that the shout from the forward picquet rang out, "They're coming." Three tanks were seen some eight hundred yards down the road, moving slowly and backed up by scores of infantry to whom they were giving cover. The Rajputs had one three inch and three two inch mortars, but no artillery nor anti-tank guns.

The lieutenant had used his time wisely along with a plentiful supply of barbed wire and dannert coils to firstly provide some defence in depth. "We'll kill them on the wire," he had told his sepoys. Secondly he had constructed some triangular dannert barriers, which he had strung across the road at three places one hundred, two hundred, and three hundred yards from their positions. His thinking was:- the tanks couldn't leave the road as the ground was too soft on either side. The tanks couldn't ram through the dannert, it would clog their tracks. Infantry clearing the dannert would be exposed to the defenders fire. If the Japs put smoke down to cover the dannert clearance the lieutenant had sited two of his Bren guns to fire on fixed lines into the dannert, no-one could live in that maelstrom – as long as the ammunition held out.

"If only we had a couple of two pounder anti-tank guns, and come to that a couple of tanks ......," the young lieutenant left his wish in mid air.

"I'm afraid as far as equipment goes, Malaya has been left sucking on the hind tit," the Aussie replied. "Well, good luck both of you."

It had been arranged that the three carriers should be hulled down behind the left hand section of Rajputs, which allowed the officer to move a few of his men across to the right hand side of the road. In addition, he had asked Harry if he would take command of some twenty men well dug-in in bunkers with overhead protection, at an angle to the central defences. One of the fixed line Brens was positioned here. Harry said he would do his best but his knowledge of the language was nil. "No problem – you have a naik who speaks perfect English, he'll interpret for you."

"You'll excuse my ignorance – what's a naik?"

The young man grinned – "that's 'corporal' to you."

Harry found his naik, about mid-twenties he judged, who to his astonishment, spoke English with a strong Yorkshire accent. He'd been brought up in Leeds, was visiting India for the first time when war broke out, couldn't get home, so joined the army. Now it looked as though he stood a good chance of dying for his king and country.

"They're coming." Those that weren't in their bunkers ran to them. There was no doubt, Harry thought, the young subaltern had made a super job of his defences. He had the remnants of three platoons, probably about sixty men. Both his flanks were secure, the left side by the mangrove, the right side by thick secondary jungle, generally acknowledged to be the most impenetrable of any in the world, not even Burma, India, nor Borneo could offer worse, or in these circumstances better.

The forward tank opened up with its 37mm main armament, which, except for splitting a few trees, did little damage. It was solid shot – in the unlikely event of a round hitting you, you knew no more, but snug in the bottom of the bunker that was unlikely. The secondary armament was a light machine gun, and again they could hose it for all they were worth but would have little effect on well dug in opponents.

The battle that ensued was almost textbook. The infantry tried to move the first dannert and was cut to pieces from the three strong points ahead. The first reply was with mortars, which caused one or two minor casualties, but otherwise was ineffective, but which resulted in the Rajput three inch mortar being brought into action – counter mortar fire to good effect.
"I reckon that's one nil to us," Harry said to his naik.
"Yes sahib, but the match has only just started," came the reply.

The next move on the part of the Jap commander was to put down smoke, attack straight up the road under its cover, and go in with the bayonet. He had three problems. One, it would be on a very narrow front, two, he had no clear idea of how many troops there were in the defence area, three, whilst he would get overhead covering fire from at least two of the tanks as he went forward, that would cease as he got close to his target or the tanks would be shooting their own men. His thinking was based on the easy victories they had had so far over demoralised, poorly led opposition. He, therefore, concluded that as these so-called soldiers saw him and his men coming, they would drop their arms and run, as had been the case on numerous occasions before. That was the last conclusion he ever arrived at in this life. He led the charge, brandishing his two handed sword, he and his men shrieking their war cries, and as he emerged from the smoke, which as far as he was concerned was unfortunately blowing back on him and the fifty or so men bunched behind him, he and his followers were cut to pieces as a hail of .303 bullets slammed into them. Not one got to within twenty five yards of the most forward position.
"I reckon that's two nil," Harry asserted.

But there was to be a lot more play before the game finished.

Chapter Fifteen

It was Friday 16th January 1942. Megan had that morning received a letter – 'it only took two weeks!' – from Harry telling her he had a new job at Corps HQ and had been made up to regimental sergeant major, W.O.I., moving from the island up to K.L.

"It's a wonder they didn't censor that," was Fred's comment, as they all assembled at Chandlers Lodge that evening.

The pride they took in his promotion was, however, very much offset by the news that during the period the letter had been travelling, the Japs had overrun Kuala Lumpur after severe fighting. "Being at Corps HQ would mean that they would get away early on," Fred reasoned, a view agreed with by the two Canadians billeted on them. It was, therefore, a question of 'wait and see' until the next letter arrived.

In the meantime, Colonel Deveson at Tampin was preparing to move again towards the causeway. He was very worried indeed about Harry. He knew from the reports from the N.C.O.'s on the lorries Harry had sent away from Malacca that they had left him behind with the Australians. He knew that the lorries had only just made it by the skins of their teeth on to the safety of the trunk road, several of them having been shot up in the process of escaping. The whole area Malacca – Muar – Tampin was under Japanese control; technically therefore Harry should be posted 'Missing.' Knowing Harry's ability to look after himself he was reluctant to make this official and give unnecessary heartache to his wife and family at home. "What a bloody life," he told himself, thinking of Megan, "that poor girl on the clouds with her beautiful new daughter, and then plunged into the depths by a buff telegram – it doesn't bear thinking about." It didn't occur to him to try and foresee what was likely to happen to him when they reached the point at which they could go no further. "I'll give him another day," he concluded.

When the day was up he officially notified the section responsible for informing the War Office and from them on matters took their course.

The family back at Sandbury now also had an additional cause for concern. Cecely and her two children had become very close. She had heard nothing from Nigel since the new year. She had cabled his brother, the judge, but had received no reply, presumably, she said, because priority cables from the government, the military and commercial concerns were naturally taking precedence over civilian traffic. Nigel's main headquarters had been in K.L. so that meant he had probably gone to Singapore. What she didn't know of course was that their lovely house on the padang at Muar was now a ruin as a result of the intensive attack over four days by the Japanese artillery, and that Ah Chin and his family were living in cellars under the servant's quarters.

Everything happened on Friday 23rd January. The two Canadians returned unexpectedly at lunchtime to say they were being moved on the next morning. Rose received a telephone call from Mark, her new husband, which used the coded phrase 'By the way, I saw Aunt Margaret the other day' which meant he was at or near the dockside on his way overseas and added 'Charlie sends his love.' David telephoned to say he would be home on Saturday, going back on Monday, would they put Maria up over the weekend, and then came the heart rending call from Megan that she had received the dreaded telegram. Fred was at home, preparing to go to Home Guard duties, but immediately jumped in the Rover to get Megan and the children. This was no time for her to be on her own. As Megan arrived, looking strained and tearful, clutching the buff envelope, Moira and Jack too drove in having been alerted by Ruth. Immediately Moira suggested she took the twins, now four years old, back to The Hollies where they would be with young John and be looked after by Nannie. The others went into the house, to join Rose, Anni, Karl and the two Canadians, Ernie being still at the factory. There was a solemn atmosphere as Ruth speedily brewed tea. Moira returned, at which Fred took the floor. "This telegram states that Harry is missing. In the conditions obtaining out there at present he could be anywhere. Not returning to his own HQ after a day or two would automatically mean his superior officer would, under Kings Regulations, have to announce he was missing, not on the strength. So it is possible he will turn up in due course."

He then pulled an envelope out of his pocket, and continued, "Another factor you should know is in this cable Harry sent to me last month." All eyes were fixed intently on Fred as he removed the cable from its envelope. "It reads:-

Dear Dad, This is a bit of cryptic letter, but I know you can read between the lines. If hostilities break out here, you may not hear from me for some considerable time. Assure the family no news is good news and when I am able I will contact you. I shall be doing a sort of David. Yours, Harry.

"Now this suggests to me two things. Firstly, if Harry got cut off somewhere there was a plan for him to rendezvous with others to live in the jungle and then to carry on behind the lines. Secondly, that being the case, it will be a long time before we are likely to know for certain if that is the case. We have therefore got to remain firm in our belief that if anyone can look after himself it is Harry – he proved that in France – and that one day we shall learn, once again, he is safe and well."

Harry passed the letter round for all to see. Moira, standing next to Ruth said to her, "I'll see what I can find out at Horse Guards on Monday. I know several top brass there who are in contact with General Wavell." It would be a forlorn hope she considered, she was trying to bolster Ruth's feelings knowing that she would be as wretched as Megan, but in her heart of hearts she knew that in the chaos that was Malaya there were thousands of people missing, many of whom would never be found.

David arrived with Maria just after lunch on Saturday having met her by arrangement at Victoria. The Canadians had gone; Mrs Cloke had come in to help get their rooms cleared ready for Maria and Cecely, who were coming for the weekend. It was a sad house. Megan's spirits had been raised a little by Fred's confidence in Harry's ability, but there was still the uncertainty hanging over them. Rose was depressed at the thought her husband was, at that moment, on some troopship somewhere or other, going somewhere or other she knew not where for certain, although she had a pretty good idea in the back of her mind. Cecely was in the same boat as Megan with the added disadvantage she had no military chain to keep her informed. Sensing this general despondency, David decided not to tell them until the last minute he would be away in a few days until sometime in the summer. Then to cap it all, Colonel Tim came in on Saturday afternoon to tell them that the Canadians were vacating their camp in about a month's time, moving down to the West Country where the whole brigade would be together. Sad to say Brigadier Halton would not be going with them, he had been promoted to major general and would be taking over a division being formed in East Anglia.

The weekend passed quickly. On Sunday afternoon David and Maria walked in the woods near the house. It was a cold, blustery day and by four o'clock was getting dark as they turned for home. They had been walking with their arms around each other as lovers do, when David stopped, pulled Maria to him, and kissed her long and ardently. In that embrace, thrilling her beyond measure, Maria had the intuitive feeling that David was trying to tell her something beyond the fact that he found her desirable. She responded in full measure, welding herself into him until, at last, he slowly released her. "I have something to tell you," he said.

"I know – you're going away."

"Yes."

There was a long silence as she snuggled her face against his chest, making a supreme endeavour not to be visibly upset. At last, she said, "I'm so proud of you; you will take good care of yourself for me, won't you?" She had not asked where? How long for? Doing what? – he answered only one of her unasked questions.

"I should be back in early summer if all goes according to plan. Keep in touch with my mother; she will be kept notified of my return."

"Your poor mother carries the burdens of us all, doesn't she? Harry, Rose because of Mark, Charlie and Kenny Barclay because they are almost part of the family, and now you. Now I suspect she is worried about Colonel Tim, Alec and Jim who are obviously being moved for a purpose."

"Yes, you're right of course, your insight is certainly far greater than mine." She reached up and pulled his head down to her, again pressing herself to him. At last he gently moved her away from him.

"You are doing dreadful things to me," he whispered, "I think we should be getting back." She kissed him lightly again.

"That's what lovers are for, and I love you so much David Chandler."

They walked on air back to the house to find General Halton there talking animatedly to Rose, Cecely and Mrs Treharne. He greeted David warmly and was particularly cordial to Maria offering her the chair upon which he had been seated. David congratulated him on his new appointment, asking him if he had any decent regiments in the new division, like the Rifles for example. The general answered his jocular question with a smile, but with also a serious answer. "I have, or will have, six county battalions and three light infantry, no rifles I'm afraid. There is one regular battalion, two territorial and the rest service battalions, so, as you can see, we've got a lot of work to do."

The onlookers were listening intently to this conversation. Ruth was thinking to herself 'how many people get the opportunity to eavesdrop on a discussion at this level?'

The general continued, "It's not only getting the battalions fit and tactically trained, I've got a whole staff, most of them new to the job, to weld together. Last but by no means least I've got to learn how to use my artillery, engineers, armoured support and so on, in the field, instead of on paper and on the sand table."

"What about politics Sir?"

"That's the part I must say I'm not looking forward to. As a divisional commander you start to get involved with our political masters. We now have the major consolation of having General Sir Alan Brooke at the right hand of the prime minister; I don't think stupid decisions will be allowed to be made as in the last war. Anyway, that's enough about boring military matters. Now Maria, I hear you have been to a tribunal, how did you get on?"

Maria was a little taken aback at being suddenly made centre stage. Quickly recovering she jested.

"Oh well, they asked me first of all if I would like to join one of the new all women tank battalions."

There was laughter followed by the general saying, "You may not know this but women do drive tanks in the Russian army. They must be damned tough that's all I can say – you wouldn't catch me in one, nor jumping out of aeroplanes for that matter," looking at David.

Maria continued, "I told them I would like to go into the forces, and as my father had been in the navy, I would like to be a Wren. What I didn't tell them was that my father had been in the German Navy, though why they hadn't guessed that from my name I don't know." There was general amusement at this account, and an immediate reply from David, in a pseudo much offended tone.

"Are you telling me that you are besmirching the family honour by becoming a sailor?"

"There are several points there to be answered Captain Chandler," she replied. "Firstly, my family honour is not affected" (accent on the 'my'), "secondly, it will do no harm for you to have an insight, no matter at how lowly a level, of a representative of what is universally known as the 'Senior Service,' and thirdly I think the uniform is decidedly fetching compared to drab khaki."

"Well, you've got your answer there David old son. What's more," the general added, stepping back a pace or so and looking Maria up and down, "I think she will look a positive cracker, as young Charlie Crew would say, in that uniform."

"Well I shan't know for a couple of weeks what the decision is likely to be. I could end up making shells or something in Woolwich Arsenal."

During the evening, Mrs Treharne took the opportunity to approach David. "Could I have a word with you David please?"

"Yes, of course. Has our cat been playing up again?" Maria made to move away.

"Oh, please stay Maria; it's not hush hush or anything." She continued, "You remember you suggested when I was first bombed out and you kindly let me come back to the bungalow, that perhaps I could take someone in as a lodger to keep me company."

"Yes, I remember it perfectly. Now don't tell me – you've found a nice gentleman friend whose wife doesn't understand him."

"Oh David, I'm afraid I don't get that sort of luck. Do you know Maria, when I'm a bit low, David can always cheer me up, and if he is not here I think of some of the things he has said to me in the past and that cheers me up. Anyway, to continue. It is obvious that Cecely is not going to be able to get back to Malaya for a long time yet. We get on very well despite her being much younger than I am. I haven't said anything to her but I wondered if you would have any objection to my suggesting she stayed with me. It is quite expensive at The Swan at Tunbridge Wells and I have no idea what her financial situation is, being cut off from her home funds."

"I think it's a rattling good idea, don't you dear?" (to Maria), noticed immediately by Mrs Treharne – one, dear? – two, bringing girlfriend into decision making? – three, putting arm round waist indicating joined up decision making? – very significant.

"As long as she likes cats," replied the ever practical Maria.

"Oh she does, she has been to tea with me on several occasions and loves Susie."

"Well, that's settled then – I'll leave it to you Mrs Treharne."

"You'll leave what to Mrs Treharne?" asked Fred from David's elbow. David explained their conversation.

"I think that's a jolly good idea," was Fred's view.

"What's a good idea, you don't have many," it was Ruth latching on to Fred's remark.

The upshot of it all was, Mrs Treharne asked Cecely straight away. She was delighted to accept the offer, and then said hesitantly, "Perhaps you will be so kind as to let me know the financial details, and whether the children will be able to come during the school holidays."

"The children can come and go as they please," David replied, looking to Mrs Treharne as he spoke, she nodding in agreement. "As for the financial details, I suggest we leave all that for the time being until you know what is happening in Malaya."

"Can I give him a kiss?" Cecely asked Maria.

"Yes, of course" was the reply, "but be careful, you don't know where he's been."

"You know" continued Cecely having planted a decorous kiss on David's cheek, in response to which David had commented he thought she could do better than that, whereupon he received a resounding smacker on the other cheek. "You know, all this kindness is thanks to Harry." And linking arms with Megan she resumed, "First of all he saves the life of my brother-in-law, then he meets up with us, gives me and the children the introduction to this most wonderful family, and then his brother provides us with a home in our hour of need. I really don't know how we are going to be able to thank you all." She was close to tears. Megan put her arm around her.

"They have done it before, nein?" Karl's voice came from the little group around the general. "First of all they save the life of my Anni after her mother was killed, then they take me in who they do not even know – how many people would do that? They should be made Lord and Lady Chandler."

There were resounding 'hear-hears,' replied to by Ruth saying, "We've been lucky to be able to help and we've been rewarded by knowing such lovely people. Now – come on in to tea."

That evening when everyone had drifted away, with the exception of the family, along with Moira and Jack, David announced, during a lull in the general conversation, "I have a short statement to make." They all knew immediately what he was going to say.

"I shall not be seeing you for a few months. I'm afraid that's all I can tell you for now." There was a silence, broken by Jack, acting as spokesman, moving over to David, taking his hand and saying,

"We won't question you old son. God keep you safe. We shall all be thinking of you every day until you return."

Ruth kept her feelings under control until at last she was alone with Fred in their bedroom. She sat on the edge of the bed and started quietly to cry. Fred came and sat beside her, holding her close. "Come on my love, this isn't like you" he was saying, "you're the bedrock of the whole family, we all rely on you."

"It's too much. First poor Jeremy is killed, then our lovely Pat. Now Harry's missing. David, Mark, Charlie, Tim, Alec and Jim all soon going into action somewhere or other. It's too much. This bloody, bloody, bloody war. It's too much, it's too much." Her sobs subsided gradually, as Fred held her. He knew there was nothing he could say to help; all he could do was to be at her side and be strong. He knew her own strength of character would pull her through this dreadful melancholy precipitated by David's announcement. When she had got through it she would be stronger than any of us he told himself. After a while she released herself, wiped her eyes and got herself to bed. In the morning she was herself again, at least to the outside world.

Moira and Jack, Anni and Karl and Colonel Tim all came on Monday morning to say goodbye to David. Ernie came up from the factory, telling Maria that if she got lonesome while David was away he had a couple of good-looking mates he could fix her up with – not both at the same time of course. David told him, and the world in general, that that would hardly be necessary as Maria kept a seventeen stone stoker tucked away for when he wasn't there.

Fred and Ruth took them to the station to see them off, Ruth pressing Maria to let her know the results of her tribunal, and to come and stay as and when she had a free weekend. As they waved them out of the station Ruth clutched Fred's arm. She said nothing, but he wagered a bet to himself she was wondering whether she would see him again, as indeed so was he.

That evening the news was again grim. The Japanese were at Kluang, only fifty miles or so from the Causeway and Singapore Island itself. Singapore town was being continually bombed; the R.A.F. defenders had been all but completely wiped out, this latter information of course not appearing on the airwaves. As the news was being read in Britain, General Percival was in the very act of telling his two corps Commanders to retreat on to Singapore Island – the Malay peninsula was lost. General Yamashita's brilliant campaign, aided by his almost total air and sea superiority, to say nothing of the ineffectual tactical ability of the British and Australian generals, would go down in history as a classic. Four hundred miles through what had been considered impassable jungle, in just eight weeks, that was his achievement. Now at the end of this part of the operation was the glittering prize of Singapore, the most important naval base in the East, the crossroads of the world, with its millions of tons of oil, huge dry docks, twenty square miles of deep sea safe anchorage, to say nothing of its workshops, ammunition dumps and factories. What a prize!

Chapter Sixteen

As a result of their train to Victoria being held up at Beckenham for some unknown reason, followed by a longer than usual wait for a taxi, David had to scramble to get his train at Euston. In one way this was fortuitous for both of them, neither of them relishing a long drawn out parting. Being apart was bad enough, day after day of loneliness, but at least this would always be offset by having other distractions. Waiting for the time to finally say goodbye on a cold draughty railway station with hundreds of other couples in a similar state of sadness, even misery, not knowing when, or even if, they would see their loved one again, was the ultimate in wretchedness. As it was, they made it with ten minutes to spare.

"You have better get on dear, or you won't get a seat." David grinned.

"If I get a seat it will be a miracle, so I will wave to you from the window. I'll telephone tonight and before I go. Goodbye, darling Maria, I'll see you again in the summer." And with that he joined countless others in kissing their wives and sweethearts goodbye, and hurried to the train.

When the train had pulled out, Maria made her way to Fenchurch Street to journey home. She felt so sick in the pit of her stomach, so near to tears, and then she thought of Ruth, who had endured this feeling so many times, of Rose who had had to endure even more in waving goodbye to her Jeremy, then to lose him. Finally again to have to part with her new husband and again with her brother. Maria recalled a snatch of an Emily Dickinson poem they had been studying at her literature classes:

> 'Parting is all we know of heaven
> And all we need of hell.'

She recovered her resolve to be like her brother Cedric had been, in David's words, 'the bravest of the brave.' But it wasn't going to be easy.

David's train pulled into Manchester Piccadilly an hour late, not to the surprise of anyone on board or to the incredulity of those awaiting it. Among those at the end of the platform was Paddy, who, taking David's bag with one hand and saluting with the other, asked, "Well Sir, did you pop the question?"

"When I pop the question you will be among the first to know." He paused for a moment. "I very nearly did a couple of times, but I chickened out and decided to leave it till I come back." Paddy knew, of course, that David was going, but had no idea where or when. They climbed into the P.U. for the trip to Wilmslow.

"Have you settled your date?" David knew that Paddy has asked his Mary to marry him during the Christmas leave and had been accepted.

"Yes, last Saturday in August. We wondered, Sir, if you would do us the honour of being my best man."

"Of course. I shall be delighted. There will, of course, be the question of my fee, but we can discuss that later."

"Mary had a long weekend pass, so she came up to see me. We stayed at the Coach and Four." Paddy paused for a few moments. "There was no hanky panky you know, separate rooms and all that, but very nice it was. I think we shall both be very pleased when August comes, she's a passionate girl."

It was past dinner time when they reached their destination, but as David was expected, a meal had been laid out for him in the dining room, included in which was a flask of soup and one of coffee, so he went to bed reasonably replete.

The next morning he was asked to go to see Robin. 'This is it my old son,' he told himself.

"David, we've got your orders at long last. Now come over here. Did you have a nice weekend?"

"Excellent, thank you. By the way, did you know that Brigadier Halton has been made up to major general?"

"Yes, I had heard." It would have been a bloody miracle if he hadn't thought David.

"Oh, and he sends his kindest regards, and said don't forget that fiver you owe him." Robin chuckled.

Reaching the wall, Robin pulled aside a curtain behind which was a large scale map of the border between France and Switzerland.

"Now, all things being equal, and as you well know they often aren't, you will leave on Friday night from Helsby in Lincolnshire. Paddy will take you there on Thursday, see you off and then come back here. You will board a Halifax which will drop you here," he pointed to a position a little north of Pontarlier. You will be met, taken over the border to be collected by a car to take you to Neufchatel station. You will then travel to Berne and will find your way to this boarding house where you will wait until you are contacted." He gave David an address on a small square of paper. "Under no circumstances will you allow that piece of paper to fall into anyone else's hands – understood?"

"Yes, understood."

"When you are contacted, you will then be given further operational instructions. Now, one or two points to remember. If you are out when your contact calls, don't worry, he will leave a message when he will return. Secondly, if you get into trouble do not, under any circumstances, contact our Foreign Office people there. All their lines are bugged. You'll just have to talk your own way out of it. And above all remember, Switzerland is full of spies from every country from Argentina to Zululand I wouldn't wonder, including, in particular, Germany and the Soviets."

David had already been made aware of the espionage systems in Europe. The British system in the occupied countries was virtually non-existent due to what was known as 'The Venlo Incident,' when the capture of two of our agents had led to the pursuit and virtual elimination of all the others. The Russians had a highly sophisticated network known as 'The Red Orchestra,' which again was eventually rounded up, and the members executed. In Switzerland the Russians had an organisation known as 'The Lucy Ring,' which was probably the most efficient and effective spy organisation ever known, with direct connections to a General in the German 'Abwehr,' or military intelligence H.Q. in Berlin. Finally, completely unknown to U.K. intelligence, the Russians had agents deep in the heart of the British establishment known as 'the Cambridge Ring,' Philby, Burgess, Blunt and Maclean.

Added to all the above were innumerable German agents from their various security branches, along with the extremely active Swiss Military Intelligence Bureau. As David had remarked to his instructor, "God they must all be falling over each other." The reply had been, "That's why you must remember you never know who you are talking to."

Robin continued with his instructions, details of money to be taken with him and where to obtain more if required, identity papers in the name of Werner Muller, which were his cover. David learnt that there had been, in fact, a Werner Muller, the same age as David, born in the town indicated on his passport, but who sadly had been killed when the British ship on which he was a kitchen hand, had been torpedoed the previous year.

With numerous other points covered Robin asked "Any questions?"

"Hundreds – but since you are most unlikely to answer them I'll keep them to two. Firstly, Hilary. Have you any news?"

"We have no news at all either of her or her immediate contacts. There are, I am afraid, only two reasons for this. She is hiding up and cannot therefore contact us, or she has been caught in which case she is in a camp somewhere. We have, in either case, to play a waiting game." He paused, "And your second question?"

"When I come back shall I be rejoining my regiment?"

"We shall see what the score is at that stage of the game and sort it out between us. Anything else?"

"No, nothing else, except a great deal of organisation appears to have been made to get me there, but up until now there has been no mention as to how I get back. It makes me feel a trifle unwanted." Robin laughed.

"Don't worry, when the time comes the Germans will fly you back – you'll see."

"I hope you are joking."

"Serious as a mother superior old boy." And with that rejoinder David was left wondering whether Robin was pulling his whatsit or whether it was some sort of senior civil service joke he was unable to fathom. Robin continued.

"Right, then will you care to join me for dinner in town this evening. Give you a chance to wear all your finery for the last time for a while. There will be one or two other people there, so get Paddy to do a good job on your buttons."

"As if you didn't know, we in the Rifles have black buttons. It is our personality that shines. Thank you very much though; I shall be delighted to join you."

"Right – 6.30 in the front hall – see you there."

David wondered who the 'other people' would be, but was not totally surprised to see one of them was Charlie's father, Lord Ramsford. "Thought I'd come and wish you good luck," he said as he shook hands with David.

"I must say I'm highly honoured Sir," David replied with a grin, "have you heard from Charlie?"

"Heard from Charlie? That blighter writes to me no more than twice a year, and then generally asking for cash."

"Is the Earl fit and well Sir?"

"He's not been too good these last couple of weeks. The trouble is he won't give in and go to bed for a few days. Thinks the estate will go to rack and ruin if he isn't checking on things. I'm going down tomorrow to try and sort him out."

"Please give him my kindest regards Sir."

"I will. And your family?" They chatted on, David marvelling to himself that he should be here in the poshest hotel in Manchester talking on equal terms with a brigadier, and he a peer of the realm at that, when in a couple of days he would be jettisoning himself into the unknown half way across Europe somewhere. They were joined by two more people who shook hands with each, obviously knowing the brigadier; Robin then introduced them to David. The first man was a civilian, short, stocky with immensely powerful looking shoulders, about forty David surmised, close cropped hair and a very hard jowl. Copper – was David's instant reaction. The second man was tall, lean, immaculately uniformed, again about forty, and a lieutenant colonel in the Intelligence Corps. He wore his hair somewhat longer than the normal military style. 'I suppose they can do that in the Intelligence Corps. Probably a don,' were David's thoughts regarding this gentleman. He was wrong on both counts. The stocky one was a Professor Cooper, an authority on codes – deciphering of. The Intelligence Corps man was a career soldier named Harris whose job was tracking down enemy agents. However the evening was purely social, no shop whatsoever, it had just so happened that they had each been in the same place at the same time, and knowing each other, had got together. However, it was plain they all knew that David was soon to be off, since at the end of a most enjoyable evening they each firmly shook hands with him and wished him good fortune in the coming weeks.

The next day David, Paddy and a somewhat dour A.T.S. sergeant from the Intelligence Corps made a microscopic inspection of all the clothes David would be wearing and taking in his suitcase. It would all be checked again before the flight as a matter of routine, just as it had been when he had emplaned for Le Mans, this original check allowing for any necessary alterations to be made in the little workroom on the premises. The day passed slowly. He had decided not to make any more telephone calls – 'probably wouldn't know what the hell to say anyway' he told himself. He listened to Frank Phillips on the nine o'clock news, had a tot of whisky at the bar and took himself off to bed.

Paddy woke him with tea at 6.30, took his gear down to the P.U. while he had breakfast and by 7.30 they were on their way, having been seen off by Robin dressed in a Crombie overcoat over rather daring scarlet silk pyjamas. It was a bright, cold, frosty morning as they made their way to Buxton, then through Chesterfield with its crooked spire. "You know Sir; they say that when the first virgin gets married in Chesterfield the crooked spire will straighten itself out." David was to get to know Chesterfield quite well in a couple of years' time. They pushed on to Lincoln, David navigating, there were no road signs of course, which made a thorough knowledge of the ordnance survey maps essential for getting from point A to point B.

Having stopped for a 'pie and a pint' at a roadside hostelry, they eventually arrived at the airfield. The R.A.F. police sergeant at the control barrier thoroughly examined their papers, checked them over the telephone with persons unknown, directed them to a building some little way ahead where they would be met, and sent them on their way with an impeccable salute which would not have disgraced an R.S.M. in the guards.

They were met by a rather pretty W.A.A.F. corporal. "Captain Chandler, will you please come with me, and if your batman can wait inside with your kit?" She turned towards Paddy. Up until now Paddy had been standing with his left arm towards her. In the Rifles, N.C.O.s wear their stripes on their right arm only, a tradition since they were first formed a hundred and fifty years before. As she spoke to him he turned and she saw his black and gold stripes on the other arm. Somewhat flustered she began to apologise.
"I'm terribly sorry sergeant. I assumed the captain would bring his batman."
"He has my dear," Paddy replied. "You see in our regiment we have some funny ways. All the sergeants are really private soldiers, riflemen we call them. All the riflemen are really sergeants. The captain here is really a colonel, and the colonel is the orderly corporal. It's all very confusing so it is. Anyway, you can call me Paddy, so that settles that." The embarrassed girl looked to David for help.
"Just take no notice of him corporal, he gets these little fits every now and then. We sometimes have to lock him up for days at a time." The corporal came to the conclusion they were both round the bend and led him off to the adjutant's office.

The adjutant was an affable chap who, dealing regularly, as he did, with a wide variety of agents, both sexes, all ages, various nationalities, some service people, many civilians, treated the meeting of someone about to climb into a bomber and drop lord knows where for what it was – an everyday occurrence.
"You will meet your pilot and navigator at dinner this evening old

boy. Then tomorrow you can have a look round the kite you'll be travelling in, have a last minute session with the intelligence wallahs at about 1300 hours, security strip search after that, and take off about 16.30 I should think." David was beginning to get the old familiar tango in his entrails as the adjutant breezily outlined his programme.

The meeting with the pilot and navigator was interesting. The pilot was young, probably about twenty-two and a flight lieutenant – equivalent to an army captain. The navigator was a good deal older, early thirties and senior in rank to the pilot, being a squadron leader – equivalent in rank to an army major. Both held the blue and white diagonally striped Distinguished Flying Cross above their right breast pockets. They described the proposed flight pattern to David. They would cross the French coastline at low level at a point where they would be unlikely to meet any flak. They would then fly at 1000 feet across Occupied France, to the drop area. By flying at this low altitude they would hope to evade night fighters as well as German radar. "That's why we have the best navigator in the business," the pilot broke in, "its all dead reckoning, you can't get much help visually from that height. When the drop zone is reached a coded system of lights, set up only hours before the drop, is brought into action between those on the ground and the navigator in the nose of the aircraft to make sure no trap exists, and then out you go," said the pilot grinning widely. David's entrails were now performing the Highland fling.

Despite his 'properly having the wind up, in more ways then one' as he confessed to himself, he slept like the proverbial log, being awakened at eight by Paddy with a large mug of tea. He saw the pilot at breakfast, who looked even younger in daylight, and who suggested he be at the dispersal point at about 10.30 for a tour of inspection. "May I bring my sergeant with me?" David enquired. "He is a paratrooper."

"Yes, of course old boy, bring your family if you like."

At 10.30 precisely they climbed into the giant Halifax. "Bit roomier than the Witley Sir, isn't it? And to think you'll have it all to yourself. I should bring a football and have a kick around."

"Are you trying to put the wind up me more than it is already?" David replied. "One thing I shall definitely not need for a few days is Ex-lax, I can tell you that."

A sergeant, who they discovered was the plane's wireless operator, came down the fuselage from the cockpit. "I'm Sergeant Lacey, Sir; I have the job of dispatcher." The sergeant then went through the procedure of hooking up, red light on, green light on – "All quite simple, Sir – I have to tell you, though you've probably done it dozens of times before." He continued, "If you come up front Sir, the skipper will show you the driving compartment and so on, then I have to take you to the parachute packing room to draw your chute. After lunch the station security officer will check you out in whatever you are travelling in, along with the stuff you are taking, then you will join the aircraft and we should be off at about 16.30 hours. It's almost dark then, flight time say three and a half hours, you should arrive at about nine o'clock, their time. We're promised moonlight so hopefully won't have to stooge around looking for the target." None of this is improving my entrails problem David told himself.

They had lunch, then having drawn his parachute, the trio made their way to the security block. First of all his case was emptied and checked – no problems except that David suddenly realised he had no idea how he was to carry the damned thing down! When he went to France before in the Lysander it went with him on his lap – he could hardly jump holding the blasted thing by its handle.

"Has no one told you Sir?" queried the wireless operator/dispatcher. "It will go down in the container. When you jump we release a parachute container a second or two afterwards. This carries your case, and tonight a new wireless for the ground people, and a couple of tommy guns and ammunition. The drop point is right near a forest so let's hope the wind doesn't blow too hard in the wrong direction so that it ends up in a tree."

"Let's hope it doesn't blow too hard and I end up in a tree," David retorted, with considerable emphasis on the 'I'.

As the search ended, the adjutant made his appearance, clutching a file from which he produced a sheaf of papers and an envelope with what seemed an enormous amount of French and Swiss currency contained in it.

"You chaps do cause me an awful lot of paperwork you know," was his opening gambit, as he shoved the first foolscap sheet in front of David to sign. The formalities having been completed, he shook hands with David saying, "Best of luck old man, happy landings," and with that to the dispatcher, "He's all yours."

Paddy drove them to the dispersal point. It would be an hour before they took off, but dusk was coming on already. In the five minute drive to the aircraft Paddy slipped David his 'Golly', given him by Maria when he first went to Ringway, and which they had named

Cedric in memory of Maria's brother, killed at Calais. David had told her he would never jump without it; Maria had made and sewn on special parachuting wings, jumping without his mascot would have been unthinkable. He reasoned that if he was searched at any time he could always find a reason for having it in his possession – that is until he realised Cedric had paratroopers' wings! They, therefore, had had to be removed and were now safely contained in his kit back at Wilmslow. Cedric would now make his first operational jump.

The preliminaries having been carried out, including the loading of the container in the huge bay of the Halifax, the dispatcher called, "Aboard now Sir."

David and Paddy shook hands. "God go with you Sir," Paddy said.

"And you Paddy wherever it is you're bound for."

The huge machine burst into life until all four engines were running sweetly. The door was closed, David was given a couple of blankets with the shouted comment, "It gets bloody parky in here Sir." Slowly they taxied from the dispersal point for what seemed an interminable ride to the end of the runway, followed by the ever increasing roar of the four engines as they gained power for take off. Paddy, watching from the dispersal point saw the plane gather speed, gradually lift off the runway and then disappear into the early evening. "I wonder if I'll ever see him again," he asked himself, and then followed with the answer, "of course you will, you stupid sod."

After flying for an hour or so, the wireless operator made his way back to David seated on a canvas chair secured to the side of the fuselage. Over the din made by the four engines he shouted, "Just to let you know Sir, we shall be testing the guns in a minute, so don't get the wind up."

David grinned and shouted back, "I've got news for you, I've had the wind up for the past two days." The wireless op grinned back, making a deprecating gesture as much as to say that he didn't believe it. "If you only knew," David said to himself.

The guns tested, they roared on. Once or twice David thought he heard some flak exploding quite close; otherwise it was, so far, uneventful. After a couple of hours the wireless op returned carrying a flask. Steadying himself against the side he poured half a cup and gave it to David. "It will warm you up," he shouted.

"Something needs to – I'm bloody frozen."

David took the cup and sipped cautiously in case it was boiling hot. It wasn't, what it was though, as far as he could judge, about fifty percent coffee and fifty percent rum. He grinned his appreciation to the sergeant and shouted, "I shall always love the Royal Air Force."

"Can't claim any credit Sir, Paddy gave it to me for you."

At last the moment of truth drew nigh. The sergeant returned. "Let's put your chute on Sir."

They fastened the parachute on, the sergeant checking every detail, then hooking the static line on to the interior retaining wire. Pointing to the connection he shouted, "Check Sir?"

"O.K. Sergeant."

They then moved closer to the hole in the fuselage, which had been covered for the flight. The sergeant took a harness from a side peg, strapped it on and fastened the umbilical cord to a stout fixture on the side of the fuselage. David had the thought that if the sergeant did fall out accidentally through the hole, how long would it be before the other crew members arrived to pull him back in? What's more, how long would he last out there in the freezing cold being buffeted about by those four huge engines? What a happy little man you are, he concluded.

Having lifted the cover and fixed it against the framework of the aircraft, the sergeant came back to David, pointing to a monitor on the ceiling. "When the red light goes on, sit in the hole, you could be there for ten minutes. When the green light goes on you go – OK?"

"OK sergeant, and many thanks." They shook hands and stood for about five minutes before the red light appeared. David seated himself on the floor, and swung his legs into the hole. Down below he could see the ground was covered either by frost or a thin coating of snow. The aircraft was dropping from its original height of about 1200 feet to between 600 and 800 feet, he could hear the engines feathering back to provide the lowest sustainable airspeed. He saw some houses flash by, a small river and then concentrated on the light above him. For fully ten minutes he sat there. He had heard tales of how sometimes the aircrew couldn't find the landing spot and had to return to England with their passenger. At other times local fog prevented the drop. At other times the recognition signal had been wrong. It could have been a genuine mistake or it could be the operation had been compromised. In any case they took their passenger back. Whilst these thoughts were going through his mind the green light came on and he thrust himself out into the unknown. The enormous power of the slipstream from the four propellers whipped his chute open almost instantaneously. He found himself swinging violently in complete noiselessness as opposed to the bedlam to which he had been subjected for the past few hours. He quickly gathered his wits about him so as to make a perfect landing. It would be monstrous to come all this way and end up crocked!

Chapter Seventeen

As it approached dusk Harry and the men at the roadblock stood-to. There was no doubt in any mind that as soon as darkness fell the Japs would try and rush them. The two inch mortar had a limited number of flares to use in such an attack, on the other hand; of course, the Japs still did not know how many men faced them. It was to be a dark night that was sure, if last night was anything to go by, no moon whatsoever and the overhanging trees making the outlook pitch-black. At eight o'clock the forward picquet threw a grenade – the signal that attackers were moving towards them. Immediately the fixed-line Brens opened up, the 2 inch mortarman put up a parachute flare, followed by a second, the 3 inch mortarman put down four H.E. on the target area in front of the dannert, and then in the brilliant light from the flares, the defenders opened up on a group of some fifty Jap troops rushing along the road towards them, shrieking and screaming. Only one reached the defenders, Harry gave him a burst with his tommy gun, which lifted him backwards off his feet to lie twitching at the mouth of the bunker. A sepoy at Harry's side within the bunker reversed his rifle, pushed the body away from the firing point and it rolled down into the ditch in front where the ants and the rats and the other small rapacious jungle predators would soon find it.

There were no more attacks that night. However, they did hear the sound of a lorry motor, and of the tank starting up. This activity invited a few bursts from the fixed-line Brens, but as ammunition was not replaceable, these were kept to a minimum. They stood to before dawn and then clearly saw what the Japs had been up to during the night. There was not a single member of the Imperial Japanese Army to be seen. The infantry were obviously dug in behind the shelter of the tanks, but the tanks had been moved so that two were side by side on the road in the form of an arrowhead pointing towards the defenders. There was a gap between the tanks at the front of the arrowhead just large enough for a 75mm artillery piece, which was obviously brought up by the lorry they had heard during the night, to allow its barrel to protrude, whilst the ranger, loader and firer would be sheltered by the tanks. The third tank was hard up against them at the rear.

"We are in for a bit of a battering by the looks of things," Harry prophesied to the two lieutenants. It was apparent that the tanks, having only the equivalent of two pounder solid shot or less, now intended to use the artillery piece either to blast smoke at the defenders prior to an attack, or more likely, were going to just blast the bunkers away with high explosive.

"I'll try and drop some 3 inch mortar bombs on them," the young Rajput lieutenant decided. As he moved back out of Harry's bunker to the mortar pit to give the necessary instructions, the first shell roared into them, caught the lieutenant in the open, he was killed instantly. The Aussie lieutenant, witnessing the tragedy, raced to the mortarmen to give them their orders, raced back again and dived into the bunker just as the second shell landed. By this time the mortarmen had ranged on to the arrowhead. It was going to be difficult to drop a bomb on exactly the spot where the gun crew were. Wherever the bombs fell around the target, the gunners were protected; a direct hit had to be made on that small triangular refuge provided by the three tanks. And they only had six bombs left.

It was not to be. Although two of the bombs hit the tanks, probably causing casualties, it was not enough to knock out the gun. Gradually the bunkers were blasted, hit again, and eventually became impossible to fire from. All three carriers received direct hits, although their crews were dug in beside them. Even so, over half of the original defenders were now either killed or wounded. They were unable to retreat as the ground behind them rose sharply for a short distance and was being continually raked by the front two tanks machine guns. Had the Japs then attacked with their infantry it would have been a walkover. As it was, presumably because they had already taken so many casualties on the previous attacks, they put down several rounds of smoke, waiting for some minutes for it to thicken before advancing into it. Harry told his naik to tell the Rajputs to retreat back to the river, there was just a chance they might find a boat and get across – a very, very slim chance he told himself, but marginally better than their present predicament. They had to leave the wounded, two of whom volunteered to fire the fixed-line Bren guns until their ammunition was exhausted. They perished brutally. Three of the Aussies, including the lieutenant, had to be left, all wounded so that they could not walk. When Harry judged all who could go had gone, he himself set off, but as he reached the little crest behind the position, he was hit in the back of the thigh, the bullet going right through and coming out the other side, and two more bullets from the same burst taking a chunk of his right rib cage away. The force of the impact bowled him over and he lay, frightened and hurting badly, for a few minutes. In front of him and a little to his left, there were two sepoys lying almost side by side, both with fatal head wounds, caught by the same burst he decided.

There was no doubt in his mind that the Japs, particularly in view of the mauling they had received, would take no prisoners. Behind him he could hear their usual screaming as they attacked what was left of the defensive position, then all firing ceased and the smoke began to thin. The nearest cover he could see was a hundred yards away, he would never make it, wounded as he was, without being seen. "I am," he said to himself, "well and truly in the cacky." He thought desperately for a minute or so, then conceiving the idea that if he pulled the two dead sepoys over him as he lay spread-eagled on the ground, marauding Japs might take him for dead as well and not attempt to finish him off. Quickly he crawled to them and pulled one of them across his legs and the other at a bit of an angle across his back. The pain from his wounds made him sweat, but at last it was done and he positioned himself with his head cushioned on one arm so that with an eye half open he could at least see partly what was happening. The other arm was flung out to the side, and it was the positioning of this arm, which saved his life.

The smoke having cleared, the position taken, the Japs dragged the twenty or so wounded to lie against a bank. In the meantime, another group was shouting and laughing as they used corpses for bayonet practice. Two of this group approached Harry and the two sepoys. "This is it my old son," Harry murmured to himself, as screaming with pleasure one of the plunged his bayonet through the neck of the sepoy lying across his legs. The other moron had positioned his rifle and bayonet to similarly take his pleasure with Harry when he spotted the leather wrist-strap to which was fixed Harry's badge of rank, the Lion and Unicorn shining brightly in the blazing sunlight. Hesitating in his thought, he plunged the bayonet into the soft earth where, fixed to the rifle, it stood upright freeing his hands to undo the strap. Harry had the immediate fear that the wretch would notice his arm was still warm, luckily in the blazing sun everything was warm, which, combined with the fact that the three small buckles securing the strap were giving trouble, concentrated what mind the looter had in other directions.

As the soldier struggled to undo the strap with his podgy fingers, his officer screamed for all the men to fall in in front of the wounded Rajputs. The man hastily dropped Harry's arm, dragged his rifle and bayonet out of the ground and followed his companion down the slope at the double. Even so, he was the last to present himself in front of the officer, receiving for his pains two almighty slaps across the face to which he submitted without demur. The officer then, with a rasping, throaty shriek, gave the command for the men to bayonet the prisoners. They did so as if they were on a practice ground with dummies – 'in', 'out', present rifles – and again, 'in', 'out', present rifles, no matter how the poor unfortunate sepoys squirmed and tried to avoid the lethal steel, in thirty seconds they were all dead, their blood saturating the light sandy soil, their executioners laughing and salivating at the depraved pleasure they had enjoyed.

But there was more to come.

The three Australians had been put to one side. They were for the officer. One of the Aussies was so badly hurt he was lying in a heap. The officer indicated to a senior N.C.O. to pull him to his knees, and to hold him up by his hair. The N.C.O. knew what was coming, and held him at arms length. The officer drew his sword and with unerring accuracy decapitated the unfortunate prisoner. As the head was left dangling in the N.C.O.'s hand, a great plume of blood squirted up into the air which, blown by the brisk wind, came back to cover the boots and leggings of the evil assistant. This was accompanied by a great roar of acclamation by the onlookers, and the holding up of the head to be blown an obscene kiss by the holder before being thrown into the ditch.

The second of the three showed great bravery by drawing himself to his knees, knocking away the N.C.O.'s hand which was intending to perform the same heinous duty as before, and stared the slit-eyed executioner straight in the eyes until he too was decapitated, his head rolling down into the ditch to lie beside that of his comrade.

The last was the lieutenant. He too knocked away the N.C.O.'s hand. He had been wounded internally and had been bleeding profusely from the mouth. As he knelt up and looked at this monster in front of him, he let go a huge mouthful of blood and saliva with all the force he could find from his damaged lungs. The jet hit his assassin fully on the chin and ran down his throat on to his shirt. There was a gasp from the onlookers, who were suddenly silent. The officer hesitated for a moment, long enough for the Aussie to shout:-

"FUCK THE EMPEROR," at which, down came the sword and another head joined the others in the ditch.

Their evil work done, the men were set to burying their own dead. This they did by the simple expedient of throwing the bodies into three of the bunkers which were the least damaged, then by pulling away the bamboo poles upon which the excavated earth had been placed to give head cover to the defenders, conveniently covered the corpses. Some additional covering up had to be done, but in an hour or so the men fell in on the road and marched away, the tanks and field gun already having disappeared. After the noise and mayhem of the past days everywhere was strangely quiet. Even the normal jungle and mangrove noises were hushed. Not for long. Soon the winged scavengers, the wild pigs, the tree rats, and the innumerable small insects, small in size but with voracious appetites, would appear to have their fill before the corpses rotted and were no more. To Nishimura's orders, over two hundred British, Indian and Australian wounded were disposed of by being bayoneted to death at the battle for Muar. In 1946 Nishimura would be hanged for this and his countless other crimes.

When Harry judged he was on his own, he lifted his head gradually to make sure he could move to cover. Lying in the sun, although he had his steel helmet on, he could feel his neck was very sore, in addition the helmet itself had become almost red hot, making him feel faint. He eased the helmet off and wiped the sweat away with his hand. He looked at his wounds, and decided if he could make it to the bamboo thicket he could then take off his equipment and his clothing and bandage them properly. He was surprised to see he was not bleeding to the extent he would have expected, the bullet having made a clean entry and exit in his leg, those which hit his ribs causing a lot more mess.

He gradually and reverently moved the two dead sepoys from him. One of them had a machete in a canvas scabbard on his belt; they each still carried their field dressings in the special pocket provided in their uniforms. Harry undid the belt of the main with the machete and took it from him, thinking he might have difficulty getting into the bamboo without it, and then took their field dressings. As he slid the machete scabbard off the belt he said to himself, "This might very well come in handy," he could have no idea of how handy it would in fact be in the not very distant future. Lastly he poured the water remaining in their water bottles into his own, which meant he had nearly a full bottle to carry him through the rest of the day.

Whilst carrying out these acts he had the uncomfortable feeling he was robbing the dead, especially when he had to roll them over to get at the field dressing pockets. Harry was not an actively religious man, he had been to Sunday school, had been confirmed, was considered by his peers to be a thoroughly decent fair minded chap, but in no way was he, what he himself would describe certain others, a 'hot gospeller.' Nevertheless, he was reluctant to just leave these two soldiers who had been instrumental in saving his life, and from whom furthermore he had taken belongings, to just be there at the mercy of animals. There was no way he could bury them, all he could think of to do was to say a prayer over them. He knelt in considerable pain from his wounds, and said:- "Oh God, please take the souls of my two comrades here, whose names I do not know, and who belong to a religion I do not know. Please see they pass into the paradise their valour has earned for them for the sake of Jesus Christ, thy Son, our Lord." As he finished his supplication he found he was crying, the tension, the fear, the horror of the day had quite overcome him. He gradually calmed, and then felt a degree of content that at least these two men had died with someone to grieve for them.

With another quick look to make sure there was no one on the road, he got to his feet, not without considerable pain, and slowly made his way to the bamboo. It was solid at the front but when he circled to the right he found a narrow gap leading into a small piece of open ground in the centre of the clump. He would be secure here, he told himself. His conclusion was shattered when in the centre of the small clearing he caught sight of a large green and amber snake, which seeing him, immediately raised its head in a swaying motion ready to strike. Harry stopped in his tracks a yard or so away keep absolutely still. After a few seconds, which felt like hours to Harry, the snake lowered its head, turned and made its way out through the thicket to the open ground beyond. The air expelled from Harry's lungs in a gasp of relief. He found he was sweating profusely, though whether it was from fear, pain or the heat of the afternoon sun, or a combination of all three, he could not tell. He then had the funny feeling he had read somewhere that some venomous snakes always go around in pairs, so he proceeded to go round the clearing, beating the bases of the bamboo canes with his machete. Having satisfied himself he had no unwelcome company he proceeded to take his equipment, uniform and undervest off, to examine his wounds. Each field dressing has two pads plus bandages. He put a pad on each of the leg wounds and bound them tightly. The wounds in his side were more difficult to get at but eventually he managed to cover them and bind the bandages from the two sepoys, joined together, to keep them in place. He felt very tired. Sitting against the bamboo he dozed off, waking an hour later with ants biting lumps out of him, but nevertheless somewhat refreshed. "Now what," he asked himself. The only way to go was back to the river. Problem One. By now the Japs had almost certainly crossed the river further upstream and occupied the town, so how can I get through then to Milestone 96 near Sulong? Problem Two. I will almost certainly have to swim that bloody, stinking, filthy river. Nigel Coates, when they were leaning on the riverbank wall together had told him of the water snakes that infested it. Some were harmless but most were big and extremely venomous. They were true snakes, not eels, and like all snakes had to breathe. Consequently although they hunted well below the surface – out at sea the larger ones could go down to 1000 feet – they constantly had to come to the surface to breathe, where a swimmer, thrashing away with his arms and legs would be an immediate target. Harry's blood turned cold at the thought of the company he might attract, but there was no alternative that he could think of.

Having cogitated, dozed, fought off the ants and cogitated further, it began to get dark. He had shed all his surplus equipment, keeping only his machete and water bottle fixed to his webbing belt. Darkness fell quickly. The frogs and the cicadas began their nightly choruses as he moved towards the river, keeping in the shadow of trees and thickets wherever he could. In a short while he reached the river about two hundred yards upstream from the sunken ferry craft. There seemed to be no movement on his side of the river, but there were lights moving about on the far side. He was almost opposite the Coates' house, or where the Coates house had been before it was reduced to rubble by the four days of shelling. A thought struck him. There was just the chance that the servants' compound had escaped the shelling and that Ah Chin and his family would still be there. If he could get to them he was sure they would be willing to give him guidance as to how to get to Milestone 96 without having to risk using roads. He waited until ten o'clock, being bitten alive by mosquitoes, then taking his boots off and tying them to his belt, in fear and trepidation he walked into the river. It is tidal at this point, he was lucky the tide was in, as a result he had only a short distance to cover of the thick, black, stinking ooze, before he slowly submerged himself into the water. He was most careful about two things. One, he had picked a particularly tall tree as a landmark on the other side, which he would be able to see as he swam. If then the current took him one way or the other he could still make the point where he wanted to emerge, that is as close to the Coates' premises as possible. Two, he was careful not to swallow, or even get the river water anywhere near his mouth. That he knew would almost certainly be fatal. He swam slowly for two reasons. Firstly his inordinate fear of attracting the water snakes, secondly so that he would, hopefully, not attract the attention of any spare Jap wandering around.

He was nearly three parts of the way over when he began to get very tired. It was difficult to tell how far he had to go, but in the darkness he felt panic coming on. "Don't give up," he kept saying to himself, and positively stopped himself from striking out to get to his landing place more quickly. The pain of his wounds, the constant action against the Japs, the fear of the river, the fear that its foul pollution would give him blood poisoning, all combined to almost make him give in. But not quite. He thought of Megan, his twins, and the new baby, and his mind settled to the task in hand. After another five minutes, he could clearly see the river wall, and the gap where there was a cobbled slipway down which the local people launched their boats. It was to this he headed, but when he reached it he found it was a slipway in more ways than one. The cobbles, covered by the river slime, caused him to stumble and splash his way up, until eventually he lay on the water's edge utterly exhausted and fearful that his noisy exit had been heard. He took several deep breaths, raised himself to his knees, and took a long look over the wall to see that the coast was clear. On the other side of the road, running down to the padang, there was a line of casuarina trees. He stood up, hunched over, and prepared to run across the road. As he took his good leg off the ground, the wounded one collapsed under him and he fell against the wall, the top of it making very painful contact with his damaged ribs. He stifled a shriek of pain and sank to the ground again. After a few minutes he tried again to stand on the injured leg, with marginal success. He looked around to see if there was a piece of wood of any sort that he could use to help support him. There was nothing to hand, but across the road under the casuarina trees there were numerous pieces of branches blown off during the shelling. He had his machete; he could quickly make a crutch of some sort and risk the noise, if only he could get there.

The tiredness which had hit him in the river started to come over him again. He so desperately wanted to lie back and sleep for a little while. The continual pain, the loss of blood, the despair at being surrounded by this evil enemy, he could understand how people faced with a plight similar to the one he was in could just give up. He pulled himself together, "Nil nisi illegitimus carborundum," he said to himself, which is the old soldiers Latin for 'don't let the bastards grind you down,' and with that he started to crawl across the road into the debris under the trees. Reaching there he searched around on his hands and knees for a piece of wood that would need the least amount of work to be done on it. Finding a straight branch with a 'V' piece on the top, he quickly cut it to length and shortened the 'V' with the minimum of noise – the former owner had kept his blade well sharpened he was pleased to find.

After waiting a few minutes to establish whether anyone had heard him, he raised himself and started to move hesitantly towards the padang. He was weaker than he had realised and had to stop time after time to get his breath back and will himself to go on. At last he reached the padang. Clearly in front of him some hundred yards or so away he saw the crumbled ruins of the beautiful house in which he had been so welcomed only a few weeks before. Just as he was leaving the shelter of the trees, he heard people coming towards him on the road twenty or thirty yards away. It was a group of about a dozen Japanese troops being marched along by an N.C.O. They were talking together but otherwise moving quietly in their canvas, rubber soled boots. Harry flattened himself behind one of the trees until they had disappeared, then lurched his way on to cover the last lap.

One end of the servant's quarters had been pulverised by a shell, but the remainder, although showing signs of damage was more or less intact. Harry made for the main door, tried the handle, but found the door locked. 'Supposing Japs have taken it over,' he thought, following that possibility up with, 'No, they wouldn't have locked the door.' He felt desperately weary, weariness brings on terrible feelings of indecision under any circumstances and he was literally at the end of his tether. He decided to knock, tapping lightly so that hopefully anyone inside would hear without his waking the whole bloody neighbourhood, as he put it to himself. There was no answer. 'They could have all run away somewhere.' He kept tapping for several minutes, which seemed like a lifetime, and all the time he could feel himself getting weaker and weaker and more and more agitated to a point almost of hysteria. As he was about to give up he heard the faint voice of someone within asking something in Chinese. In as low a voice as he could judge would be heard on the other side of the door, he called out, "Ah Chin, Ah Chin, it's Mr Chandler, Mr Chandler, Ah Chin, it's Mr Chandler, you remember me. I had dinner with Mr Coates." He heard a bolt slide back, the door opened and he collapsed unconscious into the arms of Ah Chin and his daughters.

Chapter Eighteen

It was several days, days of eagerly waiting for the morning post and of continually being disappointed, before Maria received the tribunal letter. She feverishly opened it, gave a little squeal of delight and ran back into the kitchen to tell her mother the good news. It told her she was to present herself at the Wren Depot at Mill Hill School in North London on Monday 16th February for assessment. From this she deduced that she was not 'in' yet, but if she put up a good show she would become a Wren. Places in the Wrens were much coveted; there was a certain cachet in wearing the trim navy uniform as compared to the A.T.S. khaki and Waafs air force blue. "I must telephone Mrs Chandler," she excitedly told her mother. Ruth was very pleased to hear Maria's good news, both in the course of their conversation wondering what 'David is doing now.' However, if Maria's tidings were pleasing, information from elsewhere was far from conducive to raising the morale at home.

The news from the Western Desert and the Far East was bad. Rommel's panzers were driving the British and Empire troops back relentlessly towards Egypt. Fred and Jack, guessing that was Mark and Charlie's destination wondered whether they could get there in time to take part in the campaign. Their convoy would have to go the long way round – South Africa, Red Sea, Suez Canal, to get to Egypt. Add to this the fact that a convoy had to sail at the speed of the slowest ship did not help matters when time was of the essence.

On the 8th of February, Japanese troops landed on Singapore Island. Within a week General Percival surrendered 62,000 British, Indian and Australian troops to their barbarous conquerors, of whom over a half would eventually die as prisoners of war. It was a sickening, humiliating defeat, probably the worst in the history of the British Army. Churchill told the nation they should not despair. 'We are,' he said 'no longer alone. We are in the midst of a great company. The whole future of mankind may depend upon our conduct now. We must move steadfastly through the storm.' Despite this inspiring oratory there was a deep sadness throughout the nation, particularly among those whose loved ones were involved directly in the campaigns, the Chandlers falling into that category, along with the added concern of not knowing what was happening to David.

General Yamashita, the conqueror of Singapore, had endeavoured, during the campaign through Malaya to have his troops behave in a soldierly way towards prisoners and particularly the civilian population, who they wished to incorporate into their 'Greater East Asia Coprosperity Sphere.' This was, of course, another name for the Japanese Empire, but on the surface was an alliance of the Eastern colonial peoples. As we have seen, his orders particularly in respect of the Emperor's Guards Division under General Nishimura, were deliberately disobeyed, resulting in the murder of hundreds of wounded and prisoners, and the rape and murder of even more civilians, particularly Chinese. When Singapore surrendered there was an orgy of brutality carried out by the Japanese troops, drunk with the power of victory and the liquor they had looted. At one point sixty five Australian nurses and twenty-five English soldiers surrendered. The soldiers were shot on the spot and the nurses made to walk into the sea where they were fired on by machine gunners. Only one, a Sister Bullwinkel survived to tell the story. When drunken troops reached the Alexandra Hospital, they went through each ward bayoneting the wounded in their beds. In the operating theatre they even bayoneted the doctor carrying out an operation along with his assistants and the patient. The hospital chapel was full of wounded lying on the floor. They killed them all. In the meantime they had rounded up the British nurses and after subjecting them to multiple rape, bayoneted them and burnt their bodies on a fire they made from the chapel seating. In the meantime, their leader, General Yamashita, had ordered the rounding up of six thousand prominent Chinese civilians. Over the next three weeks they had all been shot, decapitated, or taken in groups in chains out to sea and pushed overboard to drown, or to feed the sharks.

Little of the extent of these atrocities, nor those of their equally evil comrades in arms in Russia and Poland, would be fully verified until after the war. It is to be hoped they will never be forgotten.

During Maria's telephone call to Ruth, Fred came in unexpectedly. On being told it was Maria on the line, he asked if he could have a few words. Maria excitedly told him the good news, to which he asked what sort of work she would like to do in the service.

"Do you know Mr Chandler, I hadn't even thought I would get a choice, I assumed I would be placed where there was a vacancy."

"Well, they're bound to ask what you did in civvy street and use your experience in the navy. Mind you, in the army the reverse usually seemed to apply."

"Oh, I do hope not, I'd like to get away from waiting on people in general, and from food in particular."

"What else can you do?"

"Well, I got matriculation at Chingford Grammar School, with good passes in maths and English. I can drive a lorry – I've been driving daddy's Bedford trucks round the lorry park since I was about fourteen. I can speak and write more or less fluent German."

Fred put on his thinking cap. Not one to rush into a decision he analysed the problem.

"I would think that if you want a fairly cushy indoor job, working in the officer's mess would be number one on the list, but make sure you emphasise you know absolutely nothing about food preparation or you will most definitely end up in the cookhouse. On the other hand, if you want an outside job, ask direct whether you can be in the transport section or whatever they call it in the navy. I would think that the number of young women they interview who can drive a lorry must be few and far between, so you should stand a good chance. On the other hand, truck driving is not all fun, particularly in the winter. You could ask whether there were any opportunities where you could make good use of your German which could land you an interesting office job."

Maria thanked Fred for his help and advice and promised to telephone them both as soon as she had some news.

The days dragged by until on Monday 16th February Maria was up with the lark, packed a few personal things into a grip, said goodbye to her mother and father, and with a degree of trepidation, made her way to Mill Hill School, a well known public school in North London, taken over, as Maria would shortly learn to call it, to be a Wrenery. A draft of some thirty odd young women had mustered by midday, each, including Maria, surreptitiously regarding the others to try and gauge what sorts of people they had volunteered themselves to join. They were welcomed by a Wren officer who told them that for the next two weeks they would be on probation, would receive elementary drill instruction, medical examinations, be assessed, and carry out fatigue duties. Should they decide that the Wrens was not for them, they could leave at any time, although that would mean they would, of course be available for call up to another service, or be placed in industry.

Taken to their barrack room Maria had her first taste of service life. Brought up as she had been to have her own chintzy, girlish room to herself, she found herself in a noisy dormitory along each long wall of which was spaced a row of double bunks, the lower bunk about eighteen inches from the floor, the upper one, which needed a certain degree of agility to attain, being nearly six feet from floor level. She was directed to a bunk with another girl, who promptly suggested they should toss for who had the lower bunk. Maria lost. Her first two or three efforts at reaching her place of rest resulted in gales of laughter from her new friend, Enid, a doctor's daughter, this pantomime being repeated throughout the dormitory.

"It's a jolly good job there are no seamen around," Enid had said "all the top bunkers are showing their knickers off." Maria soon got the hang of things and once she had got used to being in her elevated position, felt rather superior sitting on high. Enid added to her previous remarks that it would not do for Maria to come back at night a bit tidily, and above all if she had to get up in the night to go to the loo to remember she was six feet up, and not lying on her nice comfortable Slumberland divan at home.

"I think I might buy a po," laughed Maria.

"Yes, but where would you store it?" It was obvious she and Enid were going to get on.

To their surprise they spent most of their first week at Mill Hill scrubbing floors. Whether this was to instil discipline into them, or because the floors needed scrubbing, or just the navy being pure bloody-minded, or whether it was designed to get any weak gutted individuals to go home, was the subject of conjecture. In between scrubbing sessions they found themselves out on the school playground, now turned into drill square. The drill instructor was a chief petty officer, who by the displeasure written constantly on his twenty years in the Royal Navy face, illustrated by the eighteen year long service medal for undiscovered crime worn on his chest, did not think much of women sailors in general, and his having to teach them to march in step and salute properly in particular.

"I'm going to get a photo of him one day and paste it on my po," was Maria's verdict to Enid after a particularly bad-tempered session with C.P.O. Gates. There followed then a hilarious discussion as to how they were going to get the po down from the top bunk without spilling anything. They finally decided the po hypothesis was not workable, partly because the person in the lower bunk could conceivably be the recipient of the contents in the event of a mishap.

"I'll write and ask my father if it's possible to grow a bigger bladder," were Enid's concluding remarks on the subject.

During the second week the would-be Wrens had a change of job. They were detailed to polish the floors they had previously had to scrub. Only one person had dropped out so far, but after the first polishing day another said she had had enough and would rather work on munitions. Enid and Maria had discussed together what they would like to do after they left Mill Hill. Enid had already said that after the war she wanted to go to medical school and become a doctor like her father and mother were, and her paternal grandfather before them. She hoped, therefore, she could be a sick bay attendant so as to get a grounding in the profession before she began the slog of medical school. Maria on the other hand had decided she would prefer to be in the open air and was going to try and get into the transport section.

During the second week they each in turn were interviewed by a panel of three Wren officers, chaired by a first officer, fortyish, angular jawed, grey haired, a frightfully upper crust sounding lady, who spoke in clipped sentences, and whose antecedents had obviously all been admirals. Enid's interview was on the Tuesday, she came back to the dormitory with the news that her request to be a sick bay attendant would be investigated. Maria followed on the Wednesday and received the same answer with regard to her joining a transport pool. The two discussed their prospects, wondering whether their both receiving the same decision was just a 'put-off,' or whether the panel or their minions would indeed be seeking to place them in their desired jobs. They had not long to wait. On Friday they were called in in turn, Enid receiving her posting to the Royal Navy shore station HMS Daedalus at Gosport, Maria to report to the Royal Marine barracks at Deal for driver training. They would leave on Monday.

Friday was payday. For the first two weeks they received the incredible sum of sixteen shillings per week, plus two shillings and eight pence per week on clothing allowance. They had already been made aware of the fact that their initial issue of greatcoat and shoulder bag, two uniforms, two pairs of shoes, hat, underwear etc was the last free issue they would get, from now on they had to replace worn out clothing at a place called 'Slops,' paid for from the 2/8d clothing allowance. It was generally agreed it was the Navy's way of making you look after your gear. From Monday they would be two shillings a week better off, having passed out from their probationary period.

The two girls were sad at being parted. It was a salutary example of one of the unhappy aspects of service life, in that you become firm friends with someone only to be split up, sometimes at a moment's notice, often never to see that person again. They were allowed out on Saturday afternoon and evening until 10pm. The girls decided to go into the West End to show off their new uniforms and were quite surprised at some of the extremely positive invitations they received. They had tea at The Corner House where Maria used to work, being warmly welcomed by Mr Stratton, who flatly refused to give them a bill. All in all it was an exciting day out for them, saddened by the fact they knew it would never be repeated.

On Monday 2nd March, Maria got her travel warrant, hugged Enid goodbye and joined half a dozen others waiting by a truck to take them to Charing Cross station. She was the only one going to Deal, the others going either to Chatham or Sheerness. The Wrenery at Deal was in a requisitioned hotel some little way from what she later discovered to be the barracks of the Royal Marines Depot, where she would be taking part in her driving course, 'though why I need a course when I've been able to drive for years I don't know,' she told herself. She very speedily found out. The first part of the course was learning to ride a motorcycle.

They were gentle examples of the breed, being 250cc Royal Enfields. Any hopes of travelling at 90mph along the Kentish highways and byways were definitely not to be realised. On that corner of the British Isles soon to be known as Hell Fire Corner, the weather is known to be, to say the least, unsettled. On their first day, riding round and round the barrack square, it rained, it blew, it eventually started to snow. The petty officer instructor decided to call it a day. They trooped back to their rooms; single beds here, not bunks, frozen to the core. "I just hope I am not singled out to be a dispatch-rider," Maria concluded.

Following the motorcycle course they were introduced to 15 hundredweight and then 3 ton trucks, which Maria was able to handle with a degree of expertise. Finally they had a day on Humber staff cars, as heavy on the steering as a 3 tonner in Maria's opinion. At the end of the three weeks they awaited the results of the course. There were twelve Wrens on it mostly in their twenties, but a couple in their thirties Maria judged. Two failed the course, the others, with the exception of Maria and a girl called Margaret, being posted off to other shore stations. Margaret and Maria would stay at the staff car pool at Deal. "We'll have arm muscles like dockyard workers wrestling those things," was Margaret's confirmed opinion on the posting. Having finished the course they were rewarded with a 48 hour pass. Margaret's home being in Plymouth it would have been impractical for her to travel there and back in the short time they had been given. Maria therefore suggested she should come home with her, to which suggestion Margaret was most happy to accede.

Back at Sandbury the town seemed suddenly very quiet with the departure of the Canadians, apart from a small detachment left to guard the camp. All sorts of rumours circulated as to who would be taking over the site. Where the reports came from was anyone's guess. Chandlers Lodge at present was empty of any military, the first time since the beginning of 1940 for more than a few days. Cecely had settled in at The Bungalow with Mrs Treharne. One evening she called in on Ruth and during the course of the conversation between Ruth and Rose heard that Mrs Draper, who ran Country Style in the town, was going to lose her junior sales assistant who was being called up. This was a bit of a blow as replacing her would be difficult. Immediately Cecely suggested she could step into the breach.

"But would you mind serving in a shop when people you know might come in?" queried Ruth, thinking it would be a little infra-dig from someone from Cecely's background to be a sales lady.

"Well, let's put it this way. Your lovely Pat did just that didn't she?" There was a silence for a few moments.

"As Fred would say, there's no answer to that," smiled Ruth. "Jack will be here in a few minutes, let's ask his opinion."

They did, and Jack who was totally without any degree of snobbery whatsoever, suggested they broach it to Mrs Draper – "Though we shall have to sort out what the wages will be of course." Cecely assured him that would be no problem, the job would give her something to do, and would take her mind off what was happening to Nigel and his brother in Singapore. The money was incidental.

"My dear Cecely, I have never found money to be incidental. The Good Book itself says, 'the labourer is worthy of his hire.' I admit we can hardly class you as a labourer, come to that I can't for the life of me think of the name given to a female labourer if it comes to that."

The two women regarded him with amusement.

"He's beginning to wander a bit at times these days," Ruth confided to Cecely, "'he'll be alright when he's had a glass of Whitbread's."

Mrs Draper welcomed Cecely with open arms, Cecely found the contact with the majority of their customers – it was a quality trade – to be congenial, and above all it filled all those hours when she would be often feeling sick at heart at not knowing what was happening to her beloved Nigel and his brother.

In the middle of the month Cecely had a letter from her brother-in-law in Iceland saying he was coming on leave, could she get him put up nearby. He was unsure of the date as yet, but would send a telegram as soon as he landed on the mainland. It was decided that as The Bungalow was fully occupied when the children came home on occasional weekends, he should stay at Chandlers Lodge. They all eagerly awaited the telegram. No telegram arrived, but on the evening of Saturday 7th March Cecely was surprised and delighted to receive a telephone call at The Bungalow from James to say that they were now in England – the whole battalion. He had not been able, for security reasons, to tell her this before, but they were now back permanently, permanently that is in army terms, their having been relieved in Iceland by American troops, who seemed he added, to have at least one vehicle per person, "I've never seen so many jeeps, trucks and staff cars in my life." What is more the Brits were allowed to run riot in their P.X. stores, the equivalent of the British Naafi, but containing goods, such as nylons for example, which were totally outside the range of merchandise Naafi could offer. Everyone from the youngest private up to and including the colonel, had landed with an extra kitbag full of goodies. "It's a pity fish won't keep – we could have brought a lorry load if it had been possible."

James duly arrived on Tuesday 10th, complete with an extra kitbag of goodies in the form of Spam, corned beef, tinned salmon and two dozen pairs of nylons to share among the ladies of the family. James was the archetypal tall, dark, handsome soldier, now newly promoted to major, wearing the ribbon of the Military Cross won in France at the time he was wounded. As the taxi scrunched up the driveway, all the family were awaiting him, except the men of course who were working hard on this Tuesday afternoon. After a long hug for Cecely, he was introduced to everybody, shaking hands and smiling as he went, until he came to Megan. Placing his hands on her upper arms he said, "I am told your brave husband is missing in Malaya. I owe my life to him. If I can help in any way you will let me know won't you?" He concluded with, "A man with his initiative and courage may be officially missing, but he'll turn up, you see if I'm not right."

The children were both due home on Friday afternoon for the weekend, it would be Greta's fourteenth birthday on Sunday. "We must stop calling them 'children,'" Cecely had said, "Oliver is taller than I am, and Greta soon will be." The weekend came, and Chandlers Lodge was full to the seams again, as everybody congregated there on Saturday and Sunday. It was however marred, at three o'clock on Sunday afternoon, by the loathsome wailing of the air raid siren, followed very quickly by one of the heaviest anti-aircraft barrages the people of Sandbury had so far experienced. As Fred commented to Jack, "They have upped the ante on the guns lately – I wonder why?" The immediate decision was, who was to go into the Anderson shelter?

There was certainly not room for everybody. "Women and children first," joked Fred. Quickly Megan and the twins, Moira and young John, Rose and Jeremy and finally Anni with young David, crowded in. There was no room for any one to sit down. The two top bunks were hinged upwards so that when they were fixed there was just room for the children on the bottom two bunks, the adults standing between them.

It would appear that the bombers were heading for Biggin Hill, a target on so many previous occasions, only a few minutes flying time from Sandbury. The problem in the past had been that there was an R.A.F. airfield at Sandbury, which, on occasion, had been mistaken for Biggin Hill. Today was no exception. When one bomber mistook the target and let his cargo of death rain down, others blindly followed suit. The ground shook at Chandlers Lodge as bombs missed the airfield buildings and landed in the town. One landing particularly close was followed by the tinkle of glass cascading from several upstairs windows. Those not in the shelters were seeking refuge under the stairway, always considered the safest place in the house. Another bomb falling at the front of the house blew the front door open, the blast making part of the ceiling come down in a pall of dust, choking those under the stairway. "There's only one answer to all this malarkey," Fred determined, and with that extracted a quart bottle of Whitbreads' Light Ale from his ever available stock and passed it round – even Oliver had a very professional swig, commented on by his uncle in the words "You've done that before." But to the contrary Greta, who had accompanied the menfolk, showed an expression of total distaste at her first mouthful of what Fred considered to be, the nectar of the gods.

As they clustered under the stairway, they heard the loud, deep throated bells of fire engines roaring past outside, followed by the somewhat tinnier ringing of an ambulance in pursuit. A few minutes after that they could hear the bellowing of cattle, normally at pasture in the field opposite Chandlers Lodge, but now clearly much nearer. As all overhead activity seemed to have ceased, if only temporarily, Fred announced, "I'm going to see what's going on." He ran out of the house, followed by the others, to find four cows already in the front garden, and others milling in the road outside. They drove the four intruders out on to the road, here they were met by the horrific sight of a dozen or more cattle lying in the field opposite in various stages of mutilation, two beasts walking around bellowing piteously each dragging a smashed leg, another had met the blast head on and, blinded, was staggering into the carcasses as it reeled around in agony. Most of them had shrapnel wounds. The bomb must have landed in amongst them, the same bomb which had brought the ceiling down in Chandlers Lodge hallway.

Gradually they were able to get the ambulant animals back into the field, having to leave three of their number in the roadside ditch, all too badly hurt to move further. "I'll phone Rory Gallacher," Fred told the others, "and jolly well done you two," pointing to Greta and Oliver. Rory was a Rotarian friend of Fred's, owning the local main veterinary practice. "I'm afraid he's going to have to bring his humane killer to finish quite a few of those beasts." Like all old soldiers who had seen so much death, he had such sadness for horses, cattle and sheep who were the innocent victims of man's inhumanity to man. As he spoke, the farmer who owned the cattle arrived. He knew Fred well and tearfully thanked them for all they had done.

As James commented later to Jack, "There he was, crying his eyes out, yet he would have sent each and every one of them to the slaughterhouse without another thought if they had finished yielding their milk." But then, that was the way of life, and death, in the country.

The all-clear sounded, stock was taken of the damage done. Several of the top story window panes had gone; three tiles had slid off the roof and in falling on an outhouse below, had smashed slates there. The hallway ceiling was not as bad as had been first suspected. "A bit of shoring and a few nails will fix that," was Fred's opinion on the subject. The door, door lock and door frame would all require attention, but all in all they had got off lightly, which was more than could be said for several houses in the town and around the airfield. Most people were in their shelters so casualties were light. There were a number of victims among the service people on the airfield they heard later, the raid being the heaviest they had experienced so far. The news that evening reported heavy raids on Kentish airfields with some casualties and losses to property.

"They didn't mention our poor cows," Greta complained. The next day all the carcasses were piled on to a pyre and burnt, the smoke drifting across the road to envelope Chandlers Lodge. It was days before the house was free of the noxious smell.

Chapter Nineteen

As David gathered his wits about him after his pummelling by the Halifax slipstream, he looked down and could clearly see three people running towards him, silhouetted against the frosty ground. To his right, a couple of hundred yards off he saw the container on its parachute, well clear of the trees he was pleased to note. He landed well, rolled over, and then stood up to operate his quick release mechanism and run around his canopy. By the time he had done this the three people reached him, one of them, presumably the leader, holding out his hand saying "Welcome to France Cooteman," the other two shaking hands with him in turn, the second one clearly being a young woman. They gathered up the parachute and ran to the container, which, with the wind in its chute, was being slowly dragged along the frosty surface. Detaching the chute, two of them ran to the edge of the nearby woods, each carrying a parachute, which they deposited in a hole, they had dug whilst they were awaiting David's arrival. The leader unpacked the container, giving David his suitcase and gently placed the new radio on the ground while he unloaded the weapons and ammunition. This completed, the others had returned, picked up the container, took it away, and dumped it in the hole on top of the parachutes. Five minutes furious filling in with the excavated earth, a sprinkling of leaves over the loose soil, and they were back to pick up the weapons and ammunition. During this complete operation not a word had been uttered other than the original greeting. David was most impressed with the clockwork efficiency of it all and felt he was clearly among professionals.

"We walk now for two hours, Cooteman, I am Edward, this is Maria, this is Tipo."

David nodded to them. "My fiancée is also Maria," smiling in the moonlight to the young woman.

For the next two hours, which stretched into two and a half, they followed tracks and bridle paths through the wooded slopes of the mountains, which provide the border between Switzerland and France. After an hour or so, they had a break, sitting on a fallen trunk and sampling some excellent cognac from a flask, which appeared from Edward's inside pocket. By now David's suitcase weighed a ton, the other three obviously welcoming the stop for the same reason. An hour or so later Edward signalled a halt. Through the trees David could see a fair sized group of buildings, almost certainly a farm he judged. Edward gave a low whistle, a dog barked, a muffled voice bad it be quiet, and Edward signalled to move on.

"You are in Switzerland now Cooteman. This gentleman will look after you for two days and you will then be taken to Neufchatel station. We do not know where you are going from there. Good luck Cooteman, God be with you." The three shook hands with him, turned and went back into the woods. David had a quick thought that if they were going back to anywhere near the drop point they would have covered twenty miles or so that night, to say nothing of carrying tommy guns and ammunition, plus the radio, which being the lightest load had been given to Maria.

David wondered why he had to wait two days before going on, but in line with his training did not ask unnecessary questions. He knew he could be told if he needed to know – if he didn't need to know he would not be told. It was as simple as that! His host's name was Erich. He was shown to a bedroom looking out of the back of the house into the trees from which they had emerged. Erich drew the curtains. Until now David was struck by the fact there was no blackout. The hallway downstairs, and windows next to it, probably a sitting room David had assumed, were blazing light out on to the surrounding trees and garden. Just to think, he said to himself, the whole blooming country is like this, street lamps, advertising signs and so on, just like we used to be three years ago back in Sandbury.

Having parked his suitcase and taken off his top coat, he followed Erich downstairs to the kitchen where he met Erich's wife – he never did get to know her name – who gave him soup, some venison stew and apple strudel, made sure he had had enough, said goodnight and went away leaving him with Erich.

"Well Herr Muller, you can rest over the weekend. On Monday we go to Neufchatel, it's about twenty-five kilometres from here. By the way, you have an envelope for me I believe?"

"Yes, it is in my suitcase, I will get it for you." David went and got the envelope, handed it to his host, who placed it safely inside his jerkin. David had assumed it was an agreed payment for his stay. There's a lot of organisation to this lark, he thought.

"As I was saying, we go to Neufchatel on Monday. That is the day I take my skins to my buyer."

"Your skins?"

"Yes, I am a forester, but I also hunt the chamois. Every two weeks I take the skins to Neufchatel, our local butcher buys the meat."

"He's got a nice little sideline going here," David concluded, "not to mention his B and B business."

David spent the weekend relaxing, listening to the radio to get all the background knowledge he could as to what was going on in Switzerland and elsewhere. He listened to the German programmes from Stuttgart and Munich. Apart from giving him his food, David saw very little of Erich's wife. He wandered around the outbuildings. His first thought had been it was a farm, but in fact the barn like structures contained logging equipment, a large caterpillar type tractor, a debarking machine and some other bits and pieces, the use for which escaped him. It was much more secure being in Switzerland as compared to his previous experience in France. Here there was no Gestapo, no fascist French police, a blind eye was turned to spying, except of course if you were spying on the Swiss state itself, which was heavily punished. The Swiss authorities and populace were very well disposed towards Britain. They knew that if Germany won the war in Russia and signed a peace with Britain and America, they would immediately occupy the only German speaking part of Europe they had not so far attempted to incorporate into the Third Reich, namely the northern part of Switzerland, which they called the Sudmark. The Germans had endeavoured to start Nazi movements in the Sudmark for some years with little success, and where a movement did look as though it would take root; the Swiss police quickly suppressed it. The Swiss knew that if the Sudmark was occupied the other cantons would soon be swallowed up as was the case in Czechoslovakia. They therefore were putting all their hopes on Russia, Britain and America defeating the Nazis, at the same time of course stashing away all the gold and other valuables looted by these plunderers into their deep vaulted banks. After all, business is business even in war-time, and with their numbered account system, Swiss bankers were never, and probably never will be, what you might call choosy.

On Monday Erich took his guest to Neufchatel. David bought a first class ticket to Bern (which is how the German speaking Swiss inscribe it). The only other occupier of a seat in his compartment was not at all communicative, reading his newspaper most of the time, which suited David – he was naturally a little apprehensive about using his Swiss-German. Arriving at Bern, he got a taxi to the address of a hotel close to the safe house at which he was to report. Having paid the taxi driver he waited a short while on the hotel forecourt before making his way to his new lodgings. The building was a typical four storey, pitched roof town house; it looked as innocent and faceless as any house could look. The bell was answered by a matronly looking woman who, he noted, looked him quickly but searchingly up and down.

"I am Herr Muller," he announced.

"Yes, we are expecting you. Please come in."

She led him through a hallway into a small sitting room at the rear of the building.

"If you would care to take your coat off and wait in here, I will send some coffee in to you and telephone the Count to let him know you have arrived. He will be here in 15-20 minutes."

David thanked her and wondered who the devil the Count was. He was soon to find out. A few minutes later a young man, probably around twenty David judged, brought in a tray of coffee and biscuits, complete, he noticed, with two cups and saucers. He had started to pour himself a more than welcome drink when the door opened and a tall, slimly built, well dressed man, about fortyish David guessed, came into the room, hand outstretched.

"Welcome to Switzerland, Herr Muller – better get used to being called that, what? Now, I am Count Frederick van der Heuvel. I am the head of British Intelligence here in Switzerland. All the foreign spies and the Swiss Intelligence know me, and of course I know them, so it's rather a different set up to what you might expect. Not exactly the Secret Service, what?" with emphasis on the 'secret.'

His jovial, clipped sentences, his upper crust accent, his cheerful demeanour, set David to wondering what sort of a bloody set-up have I landed myself in!

The Count continued. "Because we all know each other, the art is to find things out without the others getting to know what we're up to. I have told Colonel Masson, he's the head of Swiss Intelligence that you're here, and in fact he will come and see you, or arrange for you to see him in the next couple of weeks. When you go into Germany he would like you to do a little job for him, he'll tell you all about it."

Curiouser and curiouser David thought. First of all I am going into Germany as a Swiss national to do some sort of spying for the British, then I am co-opted by the Swiss. I suppose that makes me some kind of double agent. I wonder if they pay me double for my labours? Knowing how tight fisted the Swiss are reputed to be I would think that would be quite unlikely.

"Well now," the Count continued, "you will find a bicycle in the shed at the back of the house. If you go out of the door at the end of the yard you will see you can choose four alleyways to leave the property, each of which leads to a different road. Switzerland may be a land of milk and honey compared to the rest of Europe, but they are as short of petrol as everybody else, hence the fact that the most probable cause of death is being run over by a drunken pedal cyclist. However, it means you can easily leave the property, get lost in the crowd, leave your bicycle at a convenient spot and then take a tram, bus, or train to wherever you want to go. The amazing thing is, the bicycle will still be there when you eventually come back, they're such an honest lot!"

David poured more coffee.

"Now, to detail. You are to spend two weeks travelling around the northern canton so that you get the feel of the place. This is solely to give you a reasonable knowledge of your homeland in the event of your being closely questioned about it, which can only be obtained by walking the course. You already have knowledge of the general layout of the country, now you must see what you have absorbed from maps and photos really looks like on the ground. After that you will have two to three weeks in a factory here absorbing knowledge of the product these people make, they are, of course, friends of ours, you will then be sent to Munich and Berlin to hopefully sell these products to the Germans. Incidentally I have read with interest of your pre-war visits with Mr Phillips. While you are in Germany you will carry out another task, which we will go into in detail before you go, along with the little job for Colonel Masson. Oh! – money. You have some money I believe. Here is a cheque book in the name of Muller, it has more than ample reserves behind it, which, when you try to draw further funds, will reward you with ingratiating smiles from the counter clerks who will undoubtedly check on you. The Swiss bankers check on their own mothers before they give them a farthing!" He paused to drink his coffee.

"Well then, that's all for now. If you are going to be away overnight let Frau Kielman know, you have the telephone number, we don't want to get into a tiz thinking you have gone missing, or been snatched or something. I'll contact you in a couple of weeks." With that he stood up, shook hands again, leaving David with the thought he was facing the unimaginable hardship of having to tour around a semi-paradise with unlimited money to spend.

"I'll wake up in a minute or two," he said out loud.

His first decision was to buy some maps, the sort of concertina photo packs one buys from a stationers' shop, and rail and bus timetables. He planned to travel mainly by train, since he established you could take your bike on the train, thus ensuring you have transport when you arrived at your destination. Although it was winter, most of the roads at these low levels were clear; he had no intention of venturing into the mountains. Over the next two weeks therefore he visited Basel, Zurich, Luzern and other places of interest near these towns, collecting information as he went, and studying the booklets and leaflets he obtained when he got back at night. Frau Kielman was most accommodating with regard to his irregular meal times, the food she provided was excellent, if it wasn't for the amount of cycling he was doing, his waistline would certainly have suffered.

Two weeks later Frau Kielman told him that the Count had telephoned to say he would be visiting David the next day at 10.30 and they would be away for the day. Promptly at 10.30 the Count's Mercedes drew up outside, the Count giving a little toot, David assumed he was to get into the car.

"We are going to a factory about twenty-five kilometres from here at a small town called Saint Nicholas. They make incinerators and equipment for crematoria." He paused for a while to let this statement sink in. He continued. "The reason you were selected for the operation upon which you will embark in a month or so is that firstly you are a trained and qualified engineer. Secondly you have had considerable experience in mechanical handling, conveyors and so on, particularly relating to the use of these products in furnaces. If you wonder how we know all this, Mr Phillips who you travelled with to Germany to visit the Krupps plant before the war is, and was then, one of us." Again he waited a while for David to mull over this piece of information. David waited for the next revelation, wondering to himself what the hell incinerators had to do with the secret war effort but wise enough now not to be surprised at anything going on in this clandestine world.

"We want you to become as expert as possible in the company's products. In particular on the crematorium side to absorb all the technical details, throughput, ash disposal, bone crushing, exhaust air filtration etc, so that you can use all the jargon you need to use when talking to a prospective customer. Most of all you must get used to the fact, and talk of the products being handled as being a commercial enterprise, like baking bread, and not the disposal of human bodies. They are just a commodity to be processed, nothing more, nothing less. You must learn to think and talk of them purely from the point of view of a production problem, which has to be solved. Our enquiries about you, incidentally, resulted in our being told you had seen a fair share of death already and that you would be likely to take this in your stride."

David continued to be silent, sensing he had not heard it all.

"When you have been here for two weeks we shall have a meeting for a semi-briefing on your operation. That will then give you a further week, or longer if you need it, to sort out any technical matters you may consider necessary before you go. Right. Any questions?"

"I've a thousand questions, but if previous experience is anything to go by, you won't answer them. However, question one, do I have to leave my lodgings? Question two, if so, how do I get hold of you in an emergency?"

"Firstly, you stay with Frau Kielman and take the train to work. It will mean an early start. Everybody in Switzerland is at work by eight o'clock. Take your bike on the train, that way you will get out to the plant, which is a couple of kilometres outside the town, without having to mess about with buses. Incidentally, start thinking now in metres and kilometres; forget you ever heard of feet and inches. But then, you've had to do that before of course."

'Yes, but not for bloody years,' David said to himself, adding 'why couldn't I have been found a reason to work in a chocolate factory – a crematorium factory, I ask you!'

Arriving at the plant, the receptionist smiled a welcome to the Count; he was obviously well known there as several people they passed wished him good morning on their way to the managing director's office. Herr Brendt was a short stocky man, with piercing blue eyes, a very firm handshake, and the general aura of someone you wouldn't bugger about, this latter being David's first assessment of his new, if only temporary, boss. Everything in the office was, including the Director, solid. Solid mahogany desk, solid leather high backed chairs, beautifully polished sideboard, matching bookcase, it all reeked of solidity. Herr Brendt called for coffee. David half expected it to be brought in by a very solid Swiss lady, instead an extremely lissom, well dressed and well manicured, as David noticed whilst she was laying out the cups and saucers, young woman, mid twenties he guessed, appeared with the tray. He automatically searched her hands as she poured to establish whether she was married or not – apparently not, though to what use he intended to put this knowledge he had no conscious thought. As he said to himself later when a certain thought did come to him 'Steady the Buffs – you're spoken for!'

Herr Brendt was talking. "Helga here will take you round the plant Herr Muller, once you have finished your coffee, whilst the Count and I have some business to discuss. We shall then look forward to seeing you tomorrow morning."

Coffee finished, David followed Helga into a side office. "Shall I leave my coat here?" he asked. He was advised to wear it, she in the meantime going to a cupboard and taking out a pair of boots, a fur coat and an extremely captivating fur hat.

"We have to go outside from shop to shop," she told him. "It is reasonably warm inside, but the north easterly wind today whistles between the buildings and is freezing cold."

David found the conducted tour extremely interesting. They first of all went to the incinerator section, three largish buildings where the different components were fabricated and assembled. When he and the Count first arrived, the plant looked of medium size, but when they passed A, B and C buildings, they emerged into an open space on the other side of which were three very long bays, newly built, which housed the crematorium plant. These could not be seen from the front of the building but made the factory quite a large enterprise.

"These buildings were finished in 1939 and we hoped to do a big export business with the advanced equipment the company had patented. Unfortunately the war came, as a result it is now running at only a quarter of its capacity."

"Tell me Helga, how does a beautiful girl like you equate life and living with working in a crematorium factory?"

"Firstly I am not beautiful. Secondly it is a fact of life that we are all going to die. I look at this equipment as superb pieces of engineering designed for a purpose like an automobile engine or a milking machine. After a while you become proud of it, as proud as if you were making a Ferrari motor car."

David was silent for a few moments. "I see what you mean," he said, and then grinning mischievously, "but I still say you are beautiful."

They returned to the office block. Helga gave him a brief tour of the drawing office, printing room, and typist's pool, in the latter he being surreptitiously weighed up by a number of the younger women there. Returning to the director's office, Herr Brendt expressed the hope that David had found the tour interesting and looked forward to having him join them on the morrow.

During the journey back to Bern, the Count filled David in with more details of 'the competition,' as he called the other spy rings in the country. The most efficient and best informed was the Russian organisation, known as the 'Lucy Ring', run strangely enough by an English communist Alan Foote. One member of their organisation, who remained unknown until long after the war, had a direct line of contact with General Thiele in the German high command. The general, among others, was fervently anti-Nazi, and after the invasion of Russia, passed military information on a daily basis to his Swiss contact. He, in turn, passed it on to Lucy through an intermediary, so that Lucy never knew his identity. As a result the Soviet generals on the Russian front frequently knew of the intended German attacks before even the

German generals had been told. To make the situation more complicated, Colonel Masson was a friend of this otherwise unknown operator, from whom he also received these messages, along with details of troop movements in France, Italy and Africa. Colonel Masson, in turn, passed them on to the Count, who kept a 'pianist,' as they nicknamed the radio operator, busy sending the information back to London. General Thiele was one of the officers executed by Hitler for the 1944 bomb plot, although the Gestapo never did find out he had been the one who was sending the information from the German HQ on the Bendlerstrasse. By this time the Germans would be on the run in all directions so that the information would not have been as vital as in the earlier years.

In the course of the drive home, David happened to mention that Helga was 'quite dishy."

"You steer clear my lad," was the Count's reply, "she's the daughter of Herr Brendt, and the technical director of the company. She will, in fact, be the one instructing you, so you keep your eye on the ball, we can't afford to upset Herr Brendt, he's the prime source of our being able to get visas to get into Germany representing one or another of his companies.

"Don't worry, I'm spoken for anyway."

"Yes, but that wouldn't stop your getting a bit on the side if you had the chance I don't suppose."

David grinned, "How could you ever suggest such a thing?"

The next morning he was up and about early to get the 7.10 train out of Bern. He made the factory by eight o'clock only by the skin of his teeth, deciding therefore he would have to get the 6.50 from now on. All his life, at school, serving his indentures, and then in the army, time had been of optimal importance, it had therefore become a way of life. To be late, even if it was late in for lunch at Chandlers Lodge, was, in his eyes, almost a criminal offence. He was determined it should not happen at the Brendt plant.

For the first few days David immersed himself in the drawings and technical brochures of the equipment. He had been allocated a desk in the drawing office and soon got to know the draughtsmen, tracers (mainly girls) and printers on Christian name terms. Helga visited him from time to time. He asked her if she could loan him any books he could take home that would help him. Her reply was the first unprofessional remark she had so far made to him. "Don't tell me you have nothing to do in the evenings but read stuffy books."

"There is an answer to that, but as you are one of my innumerable bosses, I daren't give it." She rewarded him with the first real smile she had thus far bestowed upon him.

At the beginning of the second week, having spent virtually the whole of the weekend studying the equipment installation manuals he had taken back to Bern with him, he asked whether he could have two or three days in the factory to see how the plant was made, assembled, and then broken down for shipment. From his previous experience he knew that a question, which always arose from a customer about plant of this nature, was what was the size and weight of the largest bits – after all they were going to have to unload them. As a result he spent three days in overalls which he thoroughly enjoyed, although continually lifting, bending, climbing ladders and being on his feet all day, sent him back to Bern each night more than ready for a meal and bed.

On the Friday of the second week an office junior came to his desk and asked if he would be so kind as to go to the director's office. He made his way there to find the Count and another gentleman talking earnestly to Herr Brendt, who was introduced to David as Colonel Masson, but introduced to the colonel as "Herr Muller, known to us as Cooteman." This led David to thinking what a rum set up it was, and again wondering whether he was going to enjoy double pay for the next few weeks.

"First of all Herr Muller, we have been successful in getting you your visa, travel permits and letters of introduction to the people you are to see." The Count continued. "Your task is to try and establish firstly whether the rumour we have heard from an escapee from one of the concentration camps in Poland, who miraculously made his way to Switzerland, is true, namely that the Nazis are building, or have built, special camps where they are exterminating Jews and others in large numbers. Secondly you are to endeavour to locate these establishments. Thirdly to find out the means they are using to kill these people if the rumour is true. It seems unlikely they would shoot people in their thousands, if only because of the effect on the troops who would have to do the job, we know they have used carbon monoxide poisoning before the war to get rid of lunatics, disabled children, deviants and so on, but that would not be practical for the large numbers we are presently considering.

Now, the method. Your cover is a straightforward commercial one. Your company makes incinerators and has a particularly efficient range of crematorium equipment. The second product is the bait by which we may get the answers to the items we have tasked you with. If they have difficulties in getting this specialised equipment designed and made, which we suspect may be the case as there are few manufacturers in Europe specialising in this plant, they may well give you details of their requirements. This, in turn, could well lead us to the answers we are looking for. Any questions so far?"

"Yes Sir, if I get orders for this equipment will you actually make it?" he looked hard at Mr Brendt.

"Positively not, you have my word on it."

"Thank you Sir."

"The second part of the operation concerns Colonel Masson. Could you explain your requirements Colonel?"

"They are simple, Cooteman. As you will first of all be visiting Munich I wish you to carry a package to my letterbox there for one of my agents. The letterbox is a small ads department in a local newspaper. You will put a small advertisement in the paper, which I will give you, and leave the package. It's as simple as that, but as you are totally unknown in Germany, if anyone is watching the premises you will not be suspected anymore than the rest of the people going in and out. Secondly, you will be staying at the Sendlinger Hotel. The head porter there is Friedrich. When you arrive you say, 'The Colonel sends his regards and trusts your daughter is now much better.' He then will come to your room as soon as he can conveniently do so. We have some university anti-Nazi medical school graduates who actively put leaflets around Munich opposing the war. At the same time they pass us information on casualties from the Russian front that are sent back to the various Bavarian hospitals, which in turn with other information they glean from the wounded, tells us a lot of what is happening on the Eastern front. This information is, of course, passed on to the Count.

Now, the point is, we have had no information for over a month. This could be because something has happened to Friedrich, something has happened to the group, or something has happened to the pianist or his equipment. When we know which of these it is, we can act accordingly. Right, any questions?"

"No Sir, it's all quite clear."

After the meeting closed, the Count took David to a small side-room. "This is the programme. You will carry on here at the factory during next week. On Monday 9th March you will travel to Munich. On Tuesday 10th you will visit the Swiss Consulate in Munich to establish your presence there. On Thursday 12th you have an appointment with an S.S. Standartenfuhrer who is in charge of purchasing for the South German area. Because the equipment you are introducing is strictly the province of his boss in Berlin, a Gruppenfuhrer, or lieutenant general, you will be sent on there, where you should arrive at the weekend. On Monday 16th March you will visit the Swiss Embassy to register again, and on Thursday 17th you will present yourself to the S.S. headquarters to arrange the appointment with the Gruppenfuhrer. This could take a couple of weeks, so you just have to play it by ear. Keep out of trouble. Don't worry if you have the feeling you are being followed, don't attempt to evade anyone tailing you. Foreigners to Berlin are picked out at random by one or other of the security services, the S.D., S.I.S., or Gestapo, it doesn't mean they necessarily suspect you of anything. After two or three days they invariably drop off. When you have finished your business there, you have an open air ticket on Lufthansa for a direct flight to Bern." The Count concluded with, "and that's about all. Any questions?"

"Sir….."

"I wouldn't go around calling everybody 'Sir' if I were you. Address by name or position, for example Herr Direktor. Otherwise it makes you sound as though you have been in the army, which could lead an enquiring mind to wondering, at your age, why you still are not. Get my drift?"

"Yes Count. Tell me, why is Herr Brendt so very helpful?" The Count paused.

"I suppose there's no harm in telling you this in absolute confidence. His eldest daughter married a German doctor from Frankfurt in 1931. He was Jewish. They lived, and he practised, just outside the city. They had three children, twin girls and a boy. In 1940 they were rounded up and none of them has been seen or heard of since. No one hates the Nazis more than Herr Brendt. Does that answer your question?"

"It certainly does."

"One final word. If you are caught in Germany, whether the Gestapo can prove you are a spy or not, whether they can determine whether you are Swiss or not, and believe me they can be wonderfully persuasive, you will die. This is a last resort way out." He handed David a box in which there was a trouser belt with a neat oblong ornamental buckle. He took it from the box and holding the buckle he continued, "If you turn this a half turn clockwise, the cover will open and inside is a cyanide pill. It will be quicker than the Gestapo."

David felt a cold sweat on the back of his neck. This was serious, professional stuff. Until now it had been a bit 'Pimpernelish', now he was going into the lions den with only his own wits to help him. He was silent for a moment, then looked at the Count with a half smile and replied, "Do you know, I never did like taking pills."

"Don't try to be too clever and it's very unlikely you will ever have to take this one."

On the 9th March at 6.30 in the morning David caught the train to Bern to travel across the north of Switzerland to the frontier post at Lindau. His introduction papers to the S.S. worked wonders with the immigration official, he even being given a smile and a somewhat perfunctory salute. After a long, slow journey the train, at last, pulled in to the Hauptbahnhof at the very platform his great friend Dieter had arrived at only a few weeks before. As he got his things together he said to himself "Well, 'ere we go as the earwig said," or as Harry would have said, "Shit or bust!"

Chapter Twenty

Harry returned to consciousness as a result of an excruciating pain in his ribs caused, as he soon established, by the liberal application of iodine to the wound and lacerations he had received. He was lying on a kitchen table; his clothes had all been removed and deposited in a smelly heap in the corner. One of the daughters was washing his legs and feet, he could feel his body had already been cleaned, his neck and head having been left until last as, comparatively speaking, they were not as foul as the rest of him. Ah Chin, who was administering the iodine, said something excitedly to the two girls, obviously telling them Harry had come to. "You have swimmed the river Tuan?" one of the girls asked him, "you very lucky be alive." Harry smiled at her, and then it struck him of the incongruity of the situation. Here he was, stark naked, being attended by two very pretty young Chinese women who had obviously been washing all his bits and pieces for him, and he had been out for the count and didn't know a thing about it! The story of my life he said to himself, still smiling. The smile very swiftly disappeared at Ah Chin applied two more pads soaked in iodine to his leg wound.

"Must keep wounds clean. River filthy. Make flesh go rotten. Iodine very good. Good job bullet go through," pointing to the leg, "bullet left in, very bad."

The second daughter brought an enamel bowl and washed Harry's stubbly face and hair. Being clean again, the wounds having been bandaged with strips torn from an old sheet, the two girls and Ah Chin lifted Harry from the table, carried him to a charpoy in the corner, and covered him with a sheet. Harry looked around. He was obviously in a cellar, used normally he imagined as a cool storage place. There was a shaft in the centre of the ceiling, which ventilated the room, though where the replacement air came in he, could not, at present, make out. There were two electric light fitments, not at present working, the place at the moment being lit by a Tilley lamp. As he lay back, exhausted again after his treatment, it suddenly struck him that if the Japanese searched these premises, Ah Chin and his daughters would be executed on the spot.

"Ah Chin, I must get away quickly. It is dangerous for you if I am here."

"Tuan, you safe here. We live upstairs. Nobody find cellar." Harry thought for a moment. "Where are the children?" When Harry and major Deveson had visited them there were several children around.

"They sent Kampong five miles when shelling starts. With

mothers." Then realising that Harry had associated the children with the two daughters who had attended him, Ah Chin burst into laughter. "These daughters no married, no children. You first man they see close no clothes." His body shook with laughter. Harry, despite his pain and weariness, held Ah Chin's hand and laughed with him.

The girls brought him some delicious chicken soup, and helped him sit up to eat it. Ah Chin came when they had finished, carrying a chamber pot, which sight produced a paroxysm of laughter approaching hysteria in Harry.

"You go sleep now. We talk tomorrow. I leave small light." He turned the Tilley down and they left. Harry noticed that one of the girls took his filthy clothes whilst the other took his boots, gaiters and belt. And then he slept and slept, waking only once to use the chamber pot. Ah Chin looked in from time to time and let him sleep; he knew that if infection had set in, Harry would awake. If it didn't he would sleep. If infection did set in, there was nothing he could do. Harry would be dead in twenty-four hours. His temperature was a couple of degrees up before he went to sleep, when he awoke Ah Chin took it again, it was up a little more but still not enough to be seriously concerned about. Later in the day it had dropped a fraction, Ah Chin and the girls breathed a sigh of relief. He should be alright now.

For the next three days, between having his wounds dressed and his body washed by his two nurses, he dozed and slept. On the fourth day he got up, put on a pair of shorts and a singlet which had belonged to Nigel and which had been salvaged, among other items, from the rubble of the house. He walked hesitantly up and down the cellar, initially with the aid of the two girls, but soon on his own. It was clear it would be a few days yet before he could think of walking any distance, in fact even that thought was being optimistic. In the meantime the town had been garrisoned by a small detachment of admin troops who were behaving reasonably well. The Japanese wanted to give the local people confidence in the establishment of the Co-prosperity Sphere, the occupation troops therefore were under orders not to ill-treat or rob them. The Chinese were in a slightly different category although here again as long as they kept their heads down they were not molested.

It was more than three weeks before Harry's wounds were sufficiently healed for him to pronounce himself fit enough to walk any distance. He started his training with standard army physical jerks, followed by twenty circuits of the cellar. That night, Wednesday 11th February, the news reached them that the Japs had landed on Singapore

Island, there was, therefore, no further reason why Harry should not reach his guerrilla group if he possibly could. The Sulong milestone was thirty miles or so from Muar by road. God knows how many miles ducking and diving across country. Ah Chin had found an atlas of the Federated Malay States in the rubble, which showed that although there were a few swamp areas; most of the country between Muar and Sulong was rubber. "So we make you rubber tapper," Ah Chin exclaimed, his eyes almost closed together with excitement. His plan was that they would stain Harry all over with dark floor stain of which they had a plentiful supply, so that he then looked like the normal Tamil tapper employed to garner the rubber in the plantations. By now Harry had lost any surplus flesh, which may have adorned his body when he was lushing it up in Singapore. He had, like his father, always been lean and wiry, now they considered, stained almost black, he would pass as a labouring Tamil to anyone except perhaps on close inspection. This led him to ask, "What happens if I'm face to face with a real Tamil?"

Ah Chin's usual smiling countenance changed. "He either says nothing or you kill him." And then they had a setback. The exit leg wound, which along with the other lesions had been healing so well, opened up. It taught Harry a lesson. He was trying to rush things and healing will not be rushed, as a result, he was put back a couple of weeks in his endeavour to get fit for his next move. When he was able to exercise fully it was the beginning of March before they could put their plan into operation. Singapore had been overwhelmed, the war in Malaya was over, the initial barbarism of the conquerors was settling down into, if not, benevolent paternalism, mostly into live and let live as regards at least the Malays and Tamils. The Chinese were still seriously at risk.

Tamil's are usually very dark skinned. It took several applications of the stain to change Harry's whiteness and though he submitted to his buttocks and surrounding areas being treated, he positively refused to even consider having his 'John Thomas' coated. "Definitely not," he told Ah Chin "if an arm or a leg falls off because of this jollop you are putting on, all well and good, but I am definitely not risking the loss of my friend." Ah Chin laughed so much Harry began to wonder whether he would do himself an injury, but in the end agreed it should remain pristine, though he described it rather differently to that.

The curfew now was reduced to 10pm until 4am. It was dark by seven o'clock. Ah Chin had scrounged some old overalls, boots, and a length of cloth for Harry to wind around his head. After they had finished the final staining, Harry had suggested he went out to get exercise after dark. It would, he calculated, take several days of exercising, after being in that cellar for over six weeks, before being capable of covering the thirty miles or more to Sulong, and once he got to Sulong he had no idea whatsoever how many miles, or over what sort of country he was going to have to traverse to get to the camp. Common sense said it must be pretty isolated, common sense said it would be up in the mountains, common sense then concluded that the easy part was probably going to be getting to Sulong.

The Coates' house was on the outskirts of the town. There was a track, which ran alongside the river for about a mile, ending up in a hut beside a mangrove swamp, which used to contain a boat. There was a slipway into the river at this point. As it went to nowhere else it was, after dark, deserted, although during the day parts of it, which overlooked the river, attracted the odd fisherman. Harry made himself a rota. The first night, to the hut and back, two miles, increasing every night until after a week he had been successful in completing seven trips – fourteen miles. On the last night, it was getting close to curfew time; he had the fright of his life. A quarter of a mile from the Coates' house, coming towards him, he saw what were obviously two Japanese soldiers, strolling along, chattering away to each other. He thought quickly. The left hand side was the river – no escape. The right hand side was swampy but there were bushes there in which he could hide. If he could see them they could see him. If he dived into the bushes they would think there was something odd going on and possibly come after him, he couldn't see if they were armed or not but again possibly could be. He decided to walk on. The track was not very wide. As he got close to them he stopped to give them clearway, then bowed as they drew level. One of the pair uttered him a guttural remark, they walked on still chatting away, Harry turned on his way his heart racing. "Not too many like that Guvnor," he said, looking up at the heavens.

It was therefore Sunday 15th March that Harry started his journey into the unknown. Beneath his latex coated clothes he wore his service belt with the machete slung from it. He had a canvas sack in which he had the curved, razor sharp, tapping knife Ah Chin had acquired for him, along with two or three latex cups, these latter two items purely to give credence to his story should any Jap patrol stop him. He had rice with vegetables and small pieces of chicken, tied up in spinach leaves, enough for two days, and most important of all, two bottles of water. It was anyone's guess when he would find water pure enough to drink, he would have to be very sparing in the meantime. Ah Chin had been a mine of information as to where to find water in an emergency in the jungle, from the tips of large ferns, from large shallow leaves, from hollow bamboo. A man could survive for days without food, not that there wasn't a considerable amount of food around in the jungle if you knew where to look for it, but water is absolutely essential. Also included in Harry's sack was a tobacco tin filled with matches and sealed with adhesive plaster. Another tin with tobacco in it, small pieces of which to soak in water in a cloth and squeeze on leeches, pulling leeches off, and there would be plenty of them in the jungle, made them leave their jaws in the bite which then festers and leads to boils or even blood poisoning. Rivers like the Muar abound in the much larger horse leeches; prompt treatment from which being essential or an unfit person would quickly succumb. No wonder Ah Chin's daughter had told Harry 'You very lucky.' Finally his mentor had included some salt in a waterproof bag. None of these things would give rise to suspicion if he was searched. A tapper working in the sometimes swampy, low lying land would probably carry some, if not all, of these things.

They left the minute after curfew time at 4am. Ah Chin had said he would guide Harry out to the kampong where his daughters and their children were, about five miles on the Sulong road. At four o'clock in the morning there would be few people about, even fewer Japanese, and the Sulong road was not a major highway anyway. The rubber started there, Harry could then go into the rubber for say a couple of hundred yards and follow the line of the road. There would be all sorts of streams and drainage ditches to cross, but almost certainly there would be improvised bridges over them, which the planters would have positioned so that the tappers could move from one section to the next.

There had been tearful partings from the two girls. Chinese women are generally very modest and shy, particularly with Europeans. Harry hugged them both, and promised that one day he would come and repay them for their great kindness to him. When it came to saying goodbye to Ah Chin, Harry was nearly in tears. "I will never forget you my dear friend," he told him, "all my life, whether it be short or long, I shall never forget you." Ah Chin watched him make his way through the trees, the inscrutable oriental had tears streaming down his face.

He made steady progress over the next two hours, but then met his first obstacle. There was a gap in the plantation some four or five hundred yards wide running back from the road as far as the eye could see, and in that gap there was a particularly uninviting, very liquid, swamp. Trying to wade through it would, he considered, be courting disaster. Going away from the line of the road to try and get round it, even if he was successful, would be very time consuming. The only other alternative was to make for the road and risk meeting anybody on it before he came to the next rubber. Could be half a mile perhaps, he told himself, should do that in ten minutes, there hasn't been much traffic so far; I would probably get away with it.

He made tracks for the road. Looking in the direction he was to travel, the road was completely empty of anyone walking on it. There was a Chinese lorry coming towards him, he turned his back, studiously considering what he should do to this particular truck. The lorry passed giving a friendly toot; he waved in reply, climbed up the bank on to the road, and made his way to his objective. He had only a hundred yards to go when he heard a vehicle approaching from behind. It was a British army fifteen hundred weight truck. A captured fifteen hundred weight would only have Jap soldiers in it. His stomach started to churn. So near and yet so far. Ah Chin had told him of the ordinance that all civilians were to bow to Japanese soldiers; even the lowest ranks were to receive this subservience. Harry had remembered this to good effect when he met the two soldiers on the Muar River path, he decided his only chance was to climb back on to the bank, and bow as the conquerors drove past. He was so scruffily dressed it would be unlikely they would stop to see if he had anything worth stealing in his bag – or so he hoped. He was lucky; there was only a driver and a somewhat portly officer on the truck, both of whom completely ignored his presence. He got back into the rubber.

He had planned his journey thus. He would have approximately fourteen hours of daylight. He had to cover a minimum of thirty miles, mostly off-road. He then had to find the milestone and negotiate the track opposite for he knew not how far – could be miles. He therefore had decided that a couple of hours before dark, he would lay up deep in the rubber, build a 'bivvy', light a fire, eat some of his precious food and rest up for what the next day would bring – the last thing he wanted was to have to find his way along a jungle track in the dark.

By four o'clock he was desperately tired. He still was not fully fit, the country he had travelled was extremely uneven, he had had to make numerous diversions. He calculated he must be near Sulong. At first light he would go along the road to find the next milestone before returning to the rubber. He headed away from the road for about half a mile, coming to a gap in the plantation where there was a large thicket of beluka, or secondary jungle. He cut down some bamboo and made himself a bed frame about two feet off the ground, the pieces of bamboo being fastened together with vine. He put thin canes across the main supports, got a couple of large palm fronds to lie on and a couple more to lay over him, and having prepared his bedstead, set to to make a fire. The fire was to make a supply of ash – he had no means of making a hot drink. Ah Chin had told him that one way of keeping leeches from you whilst you slept was to put ash round the legs of your bedstead, and not to sleep under low bushes. The leeches would not crawl through the ash, and if there were no bushes above you, would not be able to drop on you. This left the perennial problem of the mosquitoes. There was nothing he could do about that. As soon as it was getting dark he would have to cover up completely, wrapping his head cloth around his face. He fervently hoped that wherever it was he was heading would have mosquito nets; he already had a pathological hatred for the nasty little things, a hatred that would stay with him for all his days.

He committed one cardinal error. He had not realised he had placed his bed only three or four yards from what he realised afterwards was a game trail, which skirted the beluka and made its way into the rubber. He had settled down to sleep, trying hard to ignore the thousand and one noises of the night, the bullfrogs in particular being especially cacophonous. He must have dozed off but was awakened by a loud snorting noise almost in his ear. He instantly grabbed his machete; the sudden movement startling the perpetrator of his disturbed slumbers. By the time Harry had uncovered his face from his headgear he could see, in the pale moonlight, half a dozen wild pigs hotfooting it up the game trail. They were not normally dangerous, unless cornered, nevertheless, it set him to thinking what else might be around that would use that trail. As far as he knew there were no tigers in these parts, and in blissful ignorance of the fact that one had been seen there from time to time over the past months, dozed fitfully until dawn began to show from over the eastern hills. He had a quick inspection to ensure as far as he could, he had no unwelcome visitors. Ah Chin had told him that leeches sometimes crept in through the gaps between the fly buttons. Harry, in performing his morning leak, made a thorough inspection of his pale-faced friend to confirm he was not possessed of any hangers-on. The ash preventative had obviously worked.

He made his way back to the deserted road, walking quickly to get to the next milestone. He realised he walked differently to a real Tamil. Tropical people have a different gait altogether, having all their lives been barefoot or walking in sandals, whereas in colder climates people wear boots and tend to plonk their heels down first. Their carriage, therefore, alters to suit which part of the foot reaches the ground first,

Harry deduced, followed by the thought he would write a book about it after the war – it should sell a million – silly sod. It was after these highly scientific musings he spotted the squat white milestone, the absolutely essential guide to anywhere in the Federated Malay States. In England you invariably gave directions in the form, 'take the third on the left past the George and Dragon. Follow that road until you see the White Hart,' and so on. In Malaya you said, 'take the side road two hundred yards on the right past the Milestone 108' or whatever. This milestone was numbered 107; he had eleven miles to cover before he was to find the track to meet his contacts. He went back into the rubber, which with one or two minor diversions; he was able to make good time through until he judged he must be nearing his turn off point. There was a little more traffic on the road here, presumably because he was nearing Sulong. As the track, and the river it ran alongside was on the same side of the road as he was on, he felt reasonably confident he would hit it without having to go back on to the road to check the milestone. He then ran into trouble. Clearing a stand of rubber he found himself looking at a Malay kampong some two or three hundred yards away. He had already had experience of the numbers of dogs that seemed to inhabit these villages, when he had explored Singapore Island. He could hardly walk through the village without being investigated by the dogs and thereby noticed by the inhabitants. In these early days there were some sympathisers of the Japanese among the Malays, who considered they had been liberated from the British imperial yoke, one of those might readily inform on him, though exactly how they might do it he was not quite sure, on a bicycle into Sulong possibly?

He stopped in the cover of the trees and considered the problem. He could go up on to the road, and trust to luck he would not meet anyone. People in vehicles would most likely not take any notice of him. A head-to-head meeting with Japs would probably be overcome by the crucially important bow – Japs wouldn't know a Tamil from an Eskimo he reasoned somewhat illogically – it was the chance he might meet an unfriendly Tamil or Malay that could end his adventure, and probably his life, when he was so close to his turn off point. The only alternative would be to make a wide detour of the village away from the road. But then he might very well hit another village; there were probably kampongs all around Sulong.

"It's the road," he said out loud, and made his way through the rubber back on to the highway. As he climbed up the bank on to the road, he caught his foot in a hole and wrenched his ankle. It was not bad enough to have any effect on his walking but it did give him an idea. If he limped along it would probably camouflage his faulty carriage. Perhaps I am being too fussy he told himself. On the other hand, it might just make all the difference. He kept going. One Malay vehicle passed him coming from Sulong, another overtook him. As he reached the track leading into the kampong, two Malays appeared, crossing the road just in front of him. One spoke to him. Harry smiled a half smile, put his fingers to his ear and shook his head. The Malay either understood him to be saying he was deaf, or thought he was daft, or perhaps both, and went on his way. It's funny, or if you are on the receiving end perhaps it is not so funny, that if you are unfortunate enough to be deaf, many people immediately conclude you are mentally deficient as well.

He limped on. It was, by now, getting on for ten o'clock he judged – he had no watch – and according to his calculations he should be nearing his objective. In the near distance he could see the stone walls of what looked like a bridge. A bridge should mean a river – if it's not a bloody railway line he told himself. As he got nearer his spirits rose. There was a milestone a few yards from the bridge. This must be it. He had to force himself not to speed up. About forty yards away he could clearly see the magical number 96 – he had made it, as long as a patrol of bloody Japs didn't suddenly appear to put the mockers on his day. He carefully looked round to see whether there was anyone behind him. Apart from some children playing beside the road about two hundred yards ahead, it was clear in that direction. He saw the path he had been instructed to follow and without hesitation plunged down off the road, walked along by the small river without looking back, took a sharp bend around some quite high standing beluka and was clear of being seen from the road. His sigh of relief could have been heard in Singapore. Immediately he thought of his dear friend Ah Chin. Without him he would never have made it. Without him and his two lovely daughters he would now be lying dead from his wounds or bayoneted to death by those yellow bastards. One day, God willing, I will repay you old son, he told himself.

He now had two miles to go along this path. He began to get collywobbles in his stomach at the thought of making the first contact with the sentries he had been told would be there to meet him. They would be expecting a white army man; he was now a black coolie. "I just hope they ask questions first before shooting," Harry joked, and then realised it was no joke. He had a second thought. They would be unlikely to shoot – they would be reluctant to make any noise. If they were trained in jungle fighting they would probably use a knife, or a garrot before he had time to even say a word. "I'm beginning to wish I wasn't here," he again informed himself.

The path gradually narrowed until he was brushing the undergrowth on both sides. "I'm getting bloody close," he guessed. He thought rapidly and came up with the idea that if he made a noise the sentries would know that someone was not trying to creep up on them. Not too loud a noise. I know – a military noise. A military march – that's it. He started to softly whistle his regimental march, singing the (unofficial) words in his head:

>"Wait for the wagon, the donkey wants a crap
>Wait for the wagon, we'll all have a ride
>Wait for the wagon
>Wait for the wagon
>Wait for the wagon, we'll all have a ride"

He must have whistled it twenty times when seemingly out of nowhere two Chinese, armed with tommy guns, stepped out of the undergrowth. Without hesitating, a second Harry informed them, "Sergeant Major Chandler for Mr Stewart." The Chinese looked at him up and down, looked at each other and burst out laughing.

"Brilliant," one of them said in excellent English, "absolutely bloody brilliant. I would have passed you in the street at any time as a tapper."

"Yes," replied Harry, "but would another tapper?"

They moved into the undergrowth. "I am Ang Choon Guan," the young man told him "and this is Chan Poh Chee. Poh Chee will take you to the first staging point, about three miles. You will start for the camp in a couple of days. We have two more to come, if they are not here in two days we are to leave."

"How far is the camp?" asked Harry.

"About ten days' march if all goes well," was the somewhat disconcerting reply.

"Through the jungle?"

"Through the jungle."

"I don't think I'm going to enjoy this one little bit," Harry told himself.

Chapter Twenty One

It was Monday 16th March 1942. The Chandler family was spread out all over the globe, half of them not knowing where the other half was. By pure chance Megan, Rose and Anni, each pushing her respective pram, met up at a little before midday in the town centre by the War Memorial and Memorial Garden. It was a bright sunny day although rather chilly in the light north-easterly breeze. They moved to a sheltered seat in the Memorial Garden, the one question on each mind being 'I wonder where they are.' Harry was still officially 'Missing' – somewhere in Malaya. David was goodness knows where, probably France. Mark was on the high seas or possibly in the Middle East, or possibly not. After they had settled and talked about the babies – all piddle and biscuits as Harry entitled these conversations – Rose asked of no one in particular, "I wonder where they all are?"

As no one of the three could give the answer there was a moment's silence, broken by Anni saying, "I feel guilty that I know where my husband is, all day and every day, when you two have such a cross to bear."

Immediately Rose grasped her hand. "We know that you are as worried about them all as we are – we're all family, what affects one affects all."

And it was true. That is what families are. They give help and succour to each other in times of adversity, they enjoy happiness and joy together in good times, labour together when something needs to be done and are forgiving when a member transgresses. The family is where loyalty and duty are nurtured, where tolerance and charity are instilled, where sharing and understanding are the norm, and where the sadness of one is the sadness of all. Not being part of a family is a tragedy, which should not befall any soul. Succeeding in life without having had the blessing of a family is a double achievement, disgracing the family is double disgrace.

Anni smiled her thanks to Rose. "I tell you what, let's all adjourn to the Angel conservatory and have coffee and a little something in it – on me. How's that for a good idea?" The other two agreed it was an exceptionally good idea, a convoy of Pedigree prams therefore made its way across the road to the conservatory at the back of the Angel, set aside to receive vehicles of this nature so that mums could meet and have a crafty one together whilst out shopping. As they approached the archway at the front of the building which led into the yard and conservatory at the back – the Angel was an old coaching inn – who should they meet but Fred and his accountant Reg Church arriving for their Rotary Club meeting.

"What's all this then?" he asked "my family on the booze? And what's more leading the young ones into bad habits."

Anni spoke up.

"We were feeling a bit down so I suggested we had a coffee and a little something in it to cheer us up."

Rose joined in. "What's more she said she would treat us, but then we didn't think we would bump into you, so she can obviously save her money."

"I don't see what's obvious about it. Your mother only allows me enough pocket money to cover my Rotary lunch expenses. That's why I come with Reg here – he has to buy the drinks."

Reg joined in the banter. "There's no problem. I'll tell the head waiter to send you out coffee and brandies and I will pay him, that will solve the problem." He paused for a moment. "Then I'll put it on your father's bill later when I audit his accounts."

"With your usual mark-up I suppose?"

"Of course, of course, one has to make a living you know."

With the girls enjoining the two men to have a pleasant lunch they made their way to the conservatory with its chintz covered cushioned cane chairs, its numerous pot plants and hanging baskets, and in a short while a beautiful silver coffee pot, the Angel's best cups and saucers, and three balloon brandy glasses arrived. The head waiter took a bottle of Martell from the tray and poured a generous measure into each glass. "I am told you need cheering up," he confided, "this should help," and as an afterthought added, "Though where we are going to get any more when this stock is gone Lord knows."

If they had been in possession of a crystal ball they might have divined the answer to the question consuming each of them, namely 'where are they now.' It was the 16th March. Harry had that very morning met the two Chinese and was on his way to the holding camp before making the long march to the final camp. David was in Germany, complete with a cyanide pill in his belt buckle, knowledge of which factor would have filled them with horror. Mark and Charlie had landed at Port Tewfiq on the southern end of the Suez Canal and were now at a transit camp at Gineita on the Great Bitter Lake waiting to go into the desert and join the Eighth Army. Colonel Tim, Alec and Jim were at a seaside town in Wales practising landing barge techniques ready for an attack on the French coast, they knew not when or where.

They chatted on, mainly local gossip, with some hospital gossip which Megan shared with the other two. Megan would be going back to her job as ward sister in a week or so after receiving extended maternity leave. Rose had already gone back to her job in the admin block, today being a day off because she worked the previous Saturday. After a short while Rose said, "Sister Graham had an interesting thing happen to her the other morning." Eyes were focussed on her – by the tone of her voice this was going to be interesting.

"Lucky Sister Graham," was Megan's immediate reply. "Come on, don't keep us waiting."

Rose leant forward, lowered her voice, and looked around to see she could not be overheard. She continued.

"Well, as you know, she is one of the sisters on the men's ward." The other two were all ears, their thoughts racing ahead of Rose as to what might or might not have happened to Sister Graham on the men's ward.

Rose resumed her tale.

"She was on night shift and left a little before six last Friday morning to catch her train home. The carriage was empty, but just before the train pulled out, a man of about forty got in and sat at the opposite corner. When the train had cleared the station, he stood up, opened his raincoat and exposed himself to her." There were gasps from the other two.

"What did she do?" asked Anni.

"Apparently she just looked at him and said, 'for God's sake, put it away. I've been looking at those all night.' Apparently the nutter did just that and got out at the next station." There was a pause in the storytelling. "The funny thing is that Sister Graham is now worried as to what the nasty little man wonders about the sort of job she's got."

Having laughed at the funny side of the story, they discovered further what might have been. People like that are not normally violent, but if it had been a young girl in the compartment and she had started screaming he might have tried to stop her and anything could have happened. Sister Graham apparently reported it when she got home, the police came, took a statement, said they would keep a watch but it was probably a one-off, and that was the end of the matter.

Rose finished the story by saying, "Sister Graham had the last laugh. I wouldn't have minded she said, but it really was a thoroughly insignificant little object he was putting on display – I've seen better on a ten year old."

Having drunk their coffees, downed their brandies and enjoyed their piddle and biscuits, they moved off to their respective homes. As

Rose let herself into the hall she was met by her mother.

"Hello, mother dear," she said cheerfully.

"You've been on the bottle," Ruth replied, "I can smell you from here."

Rose laughed and told her how she had met the others and that they had scrounged coffee and brandies out of dear Papa. She went on to tell the story of Sister Graham and whilst they were still laughing at this, the telephone shrilled. Ruth answered it with the usual question going through her mind "I wonder who that can be?"

It was Kenny Barclay. Kenny was one of David's section at the battle of Calais, was one of the small group who carried the French General Strich to safety and rowed back to England. He was an orphan, had been made part of the Chandler family, dearly loved in particular by Megan's twins and young John Hooper.

"Kenny, how lovely to hear from you. Are you coming on leave?"

"Well no, that is I am, but I am getting married." It all came out with a rush. "I met Hazel up here at Catterick about eight months ago. Her father's a sergeant major in the camp. We're going abroad in a month or so. I've got ten days leave; he's letting us get married. I would like you and Mr Chandler to come to the wedding, and wondered," here he hesitated for a moment or two, "I wondered if the captain would be my best man. It's on 11th April – the wedding that is."

"Kenny, that's wonderful news, and you can bet your last pound that we shall be delighted to come. However, David is away on an operation somewhere, we haven't the faintest idea where, and won't be back until mid-summer, or that's what he hoped."

"Oh, what a shame. I shall have to get that layabout Piercey to stand in."

"I'm sure he will do a wonderful job. Now let me have the details of the great day, and a present list as soon as you can."

Having given Ruth the 'details,' Kenny added, "Oh by the way Piercey and me have both been made up to corporal. Bit of a laugh really isn't it? Me a corporal. If it hadn't been for the captain I could well have been doing time now."

"Kenny, I'm so pleased and David will be thrilled to bits when he knows. Of course he will say first of all 'what's the army coming to?' you can bet your life on that, but he will be as pleased as punch for you both. I only wish I could write somewhere and tell him, but I can't. By the way, do you know where you are going, or is that a state secret?"

"Well, all the talk is the Western Desert. The battalion the captain was in is there and it looks as though we're joining them."

Ruth was quiet for a moment. Another of her family – she had had a great fondness for Kenny ever since David, then a corporal, had suggested Kenny should put his mother as his next of kin when they first went to France. Kenny never knew who his real mother and father were. He was dumped as a baby on the steps of the Royal Free Hospital in the East End. The babies' side ward was Barclay Ward; the sister who took him in liked the name Kenneth, so he became Kenny Barclay. Ruth collected her thoughts. "We will see you at the wedding" she said "oh, and send us a photo, if you have one, of your bride to be, I think Hazel is a lovely name."

"She's a lovely girl, much too good for me."

Ruth rang off, smiling, but inside she was tightening up. Another of her brood was going into danger. As she had said many times before, "Oh I do so hate that man Hitler." So little was known or understood by the average Britisher of that evil man Tojo at the other end of the world, that his name took no part in her thinking, or hating.

As Ruth returned to the kitchen, Rose naturally asked who was on the phone, to which her mother replied it was only one of her fancy men ringing up whilst her husband was at work. "I have my work cut out juggling them all I can tell you." She paused for a moment. "It was Kenny, he's been made up to corporal, and he's marrying a girl called Hazel, and your dad and I are invited to the wedding." Another pause, "– and he's being posted to the desert."

"Oh no, not another one. Why can't we have some peace?"

Ruth knew exactly how Rose was feeling. You have a pleasant interlude such as today's meeting at the Angel. You forget the anxiety, fear almost, about your loved ones for a little while, and then something else crops up that brings it all back again, tearing your composure to ribbons.

"We shall have to think of what to get for a wedding present." After further thought Ruth added, "Perhaps it would be best to give Saving Certificates or War Bonds or something. They won't be setting up home yet with his going away, so money will come in handy when they do eventually find a place."

That's a good idea," agreed Rose, "I think I'll do that."

"You will be sending a present as well?"

"Of course, since he's your 'next of kin,' he must be related to me as well – nicht war – as Karl would say? I think everyone will want to send them something – he's family."

When Fred came home that evening he agreed entirely with the plan, suggested Ruth write and ask Kenny to telephone Hazel's address, and then write to Hazel to sound out whether receiving cheques or whatever would be acceptable. The decision made, Ruth looked across to Rose and stated, "You know, your father must write dozens of letters a day at the factory, but I can't ever remember his putting pen to paper inside the house."

Fred's reply was, "You don't keep a dog and bark yourself – or I suppose in this case a -."

"Don't you dare finish that Fred Chandler or I'll crown you with this saucepan."

That evening Ruth wrote to Kenny as decided. There was no ten o'clock collection nowadays as there had been before the blackout, so Rose posted the letter on her way to work at the hospital in the morning. As a result of her being very wealthy in her own right by inheriting Jeremy's estate, as well as her army marriage allowance and an allowance from Mark, she had no need to work. Ruth, however, had pressed her to do so. It would be so easy to get depressed with time on her hands during the day, even with a baby to look after. Ruth had said that all the time they had no forces men billeted on them she could look after little Jeremy, with the help of Nanny as and when it was necessary.

Having written her letter and received a "most gracious and well written reply, she's an educated girl," as Ruth reported to the rest of the family, they each then had to decide how much to give. When you buy a wedding present you normally choose from a list, a bundle of wooden spoons if you hardly knew the couple up to a three piece suite if you are close family and can afford it. Giving money is different; you do not want to look mean, on the other hand being too lavish looks like showing off. In the end, Fred and Ruth decided to give a hundred pounds, a very great deal of money, but as Ruth said, she was his next of kin for a long time. Rose gave fifty as also did Jack. Megan, Karl, and Ernie gave twenty-five each. All in all the young couple, along with whatever was given from Hazel's side of the family, would have a nice little nest egg to start them on their way when at last the world would regain its sense and let young people lead a normal life again.

The wedding was to be at Catterick Garrison Church. Discussing the arrangements for leaving the factory, Fred had suggested to Ernie and Jack Hooper, that Ruth and he travel up on the Friday evening and come back on the Sunday. Jack's immediate reply was, "Why on earth don't you take a long weekend. You haven't had a break since ages ago when you went to Chester, neither has Ruth. Now, if you travel up on say Thursday morning and stay somewhere local, and then on the Sunday go to York for a couple of days, and then come back on Wednesday, that would make a lot more sense than rushing around like a blue arsed fly."

Ernie climbed in. "Guvnor, I reckon that's a jolly good idea. We can manage here – no problem."

"I'll put it to the boss," Fred replied, after his customary pause for consideration.

"Put what to the boss?" asked Jack, "you'll have plenty of time for that up in Yorkshire."

Fred did put it to the boss. She enthusiastically agreed the second after he had finished telling her about it, and they booked to stay first at the Kings Head in the Market Place at Richmond and then at Dean Court in Duncombe Place, almost opposite York Minster.

The day of the wedding was fine, if a little blustery. Ruth and Fred were made very welcome to the extent of being placed at the top table at the reception afterwards. Hazel was as charming as she had sounded over the telephone; her father immediately struck a rapport with Fred, being a regular soldier of the old school. Kenny made a very creditable speech, in the course of which he referred to Ruth and Fred as people who had shown him what it was like to lead a happy family life. He ended by saying that he would not be here today if it had not been for their son David, now a captain in his regiment. He would like everyone to keep David in their prayers as he served on a lonely special mission somewhere in Europe. He sat down to loud applause, as the newspapers always put it.

Ruth and Fred enjoyed their break. Despite his absence, as before when they went to Chester, the roof of the factory fell not in, the machines continued to turn, the operators operated, the materials arrived, the work in progress progressed, and the finished items went out on to the lorries. Fred's main comment upon his return being "I notice you got me back in time to pay the wages."

On the Sunday evening after their return, there was a telephone call for Fred from Ray Osbourne, the Royal Engineers' officer Harry had worked with in France. Ray's life was the first Harry saved with his German motor bike, getting him back to Dunkirk casualty centre after he had been wounded. During previous conversations with Fred and Ernie, he had asked what they would turn their hands to after the war when government orders dried up. Fred's immediate reply was, "Well, do you think we'll win?" Ray had suggested they might start thinking about the new product just being developed when the war started, namely plastics, which there was no doubt would play a large part in our lives in the future. Fred had asked him to find out all he could about the subject, they would gladly pay him for his efforts, which offer was politely refused. Ray's telephone call therefore was to say he had a couple of days off during next week, could he come and have a natter. Fred immediately jumped at the chance of learning a bit more about these magical products, as indeed did Ernie on the following morning. It was arranged therefore that he would come over from Chatham, where he was stationed, on Wednesday morning, stay at Chandlers Lodge overnight and go back on Thursday evening. He said he had quite a lot to tell them from contacts he had made with Du Pont in America and I.C.I. at Slough along with information from one or two smaller companies. Fred and Ernie therefore set aside most of those two days to be with him, Fred told Jack Hooper of the arrangements as a result he said he would join them 'to try and learn something.' Finally Fred arranged for Reg Church to come in on Thursday afternoon to answer any financial questions, which might be thrown up during the meeting.

But as Robbie Burns so rightly wrote:-
'The best laid schemes o' mice an' men
Gang aft a-gley'

As Ray lay in his bed in the early hours of Monday morning, dreaming dreams that only he knew about, and then only fleetingly, he was rudely awakened by a corporal from the duty watch. "Bomb, Sir, Dartford." Ray rolled out of bed, dressed quickly and went to the duty room. The message was quite clear.

"U.X.B. discovered under Powder Hut 12. C department. Vickers. Powder Mill Lane, Dartford.

His team were waiting for him by their 3 tonner. "You know Powder Mill Lane," he said to the driver, "we had a five hundred pounder there about six months ago."

"Yes, Sir, I remember, but that one was by the offices, this bastard is in the middle of the department where they pack all the powder into the shells. If that lot goes up half of bleeding Dartford will go up with it."

Since Ray had been with the Bomb Disposal Squad he had attended, and dealt with, some forty odd incidents, some straightforward, others not so straightforward. One at Woolwich was a relic of the Great War, dropped during a Zeppelin raid. Another, he discovered, was one of ours, which had obviously got itself jammed in its bomb bay and had finally come loose over the fair county of Kent instead of Hamburg or Berlin or wherever. One or two he had found in such a dangerous condition they had to be detonated where they were found. Up until now, however, he had not been forced to deal with a customer plonk in the middle of God knows how many tons of whatever explosive it was the C Department girls were stuffing into the shells. "I do not find this situation at all amusing," he told himself.

They reached the factory and were diverted to C Department area by the works policeman on the gate. C Department was not one large building, it was a series of wooden huts, each housing twelve to fifteen girls, each hut surrounded by a brick wall about six feet away, the brick wall being itself banked up with a thick mass of earth. By this means, if there was an explosion inside the hut, it would hopefully be contained within its own bunker, and not cause damage or casualties in the adjacent huts.

Safety was paramount. Nothing of a metallic nature was allowed to be taken beyond the entrance gate. All pockets had to be emptied of money, cigarette lighters, even the odd hair curler which might have been overlooked in the morning rush to get to work, and placed in the girl's personal safe. Random searches were made constantly, though it would be fair to say that any individual who transgressed these safety regulations would more than likely be dealt with severely by her own workmates. If a girl was stupid enough to try and smuggle cigarettes and matches in – and one or two did – and she was caught in the random search, she ended up in the magistrate's court at Dartford, plus being discharged.

The girls wore special clothing, mob caps, face covers and overshoes, all made from anti-static material. This was designed to prevent sparking, as was the construction of the hut itself, there were no steel components in the interior whatsoever. The lighting was explosion proof. Everything was designed with safety in mind.

Six hundred girls worked in 'C' Department in two shifts of three hundred. If you were in Chislehurst or Chatham, Greenwich or Gravesend, you could always tell a 'C' Department girl if you bumped into her. Her hands. The rest of her could be protected but her hands, where she was in constant contact with the explosive powder were a bright yellow. They wore these distinguishing features as a badge of pride. They were, of course, paid more than the girl inspectors in the production areas or other female operators. A girl working a forty-eight-hour shift week, including her danger money, could earn nearly six pounds a week, probably more than her husband – if she had one.

Ray was led by the works police officer to the site. "How did you find it?" he asked.

"Well, Sir, the place is empty on Sunday nights, so the maintenance people move in and do what's necessary. They earn more on a Sunday night than I do in a week," he added. "Anyway the electricians were changing one of the explosion proof lights, it takes about an hour, when the electrician's mate decided he wanted a jimmy riddle, so he goes round the side of the hut and in the middle of relieving himself, finds he's slipping down a hole. We've had heavy rain here by the way for the past couple of days, until tonight. Anyway he manages to scramble up, peeing all over himself I understand, and tells the electrician. They bring an extension light round and find this is not just a hole; it's got a bloody bomb in it. They scarpered smartish and came down to the police room, told us, and we put the wheels in motion as you might say."

Ray shone his torch into the hole. He could make out part of the rear end of the bomb. "A five hundred kilo one I should think. As always the fuse is underneath which means we've got to dig all round it, and shore up the hole before we can do anything to it."

"We've got three thousand odd workers arriving here in a few hours. I've no means of contacting them. Hello, here's the Dartford police inspector."

Ray turned to him and they introduced themselves.

"I'm afraid you've got a bit of a job on inspector. The whole plant must be evacuated of the people in it now. Powder Mill Lane will have to be blocked off, and since we're so close to the A2 you will have to create diversions there. On the other side of the works, the people in Hawley Road should be told to open their windows front and back, and stay on the side of the house away from the factory, oh and wedge all interior doors open."

"Right, Sir, I'll get that all underway." The inspector took himself off, rather hurriedly Ray thought, though whether that was in the course of duty or because he didn't like standing by a bloody big unexploded bomb Ray could not tell. He gave him the benefit of the doubt.

The handful of people working overnight were sent home, with the exception of the works police, works fire brigade personnel and two volunteer first aid staff manning the medical room. By now it was getting on for 4am. Ray and the sergeant went back to look at the hole. To get at the fuse they were obviously going to have to dig a sizeable amount of earth out. "Why is it these blighters never seem to land with the fuse on top of the blasted casing?" Ray queried. The short but descriptive answer from Sergeant Dixon was 'Sod's law.'

"Right. Get the lads to get digging. Get the timber off the lorry to shore the hole up well, that earth is as soft as a baby's bum. While you're doing that I'll see the works fire brigade people to get them to pump the water out from the bottom. If everything goes according to plan we should have it out by midday."

Sergeant Dixon passed on the orders to the six sappers, three of whom were conscientious objectors who had volunteered to do this very dangerous job. As they started unloading the timber, rigging up lighting (the blackout would have to go by the board for a couple of hours) and getting the tools of the trade ready, namely picks, shovels and wheelbarrows, Ray made his way to the police shelter, which doubled as the emergency control centre. He had a feeling inside which was quite foreign to him. Every bomb disposal man knew that if a bomb went off, the time between the explosion and when your brain realised what was happening was so infinitesimal you knew nothing of it, and he had a funny feeling about this bomb, which he couldn't shake off. He had the overpowering presentiment this would be his last bomb.

And it was.

Chapter Twenty Two

It was late afternoon when David reached the Sendlinger Hotel in Munich. Just off Sendlinger Strasse it was a modest, four storey, solid looking building needing, like most houses and buildings in wartime Germany, a coat of paint. There were three people in the lobby, two young boys around sixteen and an older man, who from the description given to him by Colonel Masson, was almost certainly Friedrich. One of the boys took his case, went to the lift and waited, whilst the second one moved off to the front door to hold it open for a lady leaving the premises. As David moved towards the reception desk he stopped beside the older man.

"Friedrich?" he asked.

"Yes, Sir, at your service Sir."

"The colonel sends his regards and trusts your daughter is now better."

"Thank you Sir, thank you very much."

David moved quickly to the reception desk, received his key and walked to the lift without giving Friedrich another glance. He unpacked, decided to put his feet up for half an hour and promptly fell fast asleep. When he awoke it was almost seven o'clock. He decided to eat in the hotel; he would explore the city tomorrow.

After dinner he returned to his room, listened to the news on the radio, all one-sided of course, and soon after ten decided to get to bed. It looked as though Friedrich was not going to contact him tonight. He had got into bed and was about to turn off the light when there was a soft tapping on the door. He quickly opened it, realising Friedrich, who he assumed it would be, would not want to hang around in the corridor. To his surprise it was one of the young lads. "I wondered if you would like me to arrange some company for you Sir?"

"That's very thoughtful of you young man, but no, thank you very much. When I want some company I will get it for myself. I'm very choosy," and with that he closed the door and went back to bed, saying to himself, "I've heard of all the mod cons, but that beats cockfighting as Harry would say." Then he had another thought, "Perhaps in view of the activity involved I should have used a different phrase to that," and then he thought, "God, I wonder where Harry is tonight?"

There could hardly be two more disparate places that a pair of brothers could be lodged in. David in semi-luxury in the heartland of the German enemy, Harry in a cellar, being coated with dark stain, in the newly conquered territory of the Japanese enemy. Neither of them it would seem was to be envied.

The next morning, as instructed, David presented himself at the Swiss consul's office. The consul was, in fact, a lady of what is often referred to kindly, as of a certain age. She was the owner and chief executive of a financial advisory business, the consulate work being only part time. She confirmed his appointment with Standartenfuhrer Eberhardt in two days time, and confirmed further that although this officer could not give a decision on this type of equipment, he nevertheless had to rubber stamp the presentation, or veto it there and then if he thought it was something with which his superior officer should not be bothered. "What the hell do I do if he's in a bad mood and slings it out," David thought, "just go back to Bern with my tail between my legs I suppose."

He thanked the consul, whose final words were, "If you have any difficulties Herr Muller, or even shall we say, abnormal difficulties, do not hesitate to contact me." She gave him a card with both her office number, and significantly her outside office hours' number. Over lunch, he studied the card and considered the significance, if any, of being able to contact her at any time. It was unlikely, as a consul, she would be involved in the Colonel's espionage set up – or was it? Perhaps since she gave him her private number, he was on to a promise? He grinned to himself, she wouldn't go baby snatching I wouldn't have thought. On the other hand, as Harry would say 'there's many a good tune played on an old fiddle!' Thinking of Harry he again wondered, as he so often did, what the devil he was up to, and even occasionally of whether he would ever see him again.

After lunch he returned to the hotel and collected the package the colonel had asked him to take to the small ads agency. He had a street map from which he discovered it was about a kilometre and a half away, he therefore decided to walk. To ensure he was not being followed, he made a detour into a street with a number of shops in it, went into a book shop, bought a small volume of poems and walked back the way he had come. By this means, if anyone was following, he, or she, would have stopped and waited, anyone loitering when he emerged would immediately be suspect, anyone who deliberately kept their face from him when he passed them would be doubly suspect. In the event, there was a total absence of any suspicious persons, which led David to tell himself he was getting too theatrical in his old age. It was however, good practice, as long as it didn't mean you ended up with a library of unwanted books!

As he approached the newspaper office, he realised he had not asked the colonel who he was to contact. He visualised walking into a big chrome and glass emporium and not having a clue as to whom to give the precious package. He was worrying needlessly as he soon discovered when he found the bureau was a small shop. Opening the one door, he found himself in an area formed by a counter and the front window and door of no more than ten feet by four feet, or as he had now automatically to calculate, three metres by one point two metres. As he closed the door behind him, a middle aged, entirely bald little man emerged from the room at the back of the shop. "Sir?" he enquired. David handed him the 'small ad.'

"Thank you Sir. We will deal with that. Is there something else?" David handed him the package. "Thank you Sir. Good day Sir," and with that he turned and returned to the back room, leaving David standing around like a spare whatsit at a wedding, as he described the situation to himself when he considered it afterwards. Taking a roundabout route through the old town, he arrived back at the hotel passing Friedrich in the lobby who politely saluted him and wished him "good afternoon." He ate out that evening, but the food was not a patch on that which he had enjoyed when he visited Germany before the war with Mr Phillips and when he had stayed with the von Hassellbeks. I wonder how Dieter is he thought, then had the depressing feeling that he could even be dead by now.

If the food was not up to much, the two steins of Munich beer he had with it did live up to his expectations. Germany might be at war he considered, the coffee might taste like strained horse manure and the butter like axle grease, but nothing was going to be allowed to ferment a revolution by doctoring the Munich beer. He made his way back to the hotel in a more cheerful mood than when he had left it.

The lad who had approached him regarding the carnal activities of the previous night, was on duty at the reception. He gave a polite 'good evening Sir,' but did not renew the offer of bodily comforts. David's thoughts on the subject were that he would never make a good salesman if he gave up at the first 'no.'

He went to his room and turned the radio on. A short while afterwards there was a light tapping on the door. I was wrong, he thought to himself; perhaps he's not as bad a salesman as I thought. He went to the door, saw Friedrich there, and quickly ushered him into the room.

"I must be quick and to the point Sir. I have to relieve that nasty little Hitlerjugend in the reception in ten minutes. He is a Gestapo informant so leave nothing lying around – he's bound to get into your room while you are out. Will you please tell the colonel that Joachim 'the pianist' was killed in an air raid. Seven of the group have been arrested, six were executed and the seventh given six years in a camp. These are the names, remember them if you can, well enough at least to recognise them again if you are shown a list, then destroy this list. It would not be wise for it to be found on you, they wouldn't worry very much at your being Swiss."

David took the list of names, but before reading it asked Friedrich "How many have you left in the group?"

"There are some twenty odd that I know, more that I don't."

"They are very brave people." He looked at the list, reading the names with a feeling of reverence knowing that these young people had paid the ultimate sacrifice in an attempt to bring decency and sanity to their beloved country. He came to the last name. There was a heading, "Six years confinement," and underneath "Frau Doktor Rosa von Hassellbek." His heart seemed to stop. In a strained voice he asked Friedrich, "Why was she not executed with the others?"

"It is said that she had well connected relatives. They couldn't save her from what they call justice but they could save her life." He paused; he looked so sad as he continued. "She was a lovely young lady; I think she would have been better off being beheaded with the others than having to spend six years in one of those foul places." He looked closely at David. "Are you alright Sir?"

David paused. "Yes, yes, I find it all so shocking, that's all."

"Just thank God you are Swiss Sir, and get back to your homeland as soon as you can."

"Thank you Friedrich. I shall always remember you, and brave people like you." David was not to know that no fewer than 33,000 anti war protesters would be executed in Germany before the hostilities ended.

With that Friedrich made for the door. David held him lightly to signify he would go first. He looked into the corridor, saw there was no one there, they shook hands, and Friedrich disappeared towards the back stairs. David went to bed that night emotionally very upset. Rosa – Dieter's Rosa – the almost carbon copy of his own dear Pat, incarcerated in a squalid evil concentration camp. He thought of the wonderful times they all had when Dieter and Rosa came and stayed at Chandlers Lodge. Because of the war, he had not heard of their getting married. With Dieter knowing that these Nazi thugs he hated so much had incarcerated his beautiful wife, how would that affect his attitude to his loyalty? And if that was in doubt would he be the next to face their so-called justice system? David went to sleep, but slept only fitfully, waking and turning over in his mind all sorts of mad ideas about rescuing Rosa and spiriting her off to Switzerland. He had to conclude there was absolutely nothing whatsoever he could do.

On the 12th March he duly kept his appointment with the Standartenfuhrer. He was a pompous ass. David decided he was one of those people who had a certain amount of responsibility and authority, and made anyone who came into contact with him very well aware of the fact. However, the blockhead would not readily admit that higher authorities than he would accept enquiries or proposals without his having positively vetted them first. The fact was that if he did not pass on these projects he would get it in the neck anyway, David suspecting this, played him along. "Best humour the gormless clot," he told himself, as a result, he got his first gem of information. As the S.S. man examined the information sheets, he started chortling to himself. David looked at him quizzically.

"Could do with a few of these at Chelmno and Belzec," he suggested to David, "especially the big ones."

"Where are those towns Sir," David enquired, as innocently as he could.

"In the Central Government – Poland. I was there a month ago."

"That must have been very interesting Sir, travelling to places like that."

"Very interesting, young man, very interesting."

"Is it in order to ask Sir, what happens there, or is it secret?"

The S.S. man hesitated. "Let's say we are starting to solve the Jewish problem there – heh?" His shifty little eyes gleamed with the thought of the inside knowledge he possessed regarding the activities in those places.

David jumped in with both feet. "Perhaps equipment can be of use in helping the Reich rid this pestilence for ever Sir?" He paused for a moment. "Just imagine, ridding the world of communism and Jews at the same time. How could you reward a nation for doing that?"

"If your plant is as good as you say it is, there will be many orders for you. Chelmno and Belzec are only the beginning. A huge complex is being built elsewhere, that alone would take everything you could make. But there, I've told you enough. You must speak to the Gruppenfuhrer in Berlin now I have cleared you here."

"I am deeply grateful to you Sir, for all your help and for clearing my path to Berlin. I wonder Sir, if you would accept this small gift as a token of my appreciation. It is, of course, for your wife, I realise you cannot accept things personally." He handed over a small box with which he had been provided by Herr Berndt. It contained an exquisite ladies watch, oval in shape, the face provided with a single surround of tiny diamonds, and a strap encrusted with small diamante chips. The piggy eyes gleamed as they examined the offering.

"Thank you Herr Muller, thank you very much, it really is quite beautiful."

"I am pleased you like it Sir, and my compliments to your wife." They shook hands, the Standartenfuhrer pressed a bell, a young uniformed woman appeared and was instructed to see that the gentleman was cleared from the building without further checks. David's last thought on the subject as he slowly strolled back to the hotel was 'I bet a pound to a penny his wife will never see that.' He then spent some time ruminating as to what sort of female would be the recipient, coming to the conclusion that if she had to copulate with that slimy bugger she more than deserved it.

He was pleased with the morning's work. Chelmno and Belzec. He would remember those names. I wonder where the big one is though. At least I know there is one. I shall certainly keep my eyes peeled in Berlin. The thought of Berlin suddenly brought him down to earth. Moving around Munich had not given him the feeling that he was walking with a noose around his neck. The Bavarians he had met in the street and in the cafés were a genial, friendly bunch. His slight knowledge, along with hearsay, of the people of Berlin led him to understand they were a stern, surly crowd. As Charlie would say 'po-faced.' Dear old Charlie, getting his knees brown I wouldn't wonder. He would have kittens if he knew I was wandering around with a cyanide pill in my belt. At the thought of it, he nearly had kittens himself, he had forgotten it all the morning – well, he concluded, they say you can forget everything after a while.

He returned to the hotel. Passing Friedrich in the lobby, he received a polite salute and "Good day Sir," which he acknowledged. At the desk he asked for information regarding train times to Berlin the next day. The young woman behind the desk asked whether it was essential he travelled tomorrow, since it being Friday the trains, since they cut the numbers back recently, were terribly crowded. Saturday would be a better day altogether, she could probably book him a seat on Saturday whereas on Friday he could well have to stand all the way. He thanked her for her help, and casually asked, "Why the reduction in trains?"

"Oh I believe it is a shortage of engines. There are carriages to spare in the sidings but the engines are having to be used elsewhere. But then, that's war. The war must come first mustn't it?"

"Yes of course it must. Absolutely."

Having got the details of his preferred travel time, the young lady said she would make the arrangements and leave the necessary papers in his post box. She then further informed him they had a hotel in Berlin called the Koenig von Preussen, which she could recommend. It was in the centre of the city, she could book for him over the telephone if he so desired. He thanked her very much again and walked to his room. On the way he got to thinking about those engines. If they were not pulling carriages what were they pulling? Flat beds possibly with guns and tanks on? Part of a big spring push? With 'the pianist' gone, there was no way to get the information back to the Count, it would have to wait. What David did not know was that in a week or so's time Auschwitz-Birkenau was to throw open its gates, and trainloads of men, women and children crammed together in cattle wagons would be taking part in a one-way journey into the most infamous place on earth. Day after day, night after night, those engines which had delivered perhaps weary travellers to their destinations, loved ones to their families, lovers to their assignations, now would deliver totally innocent people to be slave labourers and finally exterminated for no reason other than they were Jews. This manic obsession failed to take into account the cost to the German war effort. Trains were to run from places as far apart as Greece, France, and Holland and, in particular, the newly conquered eastern lands. Thousands of men had to be employed to run the trains and schedule the routes, thousands were needed as guards on the trains, tens of thousands were needed as guards in the camps. While the engines were used for these evil purposes they were not aiding the Wehrmacht, nor the war production at home. It is fair to say that the transportation of millions of Jews and the return journeys of empty wagons to all corners of Europe was a significant factor in the dilution of the support essential to the front line soldiers.

He put the engines out of his mind. "I've got a day to spare tomorrow – what shall I do? I know, I'll go to Ulm and see the von Hassellbeks." He laughed at the thought, and then wondered what they would do if he did turn up? They had called him their 'English Son,' but that was in another age. They were such lovely people, after the war he would go back and perhaps tell them how near he was to them in March 1942. It was then he realised they might not survive the war, and if they did what would have happened to Rosa, Ilse and Dieter? It would be over three years before he got the answers to this question.

On Friday he spent the day, after all, doing what all people do who go to the beautiful city of Munich, that is wandering around the old town, visiting the Liebfrauen Cathedral, the Royal Palace, the Alter Hof – seat of Munich's Dukes, finally visiting a Bierkeller to slake his first. He saw a little bomb damage – by the end of the war, half of Munich would be flattened by the allied air forces.

On returning to the hotel, the receptionist told him all had been organised for him. She had got him a nice room in the Koenig von Preussen, telling the girl in Berlin he was a most important visitor. David thanked her very much, wondered again if he had stayed any longer whether he would be on to a promise, concluding that reaching that situation would not be unlikely in view of the obvious shortage of young males to be seen so far. 'Keep your mind on your work Chandler,' he told himself, but with so many very beautiful young Bavarian madchens around it was not easy.

The journey to Berlin, although he was comfortably seated, was rather dreary in that they seemed to be held up at fairly regular intervals for no apparent reason. The hotel had provided him with a packed lunch and two bottles of beer so he was saved from wasting away on the journey, nevertheless he was glad when, having stopped at Potsdam, where his friend Dieter had commenced his military service just before the war started, the train nosed its way through the south-western suburbs of Berlin.

The hotel was a solid, comfortable hostelry of the old school. With a name like 'The King of Prussia' it jolly well ought to be David commented to himself. It appeared that the hotel attracted a more numerous than usual clientele of military and naval officers, in fact, looking around the reception and lounge areas he could only see a handful of civilian men, and they're probably Gestapo was a further unheard comment.

On Monday morning he presented himself to the commercial attaché's office at the Swiss Embassy. Normally at these places you are kept waiting around sometimes for hours while some middle ranking civil servant, too big for his boots, decided whether to grant you the privilege of five minutes of his time. On this occasion it was different. No sooner had David put his business card on the desk in front of another 'rather smashing piece of crackling' as Charlie would undoubtedly have described her, than he was told the attaché himself wanted to see him. 'What's so important about me?' was David's immediate thought. He was soon to be enlightened.

"Herr Muller, please sit down. Coffee?"

It was real coffee – David's immediate comment being, "This alone was worth coming to Berlin for."

The attaché grinned, "The acorn brew in the hotels is pretty ghastly isn't it? Now, I do not know why you are so important, but I had a teleprinter message on the machine when I came in this morning to telephone the secretary of Gruppenfuhrer Krause for an appointment for you tomorrow morning. Normally it takes two or three weeks to see him so what you have got and the others haven't, I don't know."

"Perhaps he's seen my photograph and fancies me."

"Don't joke – a number of them are like that I can tell you. Mind you, not as many as the English when they were here. God, was that two and a half years ago?" he added on reflection. "Now, down to business. If you need my help in any way, telephone me here. If you have not already been told, you have to know there are no lines of credit with us during the present hostilities. They have to pay on an irrevocable letter of credit on a Swiss bank when placing the order. This is released immediately shipping documents are presented to the customer. All clear?"

"All clear, but I've got to get the order first."

"Well, I wish you luck. Don't be afraid of them. Krause is not a bad chap – career soldier, not like some of them, just jumped us ex bus drivers. Even Reichsminister Himmler himself was only a chicken farmer until he became an early Nazi and got on to the band wagon." He paused, "And that would get me shot if I said it outside this office, so take care young Herr Muller, don't let them provoke you, though as I say you should be alright with Krause."

David's appointment was for eight a.m. He arrived at 7.45 to find the place already buzzing with people, the majority of them wearing the familiar black uniform and highly polished black knee boots of the SS, some of them wearing the skull and crossbones badge of the Totenkopf, the concentration camp officers. For the first time since he had entered Germany, David was afraid. He stood in the centre of the large entrance hall suddenly realising the enormity of the task he had been given. This was no 'Boys Own Paper' stuff, this was for real, a matter of life and death, a very nasty death at that if he didn't get to his cyanide pill. His fear was so acute he had an intense stabbing feeling in his entrails, which momentarily caused him to bend over slightly and clutch his stomach. As he fought to regain control, a cheerful voice at his elbow asked, "Are you alright?" David turned to find a youngish S.S. lieutenant or Obersturmfuhrer as they were entitled in the Schutsgestafel. David quickly recovered his composure.

"Yes, thank you. I suddenly had the gripes – must have been that dinner last night."

The lieutenant smiled. "Perhaps it was the beer you had with it. Anyway, you look lost. Can I help you?"

"I wonder if you can. I am from Switzerland and I have an appointment with Gruppenfuhrer Krause."

"I'm going that way, I can drop you off. It will give me another chance to chat up his receptionist. She's utterly gorgeous, but since there are so many majors and colonels around here – what the devil they all do I don't know – I don't suppose I stand a chance. Still, there's no harm in trying."

As they walked along a seemingly endless, highly polished corridor, the young man chatted on. "I am in the Waffen S.S. in Russia. I was wounded and then wounded again, so they sent me home for a month to recuperate. Now I'm waiting to hear where I am being posted. Right, here we are." He pushed open a swing door which led into a fairly spacious room containing a number of comfortable looking black leather arm chairs, a large photograph of Adolph Hitler, a medium sized oak desk with its attendant swivel chair, and in the swivel chair, bringing an aura of sunshine into an otherwise dull room, sat the beautiful object of the young lieutenant's aspirations.

"This gentleman is from Switzerland, to see the Gruppenfuhrer. I am from Hannover to see you. I shall soon be back in Russia so will you have dinner with me tonight?"

"Graf von Buchedel," (so he's a Count is he? David noted – reminds me of Charley) "do you never give up?" Her eyes smiled as she put the question.

"In a word – no. In fact, if these breeches weren't so damned tight I'd go down on one knee to plead my case."

"I could do it for you," David suggested.

"Now you see, there's a real gentleman. I've only known him five minutes and he will perform this singular service for me."

"We cannot have important foreign visitors denting our carpet on your behalf, so I suppose I had better have dinner with you or I shall never get rid of you."

The Graf turned to David – "We made it. Just shows you, two pronged attacks are nearly always successful." He shook hands enthusiastically, and with, "I'll collect you at six," left them both smiling, and with David mulling over the paradox as he sat in one of the armchairs, of the fact that in the space of a few minutes he had met and instantly formed a liking for this young S.S. man. In a few months time if they met again, he would almost certainly have to liquidate him.

His reveries were interrupted by the secretary. "This way Herr Muller." He was led into a large room, with the inevitable picture of the Fuhrer over the fireplace, fitted with a desk half the size of a football pitch as he later described it to the Count back in Bern. A very large, rugged, medal-bedecked gentleman rose to meet him, shook hands and offered coffee. 'It will be interesting to see whether he has to drink strained horse dung,' thought David. He didn't.

"I can only give you half an hour, Herr Muller, so we must get on. I have seen your catalogue and presentations. We need special units to be made, much larger than your largest model illustrated, but firstly I must impress upon you that every word that is spoken in here today is totally and completely confidential. Other than the technical facts, dimensions, throughputs etc which, I realise you must divulge to your design and financial people, all else is absolutely between ourselves. I understand from my officer in Munich that you personally have a strong belief in what the Reich has set out to do with regard to the Jewish question."

"Indeed I do Herr Gruppenfuhrer, indeed I do. And so do many others I know at home. We've all suffered from these people in one way or another. It is time the boot was on the other foot." And God forgive me for that lot, he said to himself.

"Right then. If these large units are successfully installed, I have a number of other smaller units needed in Austria, Serbia and the Central Government to follow, but speed is required on this project. It has the code name A/B."

"Well the first question Sir, is what is the proposed throughput?"

"Project A/B requires a throughput of 6000."

"Our Mark 3 would cater for 6000 per annum," David proposed.

"I'm talking of 6000 per day, seven days a week, fifty two weeks a year. I'm thinking in terms of four plants each to process 1500 units in twenty four hours."

David then produced the acting pinnacle of his life. Instead of showing the stomach churning shock he felt at the knowledge of the immolation of six thousand men, women, children and babies every day of the year, he smiled at this evil Nazi and said, "That is what I call doing the job properly." The general smiled back.

"I can see you and I are going to get along very well young Herr Muller."

Chapter Twenty Three

It was late afternoon on 16th March when Harry met the two sentries after his two-day, not uneventful trek from Muar. One of the sentries, Poh Chee, led him off through fairly open jungle, which closed in after a mile or so, until they reached a small encampment. There were eight other Chinese there who looked very curiously at this Tamil being led in, until Poh Chee announced, "This is Sergeant Major Chandler," at which they surrounded him, and as the two sentries had done, burst into peals of laughter. They were all obviously well educated young men, speaking very good English, eagerly demanding to know how he had got such a perfect disguise, how far he had travelled, in what actions he had taken part, all speaking at once until Poh Chee told them to shut up an and give the sergeant major some food and drink. This they quickly provided, waiting until he had finished before quizzing him. One of them introduced himself as Matthew Lee saying since it would soon be dark he would knock up a bed for the sergeant major, which he speedily fabricated from the ever-present bamboo. They had built shelters during their short stay, the benefit of which they found in no uncertain fashion that night. The monsoon season was more or less over – technically! That night it decided to give the Federated Malay States the benefit of its swan song for the year. It thrashed down on to the atap shelters, which in the onslaught gradually sprung leaks until everyone was soaked to the skin. Hour after hour it fell until, with the dawn, it eased to a steady downpour, finally ceasing altogether at about eight o'clock. Sleep had been impossible, they were all chilled to the bone, but had received one blessing – not even the mosquitoes could weather that storm, they all had a relief from that quarter. In the Malayan jungle you expect some rain every day throughout the year, but the daily deluge and the monsoon cannot be compared. The daily rain can last a couple of hours, the monsoon can go on for a couple of weeks without let-up.

In two days Ang Choon Guan gave the order to strike camp. They moved in single file, the front man being provided with a parang to cut their way through the jungle where required. Choon Guan marched behind him, pointing the direction of travel, which he obtained from compass bearings read from instructions given him by Robbie Stewart. The front man was relieved every half hour. The main problem with marching on a compass is knowing how many yards or miles you have covered. For example, if you are instructed to march for six miles on six degrees, then a further five miles on twelve degrees, it is difficult to know where to alter course. There is always a reason for making a dog's leg of this nature, either to skirt swamp areas, sudden mountainous features, or even habitation. An experienced jungle traveller will generally go by the clock, taking into account the amount of parang work which has had to be done and judging from that, whether he has covered one or two miles in the hour or whatever. He had a map, but it was not terribly helpful other than indicating major features such as rivers and mountains.

Each day they stopped an hour before dark to prepare their shelters and food. They had been steadily climbing most of the time; as a result, the mosquito menace subsided a little. Having built a fire they took it in turns to take off their outer clothes and held them in the smoke to kill off the ticks, which they had collected during the day's march. They are particularly prevalent after the rainy season and if left on clothes, will eventually migrate to the skin, burrow themselves in and cause intense irritation. On the third day they expected to reach the main north to south trunk road where it runs along the side of the main railway line. They would have to lie up and cross those obstacles in the dark, lying up again as soon as they were across – travelling through jungle at night is not the best of things to have to do, although in later days they became expert at it.

They heard the trunk road before they saw it. Ang Choon Guan went forward with one of the group and came back again in half an hour. They were both coated in thick mud up to their thighs, and what was more, because their trousers were not tucked in at the bottom, they had become the hosts to a dozen or so leeches on each of them. Martin Lee, who Harry had discovered was a fourth year medical student and was to be the camp doctor, swiftly had their trousers off and lighting a cigarette (all the Chinese seemed to smoke like chimneys Harry had noticed) touched it on the back of each leech, which promptly fell off and was stamped on. It would have been, literally, fatal to have just pulled them off since they would leave their jaws in the flesh, which then festers, probably causing blood poisoning and even death. The result of this reconnaissance therefore indicated they had to move further north so that they could find an outlet to the trunk road, hoping they would not find another such swamp on the other side after they had crossed. They moved west a mile or so into the beluka and made camp for the night.

And so day by day they gradually moved nearer their objective. On the fifth day, after a long climb up a jungle-covered mountainside, Harry found the exit wound in his leg beginning to weep. Martin had only a fairly basic first aid satchel with him, so all he could do was to soak a dressing in iodine and bind the wound up. The next day the going was even steeper and the jungle denser. They stopped two hours before dark all close to exhaustion, Harry in particular suffering very badly. From now on they could only cover eight or nine miles a day, each day a bigger nightmare than the day before. Although the Chinese were young and reasonably fit, they each came from a sedentary job, slept in comfortable mosquito-proof beds at night and were fed three good meals a day. Now a good night's sleep was an impossibility no matter how well they built their beds and bashas, the food was mainly cold rice, and the constant soaking from sweat, moisture from the vegetation, and the inevitable daily rain, combined with constant insect attacks of one description or another was sapping both their stamina and their mental processes. On one particularly difficult day, they covered only two miles, in that they had to fight their way down into a steep ravine and climb the other side, to clearly see an opening in the jungle on the opposite side they had left four hours before.

They were now nearly three thousand feet up and it was cold at night. On the ninth day they came to a largish fast running stream for which Ang Choon Guan had been aiming. "This," he said to Harry, "is a tributary of your River Muar."

"Well, firstly I lay no claim to the ownership of that stinking stretch of water. Secondly it looks a damned sight cleaner than the one I was in."

"Well now we've found it, the camp is beside it, but whether it's upstream or down I don't know, so I'll send a patrol one hour upstream first."

"You've done a great job getting us here. Well done." Harry shook hands with him.

The two-man patrol moved off, returning two hours later with the news that the stream ended in a sheer rock face, the camp obviously was downstream. As it was getting towards dark it was decided they would camp where they were and move downstream in the morning. They commenced cutting down bamboo for their bed frames and bashas whilst others found dry wood for the fire. Just as these tasks were nearly completed and the fire beginning to smoke well, literally out of the bushes four Chinese appeared led by the unmistakable figure of Robbie Stewart. Robbie made straight for Choon Guan, giving him a bear hug of welcome, in the course of this action walking straight past Harry. Having congratulated the young Chinese on the excellence of his navigation he turned to the others to tell them they were only a quarter of a mile from the camp. It was then he realised who the 'Tamil' was. As the others had done when they first saw him, he burst into roars of laughter. "Brilliant, brilliant, absolutely bloody brilliant. Would never have believed you weren't pukka –wait till the C.O. sees you. Oh bloody hell, how I wish I had a camera." His hilarity was infectious; they all started splitting their sides. Harry heard it from a distance; the world started to turn on him and gradually disappeared. He slumped to the ground.

Matthew Lee immediately took charge. "It's his wound," he informed Robbie, knowing that further explanation would be unnecessary.

"Make a stretcher Choon Guan please," Matthew asked. Quickly they made one from the bamboo and rattan they had cut, and Robbie led the way down to what they learnt to call No 6 camp. It was getting dark when they arrived. They put Harry on to a table, removed his clothes, washed him, and Matthew, having re-dressed the wound, put him to bed. The exit wound was very inflamed, but as yet, showed no signs of septicaemia. He had a high temperature. It could be caused by the wound, Matthew judged, it could be the beginning of an attack of malaria, he would keep an eye on him during the night and see what the morning would bring.

The next day his temperature had dropped a couple of degrees. He ate some food, noticing it was a great deal more palatable than the rations they had enjoyed on the march, which indicated well for the inner man at Camp 6. He slept again all the morning, and in the afternoon was visited by Robbie and the C.O., Clive Hollis, who said they would not bother him now but as soon as he felt a bit better they would like to have a blow by blow account of all that had happened to him since they last met in Singapore.

The next day the two navy men he had met at the police club came to see him, and in the afternoon Robbie and the C.O. visited him again. It was Sunday. "No unnecessary work today," the C.O. informed him, "most of the men are just bashing their charpoys," which was army talk for having an afternoon's sleep. On Monday, although he still felt weak, his temperature had dropped to almost normal and on Tuesday morning he got up to look at his new 'home.' He was met at the door by Robbie, dressed in a green uniform with a captain's pips on his shoulders. From the veranda of the hut in which he had been sleeping, Robbie pointed out the layout of the camp. It comprised a number of huts on stilts, with atap roofs, each with veranda similar to that upon which they were standing. The huts were built in the form of a rectangle surrounding an open space, or parade ground. The huts were very substantially built, all more or less from timber from the forest. A great deal of work, an enormous amount of ingenuity and what was more, a great deal of time had gone into the building of the camp. Whoever had visualised this, and the other five installations further up country, had certainly not suffered from the boneheaded stupidity of the morons in Fort Canning. Someone, or "ones," had had the kind of foresight so deplorably lacking in the higher echelons of the Government of the Federated Malay States.

Robbie pointed out the layout. Cookhouse – the far corner, long hut for the fifty odd Chinese communists, another hut for stores. Coming back ninety degrees, hut for Chinese non communists, ("I'll explain that later"), company office, turning again, officers quarters, sick bay where we now are, men's ablutions block and at the end, men's latrines, lying back from the main rectangle. All the buildings were shaded by overhanging trees, which would make them very difficult to spot from the air. It had been very carefully thought out. Despite the fact there were some sixty-five people here the camp was strangely quiet. Harry realised, as did everyone else, that this quietness was their first line of defence. If in the very unlikely event a Japanese patrol was sent into the jungle, the noise of their cutting their way through would be heard clearly from the camp, probably an hour before they actually reached it. It was so well concealed on its perimeter; a patrol could easily miss it. If it didn't, not one would be allowed to tell the tale, the bodies later being carried to a suitable spot well away from the camp area.

Over the next few days, finishing touches were carried out finishing the camp off and improving the camouflage situation. On Saturday 11th April they had their first parade. Clive Hollis, now Major Hollis, took the parade. Harry had been issued with new uniforms from the stores. He had to share a batman with the navy lieutenant and the chief petty officer, whilst the C.O. and Robbie shared another.

"Can't afford a batman each," Clive had said "but it is essential we show rank, have our meals on our own, and have nominal servants." Clive had added, "We are all on Christian name terms in the comfort of our mess but 'Sir' in front of the men – OK?" There had been nods of assent.

The parade formed up in front of the company office. Clive addressed them in English. "I know most of you understand English, those who do not will be given a translation afterward by Lee Chee Hong." He was a Mandarin speaking non-communist. Two or three of the men spoke Cantonese not Mandarin – all would very quickly have to learn basic military English that swiftly became obvious.

Clive first of all addressed himself to the communist group, telling them that as they were aware, the general secretary of the Malayan Communist Party had given direct and explicit orders that the party volunteers were to obey, without question, the orders of the Force 136, as it was to be known, officers, warrant officers and N.C.O.'s. The general secretary had made it known that any indiscipline would be severely dealt with by the force officers. Orders had been received from headquarters at Colombo in Ceylon, that no operations were to take place for six months, so that the Japanese would be lulled into a sense of false security, and then we would hit them, and keep on hitting them. Finally he introduced Regimental Sergeant Major Chandler. "Mr Chandler has killed Germans in the European War, he has already killed a good number of Japanese here in Malaya, and been nearly killed himself. Like many of you, he has seen terrible atrocities carried out by these animals – we shall have no mercy on them when we eventually go to the attack." There was immediate applause.

Afterwards, as they sat on the officers' veranda Robbie said, "There will be no trouble with them," meaning the communists, "until we win the war. Then they will carry out the second part of their plan, namely to stick to their weapons, and anything else they can get hold of, disappear into the jungle, and start fighting us to make Malaya a communist country." Robbie's prescience was borne out by events. After the war it took twelve years in what was to become known as 'The Emergency' to eventually eradicate the communist menace in Malaya. For over three years they were heroes, for twelve years they were terrorists, those that lived that is.

That evening Harry asked Clive if it was possible to get a message back to England.

"We have a set time to send messages to Colombo," was the reply, "we have strict instructions on when to send and for how long as we don't want to give any Jap listeners the chance to get a bearing on our calls. What had you in mind?"

"Well I have a pretty good idea. I've been posted 'Missing, believed killed in action.' If some way could be found to tell my wife that I'm still alive and kicking I would be eternally grateful."

"We can do that. Let's see, its Saturday today. We have a slot for thirty minutes on Sunday evenings. I'll get Eric, the C.P.O. to encode a message. How about:-

'RSM Chandler H 783290 (or whatever your number is), has returned to duties.

Please notify family UK.'

"How long they will take I don't know, I suspect they're pretty good at this sort of thing. It will be some while before we can get letters away I imagine, but even that will be possible in the dim and distant future."

And so, on Sunday evening the bicycle generator was put into action, the messages dispatched, followed by the agonising wait to hear some sort of reply to indicate their bulletin had not got lost in the ether. After some ten minutes a coded reply came in, which Eric pored over for a while, finally producing a single sheet of paper.

"Greetings friends. Messages received and understood."

Eric turned to the others and said, "We've got a right bloody joker up there. He ends the message, 'you can have the rest of the day off.'"

All laughed uproarishly at this single sally. It was not all that funny, probably even an offence under the Army Act, Signalling Procedure for the Use Of, but it gave the warm feeling that someone, miles from their enclosed little enclave in the middle of an inhospitable jungle, knew about them, would be thinking about them, and talking about them to others. They were not entirely alone.

The next weeks passed quickly. Whilst in camp the men perfected their weapon training, Robbie taught them unarmed combat, Matthew Lee taught first aid and hygiene, Harry taught them the principles of immobilising vehicles and conversely how to start a vehicle without an ignition key. These latter instructions had to be done with the use of chalk drawings on a hut wall since obviously they had no vehicle on which to practise. They carried out compass marches in groups of varying sizes from three men and a leader up to twelve, lasting a few hours up to three days. They were warned of the innumerable dangers to be encountered in the jungle and to be watchful at all times. Most of the guerrillas had never been in the jungle in their lives, they were urban dwellers. Like most 'townies' their greatest fear was of snakes and tigers, in the event most Malayan snakes are harmless and do not attack, and tigers are few and far between. They soon learned that their most dangerous enemies were ticks, ants, leeches in the lower jungle, and above all, wasps and bees. These latter were very dangerous indeed, but at least you could see their nests – like brownish paper bags hanging from branches or fixed to the trunks of dead trees. You did not necessarily have to disturb a nest. If you got too close they would go on the attack. Hundreds of mini torpedo bombers settling on a man could result in his death. You were told if you disturbed a nest to just stand still – they only attacked moving targets. Few people in that situation would, I fear, put that maxim to the test.

The main result of their incursions into the jungle was, of course, they grew less and less afraid of it. They learnt to live in it, and ultimately to know that their familiarity with it was a weapon they would be able to use against the Jap pigs when the time came. Furthermore, gaining this confidence made them impatient to use their skills to annihilate these little bow-legged monkeys, as the Chinese thought of them, from across the sea!

The time passed. When they were in camp they cultivated their garden, which had been dug on the other side of the stream. Fresh water shrimps were abundant in the stream. They surrounded the garden with tapioca plants, the tubers of which provided part of their basic diet. They grew taso, which has potato like roots which again provided the remainder of their staple food. In the garden they grew sweet potatoes, and from the jungle they harvested breadfruit, coconuts, bamboo shoots and some fruits. The general rule with jungle fruits was that if the monkeys eat them so can humans; otherwise leave them alone no matter how enticing they appear.

Meat obviously was the main problem. They were well stocked with tinned meat of all types, but this would have to be replenished by the end of the year. It was said that, provided you chopped their heads off, all snakes are edible, as indeed are lizards and frogs, but for some reason these delicacies were not particularly appealing.

In July they received a coded message that they were to expect 'Python' during that month – the code name for Colonel Llewellyn, the Commander of the ground forces left in Malaya. He arrived, along with Chua Yong Soon, the leader of the what was now to be called the Malayan Peoples Anti Japanese Army – MPAJA -, six bodyguards and to the great interest of all, two Orang Asli, or 'original people,' small, blowpipe carrying, bark clothed natives. Nomadic people, no one knew the jungle as they did. With their bamboo blowpipes they could hit a bird in flight, or a squirrel or monkey at fifty yards. The minute Harry saw them he decided to befriend them and learn their craft. He had been told in the past that a small animal hit by one of their poisoned darts was dead in seconds, human beings took only a little longer. He was already formulating in his tiny mind how, if he became proficient in its ore, this could be a very useful tool with which to noiselessly attack

Japanese sentries when the time came.

The colonel said he would be staying for five days so that he and his Chinese comrades could rest and recuperate after their long journey south. Although Yong Soon was invited to stay with the officers, he elected to be with his volunteers in order that he could then get to know and to assess each one. On the first night, seeing that the two natives were curling up on the veranda in front of the colonel's quarters, Harry went to the stores and found two fairly brightly coloured, un-army looking blankets. He took them out and offered one to each in turn. In his own mind, not knowing their names, not knowing if they even had names, of course they've got bloody names he told himself – anyway since he didn't know what they were called, he christened them Bam and Boo.

The next morning he asked Clive if he needed him for an hour and was told no, but the colonel wanted a first session with him at four o'clock that afternoon. Harry therefore sought out the two natives. Robbie had told him they came from a tribe called Negrati, from north of the Cameron Highlands area and were devoted to the colonel who had killed two Japanese in the act of trying to rape their women. They had agreed to serve with the force, their women and children being looked after by the remainder of the tribe in the deep jungle. Harry approached them, shook hands and smiling, squatted beside them. Pointing to his eyes and then to one of the blowpipes, he held out his hand. Bam handed one over. It was about ten feet long. He was surprised to find that it was not a single hollow bamboo cane, as he had anticipated, but was double sleeved, a cane within a cane. A great deal of searching he judged, would have to be done to get a pair to make a good fit, but once made it would be very rigid. The outside was decorated with carvings, intricate designs having been handed down over the centuries – these people were here thousands of years before the arrival of Sir Stamford Raffles.

They showed him the darts not, he was pleased to see, armed with the poison in which they were dipped when hunting. They were light in weight, made from slivers of the bertam palm inserted into a soft wood almost the same diameter of the interior of the tube – about half an inch. The dart, embedded in the holder, was fed into the tube, a quick puff and it was on its way. Finally there was the poison. This Robbie had told him, was obtained from the resin of the ipoh tree, and whilst these were common in the north, they were less common in their region. Harry pointed to the resin and then to the nearest tree. His new friends shook their heads, and stood up, one taking his sleeve. They moved out of the camp following the line of the stream. Harry had difficulty in keeping up. It was not as though they seemed to walk any quicker than he did, they just seemed not to meet the obstructions he encountered, swaying from one leg to the other without touching thorn bushes, being amazingly agile in overcoming rocks, tree roots and other projections. After a quarter of an hour they found the tree, they had obviously passed it on the way in since they knew exactly where to go. Pointing it out to Harry, Bam took a smaller version of a tapper's knife out of his quiver and made a delicate cut at an angle on the bark. They waited for some ten minutes before a dark, moderately viscous liquid began to leak out. The two men chatted away, pointing to it, and obviously telling Harry to be very very careful with it. "Don't worry my old pals, I'll treat it like the plague." He shook hands with them excitedly, and they made their ways back to the camp. Harry was now in, as he put it to himself, the Jap removal business. But he had a lot of hard work to do and numerous disappointments to overcome before he became proficient in this deadly act.

Chapter Twenty Four

As Ray Osbourne walked back to Vickers police room, Sergeant Dixon started to organise the muscle work required before the bomb could be neutralised. He was an old hand at this game, but just as Ray had had funny feelings about 'this one' – which he did not impart to anyone else of course – he too was not happy. He put this down to the fact that not only was the bomb a big bugger but it was right in the middle of God knows how many tons of explosive. They had once had to deal with a similar one in the Crossness sewage plant and he had not been very happy about that. The fact that he had considered he had been in 'it' up to his neck all his life didn't mean he wanted to end up in 'it.'

As they prepared the timber for shoring up, the works fire tender arrived and swiftly pumped out the water in the base of the hole. The sergeant got the men digging round the back of the bomb so that they could get a look at the fuses. They worked carefully making sure they did not hit against the casing. Some bombs had an anti-handling fuse built in which required the movement of only a millimetre to set the thing off. As soon as the fuse became visible the men climbed out of the hole and Ray went down to see what was there and how to operate further. He cleaned around the fuse with a small wooden scraper, and then slowly removed the earth lower down. "I thought so," he said to no one in particular.

"It's got two fuses," he called out to the sergeant, "a number 17 and a number 50."

The number 17 fuse was a time delay fuse, which was set before take off to explode the bomb up to 72 hours after being dropped. The Germans had found that an unexploded bomb can often cause more chaos just lying there before it goes off, than the actual explosion itself. The number 50 was the anti-handling fuse, which was designed to deter lunatics like Ray Osbourne mucking about with it. However, this bomb had been there for more than 72 hours, therefore the number 17 fuse had malfunctioned. A Major Martin of the B.D.S. had developed a method of neutralising the anti handling device. It still involved considerable danger, but where the bomb could not be exploded in situ, and this was, like the one under St Paul's Cathedral, one such situation, it had to be used.

Ray climbed the ladder out of the hole. "I shall put the B D discharger on the number 50, so warn everybody to stay well clear," he ordered Sergeant Dixon. The sergeant gave orders to prepare the B D discharger, while Ray climbed back into the hole to carry out the most delicate operation of all. With everyone now well clear of 'C' department's number 12 hut, Ray found himself all alone in the world as he had done so many times before. Just him and a bomb. But not just him. The commotion and the floodlight over the hole had brought out from his slumbers a song thrush, which, perched on a branch not more than six feet above the ground level, burst forth into a cascade of song for all the world to know how beautiful life was. Ray coughed loudly, the thrush fluttered off. If this bomb goes up I would not want the thrush to die, he told himself.

Slowly he removed the number 50 fuse cover from the casing. He had some difficulty with two of the screws, which were beginning to rust in, the extra strength he had to apply causing him to begin to sweat with the anxiety of determining how far he could go before he moved that bomb the millimetre between life and death. He told himself, as he had done on many occasions prior to this little outing, that it took more than his puny strength to move a half a ton of embedded bomb, but there was always the risk the bloody thing might move of its own volition. At last, the cover came away. He pulled the discharger towards him. Suspended on a rope from a gantry above it consisted of a container of a mixture of alcohol, benzene and salt, fitted with a plunger, which forced the cocktail into the fuse. He carefully nosed the fluid into the housing until it ran back out, took the discharger away, and climbed back out of the hole. Sergeant Dixon, watching from the entrance of an air raid shelter some distance away, ran towards him.

"All set Sir?"

"Yes, we'll leave it the usual half hour then I'll go down and take it out. By then it will be immunised." He found he was sweating despite it being a cold night.

They gave it the required half hour, plus five minutes for luck, and Ray returned to his hole in the ground. He quickly inserted his fuse key and in less than a minute he had removed the fuse. "That's one of the buggers," he said aloud. He took the fuse up the ladder to Sergeant Dixon at his air raid shelter and said, "I'm going to take the No. 17 out now, that should be straightforward." The No. 17, a time delay fuse, had obviously malfunctioned, consequently it could be treated with more robustness than the anti handling fuse, in fact it was not unknown for a disposal man to remove it with a hammer and nail if he had forgotten his key. Ray still applied this normal caution, gradually easing the fuse out of its pocket.

"All clear," he yelled, at which Sergeant Dixon and the squad doubled to the site. Ray clambered up the ladder. Just as he reached near the top, his arm holding the fuse above his head, he hit it against the staging against which the ladder was secured. He heard a click, a whirr, followed instantaneously by a blinding flash, as the fuse exploded, ripping his hand to pieces. He fell screaming with agony back into the pit.

Sergeant Dixon slid down the outside wood of the ladder, landed beside his officer, recognised immediately what had happened, took Ray's tie off and with the use of the screwdriver from Ray's belt made a tourniquet above the mangled wrist. "Get the ambulance," he yelled. The lance corporal ran to the police room, the works ambulance was there in seconds almost, and he was rushed to the Southern Hospital at Dartford where he was on the operating table in under half an hour. What had happened was the clockwork timer had originally malfunctioned only three seconds before its seventy-two hours were up – probably a substandard piece of machining somewhere. Hitting it against the timber had freed it, which had ignited the explosive charge, which would normally have set the bomb off. Ray's careful handling in taking it out had saved his life, the factory and perhaps half of Dartford, but his days as a bomb disposal officer were over.

At Chandlers Lodge on the Tuesday morning Ruth, having already seen Fred off to the factory, started to get a tray ready to take Rose up her early morning tea. It was going to be a busy day. Ray Osbourne was, after all, arriving that evening to stay for three nights instead of just the Wednesday night as previously arranged, so she and Mrs Stokes, the home help, had to get his bed ready. In addition, they had planned to get several sets of curtains down for washing or to be sent to the dry-cleaners as the first stage of the great annual spring clean. Rose was going to Bromley to see an old friend, leaving Jeremy in her tender care, which meant 'not taking her eyes off him for one minute,' and finally she had a four o'clock hair appointment at Maison Blanche, by which time Rose would be home. Fortunately she would not have to prepare dinner since Fred had said he would push the boat out and take her and Ray to the Angel, Rose included if Nanny could look after Jeremy.

As she did each morning, she wondered where David was, and whether Harry really was still alive. She was beginning to show the strain of these two and a half years of war, the loss of Jeremy and Pat, her sons she knew not where, son-in-law Mark with Charlie now probably in the thick of things, and the Chandlers themselves in 'bomb alley,' although that, thank God, had eased somewhat just lately. She poured Rose's tea. "Better get cracking I suppose."

The day passed quickly. Fred came home at around six o'clock, leaving the factory in the capable hands of Ernie Bolton. Ray had said he was coming on the bus from Chatham, to arrive at Sandbury at 6.35 and he would walk the ten minutes to Chandlers Lodge. At seven o'clock he still had not arrived. The Chandlers were not unduly disturbed by this. It was wartime. Often there were hold-ups in one district, which spilled over to another. He could have been called out on a job and was late back, though as Fred said, he would certainly have telephoned he was going to be late had he been able to – he was not the sort of chap to let people hang about. At eight o'clock Fred decided to phone his mess number.

"Officers' mess, Lance Corporal Waverley."

"Oh, Corporal Waverley. I'm trying to get hold of Captain Osbourne. He was to have dinner with us this evening. My name is Chandler."

"Will you hold the line Sir, I'll get the adjutant." There was a delay.

"Captain Tucker, can I help you?"

"Ray Osbourne was coming to stay with us tonight and has not, so far, arrived. Can you tell me whether he has been held up dealing with an incident or something? My name is Chandler."

"I'm sorry to have to tell you Mr Chandler that Ray is in hospital. He was injured dealing with a UXB last night."

"Oh no – is he badly hurt?"

Ruth and Rose, listening to the conversation looked horrified at each other.

"I can't give you details as I presume you are not his next of kin."

"As you know he has no kin here, only a sister in New Zealand – we are the nearest to kin he has."

"Very well, I'll tell you what I know. He has lost an arm I believe and is in intensive care in the Southern Hospital at Dartford. He is under heavy sedation that is all I know. We shall of course be visiting him tomorrow."

"Yes, and so shall we. Thank you very much captain for your help." He turned to the two women. "Ray was involved in an accident with an unexploded bomb last night and is in intensive care at Southern Hospital. The adjutant says he has lost an arm."

The two women burst into tears. Fred was already back on the telephone, getting the number of the almoner's office at Southern Hospital, and then booking the call. In the ten minutes they had to wait it was decided they would cancel the dinner appointment and just have something at home. The call came through.

"Almoner's office, may I help you?"

"Can you please tell me how Captain Osbourne is, he was admitted earlier today." There was a delay. "I will put you through to the ward sister." Another delay.

"Sister Wright, Raleigh Ward."

"Sister, can you tell me how Captain Osbourne is" adding quickly, "I'm his uncle, Captain Chandler, his only relative in this country."

Quick thinking had prompted him to quote his rank since this was probably a services hospital, and secondly the fib about his being Ray's uncle was, in his opinion, fully justified, saving a lot of argy-bargy.

"Well Captain Chandler. He is stable. He is sleeping. He has lost his right forearm. He will be kept sedated for some time yet."

"Thank you sister. When can we come in to see him?"

"If you telephone after midday tomorrow when the rounds have been done the sister on duty will let you know."

"Thank you very much for your help."

Fred explained all that had passed between him and Sister Wright. They were all terribly shocked and upset. They just had some soup for their evening meal, none felt like food. At ten o'clock Ernie telephoned to say all was well and that he was leaving. He too was most upset at the news; he and Ray had got on very well together. Shortly afterwards Jack telephoned. Fred had tried to reach him but he had been out for the evening with Moira in Maidstone, as a result Fred had asked Nanny to get him to call when they came home. Fred promised to keep Jack posted as to the verdict tomorrow.

The next day Fred came back to Chandlers Lodge at around 12.30, immediately booking a call to Dartford. It only took five minutes. The day sister at Raleigh Ward was only able to tell him that Captain Osbourne was not in danger, but he was nevertheless very unwell. He would be allowed no visitors probably for a couple of days but to enquire tomorrow at this time. Fred passed the news on to all who knew Ray, and made his way back to the factory.

The factory had expanded tenfold since the war began. They had been fortunate, or foresighted enough, to purchase five acres of land next to the original factory site, for which they had applied for planning permission to change to industrial use. Since this was for war production it was speedily granted, although up until now, they had not started to build on it, their expansion being catered for on the original site. Fred and Ernie were to meet senior ministry people that afternoon to discuss a new project for which they were being invited to tender. At two o'clock two large Humber staff cars arrived, discharging two obviously senior civil servants, an R.A.F. wing commander, a colonel in a maroon beret and a very attractive A.T.S. sergeant clutching a brief case and a roll of drawings.

Fred and Ernie were watching from Fred's office. Fred commented "Blimey, they're hunting in packs now."

Ernie commented, "I wonder how much an hour that lot costs?"

Miss Russell, Fred's secretary commented, "We had better get the best cups out."

Ernie went to the entrance hall to meet the guests while Miss Russell bustled around organising the removal of more chairs into Fred's office to place around his conference table. When they were all seated and had agreed that some tea and biscuits would be an excellent idea, the leader of the delegation reminded Fred and Ernie that they were subject to the Official Secrets Act, to which Fred jokingly replied, "We think of nothing else all day."

"I have to remind you of it anyway," the civil servant replied, a bit po-faced Fred thought, as Charlie would say. He continued, "Open the general arrangement drawing will you Kathleen?" The sergeant unrolled the large print, which showed what looked like a very ugly aeroplane, but which they soon realised was a glider.

"Mr Chandler, our Air Ministry friend here tells me you make component parts for the Mosquito, your work is classified at the highest standard and that you are never late." Fred kept his counsel. "This unit is called the Hamilcar. We have other gliders as you probably know for the transportation of troops. This is a new one, the prototype for which flew very successfully last month. It is designed to carry a seven ton tank for our airborne people," nodding to the colonel in the maroon beret, "or equivalent weight artillery or Bofors pieces. The major problem I imagine as far as you are concerned will be one of space. As you can see it is some one hundred and twenty feet long, one hundred and ten feet span, and around twelve feet overall height. You should base your quotation on an initial order for fifty of these on the basis of the delivery of ten per month from October onwards. Now while you and Mr Bolton look at the drawings with the sergeant" (I'd much rather look at the sergeant was Ernie's judgement) "perhaps one of your staff could show us around the plant – we have full clearance everywhere."

Fred rang for Miss Russell. "Could you ask Mr Abbott to come and take our visitors around please Miss Russell?" After a short wait, the party disappeared for half an hour while Fred and Ernie examined the drawings to ensure there were no major tendering problems. When the party returned, the view was advanced that there would be a difficulty as regards space. Fred immediately reassured them he would have a new building up on their five acres site next door in plenty of time for the first deliveries. And so it was they put in their tender and along with a small number of other wood working firms made the glider which operated with enormous success in Normandy, Arnhem and the Rhine.

On Thursday Fred came home at lunchtime to again telephone the hospital. The report was that captain Osbourne was now conscious and would be able to receive visitors on Saturday, 2-4pm, and on Sunday at the same time. It was arranged therefore that Ruth, Fred and Rose would go on Saturday, Jack and Moira along with Ernie and Anni on Sunday.

On Thursday 23rd April, the first of what were to become known as the 'Baedeker raids' was launched on England. Baedeker was a German travel guide, which listed all the medieval cities in the U.K., places with famous cathedrals and other ancient buildings. Hitler told Goebbels, his propaganda minister, he would repeat these terror attacks (they were targets of no military value) night after night until the English were sick and tired of them. He had added, "there is no other way of bringing the English to their senses. They belong to a class of human beings with whom you can talk only after you have first knocked out their teeth."

The first two raids on the nights of 23rd and 24th April were on Exeter. Also on the 24th one hundred and fifty bombers struck at Bath killing four hundred people. On April 27th and 28th Norwich was the target, also on the 28th the Guildhall at York was destroyed. Nearly one thousand people were killed in these raids. It was pure unmitigated barbarism for which eventually the cities of Cologne, Munich and others paid a heavy price.

When Fred, Ruth and Rose visited Ray on the Saturday, although he looked pale and drawn, he was remarkably cheerful. He was still being "pretty doped up, so don't expect any scintillating conversation," as he put it, with his usual grin. "Can you tell us what happened?" Fred asked. He gave them a blow-by-blow account of the night's work; ending by saying how lucky he was the blasted thing had not reactivated as it was being withdrawn. Rose was quietly crying with the stress of reliving those dreadful minutes. "You know, the first thought I had when I eventually came to and they told me what had happened to me was – how the hell am I going to learn to write with my left hand?" He paused a moment, "But I shall, you can bet your last fiver, I shall."

They were quiet as they drove out towards Farningham to get on to the A20 for home. Ruth broke the silence with, "What a very, very, brave man. We shall have to look after him when he comes out from hospital."

Fred looked at Rose; they both raised their eyebrows. "There goes mother hen – at it again." All three smiled, the first smile since they had left home that morning.

When they arrived back at Chandlers Lodge, where they were expecting all to have gathered to get 'all the news,' they were surprised to see, as they drove in, two military vehicles parked on the gravel, one a standard army Humber staff car, the second an Austin civilian car but with Royal Navy plates fitted to it. Megan met them at the door saying, "How is Ray? You've got some visitors." In the meantime the twins had rushed out to be picked up, along with young John, so obviously Moira and Jack were there as well, there was quite a hubbub. Ruth moved into the sitting room, and in addition to those she expected to be there, Anni and Karl – Ernie was at the factory until six o'clock – and the Hoopers, she found General Earnshaw, General Halton, an incredibly handsome staff captain who they learnt was named Rufus, and last but by no means least, their driver, an A.T.S. corporal, looking a little overawed by the occasion, standing beside Anni and Maria. There was further hubbub as they either shook hands or where appropriate received kissed cheeks, finally giving Maria a big hug of welcome – how lovely to see you – what are you doing here – oh what a lovely surprise, and so on. Gradually the bedlam subsided, Jack asking the inevitable question. "How is he? What happened?"

Ruth replied, "You tell them Fred." She was afraid she might get upset in front of them all if she recounted the story.

Fred ended his account on an optimistic note by saying that Ray was determined to overcome his accident, "But then" he added, "we all know he's that sort of bloke."

After a little more conversation Ruth asked, "Who would like tea?"

General Earnshaw spoke up quickly. "Now my dear Ruth, I have been expounding to Rufus here – General Halton is already more than well aware of it – of the source of the best glass of beer obtainable in these lands, or any others as far as I know. I would therefore, always assuming Fred and Jack have not drunk it all, be grateful to be able to prove my point to this initiate into the noble art of ale quaffing." There was general laughter at this, resulting in Fred bringing out a crate of Whitbread's from his store, and providing glasses of this nectar derived from the hop fields only a mile or two away from where they stood.

The girls followed Ruth into the kitchen. Inevitably the question was asked whether there was any news of David and Harry, with the inevitable answer. Ruth asked the A.T.S. corporal, nicknamed 'Sandie' apparently, how the generals came to be in Sandbury. She said she had driven her general from Colchester to a conference at Shornecliffe, General Halton being already there. Her general decided to call in at Sandbury on the way back to pick some books up from his home at Mountfield nearby. His wife, of course, Lady Earnshaw, was up at Colchester. General Halton had the rest of the weekend free, so decided he would beg a lift and spend the rest of the weekend here with his friends, the Chandlers. They were shocked when they arrived to hear about Captain Osbourne, so decided to stay on until Mr and Mrs Chandler came back from the hospital, to hear how he was.

Maria explained that she had driven a navy captain, a marine colonel and a ministry man from Deal back up to the Admiralty – "and do you know, this squirt from the ministry was in the front passenger seat, and kept, accidentally of course, I don't think, touching my knee. I kept wondering how many days I would get in chokey if I clouted him one. Anyway, as I was almost going back past your door I thought I would call in and scrounge a cup of tea."

There was general relief that Ray's injuries had not been more horrific than they were. If he had been holding the thing at a lower level, or against his chest – 'it just doesn't bear thinking about' was the accepted view.

"Well ladies, Rufus and I have got to get back to Colchester," the general stood at the door, "so I'll say goodbye to you en bloc as it were. Thank you for the hospitality Ruth. Why don't you and Fred take a weekend off and come up to Colchester? We would love to have you."

"Tearing Fred away from his factory is more difficult than you could ever imagine," Ruth replied "but thank you very much for the invitation – I shall have to get working on him."

"With your renowned feminine wiles I'm sure you will succeed," he chaffed.

They saw the general and Rufus off, General Halton remarking he had better make tracks to see if John Tarrant could put him up at The Angel, and that he would see them at church in the morning. "You will do no such thing" Ruth scolded, "We have plenty of room here, so here you will stay."

Jack looked at him grinning. "You don't get ordered about like that very often do you general?"

"When the mem-sahib lays down the law everyone obeys," he rejoined. "Mind you, I think I would rather be here than any other place I know." It was obvious he meant that so sincerely, tied in as it was with the loneliness he continued to suffer at the loss of his wife, a loss he could share with these lovely people similarly afflicted as they all were with the loss of their Pat.

Chapter Twenty Five

David had got on very well with the S.S. Gruppenfuhrer. His appointment had stretched from thirty minutes to over an hour until an aide knocked and reminded his boss that he had a meeting with the Reichsminister in twenty minutes.

"Right then Herr Muller. See my secretary and tell her to fit you in for an hour the day after tomorrow, (looking at his desk calendar) that's Wednesday 25th, and we will finalise on the delivery and commercial side of things as far as you are able, as well as discuss any technical problems which may occur to you in the meantime. She will also get you clearance to telephone your principals should you need to do so, but I should warn you your call will of course be monitored."

David shook hands with the general, thanked him for his kind reception, and made his way out to the receptionist. Having fixed the next appointment, 3pm on the Wednesday, and received instructions as to how he would be able to telephone Bern – he would apparently have to return to the S.S. H.Q. to make the call – he joked with this very attractive young lady.

"So you took pity on the poor Graf after all?" he asked. She answered him quite seriously, not responding to the jocularity in his question at all.

"So many of them are dying out there. I may well be the last girl he will ever go out with."

David had this feeling that she would never have spoken like that had he been a fellow German; she could only express her sadness because he was Swiss. His instinct was further reinforced when she added, "You do not know how lucky you are to be Swiss." She paused a moment and added, "But I shall give him a lovely evening he can remember when he goes back to fight those barbarians." David felt like screaming, 'What about that barbarian in the next room killing six thousand innocents a day?'

He walked back to his hotel, conscious of the fact he was definitely being followed. He stopped by a shop with an angled window and clearly saw the reflection of a slouch-hatted man in a dark raincoat also stop and look into a shop window. He was not perturbed since he had been warned this would probably happen.

He ate in the hotel that evening, deciding to have an early night, and not to unnecessarily take risks by going out to a bar or nightspot. At one o'clock he was awakened by the air raid siren, and ten minutes or so later the anti-aircraft guns opened up leading David to think that whatever shortages the German nation was suffering, one of them was not anti-aircraft weapons. A furious banging on his door and someone shouting, "Shelter in the basement," left him in the quandary as to whether he should go downstairs or take a chance and stay where he was. He decided on the latter – after all I am doubly protected he told himself. First of all I am one of them, referring to the people up there, so they would not drop one on me, and secondly I am supposed to be a neutral, and you are not allowed to bomb neutrals. At that point a stick of bombs screamed down only a few hundred yards away, shaking the bed on which he was lying, at which he was out of bed, slippers and dressing gown on in seconds, picked up his key and was out in the corridor following a stream of people all heading for the stairway – no one was going to risk using the lift. In the dimly lit shelter he eventually found a space on a wooden bench against a rather cold wall, between a rather large German lady and an elderly, one-armed gentleman, obviously a veteran of the 1914 war. As they settled, another series of explosions shook the building. David could see in the dim light that the old soldier was gripping his trousers with his one hand, his face was set, he sat stiff with tension. It was clear the he was again living the nightmare of the trenches of twenty-five years ago.

"I am from Switzerland," David began, and then thought, 'why should I bother to be sorry for this bloke – he is not only my enemy, he could well have been among those that my father fought.' He continued. "Do you have these air raids very often?" The reply he received left him open-mouthed.

"What do you want to know for? You Swiss are just sitting on the sidelines whilst your Jewish bankers are making fortunes out of the Reich. Why the Fuhrer doesn't walk in and snap up your little goldmine I shall never know. He could do it in five minutes, and mark my words he will one day. All the cuckoo clocks in creation won't stop him." The lady on his left had clearly heard this tirade and immediately took David's part, leaning across him (she smelt rather nice he remembered later), berating the old soldier for being so discourteous to the young foreign gentleman who must be here to help the Reich in some way or he would not be here at all, and anyway by being here he was sharing the danger they were all experiencing. The recipient of these observations having run out of invective turned his head away and said no more.

"I am sorry you were insulted in that manner," she continued to David, "it really was most discourteous."

"I think he was just very frightened by the bombing and saying things he did not really mean. Nevertheless, thank you for taking my part; it was most kind of you. I am Erwin Muller from Bern," he added.

"I am Doktor Erika Manstein, this is my husband, we are from Nurnberg. We are here on a medical conference," she added "it should have ended yesterday – I wish it had, but then nowhere is safe these days."

"You should come and live in Switzerland," David joked.

"That would be very nice. But no, we have our duty as loyal Germans." She stated this in measured terms as a matter of basic fact, not in the normal Nazi jingoistic manner.

Another series of explosions caused conversation to lapse, giving David the opportunity to study her husband for a short while. He was as small as she was large. He was thin faced with dark penetrating eyes; she was round faced with large blue eyes. He was dark, she was fair. He would be fiftyish David estimated, she fortyish. There seemed to be nothing compatible between them. This apparent state of affairs led his thoughts somewhat lewdly into the realms of how they functioned between the sheets. It would be a bit like a terrier with a wolf hound. One thing was for certain he concluded, if she turned over quickly in the night and one of her magnificent breasts thumped him, he could end up with a broken rib or two. Perhaps he wore armour-plated pyjamas just in case? Or perhaps he slept on top of her – there would be plenty of room. On the other hand if he rolled off he might injure himself that way. Not only that, he might get rolled on, that could be dangerous. David came to the conclusion that Herr Doktor Manstein led quite a hazardous life what with the bombing and sleeping with this magnificent woman. His reverie was interrupted by the lady in question turning to him and remarking, "There goes the all clear, we shall not have any more trouble tonight, they have to get home in the dark otherwise our fighters will get them. Goodbye Herr Muller, it was very pleasant meeting you, a safe journey home." She shook hands, as also did her husband. They seemed very nice people. 'Why has this bastard Hitler got everybody fighting one another?' David asked himself.

David's meeting with the Gruppenfuhrer on Wednesday afternoon produced two vital pieces of information. In the middle of discussing a technical matter, which David had discovered was impractical in the standard form and would have to be modified, a civilian having knocked on a door communicating with the general's office, and was introduced to David.

"Herr Gruppenfuhrer. I was told you were discussing the Auschwitz-Birkenau project this afternoon and there have been a couple of additions we require to be taken into account."

The S.S. man leaned back in his chair and looked at the civilian with a look which said 'You stupid loud-mouthed sod.' The civilian, instantly realising what he had done, apologised at once. "It didn't occur to me the supplier would not know the location of the project – I really am terribly sorry."

David grinned at the Gruppenfuhrer. "Sir, I didn't hear a thing. As far as I know it is somewhere on the Chinese border." There was silence for a moment.

"Well, come on then, what are these two extras you need?"

The chastened ministry man proceeded to give a requirement that nearly turned David's stomach over. How he stopped himself from retching he never knew. The civilian proceeded in a voice as matter of fact as if he was talking about a machine for the bagging up of sugar.

"On one of the lines we require an extraction plant for the removal of the body fat during the process, recovered in vats of some description. We are negotiating with a manufacturer to build a plant there to use this in soap manufacture. Secondly on another line, after the bone and clinker crushing section, we require a dual hopper system to feed the ashes into twelve cubic metre trailers, supplied by another company, who have negotiated the purchase of this commodity for use as fertiliser." He paused, "It is only fair these people should help us in the outlay of the cost of the equipment is it not?"

The general looked at David. "Any problems?" he asked.

"No, Sir, I can't see any at the moment."

"Right, I'll leave you to it." The ministry man shook hands with David, who fervently wished he had some carbolic and a bowl of water to wash them with afterwards.

"We must get on. I have another meeting this afternoon. All that is left now is to discuss the commercial side. Do you know if there is a line of credit we can use between our two countries?"

"I was advised not Herr Gruppenfuhrer."

"I see. Do you operate barter systems?"

"Yes, that is not unknown. In the past we have been paid in coffee, Hungarian wine, even Moroccan dates I believe on one occasion. May I ask what commodity you were considering?"

"Gold."

This was the last commodity David would have guessed on the answer to his enquiry. He grinned again at the general.

"Sir, if you mention gold to any Swiss manufacturer or banker, their eyes automatically shine like traffic lights."

The general laughed heartily at this.

"Do we have any indication of the grade of gold Sir? My financial director will almost certainly want to know that."

"All grades. He will have to work out a deal based on the lower grades, we shall not argue. You see, the S.S. obtains large quantities of gold from the people going to the camps. Rings, jewellery, coins and so on. And do you know that sixty per cent of Eastern Jews have gold fillings in their teeth? It's surprising how the quantities mount up."

David's stomach took another turn. He overcame it by replying, "I think the reason for that is because they have such low self-esteem, they have to put on a display of ostentation every time they open their big mouths. It's a bit like whores wearing low cut dresses." Again the Gruppenfuhrer laughed heartily, thumping the desk.

"You know young Muller, I wish to God you weren't Swiss, I could do with a chap like you here. Right now, I've got to get away. Go back to Bern and sort out the little details. The goods will be 'Free on Board' our trucks at the designated border crossing. Your gold will be placed in your bank fourteen days before delivery. I think that's about all."

"Sir, it occurs to me whether you would care to visit us to inspect the plant before despatch, assuming of course we are favoured with the order. We would look after you of course, you may like to bring your wife and have a short break together."

"Thank you Herr Muller, that would be most enjoyable. Perhaps I could telephone you in a week or so to give you an answer. In the meantime sort out the details." He paused for several seconds. "I shouldn't tell you this but you are competing against three German companies, Topf and Sons of Erfurt, the Didier Works of Berlin and C H Kori who made the plant for Dachau. They will have the disadvantage of not being able to be paid in gold, but doubtless will tender a lower price than you will. I like your mention of the fact that you would look after me and confirm that any contract placed comes over this desk." David noted the emphasis on the 'me.'

"I fully understand Herr Gruppenfuhrer, I fully understand."

David collected his papers together and slid them into his briefcase. "This has been the most interesting meeting of my life," he said as he shook hands with the general. "Goodbye Sir, I shall be in touch again soon."

As he left the building David felt a cold sweat down his back. What the hell is a one-time farm boy like me doing in one of the most evil places on earth he asked himself? Negotiating a contract to build a plant to dispose of six thousand of his fellow human beings every day, carrying a cyanide pill in his belt buckle in case he is caught, conniving in the rake-off for the Gruppenfuhrer without turning a hair, making soap out of human bodies!! Jesus Christ – what a world we live in. He was aware he was being followed again. He approached a municipal policeman to ask directions to the Lufthansa office. The quicker he got out of here the happier he would be.

The policeman was most polite and walked with him for a short distance to point out the street in which the Lufthansa booking office was situated. David thanked him and made his unhurried way to obtain his flight details hopefully for the next day. As he pushed his way through the revolving doors he noticed in the reflection that the two raincoated, trilby -hatted gents – I wonder if that's a uniform issue he wondered – had closed up on him and were following him in. He had a wild inclination to keep going round and round in the door to see what they would do but decided against it. He presumed they were Gestapo and if everything he had heard about the Gestapo was true, they would not appreciate having the piss taken out of them. As he cleared the door he paused to establish where the bookings counter was, as he did so his followers came up on either side of him. One asked him, "Excuse me Sir, will you come over here for a moment?" They moved away out of the main stream of the people going in and out.

"How can I help you?" David had quickly decided not to get on his high horse. His interrogation training had been very thorough in the hope it would never need to be put into practice, the first principle being to say as little as possible until you had established what the interrogator was after.

"May we see your papers please?" They were still being polite.

David produced his passport, following the production of this with "May I ask who you are and why you have approached me?" So as not to antagonise them, he smiled as he said this. It had been taught him that you stood a better chance of your questioners believing you if you smiled. On the other hand of course, if they had been properly trained, they would take no notice of smiles, genuine or otherwise.

His passport was handed back. "We are from the Geheimstatzpolizei" (Christ, David thought – Gestapo). "May we ask what you are doing in Berlin?"

David noticed a distinct reluctance of people going in and out to look in his direction.

"I have business with Gruppenfuhrer Krause of the Schutzstaffel."

"The S.S. heh? And what business would that be I wonder?" The politeness was beginning to wear off a little.

"I'm afraid that is secret, but please contact the General's office, they will confirm my credentials."

The senior one nodded to his companion who went to a desk, commandeered a telephone and presumably got through to S.S. H.Q. In the meantime his colleague continued his questioning.

"Who were the people you were talking to in the hotel shelter last night?"

David looked at him in some surprise. "They were residents in the hotel. I had never met them before. They were doctors attending a conference here, they come from Nurnberg I believe."

"I see. Did they tell you their name? People usually do when they introduce themselves."

"Yes of course, it was Manstein. Now look here" – David decided to start going on to the offensive – "what is this all about? I am a completely respectable Swiss businessman, here negotiating highly confidential matters at a very high level. My credentials have been satisfied fully. I am very embarrassed at being stopped and questioned in public like this. I am sure that the Herr Gruppenfuhrer will make his displeasure felt as well should I inform him of this incident."

The Gestapo man was not used to being spoken to like that, but like most bullies in a country where in virtually all domains there were bigger bullies to bully the little bullies he held his tongue. His colleague returned, whispered in his ear, at which the number one man put on a false smile saying, "I am sorry you have been inconvenienced Herr Muller, please accept our good wishes for a safe journey." They both bowed slightly and walked to the door. David had the fleeting hope that number one in the lead would walk into the wrong side and be flattened by a sixteen stone Bavarian pushing his way in, but it was not to be. However, he continued to wonder why they were watching his statuesque companion of the previous evening, and considered whether, if they were still in the hotel, he should warn them. He decided that if he bumped into them he would quickly tell them, otherwise he would not ask after them at the reception, the Gestapo had informers everywhere, in clubs, bars, societies, everywhere – even within families. The Gestapo was, comparatively speaking, a very small organisation, it relied entirely on a nation of informants, not only in Germany but in each of the occupied countries as well.

He had no trouble with his flight. The archetypal Aryan madchen behind the counter, blonde, blue-eyed, with a swastika badge in her lapel, informed him the next flight to Bern would be at midday tomorrow, calling at Dresden, Munich and Bern. David thanked her courteously as she handed him his flight tickets, receiving a manufactured smile and, "The coach for Templehof leaves here at 10.30." He thanked her again, and going the correct way into the revolving door found himself in the street wondering why some classically good-looking girls were so lacking in personality. If you shone a torch in that one's ear her eyes would light up he concluded, grinning to himself, until once again he discovered he was being followed. That took the grin off his face. He recognised he had committed the agent's cardinal sin of complacency. Having scored points off the Gestapo he had temporarily forgotten the fact that just one little false move could lead to the necessity of using that tablet in his belt buckle. He kept calm. Why is he following me? Would he be a tail put there by the other Gestapo to find out whether I would contact the Mansteins? If so they chose a pretty poor operator, he's almost hanging on to my shirttail. Could some other organisation be checking on me? He searched his brain but could not think of one. When in doubt, do nowt, he told himself, so carried on back to the hotel. Tail-arse Charlie, as he had christened his follower did not come into the hotel. David had the thought that the poor blighter was having to wait in some doorway all night to see whether he emerged. Two further thoughts. What does he do if he wants to pee or worse? What does he do if I go out the back way? There's bound to be one for the staff to use. He concluded that was his problem.

That night there was another raid. David surreptitiously scanned the occupants of the shelter, firstly to see if the Mansteins were there and to keep well away from them if they were, secondly to try and establish whether he could pinpoint the security wallah from the previous night. He had no success. The light was dim and the chap – or it could of course be a woman – would hardly be wearing a label around his or her neck. After an hour or so the raid ended and he went back to bed. He found sleep impossible. Up until now he had taken this assignment in his stride, the day to day discipline of making appointments, keeping the appointments, having technical discussions, even getting satisfaction from overcoming engineering problems, had combined to mask, except on one or two occasions, the fear of being caught and the horrific nature of the work in which he had found himself involved. As he lay wide awake he thought of those countless thousands who were ultimately the figures so casually bandied about in that office by a man who was to get a rake-off, whoever got the order. Even if I could get him to Switzerland and kill him, the juggernaut would roll on, he told himself. There is absolutely nothing I can do to stop it. He sobbed into his pillow for a long time, and eventually slid into the state of half awake, half asleep and dreaming, that deeply troubled persons suffer.

He awoke with a mild headache, looked at himself in the mirror, "God, what a wreck," immediately remembering a warning he had received in training – 'if you are feeling under par, slow down and be doubly careful.' It was very good advice, it is very easy to make an elementary slip if you are not permanently watchful.

Arriving at the Lufthansa office in good time, he selected a seat towards the rear of the bus. There were only a handful of passengers, which suited David; he had not looked forward to the possibility of having to chat to some inquisitive companion for the half hour journey. He booked in at the airport, handed in his luggage, and turning away from the desk was confronted by none other than Gruppenfuhrer Krause, accompanied by a slim, attractive, dark haired girl, David judged to be in her early twenties. His immediate thought was 'this is his fancy piece I suppose,' his second thought 'I must admit he's got good taste even if he is bordering on cradle snatching.' The general was in plain clothes and looked, again in David's opinion, almost respectable, until that figure of six thousand a day flashed through his mind. They shook hands.

"Herr Muller, this is my daughter Sonia."

Sonia shook hands with a firm pleasant grip, at the same time bestowing an open, friendly smile on the bemused David. "Have you enjoyed your visit to Berlin Herr Muller?"

"I found it most interesting, apart from a slight run-in with the Gestapo which I suspect your father was instrumental in sorting out. They were ever so polite after that." She laughed, he noted, not only with her mouth but with her eyes as well. There was no doubt she was a very pleasant girl.

"I mustn't say what I think about the Gestapo – at least not in front of my father," she said, taking the general's arm and looking up at him. She obviously adored him.

"Now Herr Muller, Sonia is going to Munich so having checked your flight plan and finding you would be on the same aircraft I thought it might be nice for you to have someone to talk to. Sonia is scared to death of flying by the way, so if she starts screaming with fright you will have to wrap her scarf around her face."

"Oh you fibber," Sonia playfully punched his arm, "don't believe a word he says Herr Muller."

The flight was called over the loudspeaker; Sonia hugged her father, telling him to take care of himself and not to get up to any mischief, at which words David could think of only one phrase – bloody hell! – the general shook hands with him and waved to them until they disappeared on to the tarmac. They boarded the JU52 aircraft, not a very pretty aeroplane in David's opinion, looking more like a corrugated iron shed with wings, but nevertheless having three reassuringly substantial looking motors up front. As he climbed in and settled Sonia in the seat against the window a thought flashed across his mind. It was a remark made to him by one of the instructors at Beaulieu – 'Always be cautious if you are suddenly thrust into the company of an attractive woman, it could be a trap.' David, pretending to study the other passengers, two in front being high ranking Wehrmacht officers, digested this thought. Sonia seemed an ordinary girl of above average looks. She had a nice open countenance, was very tastefully dressed. Ah, now there's a point. She was very nicely dressed. Unusual. Most Germans at this stage of the war if not shabby in appearance, were showing signs of it. On the other hand her father was an S.S. General, if he could not get the best, who could. I'll let her do the talking, we are going to be over two hours locked in this cabin, I would pretend to doze off but that would be rather rude assuming she is completely innocent.

"Thinking of getting home?"

He turned and smiled. "I was just wondering what all these people are doing whizzing from one place to another. I always wonder that at railway stations and when cars are racing along the main roads. We are like a lot of ants really, aren't we?"

"They are probably thinking the same about you." He smiled.

"Is it polite to ask what you do in Munich?"

"I hope you are not insinuating in that question that I might be up to something I shouldn't?" The mouth and eyes smiled again. "I am a second year medical student at the university. In two years, I shall hopefully be a doctor."

"It's a four year course?"

He continued to ask her questions, couched as well as he could so that he did not appear to be cross-examining her, but as a result getting her to do most of the talking. She willingly seemed to be accepting this role which led him to think she was unlikely to be a professional – she would be asking him questions by now. In any event, what could she be after?

"We shall be landing at Dresden in five minutes. Passengers proceeding to Munich please stay in your seats. There will be a twenty minute stopover."

"I can never understand half of what is said on those public address systems," David complained, "Lord knows what it will be like when I am old and deaf."

"At least you stand a good chance of becoming old and deaf," Sonia replied, with a catch in her voice and turning her head to the window.

David waited a few seconds. "Did I say something to upset you?" he asked.

"No, not really. You see, my brother is very much like you. He is with the Waffen S.S. in Russia. They get all the tough jobs to do. I worry about him all the time. I am glad my father has his job in the quartermasters department. Apart from the bombing at least he is safe there. He keeps saying he would rather be at the front than counting army blankets in Berlin." She hesitated for a moment. "I'm sorry, I shouldn't have burdened you with all that." He touched her arm to re-assure her. His thoughts raced – counting bloody blankets – if she is genuine, what on earth is she going to do when eventually she finds out what his job really is?

In the twenty minutes they were at Dresden they were served coffee – quite good stuff, probably obtained in Portugal he guessed – correctly as it happened. It had not been possible to serve anything on the flight due to a strong headwind making life a little unpleasant. This increased on the leg to Munich, extending the flight time to just over an hour and a half. They talked about the scenery over which they were flying, how the war had affected life in Switzerland, a sudden question as to whether his wife would be meeting him, and a self-conscious smile at being caught out asking such an innocent question when he replied that he was 'fancy free.'

Just before landing at Munich, Sonia took his hand. "I do wish we could meet again Erwin. I have so enjoyed your company."

"I will see if it can be arranged" he replied, knowing full well that they would never meet again. As she stood up to leave, she kissed him on each cheek and gave him a little hug, he hugged her back and watched from the window as she went down the steps from the plane on to the tarmac. She turned, blew him a little kiss and disappeared into the terminal building. He was left ruminating she was obviously not part of a trap, she was a very nice girl who, if circumstances had been different, he would have liked to get to know, he had only been with her for a couple of hours yet she would stay in his memory for many years. That's war, he thought, although what he meant by that thought was a trifle unclear.

After an uneventful last leg of his journey, accompanied as it was by marvellous views of the Alps in the distance and the icy blue Lake Konstanz immediately below, he landed at Bern airport. Only a handful of passengers were left to alight, the arrival procedures being therefore speedily dealt with. He felt an enormous sense of relief at being back in safety – not least safety from British bombers! He telephoned Helga at the factory to tell them he was back, knowing they would pass the news on to the Count. This they must have done immediately since when he arrived at his lodgings the Count was there waiting for him, his first words to David being "Welcome back – I had my doubts as to whether we would ever see you again."

Chapter Twenty Six

It was eight a.m. on Monday 27th April when Ruth's telephone shrilled, startling her out of her wits as she happened to be passing close to it at the time.

"Chandlers Lodge."

"Mum, Mum, wonderful news. I've had a telegram from the War Office. Harry's alive, Harry's alive." They both dissolved into floods of tears. Rose, coming down the stairs, hearing the telephone ring, and almost instantly thereafter hearing her mother crying, raced down the last flight.

"What's the matter Mummy – it's not David is it?" She was white with shock.

"No – Harry's alive. Megan has had a telegram."

"Oh, thank God." She paused for a moment. "In that case why the devil are you crying?" Ruth handed her the telephone.

"What does the telegram say Megan?" Rose asked.

"It says" – she paused a moment, obviously unfolding the piece of paper and trying hard not to drop the receiver at the same time, not however succeeding, as there was a dull clonk as it hit the hall table and a further indeterminate succession of rustling and tapping noises as she pulled it up from the floor.

"I'm sorry about that; I'm in such a tiz. It says:-

'The War Office is pleased to inform you that your husband W.O.I. Chandler H. previously reported missing believed killed in action has rejoined his unit. Stop. Operational requirements preclude his being able to contact you for the time being."

"And that's all?"

"That's all – except that I had a letter in the post this morning from the army paymaster, saying that my marriage allowance was cancelled from 28 January when they were first notified of W.O.I. Chandler being killed in action. The amounts I have received in the meantime I will be called upon to refund."

"Megan, let Dad deal with that – what an awful thing to do to someone in such stress as you have been. Let's get together and tell the world the good news about Harry, and if you will forgive my French – sod the paymaster."

Megan's tears turned to laughter.

"I'll get the children ready and come round. Will you tell Dad and Ernie at the factory? I'll see you in an hour."

The news was swiftly disseminated to family and friends. At the end of the excitement of telling all and sundry the good news there was the inevitable realisation they had no idea whatsoever as to what sort of danger he was in, what was meant by 'operational requirements,' under what sort of conditions he was living, and with whom and where. Fred came home to an early lunch to find the girls had become somewhat introspective after the initial euphoria. He immediately struck a confident note.

"This is the best news we've had this year. I always said, and particularly after I read Harry's letter to you all that Harry can look after himself better than most. Wherever he is he will make the best of it, not only for himself but also for the others who may be with him. You see if I am not right. Now, how about this lunch, I am away early tonight. Jack and I are going to see Ray at the hospital."

They found Ray in good spirits, his only complaint being that this hospital, The Southern, was in fact a Royal Navy hospital, "So as you can imagine you have to keep your hand on your ha'penny if you bend down to pick anything up, which is very difficult in my case – either you take a chance or you leave whatever it is on the floor." The jest was evidence that he was not going to let the loss of a limb rule his life. One problem he would have to face, as he solemnly told them was that he had lost his courting hand with which he had developed considerable expertise over the years, so much so that he considered it probably a professional standard. Relearning the techniques with his left hand would take not only time but a certain amount of forbearance from the lady, or ladies, receiving the approach. Jack suggested he might borrow a dummy from 'Country Style' to practise on. To a degree of somewhat raucous laughter, Fred suggested that Mrs Draper, a rather bosomy lady who ran the shop, might herself as part of the war effort, help out.

Leaving Ray with a couple of bottles of Whitbread's they had smuggled in – drink was forbidden – they got the hospital bus into Dartford, had time for a quick one in the 'Wat Tyler,' by the church, then caught the Green Line back to Sandbury, where everyone was gathered to hear how Ray was progressing. He had told them he would be at the Southern for another couple of weeks and would then be sent to a convalescent centre for a while, returning to London when he could start being fitted with a new hand. "Then I suppose they will give me a bag of allsorts and say sod off," had been his last quip.

There was a board meeting at Sandbury Engineering on Friday 1st May. The major part of the discussion was concerned with the Hamilcar project, but in 'A.O.B.' Fred raised the subject of Ray Osbourne stating that although it would be some weeks before Ray was released, they should approach him regarding his joining the firm to take over the management initially of the Hamilcar programme, at the same time commencing the development of the proposed post war plastics venture. It was minuted that unanimous agreement followed this proposal.

On Saturday morning after Fred had left for the factory, a most important looking letter arrived addressed to "Mr F. E. Chandler M.M." The envelope was heavily embossed, giving Rose, who had run to the door when she heard the postman arrive the impression of it's being of considerable consequence. Going into the kitchen she showed it to her mother with the words, "This looks frightfully posh." Ruth examined it.

"Well, it certainly isn't from the income tax people. Put it by the clock." They each conjectured during the morning what it contained, but neither was prepared for the exciting news it produced when Fred arrived for lunch and carefully opened it. It was headed:

10 Downing Street
London SW1

Ruth, looking over Fred's shoulder gave a little gasp. "Ten Downing Street – what on earth would the Prime Minister want with you? Read it out please Fred." She was as excited as he had seen her for many years. Fred read out as requested.

Sir

The Prime Minister has asked me to inform you, in strict confidence, that he has it in mind, on the occasion of the forthcoming list of Birthday Honours, to submit your name to the King with a recommendation that His Majesty may be graciously pleased to approve that you be appointed an Officer of the Order of the British Empire.

Before doing so, the Prime Minister would be glad to be assured that this would be agreeable to you. I should be grateful if you would let me know by completing the enclosed form and sending it to me by return of post.

If you agree that your name should go forward and the King accepts the Prime Ministers recommendation, the announcement will be made in the Birthday Honours List. You will receive no further communication before the list is published.

I am, Sir,
Your obedient servant

William Browne

There was a complete silence before a minor pandemonium broke loose, the two women slapping Fred on the back and congratulating him to such an extent they woke young Jeremy up who added to the noise by protesting loudly he wanted his lunch. Fred stood silent for a moment. "There's another sheet here." Ruth and Rose waited whilst he scanned it. "It says that this matter is confidential until publication time, which means that you can't get on the blower and broadcast the news far and wide. After all, His Majesty may not want me for all we know." Again he paused. "I bet this is Jack's doing – someone has to put your name forward. I'll have a word with him tonight."

When he did 'have a word' with Jack that evening, he was positively assured that his friend had had absolutely nothing to do with it. He assumed that because Sandbury Engineering had performed so well on behalf of all the three service purchasing organisations one or the other had nominated him. "And so they should – you've performed miracles at times to pull their chestnuts out of the fire when they've delayed placing contracts."

"Yes, that's true," Fred replied, "but many other people have done the spade work."

"You can't honour everybody. They share your honour, that's how it works."

The reply form was sent off over the weekend leaving the family waiting impatiently for the Honours List to be published at the beginning of June.

May was a quiet month in the skies above Sandbury. Elsewhere in the world it continued with unabated fury. The Japanese landed on Corregidor in the Philippines, leading to appalling atrocities to the surrendered American troops. British and Indian troops continued their withdrawal through the monsoon back to Imphal in India. Malta continued to endure constant air attacks, the resistance to which had won them the George Cross in the previous month. British troops attacked and occupied Madagascar in order to safeguard operations in the Indian Ocean. Himmler's S.S. deputy, Heydrich was assassinated in Prague, in the next two days two thousand Czechs were rounded up and killed, and a week or so later the village of Lidice was razed to the ground and all the inhabitants perished. Leningrad continued to be besieged. Thousands died of starvation every day. A schoolbook belonging to Tanya Savicheva contained the following:- 'Mummy May

13. 7.30 in the morning. The Savichevs are now all dead. Only Tanya remains. Zhenya died Dec 28. Granny died Jan 25. Leka died March 17. Uncle Vasya died April 13. Uncle Lyosha May 10.' Tanya herself died in the summer of 1943.

On Friday 22nd May Buffy Cartwright telephoned from Romsey. "Ruth, shall you be having the service on Sunday?" Each year since Jeremy had been killed in action in France, Rose had had a short service of remembrance conducted by Canon Rosser, the Cartwrights having a similar ceremony in their local church. Ruth replied that Rose had arranged for it after matins on Sunday morning. Buffy expressed the desire that he and Rita could join them for it. Ruth immediately welcomed the plan, suggesting they stay for a few days; they had ample room now the Canadians were gone. The Cartwrights duly arrived at lunchtime on Saturday, bringing with them a large box of hares, rabbits and several cock pheasants, who had 'done their good work for the year.'

A number of friends, having been to the morning service, joined the Cartwrights and the Chandlers for the short observance in which Canon Rosser prayed, "Not only for the remembrance of our brave young friend Jeremy Cartwright, but also for the safe keeping of Jeremy's best friend David, on operational duty in some foreign field, for David's brother Harry in the jungles of Malaya, for Mark and Charlie in Africa and for all of those you love and are far from you at this moment."

However, neither the Japanese nor the Germans were having it entirely their own way. As a taste of things to come Colonel Doolittle led sixteen American bombers, having taken off from the carrier 'Hornet,' to bomb Tokyo and four other towns in Japan. The Land of the Rising Sun learnt it was not invulnerable. A greater lesson was dealt out to the Germans. In the early evening of the 28th May Sandbury looked up to see fifteen medium bombers flying low over the town, gradually to peel off from the 'V's in which they were flying to land on Sandbury aerodrome. Aeroplanes were a daily happening over the town, but almost always they were fighters, along with the occasional Oxford or Anson. Sandbury was a fighter station not a bomber 'drome. The youngsters who knew their aircraft recognition, told their parents, who didn't know a Wellington from a Dornier, that these aeroplanes, each resembling some gigantic dragonfly with its long thin tail, were Hampdens. They were fast, rated at 265 m.p.h. and carried four thousand pounds of bombs. The talk in all the pubs that night was centred on wondering why fifteen bombers had descended on Sandbury.

They had not long to wait for the answer. On Saturday evening the fifteen took off heading towards the continent. The next day the world heard of the first '1000 bomber' raid against Germany, on the city of Cologne. One thousand and seventy four British bombers struck the greatest psychological blow the Germans had yet received, giving other cities an indication of what they were to look forward to. Churchill announced, "This is the herald of what Germany will receive, city by city, from now on." And they did. Seventy per cent of Cologne was damaged or destroyed, but the magnificent cathedral stood proud among the ruins. Accident or design?

On the unhappy side only twelve of the Hampdens returned. One was shot down over the target, one was hit and ditched in the Channel, and the third one collided with a Blenheim on the run-in, both being lost. When the aircraft flew away to their home base on Tuesday morning, the whole town turned out to wave to them as they passed overhead.

The Cartwrights went back on Wednesday after inviting Rose to bring their grandson down to Romsey in the summer and to stay for a week or two, to which suggestion Rose had readily agreed. Buffy and Rita were more like their old selves now. It may be a stock phrase that time is a great healer, it is a truism nevertheless. They could now look at Jeremy's photograph and smile fondly at the memory of their son instead of shedding tears of sorrow. They could talk of him, the funny things he used to say or do, without a catch in their throats. They could think of him, with some sorrow still, but without the heart-rending sadness of yore. Above all they could see him in the shape of the young Jeremy, beginning to look more and more like his father every day – or so they fondly imagined.

After seeing them off at Sandbury station Rose and Ruth, pushing young Jeremy in the small second-hand pushchair they had bought, new ones by now being completely unobtainable, made their way into the town centre.

"I'm going to buy you a coffee at John Tarrant's," Rose told her mother.

"That I imagine is only an excuse for you to unobtrusively slip a crafty brandy into your own cup," came the reply.

"Right first time."

"Make it two."

"Make what two?" It was Cecely, who had left the shop for her lunch and had caught them up. Being Wednesday it was early closing day, upon which she always had a leisurely snack at the Angel before going off to The Bungalow.

They all went to the coffee room at the rear of the hotel, set aside so that unaccompanied ladies could have a crafty one without having to go into the saloon bar, which would never do. Cecely had still no word of the whereabouts of Nigel, nor whether he was alive or dead. The sadness of this total lack of knowledge showed in the worry lines around her eyes, but the major problem was trying to reassure the children their father would be alright. They came home each weekend now so that she could keep a watchful eye on them, but as she said it was obvious, at times, they were sadly missing their father and uncle.

For no apparent reason Cecely suddenly wondered what had happened to Marian Rowlands, Pat's mother. She was lost in thought when Ruth touched her hand. "Penny for them?"

"I can't explain why but I suddenly wondered what happened to Marian, Pat's mother. Rowlands was well in with the Japanese, but whether that would keep them from internment I don't know. Knowing him, they've probably made him a district governor or something – he's that sort of person."

"He wouldn't co-operate with them would he?"

"That's exactly what he would do given the opportunity?"

"Then they should hang him after the war."

"He'll convince everybody that whatever he did aided the cause, you mark my words."

It was four days after the gathering at John Tarrant's that Marian Rowland's life changed abruptly. By early June 1942 nearly all British civilians had been marched to internment camps. Many died on the way, the aged, the sick, and were left for the local people to bury. The Japanese guards, although constantly urging the columns on, aided sometimes by a well placed rubber soled boot on the rear of some unfortunate laggard, did not randomly brutalise or shoot their charges as was to be the practice, or often the pleasure, of the S.S. guards escorting concentration camp victims in Europe. When the invasion was approaching Kuala Lumpur in early January, the man Rowlands, who had pirated Jack Hooper's wife Marian, had spirited away to one of his more remote properties a dozen or so of his Japanese mine owning cronies to prevent their being rounded up and sent to Singapore. As the tide of battle pushed further south, so his grateful friends took him to the local army commander to get a special dispensation for him and Marian to stay on one of their properties, a mine, work their mine for the benefit of the Japanese, and not be interned. This was granted in appreciation of the services Rowlands had rendered to the Japanese cause, both before and during the campaign.

Marian was dreadfully lonely. She had only the Malay servants to converse with. They, in view of the fact that Mr Rowlands, the Tuan, was closely involved with the Japanese, frequently gave wild drinking parties for them, as a result of which on two occasions a girl was raped, kept their distance even more than they would under normal domestic circumstances. By the end of May she had lost weight and was beginning to become clinically depressed. To add to her misery she discovered Rowlands had set up a Eurasian girl in one of the mine apartments. There was nothing she could do about it, she could not leave without being interned, she gave not a damn about the Eurasian girl, he had pursued this path many times before, but now it was being played out right under her nose. She had the consolation of knowing that at least he left her alone, she rarely had to put up with his drink sodden breath saturating her mosquito net, his rancid sweat fouling her bed linen as he vainly tried to reach a climax denied him by the excess of alcohol he had consumed.

On Sunday 31st May, Marian took her afternoon rest as usual and at around four o'clock got up, slipped on a robe and went on to the veranda at the back of the house to be served tea by one of the servant girls. This was the most pleasant part of her otherwise tedious, uninteresting day. The veranda looked out over a wide expanse of lawn, not the velvety smooth Cumberland turf of home but a rough grass known as lallang, which misappropriated the word lawn in Malaya. Beyond that was a wire enclosure containing two tennis courts, beyond that some more grass, and then – the jungle. She kept a pair of binoculars on the table where she sat, since frequently she would spot birds and occasionally animals emerging from the dense foliage, which was the eastern boundary of the property. On one memorable occasion, before the invasion, she had actually seen a tiger appear, lay down on the further stretch of grass, clean itself and then stretch out in the sun to sleep. It was a once in a lifetime experience.

As she recalled that 'day of the tiger' as she had catalogued it in her mind, she noticed some movement in one thick clump of greenery. She picked up her binoculars but could see no cause for the disturbance on an otherwise windless afternoon. She kept the glasses trained on the spot for a minute or so, was just about to put them down when to her utter astonishment, she clearly saw the face of a white man wearing a green hat. Her first thought was that it must be a soldier who had escaped from the Japs back in January and had been living in the jungle. Then to her astonishment, she saw him wave; come out of the cover at a brisk trot followed by another white man and six or eight Chinese. They were all armed, all carrying bundles of one sort or another, and most disturbingly coming straight towards her. She sat frozen to her chair as they reached the veranda and spread out along it. The most ridiculous conversation then ensued.

"Good afternoon. I am Major Leach of Force 136. I'm frightfully sorry to have disturbed you." His upper crust accent would have been perfectly at home in Whites, or the Garrick.

"Not at all, would you care for some tea?"

"Thank you no. We're here to blow up this mine, or what we can of it. Tell me, why are you not interned?"

"My husband, who owns this mine, is a collaborator, and a traitor to his country. As a result I am allowed to live here."

"Then you won't mind if we carry on?"

"Please do. Unfortunately he is in KL today or you could have blown him up as well."

"Oh, I say, how rich."

"I mean it."

The major looked at her closely. "Will you help us by telling us the layout of the plant?"

Marian proceeded to tell him that at the entrance to the workings, there was a guard hut with four Japanese soldiers in it who, when they were not raping her Malay girls, checked vehicles and people in and out. "If you come up on to the first floor landing I can point out to you where the various essential pieces of equipment are." The major and the captain with him followed her upstairs.

"That building houses the stores and the main generator. The main dredger, driven by a huge diesel engine is about four hundred yards down the hill. The guardhouse is on the corner of the stores building. Approaching it from this side you cannot be seen, as there are no windows facing this way. There is a standby generator and a reserve diesel engine for the dredger under that lean-to of which you can just see the top. Supplies of diesel for the generators are in a tank in a bund at the back of the lean-to. I think that's about all. Unless you would like to blow up that apartment over there where my husband keeps his mistress."

The major led them back downstairs, and called his small party together. Swiftly he apportioned them their tasks. Firstly he and four men would deal with the guards – "They will probably be asleep anyway." While he was doing this, the captain and his group would fix the charges to the main generator. And so the plan was swiftly formulated. As they withdrew, so they would burn all the buildings they could with the phosphorous hand grenades they had brought for the purpose – "But we shall leave the house intact in view of your help Mrs?"

"Marian Rowlands, but you can burn the house – I shall come with you, the Japs will show me no mercy, despite my husband, when they see what you have done."

"I don't think that would be practical. We have a three day march when we leave here."

"I'm fit, and with my knowledge of the country and the targets in it, I could well be invaluable to you."

The major thought for a moment. "Well, we can't leave you here, that's obvious, so you had better come with us on the very strict understanding, very strict you understand, that if you fall by the wayside, we leave you. There is no way I can prejudice the safety of my men. Do you clearly understand that?"

"Clearly."

"Then while we are placing the charges, get changed for the jungle. Pack a couple of small bags with stuff you will want, we will carry them for you."

The major beckoned four of the men, and ordered them to follow him. He had taken a vicious looking fighting knife from a sheath on his belt, the men following suit. Swiftly and silently they ran across the open ground to the stores building and then on to the rear of the guardhouse. One sentry, supposedly on duty, was seated on a bench leaning back against the wall fast asleep. The major expertly cut his throat, passing him into his Shinto afterlife without his being able to say a word in preparation before meeting his ancestors. Three of the Chinese meanwhile moved swiftly in to the guardhouse and in seconds had despatched the rest of the detail.

Swiftly they attached the explosives to the selected pieces of plant and set the timers. It being Sunday there was no work going on, they were still working to Imperial rules, British Imperial that is! A small group of maintenance people at the dredger, seeing the green clad armed men running towards them, stopped what they were doing and stood with their hands up. They were quickly bound and left in the shade of a bicycle lean to. The gate valve on the diesel tank was opened and a volume of the liquid allowed to flood into the bund, or surrounding wall. As soon as there were a few inches in the enclosure, two phosphorus bombs were lobbed in. Diesel does not burn easily but the tremendous heat generated by the phosphorus soon set it going –

after a while the tank would split and there would be real fireworks.

Having set the last of the charges, they ran back to the house to find Marian ready to go, having lined up a dozen or so bottles of Tiger beer. "It would be a shame to waste these," she said to which sentiment they all agreed, making her their friend for life! Finally, the others having left the building, the major tossed the remainder of the grenades into various rooms and caught the party up as they disappeared into the jungle. As they began the long walk back to Camp Four, as Marian found later it was called, the sound of the explosions followed them, and a pall of smoke rose to be seen clearly in the town some five miles away.

As she followed the party into the jungle Marian had a sudden thought. 'I wonder what happened to the Coates family and that nice sergeant major friend of theirs. Harry, that's right. Harry Chandler.' She would one day find out about the latter in rather unusual circumstances.

Chapter Twenty Seven

The day after David arrived back at Bern a conference was called at the factory, which lasted all day. He gave a day by day account of everything that had happened to him, including a full briefing to Colonel Masson, who came in for an hour, of the problems in Munich. When the colonel left they went into detail about the engineering requirements, which left Helga and Herr Brendt white faced and tight-lipped at the enormity of the genocide these foul animals were planning.

"This information must not go beyond these four walls," the Count pronounced. "If the knowledge becomes general they could conceivably suspect Cooteman of having leaked it. That would put him in considerable danger if I have to send him back in again."

At this statement David almost jumped out of his chair. Here he was, thinking, 'thank God that job's finished,' only to hear that he himself might well be risking joining the queue for the gas chamber again. His entrails performed the same pasa doble as they had on occasion when he was in the Fatherland. He told himself 'I'll get a bloody ulcer if they spring many more on me like that.'

Herr Brendt took the floor. "Now and over the weekend we will treat this as we would a regular trade enquiry. I, with help from Herr Muller, will do the outline drawings, so that the drawing office staff are not involved. Helga can do the costings and type up the outline specification so that we can get a proposal together for Monday or Tuesday. I will establish how much gold we shall require and what delivery time we shall give, we can then despatch our proposals to the general. So that no member of staff inadvertently stumbles on what we are doing I suggest we work at my home. I have drawing boards there. All agreed?"

They transported David in a luxurious Mercedes to a most beautiful house built in the foothills of the mountains some ten miles from the factory.

"We will send you back on the train tonight, but tomorrow bring your things for a three or four day stay. Helga will meet you at the station in the morning." And so they went to work, preparing a specification running into some thirty pages, and an astronomical quotation running into millions of deutschmarks. It took longer than they had expected, partly due to the fact that both Helga and Herr Brendt had to go to the factory on occasion to take up appointments, which they would not want to break. When all was completed, and copies had been made by Herr Brendt's totally trusted secretary, along with drawings printed by Helga and David in the evening after the staff had gone home, they sat back and studied their work. Folder after fat folder of drawings, specifications, contractual details, terms of supply, price and equivalent in gold, delivery details, detailed provision of erection drawings upon signing the contract, and so on. All the paraphernalia that goes into an industrial presentation, except that on this occasion, the end product would be the total transformation within an hour of healthy, law abiding men, women, children and babies into dust. Tears began to flow down Helga's cheeks as they sat considering the enormity of it all. Their plant would never be made, but this would not alter the fact that Didier or one of the others would make it. Nothing could stop these monsters applying what was to become known as 'the Final Solution.' With the further thought always in the back of the Brendt's mind of the unknown fate of Helga's older sister, her husband, their three children taken by the Nazis in Frankfurt two years ago, the husband being a German Jew, they were personally involved in these awful proceedings.

Herr Brendt ended the silence. "I will call a meeting with the Count here tomorrow morning," he announced. "We can then plan what we are going to do."

The following morning was a Friday. The Count was full of praise for the work that had been done; stating that one copy of this proposal would be on its way in the diplomatic bag that night to London via Lisbon. "I do hope the so-called intelligence buffs will take it seriously" he added, "the chances are that they will think it is all so far-fetched as to be impossible. I mean, who in their right minds are going to suggest that this sort of thing can take place in the country that produced Beethoven, Schiller, and so on. It has happened before. Cooteman will have to go back as soon as we can let him go to provide added weight to the evidence." At this piece of information David began to think what a lovely day it was.

"Now let us consider a modus operandi," the Count continued.

1. "We despatch the proposals, now we have succeeded in achieving our initial task in obtaining the information we set out to get."
2. "General Krause will then be left in the dark as to how much his rake-off is to be and where it is going to be deposited. There is no doubt he would prefer to have the money in a Swiss bank to having it where it can be

discovered in Germany."
3. "That being the case he will certainly wish to come here to discuss the project with us."
4. "He will, without doubt, have to bring with him to the meeting the commercial attaché from the German Embassy. We shall have to split them up for a few minutes at least in order to acquaint him of his rake-off and the bank and number therein. He will be asked positively whether that is agreeable to him. All of this we will record."
5. "We shall entertain him the following day, bring him back to the office, tell him straight that this has been an espionage operation, we positively refuse to make the equipment, he will have to place the order elsewhere on the basis of the Swiss price being too high."
6. "However, he can still get his rake-off as arranged by providing us with the top level information of SS operations he automatically receives. There is no way, with America now in the war that Germany can win. A generous nest egg stashed away in Switzerland would enable him, when the war ended, to live comfortably with his daughter Sonia. The mention of her name could well swing it. If he fails to survive the war, or the war crimes trials afterwards, Sonia will be provided for."
7. "If he baulks we will tell him of the recording, and play it if necessary, with the clear indication that should Reichsminister Himmler receive a copy of it...? He should think of Sonia."
8. "Finally, he is to make enquiries as to the fate of Herr Brendt's daughter, son-in-law and grandchildren."

The others listened engrossed at this succinct rhetoric. There was silence as he concluded, "If this works out the way I have indicated, Cooteman has not only got the information he was detailed to get, but he has also got us a top level source of information in S.S. Headquarters. That could be absolutely invaluable. With the S.S. being a law entirely to themselves, all sorts of things happen that our other sources of information in the Abwehr and O.K.W. – German high command, never pick up."

A message was therefore sent to the general on the teleprinter. 'Proposal fully sealed, handed in to your embassy at 1600 hrs today for dispatch to you alone, by diplomatic bag tonight. Regards. Muller.' Late the next afternoon a teleprinter message arrived. 'Proposal received. Will contact you shortly. Krause.'

The following Tuesday 7th April, the telephone rang at the factory, the caller asking for Herr Muller. It was the secretary from the general's office. David immediately asked her, "How is my friend the Graf?"

To which she replied, "He has gone to the front very much happier than he was." They both laughed at the meaning behind this, and again David reflected on the circumstances whereby normally they could be friends, he and this girl. "Now, down to business Herr Muller. The Herr Gruppenfuhrer will be visiting you on Thursday and Friday of next week, 16th and 17th April. Can you meet him at the airport? He may stay on over the weekend if he can manage the time. I understand you will be having a meeting at Saint Nicholas. One of our embassy officials would like to be present. Perhaps you will contact Herr Kopp and let him know the time of the meeting? I think that is all. Goodbye Herr Muller, perhaps we shall meet again," and she rang off.

David had a lazy time for the next few days, taking the opportunity to visit Lausanne, Geneva, and Interlaken. He was falling in love with Switzerland. Everywhere was so clean, so green and picturesque. Beautiful lakes with undulating hills reaching up to the majestic Alps made such an agreeable impression on him he began to think it would be nice to live here. And then he thought, 'I'll soon change my mind when I get back to Kent.' The thought that that might not be too far in the future set in motion further visions of seeing Maria again. Getting back home could not come quickly enough if only for that reason.

On the afternoon of the 16th, Herr Brendt and David met General Krause at the airport as arranged. The general dressed in civilian clothes of course since he was visiting a foreign country, carried a somewhat bulky briefcase, but recovered only a small suitcase from the hold. He shook hands enthusiastically with David, who introduced him to Herr Brendt; David in the meantime surveying the handful of other passengers to try and establish the general was not being tagged. As all the other passengers appeared to be being met by enthusiastic friends or relatives, he concluded this was not the case. They led their guest out to the large chauffer driven Mercedes, the two principles seating themselves on the rear seat whilst David pulled down an occasional. When the driver got in, having put the suitcase in the boot, he wound up the internal partition to give the occupants privacy.

It was around five o'clock when they reached Saint Nicholas where they found Herr Kopp had already arrived. Helga swiftly arranged for coffee and cakes to be served in the boardroom, informing them that she had arranged dinner for eight o'clock at a nearby restaurant, after which she understood Herr Kopp would take the general back to his hotel in Bern. At this, Herr Kopp announced that if they could discuss the commercial details first he would be most grateful, as he regretted he would not be able to join them on the morrow. He added, "Not that I would understand a word of the technical jargon anyway."

During the financial and contractual discussions in the evening, Helga begged to be excused for a short while, taking the opportunity to telephone the Count and to acquaint him of the progress thus far. The Count was very pleased to hear they would have the general to themselves on the morrow; he had been concerned that Herr Kopp might conceivably know of him, or at least might make enquiries about him after the meeting. He arranged that he would make his own way to Saint Nicholas, the Mercedes being sent to collect David and the general.

When they met on the Friday morning, the Count was introduced as the 'senior financial advisor' to the company and a minority shareholder. The general accepted this information quite readily to justify his presence at the meeting.

"General, I think we should get down to the details of our personal arrangements," Herr Brendt announced. "Our financial advisor," nodding to the Count, "has arranged that a sum of two hundred and fifty thousand Swiss francs will be placed in a numbered Swiss account in a bank of your choice at the same time as our bank receives your gold in payment for equipment we shall be supplying you. You will contact our bank with the details you have chosen to accept this money. Our bank has the money on deposit now ready for transfer. Firstly general, do you agree the amount of the commission we have stated?"

"Yes, it is very generous," came the reply.

"Are you in agreement with the payment details?" Herr Brendt asked.

"Yes, indeed."

"In the unlikely event of your death between now and the delivery date, can we arrange to pay your commission to your wife, or I believe you have a daughter Sonia."

"My wife died three years ago. I only have Sonia. However, I have no intention of departing this life for a while yet I assure you. On the other hand I suppose you have to think of every exigency, so perhaps you had better write Sonia in – not that I want her to know anything about this business or what I am involved in – you understand?"

"You have our word general." Herr Brendt paused for a few moments. "Now, as you have not had an opportunity to see our plant, Herr Muller and Helga will show you around then we will have coffee here in the boardroom, hopefully afterwards concluding the remainder of our business."

As soon as the party had left to see the factory workshops, the Count said, "Right, let's make sure we got all that on the recording." They played it back on the dictaphone. One or two phrases were a little indistinct due the spokesman momentarily turning his head away from the concealed microphones, but the important parts, especially those spoken by the general were loud and clear. 'So far, so good' was the Count's view.

The party returned from the works for coffee and when all was cleared away, the Count took charge of the meeting. Standing at the head of the table he addressed the general.

"Herr Gruppenfuhrer, it is now my duty to inform you that Herr Muller and I are agents of the government of the United Kingdom." The general started to rise from his seat. "Please sit down general and hear what I have to say."

The general slumped back into his chair. He immediately realised without their telling him they now had the power of life and death over him and over his daughter. He was pale when he replied, "You can do what you like to me, but I beg of you do not allow my daughter to be harmed."

"We do not intend for either of you to be harmed, quite the opposite in fact."

There was a lengthy silence.

"We have a proposition to put to you. As you have probably already guessed we have a recording of our previous financial discussions. Now, this war is going to get even more ferocious as America and Britain prepare to invade in the West. The Russian eighteen-year-old birth rate is three times that of Germany. They can, therefore, reinforce their troops at three times the volume of the German reinforcement capability. In a short war that would not be so important, but you know and we know that this is now going to be a long war. It is therefore a very important factor. It means you cannot win.

The work you are doing will undoubtedly mean that after the war, which I repeat you cannot win, you and others would be indicted for war crimes. Not only would you receive a long prison sentence, or even execution, but your daughter would suffer disgrace and lifelong misery as a result of your being tried and punished.

We have checked on you. You had a good war record in the 1914 war. You belonged to a good regiment, you opposed the Nazis in the twenties, why are you now in the S.S.?"

"I am in the Waffen S.S., not the Totenkopf."

"The Totenkopf I know run the concentration camps. You are doing Totenkopf work are you not?"

"One has to obey orders."

David interjected. "Do those orders not mean 'lawful' orders? If they are unlawful, as yours plainly are, can you not say so, and ask to be excused from carrying them out?"

"That may be the case in the British Army. The worst that would happen to you would be your being cashiered. In my case I would certainly be shot and my daughter would end up in Ravensbruk."

The Count interrupted. "I can assure you that following unlawful orders would not be accepted as an excuse in a British or American court, as a lawyer I can assure you of that."

There was another long pause.

"I will come to the point Herr Gruppenfuhrer. We are of the opinion that you are not a wholehearted Nazi. In fact I am aware that the vast proportion of general officers despise the Nazi clique, most of whom are ignorant, uncouth, and out for all they can get. They have committed and are committing horrendous crimes all over Europe, but particularly in Poland and Russia, crimes which besmirch the honour of Germany and which will go down in history never to be forgotten. You can help the western democracies by working for us. You would not be a traitor to your country; you would be one of the many striving to make Germany a free place to live in, for your daughter to bring up your grandchildren in peace and honour, for the Gestapo to be a thing of the past." The Count stood up. "We will leave you now for a while to think things over. I will send you some coffee."

They left the general slumped in his chair. How much of a Nazi was he at heart? If at all, that is. What difference would the money make in influencing him? Ideally of course the Count would prefer he would throw in his lot for non material reasons, but if this proved not to be the case, he would not hesitate to hold the threat of blackmail over his head, not only if he refused to co-operate, but also if his co-operation was judged to be half-hearted, or slackened off in time. The daughter is the key, he told the others, the daughter is the key – "And we would not have even known about her if it had not been for you," he determined, thumping David on the back.

They rejoined the general.

"I have been considering all you have said. I am not a Nazi, I never have been a Nazi, I detest a great deal of what they do. They had my support because they rebuilt the Fatherland after 1933 and saved us from communism, which I consider to be a far greater evil. They gave us full employment and a status again in the world. They regained German territories taken from us by the infamous Treaty of Versailles. They had my support for all those things. They did not have my support over Austria and Czechoslovakia but then you can't agree with everything the politicians do. They did not have my support over the unfair persecutions of the Jews, not that I have any love at all for Jews in general. They could have deported them not incarcerated them. This 'Final Solution' they are talking about, into which I have been precipitated, is the final straw. Being here, now, in this beautiful country has made me even more aware of the wickedness being carried on a few hundred miles away.

In short then, gentlemen, although I am well aware that I have absolutely no choice in the matter anyway, I will work for you despite that being the case."

"In which case we shall arrange for the money to be placed in the account as discussed. It will be arranged that in the event of your death, the account will be transferred to Sonia. There will be four provisos.

1. "The account cannot be used until the cessation of hostilities between Germany and the Allies. In the meantime it will, of course, attract interest."
2. "The account will be closed and repaid to our holding account in the event of your suicide."
3. "We shall pay you a monthly retainer, either direct to you or to Sonia, or to another account upon which you can draw, directly in proportion to the value of the information you send us."
4. "You will establish the fate of Herr Brendt's daughter, son-in-law and grandchildren taken by the Gestapo two years ago. This last proviso is very important indeed."

The general looked genuinely shocked at this final requirement. "Your daughter and her children in a camp? Oh, my God, how awful. How could Swiss nationals end up in a camp?"

"Her husband was a German Jewish doctor. That is more than enough reason for her incarceration. He is already dead, that I have no doubt. We live in the hope that the others are still alive." Herr Brendt added, "You can now see, you're having a daughter of your own, why I have such a deep interest in this whole project."

Krause sat back. "I will do everything in my power to find them. That I promise you."

The Count wound up the meeting, arranging to see the general again on the morrow to establish the details regarding the transmission of information to the letter box already established in Berlin, methods of payment, emergency contact systems, and a dozen or more other details to ensure complete secrecy and speed of delivery of the reports. Before being driven back to his hotel the general shook hands with Herr Brendt and his daughter, and then with David. "Herr Muller, I think you are a very brave young man to venture into the heart of the Schutzstaffel as you did. When you were there I record I said I was sorry you were Swiss, I could do with you on my staff, or something like that. I am sorry it cannot be. After this terrible war is over I would like to meet you again and find out your real name and all about you. Goodbye Herr Muller – whoever you are."

David shook his hand replying, "We must try and arrange it Sir."

The next few days were somewhat of an anticlimax. The Count was called away after his session with the general and did not return until Saturday 25th. David was reading the morning papers when the telephone rang. The landlady answered it and called to David. "For you Herr Muller."

It was the Count. "Are you free tomorrow?" David replied that he was. "In that case we will drive out somewhere nice for lunch and I can put you in the picture regarding your return." David, remembering his training, did not extend the conversation. A tap on his line would probably be unlikely, but if he knew anything at all about the dodgy world of espionage, it would not be beyond doubt that the Count's line could well be tapped – possibly even by his friend Colonel Masson!

They enjoyed a very pleasant lunch. Being a Sunday the restaurant, way up in the alpine foothills, was crowded with families enjoying the spring air, still crisp, but sunny. David contrasted the scene with the picture of life back in England. The beautiful unmarked villages compared with the battered British cities, the plentiful food compared with the strict rationing with which most British people lived, and at night the lights shining everywhere compared with the British blackout. 'They don't know they're born,' was his inner comment.

Having finished their lunch, the Count announced, "Right, down to business. We are sending you home, but there are no seats available on Lufthansa until 29th May. We could send you by train through Vichy France but that is a bit risky at the moment. Added to which Vichy visa applications are taking an age so by the time the visa came through you could be on the aircraft anyway. When you get to Lisbon you report to an address I shall give you where you will resume being Cooteman and will be allocated a seat on the next R.A.F. flight to Britain, landing God knows where."

"What do I do in the meantime?"

"Whatever you like, but report to me every other day from Frau Kielman's, just in case, I've been instructed to send you back into Germany – or Italy – or Czechoslovakia – you never know in this game." He grinned.

"I do fervently hope you are pulling my whatsit."

"I am, but funnier things have happened."

David spent his month visiting museums, galleries, travelling to the Italian speaking regions, and in particular going to concerts, recitals and operas in the evening. He had not realised how culturally starved he had become. Brought up on church music he had swiftly developed an appetite in his teens for classical music. The war had curtailed his enjoyment of the great masters apart from one or two visits to the Queens Hall before it was bombed. He thought nostalgically of the great outing he and Pat, along with Charlie and Rose had enjoyed through the kindness of Charlie's grandfather, the Earl of Otbourne, when the Earl took them to a concert at Worcester Cathedral. He could still hear the mammoth cathedral organ in Handel's Organ Concerto, and feel the spine-tingling effect of those magnificent chords, so much so that he could have cried at the memory, and nearly did.

"I must be getting weak in my old age," he told himself.

At last the day came for him to leave. To his surprise, Helga came with the car to take him to the airport.

"The Count sends his very best wishes but will be sure you will appreciate it would be wiser for him not to be seen with you. Other prying eyes at the airport who know who he is and what he is will surely be there, so it is as well you are not connected with him."

"In which case, to keep up the subterfuge, I suppose I shall have to give you a long lingering kiss goodbye?"

"Would that be a terrible hardship?"

"It might make me change my mind and desert to Switzerland."

She laughed and pointed the car in the direction of the airport. Having booked in and his luggage having been thrown, somewhat heavily he thought, on to a trolley, he turned to say goodbye before going into the departure lounge. To his surprise Helga put her arms round his neck and gave him a long, ardent kiss.

"I know you won't ever come back again, so I want you to know that if you did I would move heaven and earth to keep you here."

On the premise that he had no idea of how to answer, he kept his mouth shut, just holding her close, her head on his shoulder, her delicate perfume adding to the poignancy of the parting.

"Goodbye," he whispered, "take care of yourself."

She looked up at him. "You too, please take care of yourself, and after the war is over will you just write and tell me who you are, I would like to know that so much?"

"I will, I promise." He kissed her again, and made for the departure gate. At the gate he turned, she was waving to him; she blew a kiss, then walked away.

On the long flight to Barcelona then Madrid and finally to Lisbon, he pondered on all the strange things that were happening to him. He was flying on a German aeroplane, being waited on hand and foot by charming German girls with whom he was at war. He had just been ardently kissed by a Swiss girl, who he had known for weeks as being extremely reserved, almost distant. He had shaken hands on an almost friendly basis with an S.S. General – not many people have done that he thought – now he was on his way to go home in an R.A.F. plane which might be shot down if it got in the way of a stray Focke Wolfe over the Bay of Biscay or wherever. His final thought before the plane started its descent into Portugal was, 'Bloody hell Chandler, you do see life.'

Chapter Twenty Eight

The King's official birthday arrived, and with it the Honours List. Fred had ordered half a dozen copies of The Times, but before they had arrived, the telephone had already started shrilling. At 6.45am, when all decent people should still be in bed as Fred had put it, Buffy Cartwright was on the telephone. "My Morning Post has just arrived. The first thing I did was to look at the Honours List to see what the politicians had undeservedly awarded themselves and there was Frederick Chandler OBE. Congratulations. By jove, who would have thought when we were up to our balls in mud in Flanders I would be one day making this call. I won't hog the phone; everyone will be waiting to get on to you. Rita is saying she will be writing. Cheerio now."

From then on there was pandemonium in the house, to be continued the minute he arrived at the factory. He didn't realise he knew so many people. People as remote as Sir Oliver Routledge, his old employer when he was a farm worker after the Great War until he went into Sandbury Engineering. Doctor Carew, David's old headmaster, the deputy chief constable, the two generals from Colchester, Colonel Tim and a host of others including Alex and Jim and Charlie's grandfather the Earl, meant that he did not a shred of work all the morning and for a good part of the afternoon. As he said to Ernie, "It's a good job this happens only once in a lifetime or we would never get anything done."

Ernie's reply was typical. "Wait till you get your "K" – we shall all expect a week off!"

Other members of the family were living in ignorance of this great occasion. Harry was restless in his jungle hideout as a result of the inactivity they were being constrained to observe. Word had reached them that one of their units further north had carried out a very successful operation against a tin mine, but as a result of the attackers being identified mainly as Chinese, the Japs had taken revenge on local Chinese and killed six men between the ages of eighteen and twenty four, for every Japanese soldier killed. That added up to twenty-four innocent people. To add to the terror six had been beheaded and their heads put on poles on public display in the small local town centre. Camp Six however would very shortly now be making itself known.

As the excitement reigned at Sandbury David was waiting in a cheerless hut on a dispersal point on a Portuguese Air Force aerodrome, well away from the main buildings. He had spent three days in Lisbon, buying presents for all and sundry from shops full of goodies from the United States and South America. He had finally been told by the contact he had been instructed to reach that a Halifax was coming in on 2nd June, although they were not sure when it would be returning. He would therefore have to wait around at the aerodrome, some thirty miles north of Lisbon, until the Halifax received its further flight instructions. David by now, although he was an old hand at waiting around – he remembered with great sadness what Jessica had told him on his first day in this lark – he was getting impatient at getting home to see his family, Maria, Paddy and all the others. 'I wonder what that bugger Paddy has been up to;' he asked himself, 'something that gave his tonsils a reasonable degree of lubrication I'll be bound.'

Mark and Charlie had had their baptism of fire the previous week. Mark's company had been reformed as an anti-tank company, armed with six pounder guns, each towed by a Bren gun carrier. They were formidable weapons, but due to the company's hurried conversion from infantry soldiers to anti-tank gunners, they had had no firing practice at all. They had received a few days of 'going through the drill,' but they didn't even know how big a bang the damn thing made until they found themselves facing a combined attack of Italians and Afrika Corps, when they speedily learnt their trade 'on the job.' Things had quietened now, the heat was intense, the flies were an abomination, the sand got into everything – literally everything!! – Whilst they waited for the next assault from Rommel. As Charlie said as he slid into Mark Laurenson's slit trench – "God, I could do with one of Mr Chandler's Whitbread Light Ales right now, how about you Sir?"

It was now six weeks since Ray Osbourne had been so cruelly wounded. He was at a famous country house in the middle of Oxfordshire now given over largely to being a convalescent home for wounded officers, a mixed bag of R.A.F. wallahs, Naval types and brown jobs. Their newspapers arrived usually at about 11 a.m. As Ray had already established, the Daily Mirrors were dished out to the R.A.F., the Express and Mails to the Navy, and the Telegraph and The Times to the army chaps as they were the only ones who could do the crosswords and read the long words. It was noon before Ray was able to lay his hands on a Telegraph, and even then the Honours List was not his first priority, but as there was not exactly a plethora of news, he at last skimmed over the names of the great, the good and the deserving. And then he saw it. O.B.E. F. Chandler. Services to Industry. He almost ran to the telephone, realised he had no coins with him, they were in his room upstairs half a mile away it seemed, went up and got the necessary, came back to the telephone booth, found it and the adjacent one were both occupied, waited for, it seemed, an age, until an R.A.F. lovesick goon eventually ran out of billing and cooing, gave the operator the number, was told there was an hours delay, went and had his lunch, sat by the booth for another hour waiting for the call to come through, when it did was told 'line engaged.' He gave up and got a friendly visitor to write a letter of congratulations and to post it for him.

The Halifax did not, in fact, arrive until 3rd June, soon after dawn, flying through the darkness to avoid considerable Luftwaffe activity in the Bay. David watched the half dozen passengers disembarking at this remote dispersal point, and making their way towards the hut. "I know that one," he exclaimed to himself. Although she was well covered by a greatcoat with turned up collar, and wearing a woolly hat, it was undoubtedly Sophie – she who had been sick all over his trousers in the Lysander all those months ago. She was the last through the door, he touched her arm. "Hello Sophie, we meet again."

She turned, not recognising him for a moment, put her finger to her temple and replied, "I can't remember where."

"In a Lysander, you nearly ruined me when you trod on my vitals and then completely ruined the trousers of my government issue suit."

"Oh of course, I remember," and to the surprise of the other members of her party, threw her arms around his neck and gave him a repeat performance of the hearty kiss she had given to him, and to their pilot he recalled, when they had finally landed at Tangmere. At that time he had tentatively suggested they might meet again, to which she replied she had an eager husband waiting for her, or something along those lines.

Having been released from her embrace he said, "So, you are having to again leave that eager husband you told me about." She put her arm through his.

"When I got home I found the swine had shacked up with my best friend. Now that sort of thing only happens in novels doesn't it? Anyway, I went down to Farnham where they were and sorted the buggers out, not that it did me any good I suppose. Anyway, I am now back on the market, one not so careful owner, a good runner, but needing regular servicing."

"I'll put an ad in the paper for you, not that I think you would need it, there are not many about like you." She looked up at him.

"You really meant that didn't you?"

"Yes I did, and if I wasn't already spoken for, I would top the list."

"But you hardly know me, apart from my being sick all over you."

"Some people you know straight away, others you can be with for years and never know them." She hugged his arm.

"I must go. They are waiting. I do hope we meet again Cooteman – it was Cooteman wasn't it?" She kissed him again, hugged him for a little while with her head on his chest, turned and joined the others on the small bus outside. As they drew away she waved to him and blew a kiss. He turned back into the hut's dismal surroundings, his mind a whirl of reflection on what had happened. Poor Sophie. Fancy getting home after an operation, during which she could easily have been trapped and executed, only to find the bastard of a husband doing the dirty on her. Then having to live with that distressing situation whilst she prepared for another operation. And fancy her remembering 'Cooteman.' The only time she would have heard that name would have been when they met prior to taking off from France in the Lysander.

A jovial voice interrupted his musings. "Mister Cooteman I believe?"

"That is I, as my grammar teacher would probably have said. In which case why shouldn't it be 'that am I' not 'that is I' – very puzzling – if it is 'that is I' in the first place, which doesn't sound right somehow."

"Well you will have thirty six hours to puzzle it out Mister Cooteman. We leave tomorrow evening at eighteen hundred hours – six p.m. to you civilians."

"Never judge a sausage by its skin." was David's reply to this genial flight lieutenant with a navigator's wing on his tunic. "I could be an admiral for all you know."

"You look far too intelligent to be in the Navy. Anyway, whatever you are we leave at 6 p.m. tomorrow evening. There are no other passengers. We have to sleep on the aircraft, there are plenty of spare blankets, you can join us if you care to."

"That sounds a good idea – what do we do for food in the meantime?"

"They send us our meals from the Portuguese officers mess kitchen. Sometimes it's good, sometimes it's not so good, usually it's bloody awful. Still as my mother used to say, 'what doesn't fatten will fill.'"

"I've done a bit of shopping while I was in Lisbon. Can I dump these on the aircraft?"

The flight lieutenant regarding the multiplicity of packages, parcels and two quite bulky looking boxes saying "You know the Halifax only has a 13,000 pounds bomb load?" David grinned.

They loaded the packages and David's suitcase into the capacious body of the Halifax. As they rounded the nose of the aircraft David saw the rows of bombs painted on the fuselage below the pilots seat. A quick calculation showed a total of thirty. David pointed to them saying, "Someone's been busy."

"Yes, we've done a tour in this old bus, now we are on the soft jobs for a little while."

"Are you telling me you have made thirty bombing raids?"

"The skipper and I have scored fifty, the rest of the lads have finished their first tour in this one."

David marvelled again, as he had when talking to the Lysander pilots, of the complete lack of vainglory of these R.A.F. types. This young man, not more than twenty-five, had thirty times navigated this aircraft, and twenty times before that some other beast, through a virtual hell of anti-aircraft fire at different places over the continent, yet could talk about it as if he had just finished his paper round. The gut churning fact to David was that in the not too distant future they would be back on another 'thirty tour' into areas becoming even more heavily defended. If any earn their corn, they do, he concluded.

The flight home was uneventful. The first leg for some 400 miles was north-west into the Atlantic, thereby missing the dangers over the Bay of Biscay. They then turned north-east towards Southern Ireland for another four hundred miles and then almost due east over South Wales to land at Quedgeley, just outside Gloucester, just after midnight. It was a bumpy landing to say the least. As the aircraft wound its way around the perimeter to come to a halt in front of a large hangar, the navigator came down the fuselage to David sitting in his canvas chair and said:-

"Welcome home. I'm sorry about the bumpy landing, but we let the air gunners have a go at bringing them down every now and then." David never did find out whether this was pukka or just a typical R.A.F. leg-pull. "Anyway," he continued, "we had better get all your parcels off so that the customs people can see how much you owe them." David looked at him in the dim interior light.

"You're joking?" It was half statement, half question.

"Gospel old boy, gospel. They know when you blokes come back off holiday you always bring a load of goodies with you."

It was then he realised his leg was being pulled. "You blighter, you had me going for a minute or two."

The engines gave a final roar and petered out. David heard the fuselage door open and a set of steps placed against the opening. He walked forward to the cockpit to say goodbye to the pilot and to thank him for the ride, returning, picked up some of the parcels and put them by the doorway, then went back for his suitcase. Climbing out of the aircraft he was faced with none other than Paddy.

"What the devil are you doing here?" – as if he didn't know.

"The commandant said that if we let you get back to Wilmslow by train you would only get lost, so he sent me down to pick you up. He wants you back quick for another job the day after tomorrow."

"Now look. I've been having the urine extracted out of me for the past thirty-six hours by this sky blue gentleman here, so don't you start." Paddy laughed, stacking the parcels and suitcase away in an Austin 16, it having army plates on, David automatically noticed.

They drove the hundred and thirty miles back to Wilmslow through the night, each careful not to ask the other 'what he had been up to.' Knowing there would be nowhere to get refreshment on the journey Paddy had brought some sandwiches and a large flask of coffee. They got themselves lost at one point, which delayed them. There were, of course, no signposts, and at that hour of the morning nobody about to ask the way. Finding themselves passing a small army nissen-hutted camp they stopped. Paddy approached the guardroom.

"Halt. Who goes there?" The voice came from a very youthful sounding sentry. Paddy stopped immediately. The last thing he wanted was a bullet from an over enthusiastic rookie.

"Sergeant O'Riordan, City Rifles. We've lost our way. Can you tell us where we are?"

"Advance one to be recognised."

"There's only one of me you blithering idiot. The officer is still in the car."

With the conversation between them being heard inside the guardroom, the guard commander came out shining a large flashlight.

"What's going on?"

"The sergeant wants to know where he is." And then he added. "He's Irish."

"Oh is he. Would you mind coming into the guard room sergeant."

"He says there's an officer in the car."

"Oh is there. Blackett," he bellowed. A man tumbled out of the guardroom, carrying his rifle with one hand and trying desperately to do up the buttons on his battle dress with the other.

"Escort the officer to the guardroom."

Paddy decided he'd better humour the stupid sods, despite the fact his Irish was beginning to be roused. The still unbuttoned soldier went to the passenger door and opened it.

"Will you come to the guard room Sir?" he peered into the

darkened interior of the Austin and yelled, "It's a civilian corporal. There's a lot of packages of some sort in the car."

"Oh right, well bring him in." David climbed out of the car, becoming very amused at the performance being acted out in this back of beyond. They went into the Tilley lamp-lit nissen hut to find half a dozen bleary eyed young men sitting up on their beds wondering what the fuss was all about.

"Could I see your identity papers please?" the corporal asked David. It was then that David realised he had not got any identity papers!

"I'm afraid I have none with me," David replied, "but Sergeant O'Riordan here can vouch for me. I am Captain Chandler, City Rifles."

The corporal was not convinced. "May I see your paybook sergeant please?"

Paddy felt in his left hand breast pocket where it was always kept. Then he remembered he had put his second best battledress on for the two-way journey so that he didn't crease his best one. The paybook was snug in his best battledress, back at Wilmslow.

"I don't seem to have got it with me."

The corporal was obviously wondering what the hell to do next. He pointed for David and Paddy to sit on a bench against the wall, the two sentries in the meantime taking station at the door. "I'll telephone the orderly officer." After the field telephone bell had been ringing for some time in the adjutant's office, where the orderly officer was hopefully expecting to get a decent night's kip without interruption from stupid guard commanders, he was answered by a bleary voice.

"What's the problem?"

"Sorry to bother you Sir, but we have two people in the guard room, one an Irish sergeant he says from the City Rifles, and a civilian who says he's a captain in the same mob. The sergeant is improperly dressed with stripes on only one-arm and neither of them have any identification. They've got a black car with army registration numbers and a lot of suspicious looking bundles in the back."

"Right, I'll be there in ten minutes."

When the orderly officer arrived, he was a second lieutenant looking no more than seventeen or eighteen at the most, wearing what David could just see in the light of the Tilley lamp a most valiant attempt at a moustache on his upper lip, an appendage which David considered was going to require a very great deal of nurturing before he became nicknamed Bushy. David's final conclusion on the subject was that the war would be over long before that happened.

He addressed the guard commander. "Have you asked these

gentlemen for their identity discs – they are worn at all times?"

"No Sir, didn't think of that." The officer looked at the suspect pair. They, of course, had no identity discs. David's were still in the box of bits and pieces he had left behind when he took off from Helsby, Paddy had retrieved his after his return but had forgotten to put them on. David looked at Paddy, Paddy looked at David and they both started to laugh. They laughed until they were almost hysterical, to the wide-eyed consternation of the second lieutenant, the corporal and the now fully awakened guardroom occupants.

Eventually they gained control. "Look Mr?" he looked enquiringly at the young officer. "Hayward, Second Lieutenant Hayward."

David turned to Paddy and whispered "No wonder we're in a pickle," and they both started splitting their sides all over again.

"Look Mr Hayward, there are compelling reasons why we haven't got identification papers. Please telephone this number," he wrote Robin's number on a card from his pocket. "Ask for the commandant, he will confirm who we are. I am Captain Chandler and this is Sergeant O'Riordan."

"We cannot telephone from here; there is only a field telephone to the adjutant's office. Secondly I shall have to wake the adjutant and he will have to carry out the enquiries, he knows the correct procedure. I must leave you here under guard until that has been carried out. You do understand don't you?"

"You could just tell us where we are and let us go on our way. It would save a lot of hassle."

"I'm sorry, I can't do that. All units have had an I.R.A. alert after the bomb in Manchester last week." Paddy and David looked at each other and again started to laugh, sitting back on the bench while the young subaltern made his way back to awaken a thoroughly disgruntled, somewhat overhung adjutant.

An hour later he returned with the adjutant who had just thrown a great coat over his pyjamas and was wearing P.T. slippers.

"I am to ask you two questions each, although I must admit you fit exactly the descriptions your commandant has given me, sergeant. When you were at Winchester who was your R.S.M.?"

"R.S.M. Forster Sir."

"And what is the name of the young lady you hope will marry you in August?"

They both noted the little whimsicality and wondered whether it was his invention or whether he was quoting Robin verbatim.

"Mary Maguire Sir."

"Jolly good – that lets you out."

"Now Captain Chandler. This is a very odd question; I don't know how the devil he dreamt it up. What is contained under the stairs at Chandlers Lodge?"

"Whitbread's Light Ale, and by God, I could do with one now."

"I don't think we need bugger about with any more stupid questions. I apologise for your being held up, I'm sure that if the picture were reversed and you had come across two bloody idiots without a scrap of evidence of identity on them you might have been suspicious – what? On the other hand, there's more in this than meets the eye. Commandants don't get very polite brigadiers to telephone me from their beds every night of the week by a long chalk." He shook hands with them both. "Oh, by the way, you're at Aston Burberry." He then gave them directions to get to, "What used to be the A34 until some idiot decided to take the signposts down. What sort of drawback that would have been to invading Nazis Lord alone knows."

They arrived at Wilmslow just before five o'clock. Robin was up and waiting for them, and having enthusiastically welcomed David back told him the usual rules applied. Breakfast was ready for them both. They were then to go to bed and David was to report to Room 6 at 1600 hrs to commence de-briefing. This would continue over the weekend and when finished, probably by the end of next week you will go on leave. In the meantime you may use the telephone, but please do not leave the premises as the Brigadier is visiting at some stage in the next few days, and he wants a session with you.

Whilst the two were talking, Paddy had taken all David's bits and pieces up to his room and was waiting for him.

"There's no prizes for guessing where I've been," Paddy suggested, "but where the hell have you been? – Not that you'll tell me I know." As he spoke he pointed to a label on one of the boxes which read:-

Da Silva

Oporto – Lisboa

"Now if my geography is anywhere near the mark, those places are in Portugal. I wondered how you could be coming back on a Halifax. What the hell is there to do in Portugal?"

"It's one of those places you just pass through," laughed David, "on the way to Turkey, Russia and China." He would have loved to tell him he had been flying on German aeroplanes with German girls waiting on him hand and foot, but of course he was unable to. "Anyway, open that box up will you?" This done, David extracted a bottle from the ten contained therein and gave it to Paddy. "A little present for you." It was a litre of Constantino five star brandy.

Paddy held it up in front of his eyes. "Bloody hell," he said, "if Paddy Discroll could see me now," but Paddy Driscoll, batman to Charlie Crew, had been buried in the soft sand of the Western Desert two days before, after taking part in a heroic action against the Afrika Corps in which he had given his life.

There was a stack of mail waiting for David. He decided to sleep first and then read it. However, curiosity overcame him so that he modified his plans and decided to sort it into separate piles, the largest being, as he recognised immediately, from Maria. She must have written every couple of days judging by that lot, he told himself. There was one letter that he immediately recognised from the postmark in Aylsham, Norfolk. It was slim, obviously only a single sheet or two at the most. It must be from Pamela. He opened it. It was quite brief.

"David darling,

I am writing to tell you I am marrying in August a neighbour of ours who has been asking me on and off for the past five years. I shall never forget you.

Yours
Pamela

To say David's feelings were mixed would be the understatement of the age. He was, he told himself, like a dog with two bones – whilst he could only gnaw one, he was strongly averse to another having the other one. Then he told himself he was not only being a right shit by not being a thousand per cent faithful to Maria, but also he was being a bigger shit in resenting, however mildly or temporarily, Pamela getting spliced with presumably some chinless, swede-bashing, millionaire landowner. His next feeling was one of relief in that his nocturnal adventure with Pamela would now undoubtedly be kept between themselves – she would have as much to lose as he had if it were broadcast. This led to his feeling a shit again to think she would ever have allowed that to happen. Then he had a great feeling of elation, thinking of that night. It was akin to an Olympic runner looking back on the day he won the marathon, or a centre forward who scored the winning goal at the Cup Final. His final feelings as he completed his undressing before falling into bed, was that he hoped the new husband had plenty of staying power – he was certainly going to need it! He went to sleep smiling.

At four o'clock he presented himself at the headmaster's study, and was warmly congratulated by Robin on the success of his mission. "And before you ask, Paddy came up trumps again. I think a lot of it is due to the fact that with over eighteen years service there are very few crafty situations he hasn't met or heard talk about. He really has been an absolute gem. As you know, American troops have been in Northern Ireland some weeks now. Their security is abysmal. The things Paddy found out which we were able to send as evidence to their top brass have caused a wholesale shake-up to be put into effect. According to Paddy they reckon that if we stand aside and leave it to them it will all be over by Christmas!" It was the 6th June. It would be exactly two years to the day before they even started that great adventure, and a further year before it was completed and they would not do it all on their own by a long chalk.

At four thirty, two boffin types arrived and took David off to an upstairs room fitted with the most modern recording equipment.
"We will have a two hour general chat today," he was told, "then two lots of two hours each day until we finish. Tomorrow is Sunday – we should be finished by Thursday or Friday." David made a quick calculation – twenty-four hours of talking? What the hell can they find to talk about for twenty-four hours – you could get through the history of England in that time? But after covering, recovering, and covering again every aspect of the operation, their estimate would in fact prove to be accurate.

That evening, after dinner, he put a call in to Chandlers Lodge. His mother answered.
"Chandlers Lodge."
"Oh, I'm terribly sorry. I thought I was through to Buckingham Palace.
"David, is that you?" Not waiting for an answer he heard her call out. "It's David, it's David on the telephone. David, where are you, how are you, are you alright, will you be home soon?"
"Now mother dear simmer down. To answer your questions. I am back in England. I am as fit as a flea and all in one piece. I am hoping to be home at the end of next week. Paddy is back as well and sends his kindest regards. That's the news from this end. How are all of you? Have you hard anything from Harry? Has Maria been in touch? What news from Mark and Charlie? Tell me all."
"I don't know where to start. First of all Harry is alive and with a

guerrilla unit. Mark and Charlie have moved from their base camp. Maria has been in touch regularly and is home this weekend on a weekend pass – she telephoned only last evening. We and the babies are all well, and last but not least, your father has been awarded the O.B.E. for services to industry – how about that? And now the sad news, poor Ray Osbourne removed a fuse from an unexploded bomb and it exploded in his hand, which had to be amputated. He is terribly, terribly brave, but of course he will be discharged in the not too distant future. Anyway we will tell you everything in detail when you come home. Rose and your father would like a word. Bye bye dear, I'm so happy you are back."

Rose took the phone. "I won't keep you long," she started to say.

He interrupted, "You can talk all night if you like – it's on the house."

"Yes, but as I seem to remember saying to you once before – which house I wonder? Anyway to answer your unasked questions, I am fine, young Jeremy is getting bigger every day. I have not heard from Mark for over three weeks now – I think they must have been moved up into the action, there's an awful lot going on out there at the moment. Still I expect you know that already."

Without thinking, or because he was still very tired after the journey and his first debriefing, he answered, "No, I heard little of that news where I was."

"And where was that?" she paused for several seconds, and continued "It's alright, I know you can't tell me, but I'll worm it all out of you one day even if I have to get you drunk to do it. Anyway, Dad wants a word. See you soon. Bye bye."

Before Fred could speak David greeted him with, "What's all this O.B.E. lark then? You realise you will have to move up all your medal ribbons on your battledress blouse now don't you? Anyway, congratulations, you deserve it. If anyone has moved heaven and earth to get things done for the war effort you have."

After chatting for a while, David quizzing Fred in particular as to what they knew about Harry, David rang off and put in a call to Maria. Mr Schultz answered. "David, my boy, how wonderful to hear your voice." David thought – you would think it even more wonderful if you knew in which country I had been!

"Maria is out this evening. She and a friend have gone to a wedding reception today at Romford and will not be back until late. Can she telephone you?"

"No, not really. If I ring at about nine o'clock tomorrow morning, being Sunday I should get through fairly easily, do you think she will have sobered up by then?"

Mr Schultz laughed heartily. "I will tell her what you have just said. But yes of course, that would be fine. If I know Maria she will set her alarm for six o'clock so to make sure she is not late – nein?"

It was still only nine thirty but David had become so tired his only thought was now to get to bed. Paddy was waiting for him in his room, with the perennial question "What will you be wearing tomorrow Sir?"

They chatted for a short while. David becoming more and more weary until he announced "I'm going to bed now. Give me a shout at 7.30 will you?"

"7.30 on a Sunday – surely Sir that's against your religion?"

"I have a date at nine o'clock. Only a telephone date, but an important telephone date for all that."

"Right Sir, 7.30 it is. Don't dream of her tonight Sir, it might make you too weak to get up in the morning. By the way Sir, how is the young lady from Norfolk these days?" (He had obviously seen the postmark on Pamela's letter).

"She is getting married in August."

"But then, won't she want you there as her best man Sir?" and with that he scampered out of the door before David could find anything to throw at him.

He got through to Chingford quickly the next morning. "David, David, how lovely to hear your voice. Will you hold on a moment?" He heard her addressing someone in the room 'you can go now, I shan't need you for a while,' she returned to David, "it's alright; I'm just giving my stoker friend his marching orders for the time being."

"Has he put on any more weight?"

"He's seventeen stones and a bit now."

"You need nourishment not punishment."

"David Chandler you are very naughty."

The bonhomie he shared with Maria was something he valued so much. Their relative senses of humour were so finely turned to be almost identical.

"So when are you coming home?"

"At the end of next week, for three weeks I am told, although I will believe that when it happens."

"My next seven days is on Friday 19th June, so we shall be able to see each other. Oh, how exciting."

They chatted on until David looked at his watch and said he had to be away to a meeting.

"How long will that last? Can I telephone you tomorrow evening?

You see, you can't get hold of me where I am."

"Getting hold of you I can assure you is my top priority at the moment – they will eventually have to prise us apart. But yes, the number is Wilmslow 400 as before."

"I'm wondering who the 'they' will be. I shall ensure there is no one within fifty miles when I next meet you. Bye bye darling David."

For the next few days the routine hardly varied. Despite the fact he did little active work, the psychological strain of the intensive cross questioning by the two dons, for that's what they turned out to be, sent him to bed each night ready for sleep. On Wednesday Robin told him that the brigadier would be arriving that afternoon, and would spend some time with him, but it was in fact early evening before Lord Ramsford arrived, just as David was going in to dinner.

"David, this is Brigadier Sandford, he will be sitting in on our conversation, with your kind permission."

David shook hands with them both, grinning at Lord Ramsford, as much as to say, 'do I have a choice?'

"Right, dinner first – I'm starving," they all three trooped into the dining room. There was no 'shop' over the meal. David asked after Charlie, to be told the battalion had seen some heavy fighting, Charlie's company was now an anti-tank unit armed with six pounders, but he had had no correspondence from him since the action. He continued "But as you know only too well, if his penmanship was a fraction as prolific as her verbosity, I would receive a letter every day instead of every month."

After dinner they retired to one of the interview rooms. There was no cross-questioning of the type carried out by the dons. The brigadier was very interested in General Krause.

"You know David; getting Krause is a major coup. As a result of his being on the payroll, as our quaint American friends put it, we have a direct lead to what Himmler is planning. Most people here, even in high places, do not appreciate that the S.S. is so independent of the Wehrmacht and the Reich Chancellery, that they could, and would, if anything happened to Hitler, take over the country. Goering, Bormann, Goebels, Ribbentrop, are all secretly running scared of him. If you do nothing else of consequence during this war, getting us Krause was a stroke of genius. Tell me, when did you first think you might land him?"

"I think it was during my second visit to the S.S. Headquarters in Berlin. It looked to me that in our being awarded the contract a straightforward back-hander would be expected. I then thought if we could get him to come to Switzerland and get him accepting the bribe registered on a recording machine we would possibly have a means of coercing him into working for us. It was then that I met his daughter. It was plain she had no idea whatsoever of the evil work he was involved in, she adored him and he patently loved her very much. We decided she was the key, and the rest as they say is history."

No one spoke for a minute or so. Brigadier Sandford broke the silence. "You say you went into the S.S. Headquarters?"

"Yes Sir, on two occasions for consultations and on a couple of other occasions to use the telephone to Switzerland, which was of course monitored."

"By God, you've got some guts."

"I wore my brown leak-proof underwear Sir." The two brigadiers laughed uproarishly. "However, I did get a serious fright just before I returned to Bern. I was arrested in the Lufthansa offices by two rather unpleasant Gestapo people. I immediately referred them to my friend General Krause who one of them telephoned, as a result they released me, somewhat reluctantly it seemed to me since there was no apology. It occurred to me that if they could go around arresting people who were patently as innocent looking as I was, who else would stand a chance?"

"Now, what about these extermination camps you've confirmed exist," asked Brigadier Sandford.

"Well Sir, the Standartenfuhrer I saw in Munich S.S. offices told me plainly they had started gassing in Chelmno and Belzec, but that a huge one was being built elsewhere. I found out by a stroke of good fortune, that it was at a place called Auschwitz – Birkenau. It was General Krause who of course gave me the figure of six thousand a day – I was almost sick when he told me that. Six thousand innocent people every day of the year. How could civilised human beings even think of such a thing, let alone carry it out?"

Lord Ramsford stood up and walked up and down. "I must get on to the Poles and get them to give us all the information they can about the progress on the project. I will talk to the R.A.F. about bombing it. There are two obvious problems there, firstly the distance involved and secondly they may well have many thousands of potential victims in the area waiting to be processed. Processed! – Good God even I am talking as if we are discussing some sort of article on a production line."

"That to them Sir, is what it is."

They were all silent, trying to absorb the enormity of this wickedness, about which it was becoming obvious nothing could be done.

Lord Ramsford broke the silence. "I think we'll pack it in now, it's nearly ten o'clock. I shall have another meeting with you after your leave, probably in London. Come to that I may pop down to Sandbury while you're there, Charlie has so often drooled over that drink of the gods your father keeps hidden away. I shall not rest until I have sampled it!"

"You will be most welcome Sir." They shook hands. David was up at seven the next morning; the two brigadiers had already breakfasted and gone on their way.

Chapter Twenty Nine

David was told later that morning he would be able to go on leave on Saturday 13th June. A P.U. needed to be returned to Roper Street, so Robin suggested, in view of the quantity of merchandise he had apparently obtained, that Paddy should drive him down, take the P.U. back to Roper Street, and then he himself would go on a ten day leave before coming back to Wilmslow.

"So this means you are keeping your claws embedded in me does it?"

"Only for a short while I suspect. Two brigadiers don't turn up especially for a tête-à-tête with one, Captain Chandler, without something being in the wind. What that is, I shall probably be the last to know."

"You know a blooming lot more than you let on I fancy. Anyway, thank you for letting me have the vehicle, it will save me a lot of trouble."

When he telephoned Chandlers Lodge that evening to tell them he would be home late on Saturday evening and could they find a bed for the night for Paddy, he asked how Ray Osbourne was getting on, and where exactly was he. Told he was in a large country house, Bramcote Place, three miles out of Oxford, David said they would call in and see him on the way down, as they would be travelling on the A34 to Oxford and then the A40 into London.

They left early at seven o'clock, seen off by Robin, already dressed. David took over the driving at Birmingham and by midday, having enquired the way to Bramcote Place, and being told they had passed it a mile or so back, they turned into the long drive leading up to the large manor house. It was a glorious day and as they drove up to the front of the building and parked, Ray got up from one of the many seats on the lawn and walked over to them. His right arm was still in a sling. Holding out his left hand he announced with a grin, "I've joined the Boy Scouts" – scouts of course always shake hands with the left hand. David gave him a hug and Paddy shook hands.

"Now I understand you've been on another of your little overseas holidays."

"We both have" nodding towards Paddy. "I've brought you this," and he handed a bottle wrapped in tissue paper. Ray put the bottle into the sling and began to peel of the wrapping with his left hand. David immediately jumped to assist him.

"No, no, I have to do it myself. I have to get used to doing everything I can for myself – matron's orders – and she's a right martinet I can tell you. There's one thing I find very difficult and that is undoing my fly buttons when I want a pee. Now you can help me with that operation if you like. No? Oh well. What have we here?" He looked at the bottle – "Constantino five star!! Now that is going to be very carefully hidden away. I'm an extremely generous chap most of the time but not a drop of this will touch the lips of anyone but me. Thank you very much."

They walked across to the seat Ray had left to come and greet them.

"Would it upset you to tell us what happened?" David asked.

"No, I've got over the shock of it now. Briefly I took a fuse out of a rather large bomb, which was in a muddy hole in the ground. It was a clockwork time delay fuse, which had obviously malfunctioned. As I climbed up the ladder out of the hole I must have whacked it on some woodwork, which set it going. Unfortunately the malfunction had occurred only a second or two before it was due to explode and set the bomb off, so it went off in my hand. The only consolation I have is that it could have got going when I was getting it out of the bomb, in which case they would have been having a bit of a treasure hunt to find some bits of Captain Osbourne to bury. Anyway I fell off the ladder apparently – I don't remember anything much after the bang – and into the mud in the bottom of the hole." He paused for a moment or two. "They rushed me to a nearby naval hospital and carried out the first amputation. Because the injury had been covered in mud they had to leave the surgery open for five days, all wrapped up of course, to make sure no infection had set in. After five days they sewed up the flaps, as they call them, from the loose skin, over the end of the limb, and now I have to wait three months or so before it all heals up ready to start being fitted with a replacement."

Ray's matter of fact, almost cheerful in fact, statement of what happened prompted Paddy to say "Well, you've got more bloody guts than I have Sir, I would be crying my bloody eyes out."

"I don't mind admitting to you Paddy, that I have in fact had a couple of little weeps about it, but it's no more use crying over lost hands than it is over spilt milk."

"Any plans once you're out of here? Will they keep you on as an instructor? Your knowledge must be invaluable."

"David – the last thing they will want around the depot is a limbless bomb disposal officer. It gives the place a bad name. They may offer me a staff job, but I think that is unlikely since I am not the only one afflicted in this manner by any means, in fact I doubt whether there are enough staff jobs to go round judging by the number of amputees I have seen floating around even here. No, I shall probably be discharged."

"Well, we had better be making tracks. I'll keep in touch."

"Yes, please do that David, and please" he emphasised the 'please' – "please let me know immediately you have further news of Harry."

"I will do that. Cheerio now." He and Paddy shook hands, Boy Scout fashion, and climbed back into the P.U. They had an uninterrupted journey to Sandbury, crunching up the drive just before six o'clock. Ruth ran out to meet them, whilst the rest of the family piled out on to the flagstones in front of the porch. There was the usual bedlam which accompanies an arrival to the midst of a large family, everyone talking at once, children excitedly ducking and diving between the adults, until in a lull in the tumult the voice of the matriarch is heard to say 'Come in and have some tea,' the signal for all to troop back into the big kitchen and simmer down.

Young John, and Mark, one of Megan's twins, each nearly five years old, were fascinated by the huge gold and black stripes on Paddy's battledress. They stood together beside him as he drank his cup of tea. At last young John ran his fingers over the gold edges and looking up at Paddy said, "Uncle Paddy, is this real gold?"

"Yes, of course it is, real as real."

"Does that mean you are very important?"

"Very important. You have to stand to attention when you speak to me."

The boys looked at each other. They obviously had some idea of what standing to attention was from the time they had played at soldiers with Kenny Barclay when he was on leave at Chandlers Lodge. They promptly did a passable attempt at standing to attention.

Mark this time. "Are you more important than Uncle Kenny and Uncle David?"

"I'm a bit more important than Uncle Kenny and a lot more important than Uncle David." The boys looked at each other again meaningfully, while the remainder of the family hid their smiles. John whispered something into Mark's ear, cupping his lips over to ensure Paddy could not hear what he was saying. Mark, repeating the action, whispered something back, and then turned to Paddy.

"Uncle Kenny and Uncle David always give us two shillings each when they come home, but as you are more important will you be giving us half a crown?"

Amidst the laughter from the listeners, combined with the

immediate scolding from Megan, Jack and Moira at their 'asking for money,' and that combined with the look of innocence as to what all the fuss was about from the two boys, Paddy was heard to say, "I know one thing, you two will never grow up to be hungry" promptly diving into his pocket and producing, fortunately, three half crowns, two for the boys and one for Elizabeth. The three clustered together looking at the treasure they had acquired, then all clambered up to give Paddy a kiss.

David murmured in his ear, "That will teach you to keep your gob shut!" one of Paddy's own favourite expressions.

Paddy departed early on Sunday morning. David went to see Pat with flowers his mother had picked fresh for him from the garden, then met the rest of the family for matins. After lunch he got his parcels out. A bottle of brandy each for Fred, Jack and Ernie, three pairs of American nylons for each of the ladies, and last but not least a box of the small cigars that Karl so much enjoyed. David had bought them in Germany, and as he gave them to Karl, having his back to the rest of the family, he put his finger to his lips indicating that Karl should not ask how he acquired them. Karl gave a slight nod of understanding, thanking him profusely for his kindness.

David went to bed that night, having had a long, reversed-charge talk with Maria, unable to get to sleep. His mind kept going over his deepening feelings for her, these suddenly becoming interlaced with the fact of those innocents even at this very moment arriving at the extermination camps, wives being wrested from husbands, children being parted from parents. His fury at not being able to do a thing about it tortured him beyond belief. It would be better if he had never discovered what was going on – ignorance is bliss. Supposing Maria had been born in Germany and caught up in their iniquitous 'Final Solution' for some reason or other. His mind started to visualise the horror she would face, the horrendous journey to the camp, the degradation of being stripped naked, of being a part of the mass terror of other women and children, of having no conception of what was to happen to her except that she was facing a horrible death. He sat up, sweating, his throat dry, his head throbbing, and switched on the bedside lamp. His travel clock told him it was eleven thirty-five. He decided to go down to the kitchen and have some hot milk with a drop of brandy in it – 'perhaps it will make me sleep.' He switched on the light on the landing and stairs, and as quietly as his thirteen stones would allow, crept down to the kitchen, poured some milk into a saucepan, put it on the Aga, took Fred's bottle of brandy and poured a measure into a glass. As soon as he had judged the milk was warm he poured it and the brandy into a tumbler. It was as this part of the operation was being put into effect, his mother appeared in the doorway.

"David, are you alright?"

"I felt restless, so I thought I'd get some warm milk."

The next question came like a bolt out of the blue. "David, have you seen, or done, some terrible things that are praying on your mind?"

David looked at his mother, distress showing clearly on his face.

"I haven't seen or done such things, Mum, but I have discovered such wickedness that you and other decent Christian people could not even begin to comprehend. What is more I am bound not to discuss it with anyone. What is even worse not I, nor my superiors to the very highest level can do anything whatsoever to prevent its going on. I thought when I had been de-briefed I would leave it all behind me. Tonight for some reason it all came back." There was a long pause. "I'm alright now, mum, your catching me out, and being able to talk to you without being cross-examined, has somehow levelled me off again. I've heard before that sometimes people coming back off these jobs get the heebie-jeebies for no reason at the most unusual times and under the oddest of circumstances." His tone changed markedly to almost his usual cheerful self. "Anyway, you've done the trick, I feel alright again now," he paused again briefly. "I would be grateful if we could keep this to ourselves?" put as a question rather than a statement.

"Of course dear, of course."

"Oh, and mum," Ruth turned as she reached the door.

"I am seriously thinking of asking Maria to marry me."

Instead of a show of surprise, pleasure, congratulations, discouragement, shock or any other one of the innumerable feelings a mother might have at such an announcement from a member of her family, Ruth merely replied, "Oh, are you dear, I thought you probably were, in fact we were all thinking you probably were."

With that she went to bed, leaving David open-mouthed and convinced "There can't possibly be two people like my mother!"

David had one other bad night that week. Each morning his mother asked him whether he had 'slept all right?' At the Thursday morning mild interrogation he had to admit he had not.

"Have a word with Doctor Power, perhaps he can give you something to help."

"You know I hate taking pills. Before you know it you can't do without them – I don't want to reach that stage."

"On the other hand disturbed sleep doesn't do you any good. Now what are your plans while Maria is on leave?"

David outlined the arrangements they had made, all of which could be altered to suit other parties' convenience of course.

"I take it I'm included in the 'other party' category?"

He went on to say that he was meeting Maria off the train at Charing Cross on Friday lunchtime, and they would be going on to Chingford until Tuesday 23rd. They would then come to Sandbury for the rest of the leave if that was O.K. – Maria had to be back on Friday 26th. There were no problems in respect of these arrangements, his mother assured him and perhaps they could have a family get-together on one of the evenings?

David waited at the barrier for the arrival of the Dover Priory train 'as excited as a two year old,' as he told himself. When the train arrived it disgorged an absolute conglomeration of navy-blue, male and female, interspersed here and there with a civilian or a brown job looking entirely out of place. David's eyes became almost blurred with the effort of switching from one face to another. I should have stood further back he told himself as he found himself in the midst of a stampeding throng of sailors rushing to get a beer, rushing to catch the underground, rushing to fall into the arms of their wives, or in a number of cases, somebody else's wives. At last he spotted her, walking along with another very attractive wren. At the same moment she saw him, which recognition triggered such an uncontrollable acceleration in her deportment she virtually took off, landing in his arms with such impetus as to require all of David's substantial mass to prevent their both ending up in an unseemly prostration on the forecourt of Charing Cross Station. Fortunately decorum is not the highest requirement on the forecourt of Charing Cross, or any other main line station, in time of war, the lingering kiss of welcome therefore being hardly noticed by the passers-by. One or two, obviously going kiss-less, thought 'jammy sod,' or something similar, but apart from that, and apart from Maria's friend, patiently waiting for the osculation to come to an end, at least for the time being, the rest of the multitude took not a blind bit of notice.

The greeting made, Maria introduced her friend. "David, this is my friend Emma Langham. She lives near us at Buckhurst Hill, so we shall be travelling together."

David, shaking hands, issued a polite, "How do you do," then added "and do you have a seventeen stone stoker as well?"

The girl looked at him as if he had a screw loose, then looked enquiringly at Maria, who laughingly informed her "Don't take any notice, by four in the afternoon he becomes quite rational." Emma shook her head in bewilderment; the reunion has deranged them she concluded. During the journey to Chingford, David established she was a couple of years younger than Maria; she had no particular boyfriend, which was surprising in his view since she was undeniably a bit of a corker as Charlie would have opined.

The thought of Charlie led him, out of the blue, to ask her whether she would be interested in having a pen pal at present with the Eighth Army in the Western Desert. "He's about your age, an officer in my regiment, the City Rifles, super company and absolutely fancy free."

"David are you starting an introduction agency?"

"That's not a bad idea. I could earn a few shillings on the side, couldn't I? Mind you, I would have to interview all the young ladies to ensure they were a suitable match for my extremely vulnerable soldiery. After all, there is no point in starting a business if you don't get any of the perks." Maria thumped him. Emma laughed.

"I would be pleased to write to him David, those chaps are having a rough time of it out there at the moment. One question though – is he as mad as you?"

"Madder – but lovely with it."

David did not mention that Charlie was an 'Hon,' the son of a lord, he later asked Maria not to do so either with which she fully agreed.

It would be difficult to describe the welcome Maria and David received at the hands of Mr and Mrs Schultz. They were naturally delighted to see their daughter, looking so neat, trim and so very attractive in her Wren's uniform. Looking at her made them feel so proud their daughter was serving their country in what they, and others, considered a prestigious service. Mr Schultz, like most naturalised foreigners was more English than the English. If he could have had a flagpole at the front of his house he would have run the Union flag up it every day. As for their welcome to David – had he been royalty it could not have been more lavish and unrestrained.

The three days at Chingford passed quickly. On one of the days they went into town for the day, deciding to have lunch at the Corner House. Mr Stratton was delighted to see them, had them seated at his private table, raided the brasserie downstairs for a very good bottle of St. Emilion du Croix, finally flatly refusing to provide them with a bill. It was probable that never in his whole career, before and after Monday 22nd June in the Year of Grace 1942, did Mr Stratton spend so much time away from his managerial duties as he did on that day. There was, however, no noticeable difference in the share price of J Lyons and Co

Ltd on Tuesday 23rd as a result of this neglect of duty.

On Tuesday they said goodbye to Maria's parents and made their way to Sandbury. The news that evening was grim. Rommel had captured Tobruk. The South African general commanding the garrison, General Klopper, surrendered thirty thousand men, over two thousand vehicles and thousands of tons of petrol and rations. Hitler made Rommel a Field Marshall. Churchill said, 'Defeat is one thing, disgrace is another.' It was without doubt an appalling disgrace. Tobruk could and should have been defended and become a thorn in Rommel's side. At the same time Tobruk was being given away, the Russians were being besieged in Sebastopol in the Crimea, the Germans using flame-throwers to drive them out of, or incinerate them in, the ancient forts surrounding that city. They held out for nearly a month before the last man was killed.

June 23rd marked another day in the infamy of man. On this day an advance party of three hundred British prisoners of war arrived at Bampong in Thailand to start the building of the Siam – Burma railway, an undertaking, which would eventually claim the life of one man for every sleeper laid.

Maria had been studiously avoiding asking David where he was to be stationed or what he was going to be called upon to do next. He had bought her a beautiful wristlet watch in Switzerland, but since all watches seemed to come from Switzerland anyway she had not connected his previous absence with his presence in that country. When she had been at Chandlers Lodge for a while and the fact that David had brought the men bottles of Portuguese brandy, she became somewhat puzzled. Why Portugal? We were not fighting them – very odd. On the day before she was due to go back she asked him if he knew what was being planned for him. He had to honestly answer he hadn't a clue. The brigadier had said he might possibly be visiting them next week – perhaps he would put him in the picture, though the probability would be he would leave it to the commandant at Wilmslow.

They were walking in the woods with their arms around each other as they discussed this and other matters. They reached a glade where a fallen elm had left enough seating room to accommodate a complete wrenery. They sat silent for a while, her head on his shoulder, his arm around her with his hand touching against her breast. There was a scurrying in the bushes and a fox ran into the clearing not six yards away, looked steadily at them, turned and loped off. Maria looked up at him.

"I could stay here for ever."

"It would be pretty cold in the winter."

"You would keep me warm."

"I would do more than that."

"You mean you would provide this nourishment you were talking about?"

"Continuously."

She threw her arms around his neck and kissed him long and hard. They were silent again for a while.

"Maria, I have no idea what I am doing on my next assignment, or when or where I am going or for how long, but if it is not the week after next will you marry me?"

"I will marry you even if it is the week after next."

"I may be away for a long time for all I know. Would it be fair on you?"

"Is it fair on Rose, on Megan, on Cecely? Of course it's not fair, but I love you and we will have the rest of our life together when you return."

And if I don't return, he said to himself.

"Then will you marry me? Always assuming your parents feel that I am a fit and proper person to take their indescribably beautiful daughter from them?"

"Yes, yes, yes, yes, yes. As for my mother and father, they see a halo round your head every time they look at you. They will be walking on air when they hear the news."

"Then let's go into Maidstone this afternoon so that you can choose a ring."

They returned to Chandlers Lodge, but said nothing to either Ruth or Rose, and strangely enough neither his mother nor Hawk Eye discerned anything different in the atmosphere between them or in the slight flush of elation on Maria's cheeks. They caught the 1.15 bus from the Angel, on arrival in Maidstone spent the first hour window-shopping in the High Street and Fairmeadow Street. They saw innumerable engagement rings, but it was not until they saw a large tray in the window of the second shop they came to that Maria said, "You know darling, you have said we will buy an engagement ring – I have no idea what sort of money we are talking about. We have seen them priced so far from five pounds to a hundred pounds." David broke in.

"If you see what you like the money is secondary – and I mean that."

In the event, Maria chose a simple solitaire mounted in a

beautifully chased claw in the lower price range. She asked if she could wear it straight away.

"While we're here, we had better get the wedding ring do you think?" David took the opportunity to ask this question whilst the proprietor was addressing the till.

She hugged his arm. "Yes, let's." Again they settled on a simple nine-carat chased ring. It being wartime no new rings were made in more than nine carats. The salesman had offered them rings up to twenty-one carats, but these were second-hand and Maria said she would feel uncomfortable in wearing a ring that had been used before. So nine carats it was, carefully tucked away in its plush box in David's pocket to await the great day.

They made their way back to the bus stop with the congratulations of the proprietor ringing in their ears and a look of abandoned joy on both their faces. Arriving at Chandlers Lodge they walked into the kitchen to find Fred there in his Home Guard uniform. There was to be an exercise that evening in which a platoon of West Kents from Maidstone barracks were being trucked over to Sandbury to make an attack on the pumping station and main transformer station, to be heroically defended by Sandbury company of the Home Guard. Afterwards they were to have a booze-up at the Angel – not quite what would happen should the Wehrmacht decide to attack!

The couple walked to the centre of the rug in front of the Aga. Fred started to say something about – "We are losing you tomorrow then Maria," when Maria held her hand out, back uppermost, to show her ring to Ruth. Immediately there were squeals of excitement and delight from Rose and her mother, followed after a decent interval by Fred putting his hands on Maria's arms, kissing her on the cheek and saying, "Welcome to the family, he's a damn lucky chap."

That evening, the telephone wires having fairly hummed, everybody came round to Chandlers Lodge to drink the couple's health, David in the meantime having telephoned Chingford to an excited Mr and Mrs Schultz – with the final word from Maria's mother, "We lost a son, it was so sad, we have now gained a son, our Cedric will be rejoicing in who it is."

David went back to Deal on the train with Maria the next day. They said their goodbyes at the station before David put her into a cab for the depot. As she pulled away from the forecourt she wound the window down and held her hand out showing the third finger of her left hand. He smiled and waved until the taxi turned away.

On Sunday, before matins, he went to see Pat and told her he was marrying again, but that he would never ever forget her and the love they had had together. His head in a turmoil, he went on to church where the presence of his family, the familiar voice of Cannon Rosser, the voices of the choir, the adult section augmented by two or three choristers from the local army detachment on the airfield, and finally the organist filling the church and his head with music he missed so much while he was away, brought him back to his normal level of reasoning.

It was whilst he was visiting 'Country Style' on Monday that the brigadier telephoned. Rose answered the call, explaining David was out for an hour or so. The brigadier said he had to get away but would it be convenient for him to come down the next day to have a chat with David. Rose said she would make sure David was there – at what time approximately? Told that it would be about four in the afternoon Rose immediately asked whether he would care to stay overnight. Lord Ramsford, having asked if she was sure that this would not cause inconvenience, gladly agreed with the suggestion.

The stir this caused when Rose told her mother and later the rest of the family would have to be experienced to be believed. A real lord staying with them! When David arrived, expressing no excitement whatsoever at the news, his mother suggested that since he mixes with lords, earls, etc all the time, he could give them a quick course in etiquette respecting the method of conversation with such an august personage. To David's reply, "You just say "Oi, you," they both gave him a clipped ear. The penny then dropped. He was coming to see David. Bosses don't visit underlings for no good reason. The only reason they could think of was that David was to be taken away again. To questions from them both, David could give no answer, although their having asked them, started a momentary rumble in his entrails again. Oh well, the morrow will tell, he told himself, then realising that that rhymed he told himself, 'I'm a poet and don't know it.' He called out 'Any tea going mum?'

Chapter Thirty

By the beginning of July 1942 the occupants of Camp Six were becoming restless at their enforced idleness. Really, idleness was entirely the wrong word. They trained daily, they ventured into the jungle on exercises, they cultivated their garden, which they were constantly enlarging. Knowing their tinned meat stores would not last forever, major Hollis had sent a number of Chinese who were known in the nearest Kampongs - up to two days away - to buy piglets. These were brought back, penned in a secure area and told, as the Book of Genesis puts it, to 'Be fruitful and multiply,' which in due course they did. Despite these diversions, the Chinese, in particular, were anxious to get at these barbarians who had invaded them and who, furthermore, had ravished their homeland of China, raping and murdering, destroying and pillaging for so many years past.

At last the good news came on Sunday evening, the 5th of the month. It was a simple message – 'Proceed, repeat, proceed. Please acknowledge.' The message was duly acknowledged. When Colonel Llewellyn and Chua Yong Soon, the M.P.A.J.A. leader, had visited them a number of targets had been discussed. Since the main railway line from Singapore to the north, and the main trunk road running close to it at places, fell into the Camp Six area, these would naturally select themselves as prime targets. So also would the only main east to west road across the peninsula from Kluang to Mersing, on the east coast. Selection of which targets to hit, and when, was left to the camp commander, Major Hollis, the main criteria being to carry out the operation and then to disappear. No wounded were to be left behind. Since they would impede the progress of those withdrawing they could not be carried away but would have to be killed. Each man, up to and including the major, knew this, accepted it, but secretly wondered how he would react if the dreadful situation ever arose. Surely no man would be able to wilfully end the life of one of his comrades. On the other hand, left still alive to the tender mercies of the Kempetai a wounded man would beg to be despatched.

The major, Robbie, Harry and Choon Guan, leader of the camp communist faction, held an 'O' group the next morning. The camp was only a day's march to the nearest section where the Singapore railway and the trunk road ran side by side through steep sided defiles. It would not be impossible to find a suitable place where a train could be derailed in such a fashion that it would spew over on to the road and block that as well. The main problem would be in the choice of train. The last thing they would want to do would be to operate against a passenger train. As it was, all the train drivers were Malays of one sort or another, frequently Eurasians, each as a result would have to be sacrificed. Ideally therefore, they should select a troop train, but since these were few and far between, troops being posted travelled in the normal passenger services as a rule; it looked as though a goods train would be the best bet. The drawback to this latter operation was that goods trains travel at much lower speeds than passenger trains therefore the resultant pile-up after a derailment would conceivably be less.

"Whatever we do we've got to do the job properly," the major decided. "The old military axiom applies here I think - 'Time spent in reconnaissance is seldom wasted.' I propose therefore that the R.S.M. takes four good men to do exactly that. Record the number of trains, the pattern over a period of say three days, and nights of course, all of which we can analyse on his return, then put a plan into action. It is highly probable of course that this information will be of value to us in carrying out later operations on the line at other places. Any questions?"

Having dealt with a number of matters he concluded. "Right Mr Chandler" (it was always Mr Chandler in front of Choon Guan), "sort out who you are going to take, and move off at dawn tomorrow. I'll give you the map reference to head for, purely as a suggestion. I'll leave you to make the final recommendation when you have carried out your patrol."

The Chinese almost fought to get on the patrol with Harry. One man, Choong Hong, was an automatic selection in that he had worked for the railway authority in the offices of the permanent way department, organising maintenance, track re-laying, bridge inspections and repairs, and so on. He would know what to look for to see if they could make the eventual operation look like a real accident instead of sabotage, thereby reducing the possibility of reprisals or a hue and cry. The Japanese would know soon enough they had a hornet's nest stirring in their midst.

Choon Guan soon sorted out two more of his men, who with him and Choong Hong would make up the patrol. The major queried whether he should not let one of his deputies go but Choon Guan intimated he must lead from the front as everything that happened at Camp Six would be notified to Chua Yong Soon, the leader of the M.P.A.J.A., by the camp commissar in due course. As the major said to Robbie later, "Pity they don't get that blasted commissar up the front end; he is one I could well do without." But commissars, whether here, or in Russia, worked on the principle 'follow me lads, I'm right behind you.' Their job was to drive the foot soldiers into action and shoot them if they tried to retreat. Nikita Krushev was one such who was decorated for it with the Order of Lenin.

At 5am the party broke camp carrying five days' rations and double water bottles. Water was not a major problem as it rained most days, though you could never be absolutely certain this would be the case. Marching on a compass bearing they reached the railway line by late afternoon, how far from their intended point of contact they had yet to establish. Harry immediately mounted one well concealed observer, complete with map case and chinagraph - very appropriate name, thought Harry, for the special crayon which would not be affected by rain on the shiny map case exterior - then pulled the remainder back about fifty yards into a thicket to prepare their bamboo beds for the night.

Trains passed on the single-track line at about half hourly intervals until nine o'clock. Then they became spasmodic, and with the exception of one night express at just after midnight, they were all goods trains. One of particular note going north consisted entirely of fuel tankers. The observer noted the number and the fact that it also included two guards' vans, one behind the engine and one at the rear. In each of these he could see a number of Japanese soldiers, two in each van looking out on guard and others seated inside the brightly lit interior. When the train was well past he used his small torch to get all this information down.

And so the information built up. Transferred, after every man came off duty, into a record book, patterns soon began to emerge. After three days and four nights of observations they had a considerable amount of movement information. In addition, during daylight Harry and one of the Chinese patrolled for three or four miles in each direction on successive days to get a picture of the track layout, and above all to establish exactly where they were in relation to the point at which they had originally intended to hit the railway line. Despite the distance they had had to travel from Camp Six and the difficult terrain they had had to traverse, they were in fact only half a mile from their original intended destination. 'Not bad for an amateur,' was Harry's self-congratulatory comment. On the fourth morning they set off back on the long climb. It was dark as they hit the stream, the last two hours to the camp being accompanied by torrential rain, continuous vivid lightning which did at least illuminate their way to a certain extent, and horrendous thunder that only the tropics can produce, noise so violent it seemed to be stoving their very skulls in.

The camp turned out to greet them. They rubbed down, got into dry clothes and were given their first proper meal for five days. Then into their mosquito proof beds. Not one of them had slept for more than an hour or two at a time whilst they had been away, yet sleep came slowly to them, when it did, it was more like a bout of unconsciousness, so much so that Harry's batman had virtually to punch him to awake him the next morning.

The 'O' Group went carefully over the details collected so meticulously by Harry and his party. An hour or so later the major expressed his congratulations on a well carried out and superbly documented operation.

"We could have charged in and got some sort of result but now we can really plan our first attack. Now Mr Chandler, let's have your view on what we should attempt."

"Well Sir," Harry began, "about a mile north of our observation point a section of the line runs over a short steel bridge, not more than say fifty yards long. It spans a ravine running back into the side of the mountain. Parallel to it only about fifteen yards or so away but at a lower level the road spans the same ravine. Both of these bridges have only low side structures. If therefore the train could be derailed as it reached the bridge, the chances are it would topple on to the road below. If we could derail the petrol tanker train that would not only cause havoc but kill Japanese guards as well, which in my opinion would be an excellent bonus. Perhaps Choong Hong could advise us as to method. The disadvantages to this operation would be we would have to be certain we get the right train. As you have already noted, the schedule they run to is not particularly regular, and they run only at night. Two of us could remain behind until daylight to establish accurately the results we had achieved, but the remainder of the attack force would have to get clear in the dark. We could consider having guide tapes back to a safe distance and then wait for daylight to continue back to camp I presume, it wouldn't be much fun thrashing about in the darkness."

"What do you think?" the major asked Choon Guan.

"Well Sir, I have two men who were telephone engineers. They have handsets they used to test lines with. They have suggested that they use the existing telegraph wires that run along the track to send a signal that the right train is approaching. It would work like this. They would select say the bottom right hand wire of those on the poles. One man would take station say two miles south of the derail point, the other one with the derailing party. Each would climb a convenient telegraph pole - they have their spiked boots, which enable them to do this - and tap in to this selected wire. When the first observer sees the train coming and confirms it is the fuel train he rings the man at the main party. Now, Choong Hong says that to derail the train, since there are no points anywhere near the bridge which could be interfered with, is not as easy as it sounds. The Ward fishplates, which join the lengths of rail, can easily be unbolted, but the rail itself is still pinned into the sleepers. It would be necessary therefore to remove the pins on one length of rail well before the arrival of the target, as this will take some time, but leave the fishplates still attached. Any train passing over the one loose rail would be unlikely to cause any problem as long as the fishplates were still secure. Now, as soon as the signal of the approach of the target is received, the fishplates would be very quickly removed, the nuts having been loosened before hand, the rail would be toppled over and the train would keel over to the left."

There was a silence for a few moments.

"Anyone got any comments?" asked the major.

The others were still digesting all that had gone before. It was no longer a case of being part of Force 136, it was now crunch time. They were now going to have, not only to put into practice what they had learnt at arms length, they were now undoubtedly going to start learning their craft the hard way - on the job!

Harry made the first comment. "Having the first lookout man two miles down the track will give us roughly five minutes to take the bolts out of the fishplates. There are eight half-inch bolts in total to remove. We shall have to move fast. Secondly we cannot risk standing up on the track to do this as we shall be silhouetted from the road. It is unlikely that there would be traffic at that late hour; nevertheless, we must work on our bellies.

And so the planning went on. It was decided the operation would take place on the following Wednesday night, the 15th, when with luck they would have a good moon. An hour before dawn on the Wednesday, Clive Hollis led his party out for their first strike against their Nipponese adversaries. They reached the intended base in the jungle from which the assault would take place, and to which they would return in the dark to await daylight. A white tape was laid out almost to the railway line some four hundred yards away. Clive, Harry and Choon Guan patrolled forward to study the track through field glasses, firstly to make sure nothing had happened in the past few days to alter the plan, and secondly to decide which rail to remove.

As darkness came the first observer was despatched along with two comrades to follow the line of the track keeping just in the jungle fringe. The men at the derailing point were sent in pairs on their stomachs to remove the pins, others to free the nuts on the fishplate bolts. Traffic on the trunk road was fairly continuous until nine o'clock reducing to the odd military vehicle every few minutes after that. Trains passed interrupting the work on the pins. Midnight came and the trains became few and far between. The bolt removing squad were beginning to feel the tension knowing that when they got the word they had to move like greased lightning to get the bolts out and get back into cover so that a watchful driver or fireman did not catch a glimpse of them as they came round the curve in the track some two hundred yards away. Clive Hollis thought of the poor sodding train crew being sacrificed and wondered again whether they should be doing this if only because of them, then hardened his heart.

At 1.15 a long northbound goods train carrying road-making materials rumbled past. At 1.40 a southbound train pulling only a dozen or so ordinary goods wagons clattered through. At 2.10 the bell on the telephone shrilled out – 'enough to waken the bloody dead' as Clive exclaimed afterwards - and it was all systems go. Working on their stomachs the bolt removers got to work, and got back into cover - except for one. One was giving trouble and there was, at the most, two minutes to go. Harry jumped up and ignoring his own previous comment re silhouetting, ran along to the sweating young Chinese desperately trying to free it. He saw the trouble immediately. Taking the other bolts out had put all the weight of the rail on this one bolt. He called out, risking the unlikely possibility of anyone passing on the road.

"Lift the rail that end, only an inch or two."

Four men ran out and did exactly that. They could hear the train coming. The rail was very heavy. The men had to drop it. As they dropped it the bolt slid out. It was all over. They dived back into cover, hastily moved back into the jungle, kept on moving until their lungs were bursting. If thousands of gallons of petrol were going to blow up in a couple of minutes they wanted to be as far away as possible.

The sequence of events that followed could be likened to a giant playing a malicious game of 'crashes' with his train set. Everything that happened seemed to do so in slow motion. First the engine, a typical imported British 4-4-2 work horse, toppled on to its left hand side, slewed round to its right and slid on its side amidst showers of sparks along the railway lines. The tender hit the side of the bridge and toppled over on to the road below shedding a ton and a half of coal in the process. Next came the guards' van containing two soldiers on the observation platform and six others inside. The two on guard had a clear view of what was happening, shouted a warning, then jumped for their lives. As they landed, the first of the tankers swung off the track, toppled over the edge of the bridge and mangled their bodies between it and the bridge steelwork. In the meantime the guards' van balanced itself on the edge of the bridge until, with the men inside running to the front to jump off overbalancing it, it keeled over headfirst on to the road below. The second after this happened the first tanker landed on top of it, the final and total flattening of the van and its screaming contents being ensured by the second and third tankers following suit, bursting open at the welds and decanting some five thousand gallons of fuel oil over the wreckage and down the road. Three more tankers followed suit. It was a monumental pile up.

By now, with the sudden coming to a stop of the front of the train, succeeding tankers had either slewed over, or jumped the rails but remained upright. The last few remained on the rails, as did the rear guards' van. As this came to a halt the N.C.O. in charge jumped down shouting to his men to follow him. His first thoughts were that this was sabotage and that the saboteurs could only have retreated into the jungle. He gave the order for rapid fire to the sprayed into the jungle, but as no return fire came he ordered the ceasefire, and moved forward to investigate the scene of the derailment. As he did so one of his party gave a warning shout. These were not petrol tankers; as a result, nothing had been ignited by stray sparks. However smoke was beginning to rise from the road below. As they reached the bridge it became clear that hot coals from the engine were strewn all down the embankment, some of them having reached the spillage below. They moved back quickly as the fire took hold and gallons of fuel oil began sending thick black smoke up into the moonlit sky.

As there had been no explosion, Clive beckoned to Harry and Choon Guan to follow him as he moved forward to get a closer view of the site. He quickly sized-up the situation and indicated they should go back. It was now 3.15 and would be dawn in an hour. It had been planned that the main party would follow the tape back to a waiting area, where hopefully they would be joined by the first observers, the whole party moving off back to camp at first light. Harry and Choon Guan would stay on for a further day and night to make a full appraisal of the results of the operation. As the main body prepared to move, they could clearly see the smoke increasing - any minute now the area would be swarming with

Japs - "It's time we weren't here. Take care you two," said Clive, and they were off, the last man rolling up the white tape as they went.

As it got light Harry and Choon Guan, with an excellent view of the havoc their party had caused, concealed as they were in a hide overlooking the bridge only a hundred yards away, were glad that the wind was in the east. Thick black smoke was blowing away from them, although the smell of it was, to say the least, somewhat unpleasant. It had been a super night's work. Both the railway and the trunk road were blocked and would remain so for days to come. Harry drew a sketch on his pad of the position of the fallen tankers, along with copious notes of the state of the track, the state of the road, the surface of which was burning over a length of two hundred yards or more as a result of the burning oil having set fire to it. Traffic from both directions was being turned round and sent back. It would have to divert right back to the coast road in a huge circle of one hundred miles.

During the day they witnessed the Japanese attempt to put out the oil fire which the firefighters, both Jap and Malay accomplished by mid afternoon. Railway people arrived, with a small engine and moved the still standing tankers away but it was dark before a large crane arrived which Harry confidently judged would not be man enough to lift a laden tanker back on to the tracks. In this judgement he was wrong. The recovery crew had met this problem before. They had no intention of trying to reposition a full tanker in one lift, they jiggled one end at a time, and with patience, know how, and a certain amount of luck, combined with voluble profanity in a number of languages, got the four tankers back on to the track, having worked all night under their own arc lights. Dawn came. Harry and his comrade had managed a couple of hours sleep during the night whilst the other kept watch, but were beginning to feel tired after being awake for most of the past forty-eight hours. They now faced the prospect of a day's march through jungle, up hill most of the way, and as it happened, in pouring rain for most of the time. They hit the stream, waded on to the camp, were met by Clive and Robbie, handed in their reports in a haze of exhaustion, then collapsed into their beds until noon the next day.

The first operation of Camp Six had been a great success. They had put the main trunk road and railway out of action for several days, destroyed thousands of gallons of fuel oil, to say nothing of the rolling stock, and as a bonus had killed some Japanese in the process. Harry's final comment to Robbie was, "What a pity it wasn't a troop train" - but that would come one day - that would come.

Chapter Thirty One

General Sir Bernard Law Montgomery sat in his office at Southern Command. It was nine o'clock on the evening of the third of July 1942. He was concerned at the weather reports he was receiving from various stations on the south coast and at sea, they were bad and were not improving. Off the ports of the Isle of Wight over 6000 soldiers, plus considerable numbers of sailors, were aboard vessels waiting to take part in Operation Jubilee - the raid on Dieppe. Most of the soldiers were Canadians, plus about a thousand British and a handful of Americans and Free French. Elsewhere a battalion of paratroops was standing by to drop outside the town during the seaborne assault in order to prevent German reinforcements reaching the beleaguered defenders, and R.A.F. bombers were standing by to soften up the target prior to the landing.

The weather not abating, the attack was put back a day, then another, then another, until on the 7th July, knowing that the 8th was the very latest day that conditions would be suitable for the landings, the operation was aborted.

Bernard Law Montgomery was not sorry about this happening. He had been part of the army side of the combined operations headquarters, who were responsible for the overall plan. This was headed by Admiral Mountbatten of whom the general did not have exactly the highest regard. There could not have been two people more unalike. Montgomery was outspoken, domineering, religious, a non-smoker and drinker, who made attention to detail and dogged persistence the centre of any undertaking in which he was involved. He had been in the trenches in the Great War and had been one of the few divisional generals who emerged from Dunkirk with distinction. Mountbatten on the other hand was a lieutenant in the Royal Navy before the war and was now an admiral; largely it was conjectured as a result of his royal connections and his mentor Churchill. He was known as a bon viveur, a party man, a high society man who kept getting his ships sunk from beneath him and was not over-endowed intellectually.

The men sealed in the ships were disembarked. They were disembarked being in possession of full knowledge of the objectives of the raid, the method by which these would be met, and the forces to be used. Six thousand people were sent ashore with all this knowledge, when combined operations headquarters, headed by Admiral Mountbatten, decided they would have a re-run on the 19th of August.

General Montgomery immediately protested to his boss, General Paget, commander in chief of Home Forces, that the security of the operation had doubtless been compromised in every pub and billet in the South of England. He suggested therefore that either the raid be cancelled or alternatively provided with a different target. He was overruled. He was further, greatly upset by the knowledge that paratroops were now not to be used, and secondly there would be no preliminary bombing of the defences. He protested strongly at these omissions but again was not listened to. On the 10th of August, nine days before the raid, he was flown to Africa to take over the Eighth Army where he would demonstrate shortly how an operation should be planned and executed, and where he became Montgomery of Alamein.

On the 18th of August, Colonel Tim, Alec, and Jim were back on board the peacetime Isle of Wight ferryboat, packed to the gunwales with their battalion. There is always an apprehensive feeling about having a second go at things, as paratroopers in later times found when having to stand down for twenty-four hours or longer because of weather conditions before they could take off on an operation. Colonel Tim had called his 'O' group, had informed his incredulous company commanders there would be no softening up and no paratroops, this information adding to their previous apprehension. Late that night the convoy of boats, landing craft, and Royal Navy escort vessels moved out to cross the sixty-five miles to Dieppe. The small armada arrived on the French Coast without incident; the landing craft were loaded with the first waves and headed toward shore. It was only then that the German lookouts realised what was afoot and fired the seven-green-starred alarm rocket which immediately alerted the crews in gun emplacements built into the cliffs overlooking the beach and harbour at Dieppe, and the beach running south to Pourville and Quiberville.

Colonel Tim's battalion had been given the task of capturing Quiberville, then climbing the cliffs overlooking the town and preventing reinforcements from the direction of Rouen reaching Dieppe whilst the docks were being blown up. Originally he had been allocated a squadron of Churchill tanks, but these had been switched to another unit attacking the docks. In the event, it made little difference. The Churchills proved utterly incapable of overcoming the steep incline of the gravel beach so that the clutches burnt out trying to move thirty odd tons over such an angle, or the tracks, fitted with connecting links, which were not man enough for the job, simply shattered and lay in rows along the beach. Once they had fired all their ammunition, the tanks were finished. So much for planning.

Jim Napier's company led the battalion assault. Jim never even reached the beach. Although smoke had been laid, the beach was covered from the cliff emplacements on fixed lines from machine guns, light artillery and mortars. The German defenders fired into the smoke and into the sea lapping the beach. Jim was killed instantly. Colonel Tim, following him in with his battalion headquarters reached the steep gravel, ran through a hail of bullets, and established his HQ against some buildings sheltered from the cliffs. As he waited for his other two companies to arrive, a squadron of Spitfires flew in firing their cannons into the cliffs, wheeled out to sea, came in again, the temporary respite provided by the gun crews having to keep their heads down allowing Alec and his men some let-up from the carnage taking place on the beach and in the water.

As soon as a goodly proportion of the battalion had assembled under the lea of the cliff, Tim yelled to start climbing. The cliffs sloped steeply but were not vertical. At first they were shielded from the top, but as they reached the half way mark they came under fire firstly from a unit on top of the cliff, and secondly from one of the emplacements which could just see them from their position on the face. Tim ordered smoke to be put down to shield them from this disturbance. They reached a small shelf or plateau to find it was thick with barbed wire coils. Even worse, hanging on the wire were the dreaded signs 'achtung minen.' Although they had been given no information regarding wire entanglements they had as a matter of form, brought Bangalore torpedoes with them, long tubes filled with explosive which were pushed under the wire, detonated, hopefully blowing a gap in the wire and exploding any adjacent mines. He called the Pioneer section forward to carry out this task whilst they all kept their heads down. With a tremendous roar the Bangalores went off, blowing a four feet gap in the wire, which the men charged through to assault the positions fifty feet above them.

There was scattered resistance on the top of the cliff, which Tim's men swiftly dealt with, pushing on to their objectives astride the roads south. They had been ashore less than an hour. He had lost a third of his battalion already, and now dug in furiously to await the onslaught of the crack S.S. Adolf Hitler Division which intelligence had told him was positioned some thirty miles to the south. This was only a raid; they were not there to stay. It was hoped that the special objectives at the docks, and the obtaining of vital secrets from the Radar Station positioned on the cliff top between Pourville and Dieppe, would be speedily successful, then they would make a speedy withdrawal, hopefully before reinforcements arrived. This was not to be. The code word over the battalion radio ordering the retirement to the landing craft at the beaches was 'Vanquish.' It was received at 10.30 am by which time Tim was being heavily engaged by infantry, although luckily they were not, as yet, supported by tanks. He gave the order to retire down the cliffside, platoon by platoon until only his headquarters and the battalion HQ defence platoon were left. Finally they slipped away, and twenty minutes later found themselves back among the houses of Quiberville. They were out of the frying pan and into the fire. To get into the water and wade out to the landing craft meant traversing a rain of death from the cliff emplacements and from the new arrivals on the top of the cliffs. The Navy put smoke down, but this did not prevent the weapons, firing on fixed lines, from wreaking havoc. At last a destroyer moved in closer and began to fire broadside after broadside into the front of the cliffs. Weapons, corpses, concrete blocks, began to fall on the men sheltering below. Tim yelled for the men to run now into the sea, his orders being taken up by the remaining officers and N.C.O.'s spread along the top of the beach. They slid and scrambled down the steep shingle into the smoke covered water and started to wade out to the boats - or to where the boats should have been. Two had been sunk by Junkers 88 bombers and were just visible, another had its landing ramp shot away and was stuck, full of troops, but unable to get away since as it withdrew, it would immediately fill with water.

Tim turned to wave the men back as another murderous fire was set up from the emplacements which had remained undamaged but had gone to ground when the Navy plastered them. As Tim waved and shouted so a burst of fire from an MG42 ripped into him leaving his body floating slowly out to sea, from whence four days later, it was washed up some eight miles along the coast. He was accorded the respect of being given a military funeral by his former opponents in the S.S. Adolf Hitler Division.

Alec Fraser had been just a few yards from Tim when the colonel was cut down, immediately taking command of the hundred or so men still unwounded and waiting to get to the boats. However, it soon became apparent the boats that remained were not coming in to the beach to collect them, being subjected now not only from fire from the emplacements but also from troops and armoured vehicles which had arrived on the cliff top. They waited four to five hundred yards out, whilst the Navy continued to plaster the cliffs. In the shelter of the houses, Alec became fully aware that if they couldn't swim to the boats they were going to be captured. He called a hurried 'O' group of the one or two officers, and a number of senior N.C.O.'s and told them bluntly that it was swim for their lives, those that couldn't swim the distance to stay behind and surrender in due course. There was no other way. The navy was still laying smoke, Alec's orders were to dump all equipment and boots, when the smoke thickened to spread out and make a rush for the sea. After a few minutes the smoke thickened again, blowing back in to the cliffs. Alec yelled, "Now," at which some seventy or eighty swimmers ran into the sea. There were half a dozen casualties from the fixed line firing which had continued, mostly wounded, the rest reaching the water, plunging in, and furiously trying to cover the danger zone of the waters edge. Some thirty yards out Alec raised himself in the water and yelled, "Take it steady now, don't wear yourselves out." Five hundred yards might not be a long swim for some, but to many it was going to tax every ounce of strength they had, so conservation was the watchword.

One or two didn't make it and sank out of sight. Several would not have made it without the help and literal support of their comrades. Alec covered the last hundred yards pulling a young lance corporal who had been hit as he went into the water, eventually losing consciousness as rescue was in sight. Willing hands from the landing craft crew and previous arrivals dragged the men from the water where they lay or sat in the bottom of the boat in varying stages of breathlessness through to utter exhaustion. Nearly a thousand Canadians had been killed, nearly half of those being washed up on beaches days later up to ten miles either side of Dieppe. Nearly two thousand were taken prisoner mainly as a result of not being able to get to the boats. Mountbatten said to the War Cabinet the next day, "Very valuable lessons have been learnt." The truth was that the planning had been abysmal. Instead of appointing a task force commander to be solely responsible from start to finish as Monty had wanted, there were too many people in the decision making. We all know what happened when a committee set out to design a horse - they ended up with a camel!

Alec landed back at Portsmouth in the early hours of the 20th of August. The news at seven o'clock from the BBC that morning was awaited impatiently by all at Chandlers Lodge. The announcement of the raid had been made the previous evening, but little detail had been forthcoming. Further details now emerged. Casualties had been heavy but all the objectives had been achieved.

"The usual..." he was just going to say bullshit, but checked himself. "The usual jargon' Fred fumed.' It will be days before they tell us the truth - if then. Still, perhaps we will get it from Tim or one of the others. Well, I must be off. See you later."

Just after eight o'clock David telephoned. Since he had gone back off leave, during which Lord Ramsford had visited Chandlers Lodge, he had been carrying out routine tasks at Wilmslow, including a four-jump refresher course at Ringway along with Paddy. Paddy had been very cut up on hearing of his pal Driscoll's death in the Western Desert; they had soldiered together for close on fifteen years. Contrary to the wild conjecture passing through David's mind as to the reason for the brigadier's visit, it did not end with an invitation to him to assassinate Hitler, to recover the Belgian and Dutch crown jewels, or blow up Peenemunde, it seemed, although they had long conversations in which at times he felt he was being asked things with some ulterior motive, it seemed the brigadier really was at Sandbury on a social visit. He asked Fred if he could visit the works. Fred was delighted to show him what they were doing.

He met Ernie, his first words to him being, "I've heard all about you from Charlie. Apparently you're the brains of the establishment!" this latter with a conspiratorial grin at Fred. He stayed two nights instead of the single night they had first arranged, meeting Anni and Karl, Megan, Jack Hooper, Cecely and Mrs Treharne. All thought what a courteous, pleasant man he was. Having some indication of the job he did they wondered how it was that one person could carry all the responsibility of the lives he controlled, the inevitable sadness at the loss of people from time to time he knew intimately, being surrounded all his waking hours by secrecy, secrecy, secrecy. That alone, Fred remarked after he had gone, would be enough to drive a bloke up the wall.

Yet his conversation was intelligent, lively, and when Cecely happened to mention a travelling opera company was coming to Maidstone in a couple of weeks, showed a keen knowledge of Verdi's 'Nabucco,' which was to be performed. "Only the tickets are like gold dust," she had mentioned in passing, "and I've had to go on to the returns list - not much hope I'm afraid." This led Lord Ramsford to talk to Cecely about her favourite operas, whether she had the opportunity to see performances living in Malaya, and so on. She had to confess that her love for them had, in the main, to be satisfied by her collection of HMV, Decca and Columbia recordings, although her husband always took her to Singapore on the occasion of visiting companies, unfortunately these were not frequent events. "On the other hand I developed a taste for Chinese Opera," she went on to tell him, which provoked another long discussion, until Cecely told him she was hogging his company, at which he smiled at her saying it was a long time since he had enjoyed someone's company so much. The following week two tickets to the performance of 'Nabucco' arrived at The Bungalow, with a short note from Lord Ramsford.

"Dear Mrs Coates

Strings are designed to be pulled. I do trust you and Mrs Treharne will enjoy your evening. With kindest regards to all at Sandbury.

Your friend,
Hugh Ramsford"

There was a certain amount of leg-pulling at Chandlers Lodge when the note was shown to the family, particularly as the seats were in the most expensive block, Cecely weathering it with her usual good humour. She and Mrs Treharne, for whom this was an exceptional and unexpected treat, thoroughly enjoyed the performance, an oasis of culture in a world of harsh reality.

On the 20th of August the midday news brought the first intimation that casualties at Dieppe had been high, although of course, all objectives had been met. In the late evening news, little further detail was announced. At nine-thirty the telephone rang at Chandlers Lodge and was answered by Fred who had just come in from Home Guard duty.
"Mr Chandler, its Alec."
"Alec, how are you? We've all been so worried, feeling pretty sure you were all in this raid. How are all the others?"
"I've got bloody awful news for you Mr Chandler. Both Tim and Jim were killed. I'll give you all the details when I come on leave to the Bolton's at the weekend. We have lost over half the battalion, a lot of them taken prisoner. Anyway, I won't blab too much over the phone, I'll tell you more when I see you. Will you please tell the family. I'm sorry to be the bearer of such rotten news. Most of us feel there is someone up at Horse Guards who deserves to be shot, but then I suppose it would be treason to say that. Anyway, I'll ring off now. Give my love to everybody."
"I'll do that Alec. My God, they are going to have a shock."

And have a shock they did. Losing Jim and Tim was like losing family. Rose and Ruth in particular, who had been so close to them ever since they landed at Christmas 1939, over two and a half years ago, were devastated. Although it was late, they telephoned David, getting through quickly at that time of night. He was greatly saddened at the loss of two fine friends, in addition being very concerned as to the effect their deaths would have on Rose and on his mother, both of whom he knew having the greatest affection for the two men. Rose went to bed and cried into her pillow until sleep overcame her. Ruth too cried and cried, being comforted as best she could in Fred's strong arms. But it was no use. She would stop crying, try to get to sleep, then another wave of sorrow would overcome her, setting her off again. In the early hours, Fred got up and heated some milk for her, laced it with a good measure of brandy, brought it up to her and sat beside her whilst she sipped it, but even in the middle of drinking it she dissolved into sobs of despair at having lost two more of her brood. "And what must Jim's wife and family be going thorough?" She asked "and Tim's parents?" There was no answer to these questions, but the thought of the pain of others induced in her a calming effect to the extent that she eventually settled into a disturbed, dream filled sleep. When the morning came the great sadness was still there. Every now and then she dissolved into tears, not only at the loss of these two dear friends, but also for the thought of the futility of it all. Jeremy, Pat, Tim, Jim, Maria's brother Cedric - why? These were all people who should still be enjoying the life God had given them. Instead they had been sacrificed - why? From that day on Ruth began to retreat into herself. Fred became aware of this and kept a careful watch on her, coming home more frequently than had formerly been the case, manufacturing excuses to telephone during the day. Rose weathered the storm but she too was not her usual bright vivacious self. Underlying the sadness of the loss of her friends was the fear for her husband and dear Charlie facing similar dangers to those, which had just taken Jim and Tim from her. There seemed no end to it all, not even the prospect of an end. The tension and sadness was almost physical.

Over the weekend, Fred was so concerned at Ruth's depression and listlessness, he buttonholed his doctor at the Monday lunchtime Rotary meeting, asking him to come in and check Ruth over. John Power was not only their doctor; he was also a good family friend. "You will have to tell her I'm coming you know Fred. I can't just creep up on her. Tell her straight you are worried about her and want me to run the rule over her. That will do to start. It will be then we may have a problem. The chances are there is nothing organically wrong with her. That being the case, I would have to call in a specialist who deals with depression and related diseases, depression is an illness in its own right and often very difficult to treat, but in a great number of cases rights itself in time. Anyway, first things first. Fix a mutually convenient time and we'll take it from there."

David rang that evening, firstly to make sure that Rose and his mother were feeling less distressed at the news of Tim and Jim, and secondly to finalise arrangements regarding their presence at Paddy and Mary's wedding on Saturday. Fred told him of his mother's state of health and doubted whether they would be able to make it. Doctor Power had telephoned earlier that evening to say that a Doctor Fielding could call on Wednesday afternoon:- if it was convenient, and that being the case it was therefore so arranged. He would wait until he had had words with the specialist and then decide whether to telephone Mr Maguire to apologise for not being able to attend the wedding should that be necessary. He ended by saying, "I'll let Rose have a word with you."

Rose was subdued but told David she had now got over the initial shock. She was, however, worried about their mother. David asked whether she thought she would be able to be at the wedding. Arrangements had been made for them to travel to Aylesbury on the Friday afternoon and stay at The Bell on the Market Square until Sunday, Paddy initially being with them. They were having a "bit of a stag party" on the Friday evening - "nothing too riotous you understand" as Paddy had put it.

David replied, "When did leopards start changing their spots?"

Talking to David rallied Rose's spirits. She said she would come, and meet him there. Maria had got a forty-eight hour pass and would arrive during the evening, but had insisted that David should not interrupt his stag party to meet her, or indeed even see her until he was properly sober in the morning. Rose and Maria were having to share a room so would be company for each other. "You never know, we may be lucky enough to pick up a couple of Americans, I understand some are stationed up that way now," Maria had told him.

"If I could think of a polite enough reply I would answer that," had been David's riposte.

The specialist duly arrived along with Doctor Power at two o'clock on Wednesday, carried out all the usual medical checks.

"Which I know Doctor Power has already put you through, but we doctors have to earn our fees and do everything twice you know," he said cheerfully to Ruth. It was obvious he was not one of the 'oh! so solemn' brigade trying to make everything look more serious than it probably was.

"I understand you were terribly shocked by the loss of your friends," he had of course been fully briefed by John Power before the visit. "How were you feeling before that shocking news?"

"I was beginning to feel under the weather. This war is going on and on. We have lost two of our family already. Another, near and dear to us, has recently had his hand blown off, our son was posted missing believed killed in the Far East, our son-in-law is in the fighting at this moment in the Western Desert. I had the feeling it was all never going to end. I am lucky that I have wonderful people around me, but knowing that each of them has a worry or worries of some sort, just as I have, made me feel even worse." She paused. The description of her feelings had been given in short, staccato phrases, the specialist noted her tightly gripped hands and the tremble to her chin as she hesitated. "I know others are in the same boat, but knowing that doesn't seem to help. I know I'm better off than many since I have a comfortable home and am reasonably well off - others have lost everything they possessed in the bombing."

Dr Fielding let her talk on. She poured out all her built up sorrows to him, all her concerns for others, the fact she could do so little to help others in distress, her fear of the future regarding David, Harry, Mark and all the others, her guilt at having a comfortable life while others throughout the world were being mindlessly destroyed, her distress at the dreadful loneliness of her friend Cecely and the two children and the thousands like her she didn't even know. At last she stopped. Her hands had unloosened somewhat. She looked wildly at him and started to cry, silently but intensely. He took her hand and held it for several minutes in silence until slowly she became more tranquil. She took a number of deep sighs without saying more. When he considered it apposite he spoke softly to her.

"Mrs Chandler, it would do no good whatsoever for me to take each phrase of what you have just told me and prove you have either nothing to worry about, or that your worries are exaggerated. I know from my experience of the feelings of many many others, that those apprehensions are real - terribly, terribly real. This syndrome, this war weariness, is being suffered by all manner of people. You are not alone. People at the highest level of responsibility for our affairs down to a number of those individuals at the sharp end are beginning to be afflicted by it, particularly those in possession of secrets about which we ordinary people cannot be allowed to know." Ruth's mind immediately flew to David. "I say this not in the sense of telling you

'you're not the only one,' but in the sense that what you are suffering is an illness, it is known to us, and we can help you. On the reverse side of the coin we have no magic instant cure; it will take time and patience. I cannot give you a bottle of beautifully coloured, or horribly tasting medicine and say that will sort you out by the end of the week." He smiled at her; she gave him a watery smile in return. "Now - how do you sleep?"

And so the consultation went on for over an hour, at the end of which it was decided he would prescribe a mild sedative to help her with her sleeping "Although I don't want to dope you up," as he again cheerfully put it, some medicine designed to 'buck you up a bit,' and an appointment for her to see him at his clinic in Maidstone in a week's time. He shook hands, and was shown out by Fred. As they reached the front door he took Fred by the elbow and said, "Get everyone she has told me she worries about to write to her cheerfully. Don't let her be overwhelmed with visitors. Try and get her away from the house into the woods and countryside around, and make sure she has a good lie-in every day, not up at the crack of dawn to see you all off. One day I suppose we shall have all sorts of magic pills to stabilise these sorts of nervous breakdowns, at the moment, apart from one or two drastic treatments, there is little we can do beyond rest and as they say at medical school, T.L.C. - Tender Loving Care!"

Fred thanked him for all he had done, asking whether it would be beneficial to take her away somewhere. "I don't think so," was the reply. "I think that would, at the moment, even be detrimental to her condition in the sense she would be worrying about your being away from the factory. I suggest you organise a system to keep her as occupied as you can without her having to be responsible for running the house, getting the meals, and the normal chores around the house. Get her out in the fine weather, otherwise sit her with her feet up and rest. When she visits me next week I shall carry out blood tests and so on, and take some X-rays. Then we'll have another talk."

And so it was arranged. Almost everyone, with the exception of Moira who was away most of the time now visiting various War Ministry establishments, was placed on a rota carefully calculated to ensure that she was not overwhelmed with people or visitors at any one time, conversely was not left on her own for long periods. That evening Fred telephoned Mr Maguire who was extremely sympathetic, asking Fred to tell Ruth they would miss the company of, according to information supplied by Paddy, the most elegant of all their guests. "I'll tell her those exact words," was Fred's reply, "it will probably be the start of her recovery."

Everyone telephoned that evening. David informing his father that he had scrounged two extra days on his forty eight, "On compassionate grounds, although I've so little to do here at the moment I could disappear for a week and no one would notice." He would therefore come back on Sunday with Rose and Maria, taking Maria on back to Deal in the evening and return to Wilmslow on Tuesday.

Saturday dawned a glorious sunny day, glorious that is except for those who were physically incapable of looking even obliquely at or anywhere near the sun. There were certain people who had difficulty in raising their heads from their pillows, who complained bitterly about the hotel cat stamping around, who compared the state of their mouths as resembling the bottom of a parrot cage, who vociferously claimed it was all Paddy's fault, who just as confidently doubted they would be able to get to the wedding, and to a man said 'Never again.' High on this list were Mr Maguire, father of the bride, and one Captain Chandler, hopefully to be best man if he could get his trembling legs to support him. The utterly infuriating thing about it all was that Paddy was striding about like a two-year-old at Newmarket, confidently assuring them some eggs, bacon and fried bread for breakfast would soon put them right. One thing they all agreed upon was that it was a stag night right at the top of division one of stag nights, although to be fair, few of them remembered actually going to bed, even fewer who had got them there.

When David managed to get some flannels and a pullover on to get down to the breakfast room before it closed at ten a.m., he bumped into Rose and Maria. They looked at him, they looked at each other, they burst into screams of laughter.

"Oh my God, what a wreck," hooted Rose.

"Why have you still got your pyjama jacket on?" asked Maria.

"Are you going to have some nice fat rashers?" spluttered Rose, between her gusts of laughter.

David produced the best apology of a smile he could muster. "I do wish you wouldn't talk so loudly" he asked, "you are not being very kind to a man who has, against his normal abstemious way of life, carried out the duties of a best man in giving a comrade a good send-off into marital bliss, above and beyond the call of duty."

"Certainly above, and undoubtedly well beyond, to judge by the colour of your eyes," concluded Rose. "Anyway, go and get some coffee down you, we'll see you later." With that they walked away arm in arm, laughing together. David thought, 'I didn't even get a kiss!'

The wedding passed off without a hitch. Paddy still possessed his peacetime black and green dress uniform now with its huge gold stripes on the right arm, although it had required a certain amount of extremely clever needlework on the part of Mrs Maguire to expand the waist line of the trousers, and one even more clever piece of needlecraft to perform the same result on the tunic. Paddy assured her, "Its all muscle, so it is."

The speeches at the reception went well and were warmly received, Paddy including in his that all that was happening today was as a result of his meeting, and having the privilege of looking after his officer, his best man, Captain Chandler. "I've met many gentlemen in my years in the City Rifles, but he is head and shoulders above any one of them," this received with loud applause. He continued, "I would not now be a sergeant if it had not been for him, and above all I would not have met my Mary if I had not been with him when he went off God knows where. As you all know, Mary and me and the captain cannot tell you what we do, but I can tell you that this man is the bravest of the brave." Again there was thunderous applause.

David was taken aback by this obviously well prepared speech, given without the recourse to notes, and totally unexpected. Finally Paddy added, "Mary has particularly asked me to express our great sadness that the captain's mother, Mrs Ruth Chandler, cannot be with us today. When I have visited Chandlers Lodge, where I have met people from private soldiers up to brigadiers and generals, I have always been welcomed by Mr & Mrs Chandler as if I was as important as any one of their high ranking guests. Mary and I therefore would like Rose and the captain to take our best wishes, and I'm sure those of you all too, wishing Mrs Chandler a speedy recovery to full health." There were loud 'hear - hears,' and applause, after which Paddy sat down, suddenly weak at the knees after making the only speech of substance he had ever made in his whole life, which he had carried out with confidence and aplomb, and which would not be the last speech he would make in the years to come, but that is another story.

The evening went with a swing, the happy couple leaving at eight o'clock for Birmingham where they would stay at The Midland overnight, going on to North Wales for their honeymoon on Sunday in a small rented cottage on the coast of Bangor. The party, under the considerable persuasion and example of Mr Maguire, developed into almost a repeat of the stag night to the extent of providing the most riotously funny incident any of the people there had ever seen in their whole lives. The priest who had conducted the service - a friend of the

Maguires as well as their father confessor - was a bulky person and known to like a drink or two. On this occasion, being as it were almost one of the family, he was naturally invited to the festivities, at which he let his hair down well and truly, aided and abetted by Eamonn Maguire to the extent that his glass was not only never empty but not even left half-empty! By eleven o'clock when the party had to end, Father Kelly was slumped back on a chair against the wall totally incapable of standing up, singing 'Mother Macree' at the top of his voice. Mr Maguire and several of his catholic friends stood looking down at this mountainous heap of clerical inebriation. Attempting to lift him to his feet was Herculean in itself, until they found that there was to be no assistance whatsoever forthcoming from the functioning of the priest's legs. Whatever message to indicate locomotion was coming from Father Kelly's brain was being waylaid somewhere, since it certainly was not reaching his lower extremities. They let him slump back onto his chair whilst Eamonn myopically sized up the situation. "It'll take six of us to carry the bugger," was Eamonn's judgement.

"I'll get a barrow and some four by two," one of Eamonn's friends - a builder with a yard not fifty yards from the hall - announced to his companions in the newly constituted ecclesiastical relocation committee. He hurried off, accompanied by another of the guests, neither moving in what could be described even loosely as a straight line. They returned in about ten minutes with a huge wooden wheelbarrow, the accomplice carrying two lengths of four by two on his shoulder. Six of them, David being one, picked the padre up and lowered him not too reverently into the wheelbarrow, one of the ladies slipping the cushion off the piano seat under his head a second before it would have made contact with the front edge. David volunteered to wheel the barrow but as soon as he lifted the sixteen stone cleric along with the wheelbarrow which itself felt as though it weighed a ton, he urgently regretted his foolhardiness. Nevertheless there was no going back - there was no way he could announce the task was beyond him, particularly with his sister and fiancée watching him through their uncontrolled tears of laughter.

He wheeled the barrow through the door from the hall to find himself confronted by four broad steps down on to the pathway. He then saw the purpose for the pieces of four by two. The builder guest had met this problem before. How do you get a barrowful of wet cement, or in this case, a thoroughly soaked man of the cloth, down a flight of steps without spilling anything?

"Turn the barrow round captain, so he goes down feet first," bade the builder in charge of this delicate operation. David complied.

"Now put the four by two under." This was accomplished.

"Now, two on each end of the wood. When I say lift, lift slowly. No, not yet Michael you blithering idiot." Michael was a big strong fellow, and in lifting his end had dislodged the grips of the two on the other end of the timber, which fell to the floor, in the process turning the baulk of wood into a lever, thereby almost turning the barrow over and dumping Father Kelly on to the top step of his own parish hall. They reorganised.

"Now lift slowly." This was now accomplished without further mishap.

"Now slowly down the steps - and KEEP IT LEVEL." This was easier said than done. It must be remembered that each and every one suffered a height differential from his companion on the timber. Secondly each and every one had had copious quantities to drink. Thirdly half of them were so close to hysteria at the whole bloody shebang they were almost useless anyway.

Somehow or other Father Kelly arrived safely on the pathway, by this time snoring loud enough to wake half the neighbourhood. It was about a hundred yards along the main road to his lodgings at The Priory, once he got going David finding his task to be not utterly beyond him. It was a bright moonlit night when two policemen on bicycles coming from the opposite direction spotted a most unusual cavalcade of men, talking loudly, some carrying baulks of timber, followed by a cortege of well dressed ladies, most in hats, the whole preceded by a somewhat bulky army officer in full service dress wheeling a large wheelbarrow containing a body. It was not a sight they normally met, even on a Saturday night, in the fair borough of Aylesbury. They decided to make a 'U' turn on their velocipedes, which they really should not have done. As they completed their turn they both took their eyes off the road, and off each other, to look at the body in the barrow, to their astonishment recognising the extremely well known, if at present recumbent figure of Father Kelly no less. Their surprise compounding their previous inattention caused their front wheels to become interlocked as a result of which from the elevated seats of their sit up and beg machines they were deposited on the pavement right in front of David's barrow. David stopped; let the barrow down with a bit of a bump, which in turn disturbed his cargo, who promptly started to sing 'Mother Macree' all over again.

Things went from bad to worse. Two of the guests ran, or rather staggered, round to help the policeman up. However, Buckinghamshire policemen are not recruited unless they have the build of heavyweight boxers. As a result the aforementioned guests found the task beyond them. In bending down to perform the enterprise, their equilibrium being somewhat disturbed by the adverse ratio of alcohol to blood within their systems, they found their good intentions did not compensate for the marked lack of physical strength they had previously considered they possessed. To put it plainly, they were too pissed to be of any use to anybody, as a result they both found themselves prostrated on the unwelcoming bodies of two members of the constabulary; a race which normally considers it is at the top of the pile, not the underdogs. Willing hands pulled the would-be helping hands up, thus allowing the pride of the Buckingham Constabulary to re-establish the vertical thus bringing some pretence of law and order to the streets of Aylesbury.

By now Father Kelly had gone back to sleep. The senior policeman announced in suitably officious tones they had better get 'him' home before they were all in trouble. One wag from within the party proclaimed, "When the super sees your bikes I reckon you will be the ones in trouble." All eyes turned to the specimens of police mobility lying in the gutter. Each front wheel instead of presenting a perfect circle now curved in altogether different directions. Buckled, bulged, contorted, warped, however one might describe them, there was no way they could be wheeled, let alone ridden. The party had the highly satisfying sight of two burly policemen each carrying a bicycle back to what would undoubtedly be a committee of enquiry constituted from on high after which they would be court martialled, or whatever it is they do in the police force to people who marmalise property belonging to the 'Old Bill.'

The evening was not over.

David's arms felt they were being slowly but painfully removed from their sockets, he was therefore mightily relieved to hear Eamonn announce, "We're here. Well done David my boy." They were at the bottom of a flight of some half a dozen steep steps leading up to the front door of The Priory.

One of the crowd asked, "Who's going to ring the bell?" David thought this question was surely unnecessary; anyone could ring a blasted doorbell! However, as he soon was informed it was not the actual ringing of the bell, which presented a problem; it was the facing of Sarah McGonicle, Father Kelly's housekeeper, who would be the one to answer it. The fierce, and utterly devoted Sarah had looked after the Father ever since he came to the parish in 1919. It was firmly believed that she was descended from a long line of inquisitors, since no one could disturb the peace of Father Kelly without undergoing a third degree grilling to establish whether their business was a matter of life or death before they were allowed beyond the front door.

David heard himself saying, "I'll ring it," and then discovered himself thinking, 'you silly sod, you've volunteered again!' Having made the statement, to the unbounded relief of the parishioners, he climbed the stairs to carry out the enterprise. He had not long to wait after tugging the jangling bell-pull.

He could hear footsteps slap-slapping across the bare boards inside, the door opened, and a thin faced, grey haired lady, wearing a housecoat and a mauve coloured hair net, faced him, with a mouth half open to declare "What do you want?" in no uncertain terms, until she saw a handsome army officer in full service dress, Sam Browne, medal ribbons and all standing there in the moonlight. Instead of the expected tongue-lashing, the guests on the steps heard her say, "Good evening to you Sir, can I help you at all?"

"I have been a guest at Mary Maguire's wedding. Father Kelly was also there, as you will doubtless know. It was very warm in the hall, in fact it has been a very warm day altogether, has it not?" Not waiting for a reply he continued. "As a result of the hot room and the fact that Father Kelly was very tired after a long day, he fell soundly asleep, so we've brought him home."

Her attitude changed. "What you are saying captain - you are a captain are you not? - is that you and the Maguire clan have got him drunk. You all ought to be ashamed of yourselves so you should," she yelled at the crowd assembled around the wheelbarrow, which she discerned for the first time. "And wheeling him through the town in a wheelbarrow - oh the shame of it, oh the shame of it."

"He really was quite comfortable," David assured her, and then could not help adding for sheer devilment, "Even the two policemen who stopped us agreed he was quite comfortable and being well looked after."

At this, Sarah was speechless, at last spluttering, "Bring him in."

The four by two wheelbarrow raising party fell in. They found it was much more difficult carrying their load up the steep steps than it had been carrying it down the shallow steps at the hall. Eventually, after what would have seemed an extremely hazardous flight had the passenger been capable of experiencing it, they reached the top level by the front door.

"You are not bringing that blasted thing in on my polished floor," harangued Sarah McGonicle.

Adding fire to the flames Eamonn called out, "Sarah, you've just said a naughty word, I shall have to have a word with the Father tomorrow." She looked at him, unable to find words with which to chastise him.

"Wait here," she commanded, and scurried off, returning a minute later with a long narrow Persian hearthrug. "Lay him on the end of that," she ordered. Half a dozen of them picked the Father up out of the barrow and laid him as gently as they could on the rug. Sarah picked up the loose end and started to tug the recumbent incumbent on his rug across the highly polished floor. David, seeing that she was making very heavy weather of it, jumped to her aid and they dragged him down the hallway into the sitting room and across to the fireplace where the remains of a wood fire were at their last gasp. Quickly Sarah put a cushion from the sofa under his head, got two travelling rugs out of a sandalwood box against the wall and put them over him. It occurred to David that this was not the first time she had performed this service for her beloved padre. She looked at David. "He'll be alright there. He has slept in far worse places. He was three years in the trenches and won the Military Cross you know." Her voice was that of someone having a deep love for another. It lasted only a minute. She went back to the door. "Away with you all, you should be ashamed of yourselves," and with that slammed the door on them.

They made their various ways to their beds, sides still aching, and with a story that would be told from Lands End to John O'Groats and even further for years to come.

Chapter Thirty Two

David returned to Wilmslow after his two days at home, most of which he spent with his mother. He was most concerned at the marked deterioration in her state of health, although she constantly tried to assure him that it was just a temporary reaction to all the bad news they had received lately. He found it difficult to judge whether he should be ultra-cheerful and try to jolly her along, or to be quietly sympathetic. He decided on the latter on the basis that as he knew well, there is nothing worse in a group of soldiers in a hole than having one comedian cracking senseless jokes; you end up threatening to murder him. The last thing he would want would be to add to his mother's distress with a lot of irritating chat. Ruth was due to see Doctor Fielding on Wednesday afternoon, David arranging to telephone that evening when he got back to his unit.

The news that evening provided him with no further indication of his mother's condition. The afternoon had been spent taking blood samples, having X-rays, including three of the head, undergoing heart tests and so on, at the end of which Doctor Fielding said he would be away for the next ten days, would make a further appointment for two week's time, by which date all the results of the tests would be in his hands. In the meantime she should just rest, relax, read a good book, listen to the wireless and go for walks when it is fine weather.

The next day was September 3rd 1942. The war now was commencing its fourth year; no wonder people were becoming war weary, or at least a goodly proportion of them. The spivs and black marketeers, a proportion of the base wallahs, the girls who were servicing the ever increasing number of American troops arriving here with money to spend, for them it could go on for ever.

On Friday 4th, Robin called David in to his office to tell him that the brigadier would be visiting them on Sunday 13th - well at least it was not a Friday was David's immediate reaction - and wanted to talk to him, ending with, "And I think Paddy may be involved."
"I know it's absolutely ridiculous to ask you if you know what it is all about?" David complained, the utterance having been made more as a question than a statement.
"Cross my heart - I haven't the faintest."
"I'll believe you - thousands wouldn't."

Paddy returned on Sunday 6th, was warmly welcomed by all at Wilmslow with whom he had become extremely popular. After the usual ribbing of a comrade just returned from honeymoon, David asked, "What did you think of the scenery in that part of North Wales - it's very beautiful I believe?" To which Paddy hesitated before replying.

"Well you see Sir; you know we had rented this little cottage." David nodded.

"Well Sir, we only went out twice, that was to a little shop along the road to buy bread and milk and a few odds and sods. There was no point in wasting time looking at scenery now, was there?"

"Did you bother to undraw the curtains at any time?"

"Not at all Sir, not at all."

"You probably hadn't got the strength by the time you came away." Paddy grinned.

"Well, all I can tell you is that the brigadier is coming in a week's time. It looks as though he may have cooked something up for both of us."

"Do you mean together Sir? Holy Mary, I shall look forward to that."

"The state you must be in, I don't know that I should risk taking you, wherever or whatever it is."

Paddy grinned, he had a pretty good idea that the captain would look forward to a caper together with him as much as he would with the captain.

The days passed slowly until the next Sunday. Lord Ramsford arrived late on Saturday night, calling for a meeting with David at eight o'clock on Sunday morning. David's first reaction to the message, given to him by Robin, was, "Doesn't he know the union rules? There is no such time as eight o'clock, dressed, shaved and fed, on a Sunday morning."

"You're lucky he didn't call it at midnight when he arrived. It wouldn't have been the first time," was the unsympathetic response from Robin.

At five minutes to eight they duly presented themselves at the reception desk. The duty sergeant answered the internal telephone.

"Yes Sir, they are here. Very good Sir. Will you please go on in."

David led the way into Robin's office - the 'Headmaster's Study' as he always called it - once inside they both halted and saluted.

"Sit down both of you. Before we start, what news of your mother David?"

"Well Sir, she has had further tests, the results of which will be known during this week."

"Right. I will telephone your father later." He made a note on a pad.

"Now I know you two want to get back to your unit for the invasion. This still will not be for a while I am afraid. We have to get a lot more Americans here and train them before that can happen. In the meantime I have loaned you to a friend of mine, Brigadier Hopgood who you met when I was visiting before."

"So he brought that bugger here to size me up," was David's immediate conclusion.

"Now, he is the head of intelligence for the section dealing with Tito and the Yugoslav partisans. He wants you to do a job for him, the pair of you that is, which entails your being dropped into Yugoslavia. It will last about six months. I am unable to tell you any more. There is a flight to Cairo the day after tomorrow, your tropical kit will be here today, the rest of your gear for the winter in the Balkans will be made available to you in Cairo where you will meet Brigadier Hopgood and others who know the area, and will be given your orders. Now, any questions?"

"Can we tell family and friends where we are going Sir?" David asked.

"I don't see why not. This is not the sort of affair that can be compromised."

"Sir," asked Paddy. "I see we are dropping in, is it in order to ask how we drop out in six months time?"

"We have a regular submarine service for that purpose sergeant. Oh, and by the way, you are both being promoted as from today, for two reasons. One, in appreciation of the excellence of the work you have both recently carried out and two, to give you greater status with the partisans.

"They looked at each other, the new major and the new sergeant major, chorusing, "Thank you Sir, thank you very much."

"Right, that's it then, clear your decks and be ready to leave first thing in the morning for the airfield." He stood up and shook hands with them both; they saluted, did a smart about turn and marched out.

Outside the door Paddy turned to David. "Do you know what Sir? I am damned glad I didn't waste any time last week." He paused, smiling, and continued, "Do you know Sir, I reckon if I stick with you I'll end up a bloody general, so I will." They laughed and headed for the telephone booths.

Rose answered the telephone when David called Chandlers Lodge. After giving him the latest news of his mother, which was little different to the news he had been given the day before, he told Rose he was off again, this time to Cairo and then into Yugoslavia.

"How is it you can tell us all this when we have no clue at all as to where you have been before?" She questioned.

"I have ceased to try and understand the workings of the military mind," was David's reply, "all I can conclude is that the dropping of two of His Majesty's riflemen into Yugoslavia would not constitute any feelings of fear into Mr Hitler's field commanders."

"Two riflemen? Who is the other one?"

"Sergeant Major O'Riordan, oh and by the way, I am now Major Chandler, so I shall expect a little more respect from you from now on."

They chatted on for a while, until Rose told him his mother and father were arriving, having just come from the eight o'clock Holy Communion service, after which they had been invited, along with the other communicants to a cup of tea and biscuits in the church hall with Cannon Rosser. Rose briefly told her parents of David's news, Ruth then taking the telephone. Apart from asking firstly how long he would be away, a detail which he had forgotten to impart to Rose and she had not thought to ask of him, then saying how pleased she was Paddy was going with him who would, she was sure, take good care of him, she did not appear to be as upset as he feared she might be. Thinking of that point later he wondered whether the medication she was being given was, in fact, reducing her worry factor along with the depression with which she was afflicted.

Having got over the difficult part of saying, "Goodbye - I'll see you in the spring," he rang the Schultz household.

"Mr Schultz - it's David. Will Maria be telephoning you at all today?"

"Yes David, she rings at about eleven o'clock every Sunday morning."

"Will you ask her to ring me as soon as she has finished her call. It is important."

"Certainly I will David. Am I right in fearing you are away again?"

"Yes, tomorrow. I'm afraid it has been sprung on us."

"Us?"

"Yes, Paddy and I are both going. That is we're on this job together. I'll tell Maria all about it, then she can pass the news on to you. Please give my kindest regards to Mrs Schultz."

"I will David. God bless you both and keep you safe."

David went off to his room where he found Paddy sifting through his kit, making two piles, one to take, one to leave behind.

"Now Sir, what's this Yugoslavia like. Is it a hot country like Egypt or cold or what?"

"I'm damned if I know. But hang on a bit. How can we have a company sergeant major, a warrant officer class II, sorting out somebody else's kit?"

"Well Sir, we've had this out before. I'm here to look after you and that's what I intend to do. Mind you it might alter when I'm a general."

"Well, we haven't time to argue about it. I'll go and find out from Robin what we should take."

He ran down the stairs, knocked on Robin's door, being bade to enter, went in to find the brigadier there as well. Before he could say anything the brigadier told him he had just been talking to Rose, in addition having had a few words with Ruth. "She seems a little brighter than she did last week," he concluded. David thought of the myriad things the brigadier would have on his mind, yet he could think of and take the time to enquire about his mother's health.

"Now, what can we do for you?" Robin asked cheerfully.

"What sort of weather are we likely to expect in Yugoslavia?"

The brigadier answered.

"From now on it's very cold. You'll be high up in the mountains. Virtually everywhere you go you will have to walk. So take warm clothing, puttees, and two or three pairs of good boots, and daft though it sounds, a couple of gas capes each - they will be worth their weight in gold, you mark my words."

A gas cape was issued to every soldier until quite late on in the war. It was carried rolled up on the haversack worn on the soldier's back, was fitted with a quick release string which when activated, allowed the cape to unroll for the soldier to slip his arm into the sleeves and button it up like an ordinary mackintosh. It was fabricated from very durable material, made to be proof against attacks from mustard gas, was therefore totally waterproof and tailored to cover the soldier and all his equipment. David could instantly recognise therefore how invaluable one would be in the rain and snow of mountainous Yugoslavia.

"Thank you Sir. Robin, could I borrow your Britannica with Yugoslavia in it please. You shall have it back later today." Robin walked across to one of the shelves in the book-lined room and reached down the X-Z volume. David thanked him and made his way back to his room.

The brigadier turned to Robin. "What I like about young Chandler is that he never leaves anything to chance. In all the reports I have received from his various tutors and instructors, he never fails to ask the pertinent question or to query anything about which he is not a hundred percent clear."

Soon after eleven, a mess waiter knocked at the door. "Telephone for you in number two booth Sir."

David raced down the stairs to take Maria's call, only it wasn't Maria. It was Jack Hooper. "David, I had to ring you to wish you well. I thought too I could give you one or two addresses in Cairo which you may well find useful."

"That is most thoughtful of you, but I think I will decline your kind offer - after all, I would not like to be declared medically unfit to continue my duties and be sent home before I had ever started."

"I was, of course, referring to museums."

"If they have the same personnel who were there when you spent your dissolute hours in them they probably could be classified as museums by now."

The banter went on for a short while, Jack ending by saying, "I'll not keep you longer. Good luck to you both, we'll see you in the spring."

As David walked away from the booth the bell rang again. It was Maria.

"Darling, Daddy tells me you're going away tomorrow." She sounded very upset.

David explained what was happening, that he would be back in the spring, then they would fix the wedding date. It was a tearful Maria who said goodbye.

Their tropical kit arrived during the afternoon complete with badges of rank, parachutist wings and medal ribbons. Paddy stowed all the gear neatly in the two kitbags they had each been given, saying, "If we need anything else we'll get it in Cairo."

"I think we may find we can only take what we can carry," was David's gloomy reply.

After dinner that evening, Robin told David to have all their kit down to leave in a truck at eight am the next morning. Paddy had the kitbags down promptly; they breakfasted, then waited in the hallway for the truck to arrive. When it did so, and the driver alighted to announce her arrival, Paddy called out to David, "Look who we have here Sir, and with two stripes now and all." It was none other than their old friend Amanda from Ringway days. They both hugged her, which looked rather incongruous and most definitely un-military to the two or three people passing through. After all, it's not often that sergeant majors or majors hug corporals - well not in public anyway.

"Now then, how's that staff sergeant of yours?" asked David. "We did a refresher but didn't see him there. I put that down to the fact that the place has grown enormously and we were only there a short while anyway."

Amanda looked downcast. "I'm afraid it's all over Sir."

"Oh no, I am sorry Amanda. I really am. Despite our leg pulling, I thought you were a couple, and so did Paddy."

"You're right Sir, you're right indeed."

She put on a brave face. "Well, I thought so too, but unfortunately Alistair had his eye on the main chance. One of the station officers, Waaf officers that is, is a daughter of an air vice-marshall. Apparently he started to get his feet under her table behind my back despite the fact we were engaged. Eventually someone told me what was going on, I tackled him about it, and he told me he was breaking off the engagement. Since then he has been put on an air crew course and given a commission."

Paddy put his arm round her shoulders. "You alright now my love?"

"Yes, I think so."

"Well, if you weren't such a lady, I would tell you exactly what I think of him, but you wouldn't understand half the language if I did."

Amanda smiled. "I'll survive, it's happening all the time I suppose. I wasn't the first one and I shan't be the last. Anyway, I've got to get you to Quedgeley I understand."

"Quedgeley?" they uttered in unison.

"Yes, why, do you know it?"

"We got lost coming from there some time ago and stopped at an army camp to ask the way. They thought Paddy looked suspicious."

"Well, he does at the best of times, doesn't he?"

Paddy again put an arm around her shoulders. "That's my girl," he said rejoicing to see her sense of fun had not deserted her.

"Anyway, just coming back from, well from wherever it was we came from, we had no identification papers, so they threw us in the guardroom, until eventually Robin got us bailed out."

"Oh, I would love to have seen that," she giggled, "it would have been better than the Marx Brothers."

Paddy tightened his hold. "Well Sir, she may have had a dirty trick played on her but she's still our loveable cheeky little Amanda, is she not?"

Robin came out to say goodbye, and by half past eight they were on their way to Quedgeley in the capable hands of Corporal Dudley, as a result failing to get lost.

The guard commander at the main gate had notice of their coming and directed Amanda to Block 28, where they were to be billeted until take-off the next afternoon. They both kissed their driver goodbye, again much to the curiosity of several passers-by and nosey parkers looking out of the barrack block windows, before she drove off on the long journey back to Wilmslow with a little prayer for the safety of those two lovely men going into all sorts of dangers and discomforts. In her wildest dreams she could not have imagined the dangers, and particularly the discomforts, they were to meet, as indeed neither did the two men themselves, as they waited the inevitable wait for the next stage of their journey to take place.

On Tuesday evening, they boarded a Halifax along with some half a dozen others they had not previously met, including a brace of women they observed. However, since noise and general discomfort did not encourage socialising they found out nothing of what they were up to, particularly since they were bundled in to a fifteen hundred weight truck and driven away when they arrived at Gibraltar soon after dawn, leaving David and Paddy standing on the tarmac 'like two pricks at a wedding,' as Paddy succinctly put it. The use of this phrase started David chortling away until Paddy asked, "What's so funny Sir?"

"Your talking about a wedding reminded me of Father Kelly in the wheelbarrow."

This started Paddy laughing. "I heard about six different accounts of that when Mary and me came back, and we both got a right earful from Sarah McGonicle when we went round to see the Father."

"Did you go round to book the christening?"

Their banter was interrupted by a captain in the Intelligence Corps arriving in a pick-up.

"Major Chandler? Welcome to Gib, albeit you will only be here for today, flying out to Malta tonight. If you would like my driver to show you round after you've had some breakfast and a few hours' kip, I will gladly arrange it and come with you both."

They arranged therefore to have breakfast, sleep until midday and then sight-see during the afternoon, after which the captain brought them back to the airfield for the next stage of their journey. This was to be in an Anson, infinitely quieter than the massive four-engined Halifax, fitted with six comfortable seats and provided with a luxury that David had not experienced since his Lysander flights, namely windows in the sides of the fuselage. It was roughly eleven hundred miles to their next landing point - Malta. As the Anson had a normal range of some eight hundred miles, it meant it had two spare fuel tanks slung beneath which looked perilously close to the ground on an airplane already set low on its landing wheels. David had a quick look at them and was disappointed to find they were made by a competitor of Sandbury Engineering. Paddy looked at him quizzically.

"I thought my Dad may have made these," following this statement up with, "I hope there are no humps in the runway."

They climbed aboard, sat in the rear seats awaiting the arrival of the remaining passengers, the crew being already in their places. In a few minutes a large Humber staff car swept up, from which emerged two Generals, each with his attendant A.D.C. They were obviously base wallahs dressed in service dress, the Generals being covered in red tabs and the A.D.C.'s - both captains - each wearing a large red armband on the left upper arm designed obviously to make them look infinitely more important than they really were. Getting into the aircraft the generals just nodded to David and Paddy, sitting themselves in the front pair of seats. The errand boys, climbing in after them, followed in their master's footsteps, just nodded and sat in the centre pair of seats. David sat with his first two fingers of his right hand pointed upwards in recognition of the courtesies they had just been accorded. Paddy sat killing himself with laughter at the little pantomime.

They took off just as it was getting dusk; flying at low level across the Mediterranean, with the intention of arriving at Malta at day break before the daily bombing started. Arriving at the R.A.F. station they were hustled away to breakfast and bunks in an underground shelter, this time without even a nod from the chair borne warriors with whom they had just spent the night.

They rejoined the Anson at six o'clock that evening in its concrete canopy on the edge of the drome. The canopy would be no protection from a bomb but would prevent damage from the multitude of pieces of shrapnel falling from anti aircraft fire during the continual raids. Wreckage of other aircraft around the perimeter of the airfield gave a clear indication of the effect of previous attacks.

They were both rather travel weary at the end of the seven hour flight to Cairo, a flight not improved by considerable turbulence for half the journey leaving both David and Paddy wondering whether the meal they had been given before the flight would stay with them. Fortunately it did. Just before they landed, they experienced one of the most beautiful sights on earth, that of the sun rising out of the desert. Miles upon miles of black land slowly being lit up by an enormous shining orb of gold in the east. From the ground it is a magnificent scene, from the air it is a spectacle beyond belief.

The Anson taxied to the reception area, swung round and cut engines. The cabin door being opened a wave of dry hot air hit them, which even at that hour in the morning, made them realise they, would soon have to get out of their serge battledress and don their tropical kit. On the tarmac to meet them was a young captain who smartly saluted David, saying, "Welcome to Egypt Sir, and to you Mr O'Riordan. The brigadier presents his compliments Sir, and says he will see you this evening when he returns from Alexandria. In the meantime I am to take you to a hotel where you can rest up after your journey and he will come and see you there at around eight o'clock." David instantly understood the reason for this arrangement. If they had been taken to army quarters Paddy, not being an officer, would not be able to be billeted with him, nor be able to be with the brigadier for a meal together. At a hotel that would not apply. Attention to detail, thought David, attention to detail. The brigadier knows his business, that's obvious.

The hotel turned out to be of medium size, in a well kept street - well kept by Egyptian standards that is - in Heliopolis. Their rooms were lofty, fitted with ceiling fans and overlooking a large garden. Their young companion saw them through reception and onward to their rooms, leaving them with the injunction to order whatever they required as it was "on the house," to which David replied to a mystified captain "But as my sister would say, 'who's house I wonder?'"

"Do you know Sir," Paddy added, "tis lucky you are, I am now a teetotaller otherwise you might have regretted saying that."

"He's also the biggest fibber under the sun too."

"All I can say Mr O'Riordan is that if you can keep pace with the brigadier you will be numbered among a tiny few in the Middle East."

"I won't take that as a challenge Sir, there's no way I'd get on the wrong side of a brigadier."

Leaving his contact telephone number with David, with the warning not to say too much over the phone, the captain left them to strip off their serge, shower, have breakfast together in David's room, then each to dive into a pair of crisp, clean, cool, Egyptian cotton sheets. It was a luxury that in a few weeks' time they would look back upon with nostalgia, the cleanliness, the soft whirring of the ceiling fan, the occasional movement of the mosquito net hung from a central point in the ceiling above, the well sprung mattress, the sensation of knowing, at least until eight o'clock, their time was their own and they only had to pull a satin covered cord to have a room servant arrive to wait on them hand and foot. There could hardly be two different worlds than this present one, and the one, which they would join in a few weeks' time.

Chapter Thirty Three

Camp Six, still flushed with the success of the trunk road operation, or as it became officially known 'The First Trunk Road Operation,' was eagerly awaiting the call to carry out the next attack. None more so than those who were left out of the July strike and who were now champing at the bit. Major Hollis and Choon Guan assured them they would soon have all the action they could cope with, secretly hoping the all clear would be given soon for them to make the next sortie. On the 23rd August, the go-ahead was given. Clive called his 'O' group to inform them of their next objective, which immediately became obvious was to be a definite 'hands on' operation, that is to say the objective was to kill Japanese, not just to cause mayhem.

The plan was simple. The force numbering some sixty active troops was to be divided into four parties. A base party of ten plus cooks and any sick would be left behind under the navy lieutenant to guard the camp. A second party of ten would travel with the barest necessities, they would not carry weapons but would have specially made back packs to carry back certain items of loot to be obtained from the objective, details to be provided later. The objectives were twofold. The main objective was a Japanese army supply, storage, and petrol refuelling point at the small town of Kabang, halfway along the only east to west road across the state of Johore Bahru, which ran from Ayer Hitam on the Grand Trunk Road in the west to Mersing on the east coast. Five miles beyond Kabang towards Mersing the road passed over a bridge over the River Endau, a single track combined steel and timber structure, which was to be the secondary objective. If this could be destroyed it would completely halt traffic across the southern peninsula.

The whole force of forty odd men would move out of camp south east through the jungle and establish a firm base on the fringes of the lower jungle where it met a large area of cultivated oil palms, some eight miles of comparatively easily negotiated country from each objective. Clive had given considerable thought as to the timing of the two operations. A dawn attack would provide them cover of darkness up to the targets, after that they would have the disadvantage of a daylight pursuit. If they attacked in the late afternoon when the enemy's watchfulness would be at its lowest point, they risked approaching the targets in daylight, being detected, thereby losing the element of surprise. He decided on the dawn attack, trusting they would eliminate any Japanese in the immediate area, and would have melted back into the jungle before reinforcements could arrive from Kluang, the nearest garrison, some twenty-five miles away.

Calling the 'O' group to order, Clive gave out his orders. He would command the main attack force of twenty-four men. Each man in addition to his weapon would carry four phosphorous bombs and two hand grenades. He would give the detailed attack plan to his own men immediately after the 'O' group. Captain Stewart would command the ten man carrying force. On a signal from the attack force that the godown had been cleared of Japanese he would select what was to be taken away and get his men loaded as speedily as possible, getting them back to the firm base while the attack force proceeded to demolish as much as they could. In the meantime R.S.M. Chandler would take a party of twelve men due east to the bridge where eight of the men would give him protection whilst he and the men he had already trained would fix the explosives and blow the bridge. The cover party too would carry phosphorous bombs to assist in destroying the wooden part of the structure if necessary. The bridge destroyed, they would make their own way as speedily as possible over somewhat open country back to the palm plantation and then on to the firm base. They would move out from the high jungle in three days time, Thursday 27th August, the attack would take place at dawn on Sunday 30th August. As David and Paddy were standing side by side before a completely sober - for the time being - priest, as Ruth stretched out on the sofa at Chandlers Lodge having a cup of tea with Karl and Anni, as Mark and Charlie waited in their sand blown emplacements for the next Afrika Corps attack which was to go down in history as the Battle of Alam Halfa, the beginning of the end for Field Marshall Rommel, as all these happenings were taking place, Harry and one man were carefully reconnoitring their target through field glasses from the cover of some beluka some six hundred yards away.

"Piece of cake," was Harry's verdict. His Chinese companion grinned excitedly. It was his first operation; it would not be his last.

Clive called a last minute meeting before they settled down for the night, though in fact, with one or two exceptions, settling down was perhaps the wrong expression. Clive had reminded the leaders, British and Chinese, that no immobile wounded men were to be left alive to the Japanese. This directive had somewhat taken the froth off the excitement of the prospect of killing the sons of Nippon; the thought that one of their own unfortunates could be you was to say the least a sobering prospect. The contemplation having to be the one to carry out the dreadful act was even worse.

Three hours before dawn they moved out, Clive and the main party following the markers they had laid during their previous day's reconnaissance in a southerly direction, Harry and his small party in a south easterly direction. They each reached their attack start points before dawn, to find the road, as they expected, to be empty at that time in the morning. They swiftly cut the telephone lines. The resupply godown, petrol store and small barrack room which they had determined housed some dozen Japanese, with two officers and clerks housed in a small adjacent bungalow, all were situated on the eastern outskirts of Kabang. Each of Clive's sections had been allotted its individual task - they had almost fought among themselves to be in the section, which was to destroy the monkeys in the barrack room. Clive gave the signal. The four men detailed to kill the two sentries moved forward, quietly and efficiently grabbing their unsuspecting victims and slitting their throats. The barrack room squad moved past them simultaneously throwing a total of eight hand grenades through the open windows amongst the sleeping soldiers, having thrown themselves to the ground to avoid the blast. One inmate had obviously been awake and having seen the incoming hardware ran out of the single exit to be blasted by half a dozen trigger happy Chinese. At least four of the men inside had been wounded but were able to jump out of bed to get to their weapons. These however were in a chained rack at the end of the room, the key to the padlock which secured them being in the possession of one of the officers in the bungalow nearby. As they stood there wondering what to do next, the decision was taken out of their hands by Choon Guan's Tommy gun. Swiftly he and his squad moved through the hut finishing off those still alive, then raced out to accomplish their second task.

Simultaneously Clive and his squad burst into the bungalow to see a half-dressed signaller racing to his field telephone, and the incongruous sight of a portly officer, seemingly well past retirement age, stark naked but wielding his officer's sword coming straight at them. Clive removed him with a short burst whilst the signaller was swept off his feet by Choong Hong, the railway man. The second officer and the two clerks had, in the meantime, broken out of the back of the bungalow heading for an overgrown plantation. They were brought down by rifle fire, two men being detailed to ensure they were dead, if not to deal with the matter. In the space of six minutes, they had killed twenty Japanese, now they must get a move on, there could be sympathisers in Kabang, even Japanese sleeping out with mistresses or with the newly arrived Korean comfort girls who were being kidnapped from their homeland and being brought to the peninsula to staff the officer's brothels.

Clive gave an order. "Get moving!" Each man knew what he had to do. Robbie was already examining the godown. It had a large stock of rice, cooking oil, sugar and salt, all of which headed his shopping list. Quickly he organised the loading of his carriers. They would each carry roughly one hundred pounds weight to the assembly area, where half of it would be taken from them and distributed among the remainder of the force into gunny sacks brought especially for the purpose. In twenty minutes the carriers were laden and were moving away towards the oil palms. In the meantime the large petrol tanker had been allowed to leak. Clive gave the order to burn the buildings at which a dozen or more phosphorous bombs were hurled through the windows of the huts and into the godown, the men then clearing the site at the double whilst Clive himself retreated to the edge of the road. He watched for a minute or two from the safety of the monsoon ditch until the rivulet of leaking petrol was some thirty yards away, when he primed his phosphorous bomb, judged his distance carefully and lobbed the bomb into the approaching liquid. It resulted in the mother and father of all firework nights. The end of the stream of petrol ignited, providing a veritable channel of fire back to the tanker. With a huge roar and a cloud of smoke and flame, the tanker exploded throwing pieces of steel and balls of burning gases hundreds of feet into the air. Clive huddled in the bottom of the storm drain wishing fervently he had thought of a better way to blow up the confounded petrol as pieces of metal dropped perilously close to him. In seconds almost it was all quiet except for the ferocious burning noise of the residues which had been conglomerating in the base of the tanker over the past few years. He clambered out of the drain, ran to rejoin his squad, who when he caught up with them, he found were grinning excitedly.

"On now, on," he called "we must get away." They moved on as fast as the carriers could travel, through the oil palms, on to the beluka until at last, the carriers thoroughly exhausted, they reached their firm base where they would sub-divide their loot and wait for Harry.

Harry had reached the bridge before daylight and in the half-light as dawn was breaking got his 'shopping list' laid out on the teak decking. He despatched four men in either direction along the road which, when fully light, gave observation in either direction for almost a mile. The bridge would be about five miles from their colleagues in Kabang.

Quickly his party of four men assembled his bundle of gelignite and tied it to a vertical stanchion carrying the main decking supports. The plan was to blow these uprights outwards, which would cause the longitudinal members to collapse into the river, taking the decking and cross members with it. The Japs would not clear that lot in five minutes! As they finished off on the bridge, and ran their cables back to the plunger, Harry gave a last inspection and called the picket back from the eastern side. As they doubled in they heard the dull explosion from the direction of Kabang, which they guessed was the petrol depot going up. They looked at each other giving an excited thumbs up.

Harry had been surprised there had been so far no traffic or pedestrians on the road. Admittedly it was Sunday and anyone with any sense he reasoned, would be having a lie-in. As he made the final connections to the firing mechanism, some seventy-five yards from the bridge - he remembered what had happened at the last bridge he helped to blow, back in France. Bits of metal had come clonking down and nearly put an end to Ray Osbourne. 'I wonder what Ray is up to now,' he asked himself. As he told the men to get as much cover as they could in the storm ditch, in itself not a particularly healthy place to be in view of the unpleasant creatures who tended to live in it, one of the lookouts called out, "Truck coming from Mersing direction Sir." Harry told them all to keep down, gradually raised himself above the level of the bank, training his field glasses towards the oncoming vehicle. He instantly recognised it as a Bedford 3-tonner, and if it was an ex-army vehicle it would without any doubt whatsoever, now be the property of the Imperial Japanese Army. As it was head on to him at this moment he could not see what was in the back of the truck, but in a hundred yards or so when it negotiated a curve, he could see a row of armed Japanese troops sitting on benches along each long side. He estimated twelve each side, two in the cab - twenty-six or thereabouts. Harry thought quickly. His only chance he could see would be to blow the bridge with the truck on it. If he blew the bridge now, foot soldiers would almost certainly be able to scramble across the debris or wade or swim the river and pursue them. He had at least five hundred yards of open country to cross to get to the beluka, if his pursuers were any good at all, he and his twelve men would stand little chance of making it. If he could blow the bridge with the truck on it, that would be a bonus none of them had remotely considered. If however the commander approaching them even considered the possibility of sabotage and sent a recce party forward to inspect the bridge, the game would be up. There was nothing Harry could do he had to await events. He had not long to wait, he watched the truck approaching, saw it slow down as it approached the bridge, realised all trucks do this as the decking makes a dreadful rattling noise as it is traversed, and as it moved on towards the centre where the explosive was positioned on the side frames, suddenly boosted its acceleration. Someone had spotted the gelignite and shouted a warning to the driver. At that instant Harry pushed the plunger, there was a tremendous roar, the bridge disintegrated, the truck was hurled upwards, bodies of Japanese soldiers hung suspended in mid air before falling back on to the steelwork or into the river.

The Chinese started to run towards the bridge. Harry yelled, "Keep down, keep down," when the debris started falling around them they realised why. When the dust had settled a little, they all moved forward. Miraculously two of the soldiers had survived the explosion and even more miraculously retained their rifles. As they crawled out of the water and up the bank they were liquidated without a second thought on the part of the Chinese. Harry gave a quick order, "Check no more are live," this being carried out, he called, "Let's go before anything else turns up," having done a quick body count they moved across the open country to get to the safety of the beluka. As much as they hated the jungle, they were pleased to see it.

The three parties having successfully joined up at the firm base, they quickly made their way into the high jungle, using streams and game trails as much as possible to lessen the possibility of being successfully pursued - an unlikely possibility but one which always had to be considered. After an hours steady climb, it started to rain, then it started to bucket down, then for the next three hours stair rods of water deluged them making them slip and slide under their loads, but ensuring that any tracks they may have made would have been obliterated.

When the force reached Camp Six in the early afternoon of Tuesday 1st September, they were eagerly greeted by the camp protection group, each and everyone casting an eye over their mud stained, weary comrades, to establish there were no missing faces. Their loads were taken from them, this having been carried out Clive commanded.

"Now listen everyone." There was immediate silence. "I know you are wet and tired, but there will be a weapon inspection here in half an hour. You will then be dismissed until nine o'clock parade tomorrow morning." One or two started to protest to one another.

"QUIET!" The authority in that voice was indisputable. "You are soldiers. You are now battle-tried soldiers. You will act as soldiers. Your weapons always come before your personal comfort. If you were a cavalryman your horse's comfort would come before your own, so thank goodness you are not cavalrymen. There will be weapons inspection in thirty minutes - MOVE!!" They hustled away, most of them smiling, most of them revitalised by the thought they were considered to be a fighting unit, one or two with sullen looks at being ordered about by a white officer, faces noted by Harry to have a word or two about with Choon Guan, their camp leader. They could not afford to have a bolshie clique in a unit like this he thought - then he had another thought 'You silly sod - they're all bolshies aren't they?' - and yet another thought "well what do they call bolshies in a communist army?" The profundity of this problem failed to wake him once during the twelve hours sleep he enjoyed after the inspection, a shower and a meal before collapsing on to his charpoy.

At the parade the next morning Clive congratulated the men drawn up before him on a superbly carried out operation. They had destroyed a supply post, demolished a strategic bridge, obtained vital supplies of food and above all killed between forty and fifty Japanese, all without loss to themselves. "But," he continued, "there will come a time when things will not go as well as they did on Sunday. We must therefore keep at our training, our field craft, jungle training, weapon training, even house to house fighting practice so that if we do have casualties they would have been unavoidable."

Afterwards when talking to the other officers he made the point that because everything had gone well on their first two operations he wanted to make sure the men did not get complacent - that could lead to disaster. So far they had had the element of surprise, one day someone may surprise them!!

Two weeks after their return Harry developed a temperature. He was practising with his blowpipe, a routine of one-hour duration he set aside each day. The blowpipes his Orang Asli friends had carried were around ten feet long, far too long to serve the purpose for which he ultimately intended. After considerable searching he at last found four pieces of bamboo to make two pipes, one four feet long when finished, the other five feet. Day after day he practised, much to the interest, and amusement in some quarters of the camp inmates, until one day a tree rat scampered across the parade ground some thirty yards away, travelling fast. Harry aimed just ahead with his five footer, puffed, the dart whistled through the air and the next thing the handful of watchers saw was the tree rat rolling over and over until it lay dead, pierced through by the dart. The Chinese ran to the target, standing around it in admiration as though Harry had just shot a tiger. It was the beginning of

Harry's reputation as 'The Silent Executioner.'

However, on this day, he found it impossible to even hold the blowpipe steady, added to which his shoulders were aching like the very devil. He tried to fight it off, found he was not succeeding, got up from the piece of rock upon which he had been seated, found his legs refused to carry him, and flaked out on the parade ground. Willing hands carried him to Matthew Lee's medical room, where malaria was swiftly diagnosed. The camp had a plentiful supply of quinine, this commodity having been considered to be one of the top priorities when the camp was first being planned. Matthew sat at the single patient bedstead for hours, dosing Harry with thirty grains each day, continually changing his sheets soaked with perspiration from the fever, continually getting him to drink to replenish the liquid he was losing. For the first two days Harry knew little of what was happening to him. He hallucinated, tried to get out of the bed, as a result had to be forcibly restrained, he called out, but sometimes was so comatose they thought they had lost him. At the end of the second day, just as dusk was falling, they heard a voice say,

"Matthew, what's up?"

Matthew ran across saying, "Lie back, I must take your temperature."

The thermometer showed a marked reduction to that of mid afternoon. Matthew changed his sheets again, then held him up to drink some water. As he sat up, he cried out in pain from, it seemed, every joint in his body. Matthew gently lowered him.

"We need one of the girls from the massage parlours in the Happy World" he told Harry. Despite his total exhaustion, a little of the old Harry surfaced.

"What does a good Christian boy like you know about a place like that?" he asked feebly, accompanying the question with a gallant attempt at a grin. The Happy World was a large amusement centre in Singapore catering for every requirement of a large garrison and visiting ships of all nations.

"When you were delirious, you told me all about it, and a lot of other things too including some language I had never heard before. Who was this girl in a place which sounded like Mouthfield you used to take into the apple orchard?"

Harry lay back laughing weakly, but even this made his stomach and chest muscles ache.

"Since we have no massage girl, I shall have to deputise."

He gently turned Harry over, moistened his hands with palm oil and gradually worked up and down Harry's spine and across his shoulders. Although Matthew was, like many Chinese, slightly built, his hands and fingers were surprisingly strong. For over half an hour he searched out the little pockets of stiffness and pain particularly in the neck, until Harry became so relaxed he almost dozen off again.

"That will do for now. I'll go over you again before you go to sleep tonight. You have been close to death's door, but our Good Lord has kept you with us. Praise be to God."

Harry smiled to himself. "Amen to that."

He got up, albeit shakily, the next day, but it was a week before he felt really fit again. He wondered about the troops living in the jungle - what happened if they were unable to be evacuated to perhaps a tented hospital? He, at least, had a roof over his head to shelter him and regular hot food when he at last was able to take it.

At the end of September, Clive announced a further operation, or rather a series of operations.

"We are going over the next two months to carry out a series of pinprick attacks," he told the assembled guerrillas. "They will be carried out in widely dispersed areas with different types of targets so that we have the Japanese chasing around all over the place not knowing where they will be hit next. To quote the old army phrase, they won't know their arse from their elbow."

The first sortie was led by Harry. Some ten miles north of the camp, way up in the high jungle, a power line stretched from the main grid in the west across to the east coast. At one point it descended into an almost inaccessible ravine. How the original British engineers had got equipment and material down there to build the thing in the first place was itself a miracle. To cause the maximum amount of tribulation to the Japs it was decided to blow it up deep in the ravine. It meant that Harry and his four men would be away for nearly a week. They made a first class job of it.

Other parties attacked and burnt down an electricity substation, a telephone exchange, and most audaciously a Japanese officer's club in broad daylight when the members were all elsewhere about their duties. However, here they suffered their first casualty. Part of the facilities of the club were five Korean comfort girls ruled by a Japanese Madame who when the first explosions took place, ran out from their beds completely naked on to the lallang in front of the building - their work in the establishment having been concerned with the night shift of course. Behind them three of the Japanese club staff emerged firing revolvers at the attacking Chinese. The raiders hesitated to fire momentarily for fear of hitting the women; in those fatal seconds one of their comrades was hit and died instantly. Robbie, who had run round the left of the group, cut all three of the Japanese down with one long burst from his tommy gun, killing one and wounding the other two, who were speedily despatched by Lo Chee and Chee Hong following close behind. Having fired the building and the stores behind it, they were not in a position to remove any of the contents much as they would have liked to, they retreated into a neighbouring plantation, from there into the beluka, then back into the jungle, leaving flames licking up into the heavens and six naked women huddled together on the lawn. As Robbie remarked to his comrades,

"Well, they are used to having no clothes on are they not?"

Whilst the planning of these minor operations provided Harry with plenty to occupy his mind - he was involved in the planning of each project even if he was not taking part in it - there still remained those long hours, particularly in the evening and at night when he experienced a deep and bitter longing for Megan and the children. The resentment at missing their formative years, the bitterness of having to sacrifice the wonderful bodily contact he enjoyed with his wife, the anger he felt against these hideous Japanese for causing all this time wasted, never to be regained, instilled in him a hatred which became more and more ingrained to the extent he would no more flinch at killing one of them than he would of swatting a mosquito. He recognised this gut feeling within, reminding himself that it must not take over and control his judgement in any way. He was responsible for the lives of many others, several of whom had even more cause to hate their enemies than he had. A number of them were fatherless through the horrific actions of the invaders, some even having lost their whole family; he therefore curbed this burning desire to kill so that when the opportunity arose to put his anger into action it was exercised in a professional - almost a clinical - manner.

By the end of November the Camp Six force had ranged far and wide over Northern Johore, the enemy never knew where they were going to strike next, neither did they know where they had come from. They made attempts at infiltrating the jungle but searching in that environment was like looking for a needle in a haystack, particularly since the guerrillas had become past masters at covering their tracks. It would be possible for a Japanese patrol to pass within two and three hundred yards of the camp without knowing it was there. If they should stumble upon it they were dead men.

And so New Year 1943 approached with them all more than satisfied with their successes in 1942, but deep inside them the unhappiest of feelings of being unable to see any light at the end of the tunnel.

Chapter Thirty Four

Brigadier Hopgood came to the hotel in which David and Paddy had been installed, rather late that evening. He apologised for keeping them hanging around - brigadier's apologising again - the world's turning upside down thought David - saying that tomorrow they could have off as his Yugoslav specialist was at present in Jerusalem and had been delayed. "Toby will take you on a sightseeing trip" he said. "We are issuing you with paratroopers' maroon berets," he added, "there are, of course, dozens of axis agents in and around Cairo. Upon seeing two paratroopers being shown around they will immediately inform their controllers who in turn will assume you are some sort of advance party and that the Western Desert is being reinforced with divisions of airborne troops. It is surprising how effective a little disinformation can be."

And that was how they obtained their so-called red berets, with which from then on they would not be parted - except on rare occasions in Yugoslavia where they would have stuck out like a sore thumb and would have been selected for special attention by an inconsiderate enemy. It sometimes pays to be anonymous.

Toby took them to the Cairo Museum, where as David said, they could have spent a week, and then on to a restaurant at Giza. They had a wonderful lunch after which they needed, as Jack Hooper always described the operation, 'to water the horses.' Having performed this necessary exercise they turned to wash their hands, only to find the towel beside the cold water tap was as black as night, or as Dylan Thomas would have said 'Sloe black, crow black.' Toby, who up until now has been frightfully, frightfully proper, expressed the view, "I'd rather have the germs off my cock than off that," and walked away with hands dripping onto the marble floor. David and Paddy looked at each other with raised eyebrows and roared with laughter.

They saw a lot in a short time, but it left David with an intense desire to spend real time here in this wonderful country which up until now, he had been led to believe was just the pornographic centre of the world. It probably was both.

The next day a meeting was called for 8am. The 'Yugoslav specialist' turned out to be a middle-aged, very seedy looking gentleman who, David thought, one might well not be surprised to meet frequenting the underground lavatories in Leicester Square. He speedily kicked himself in the pants, metaphorically speaking, telling himself that he of all people should know better. In this business you can never tell a sausage by its skin, the bravest of the brave often looked like a gutless wonder, a gormless look could conceal a brilliant intellect, a frail frame could mask incredible endurance. On the other hand, he consoled himself; a prat was often what he seemed to be - a prat.

Brigadier Hopgood introduced the newcomer as Doctor Lazic, who would give them a run down on the present position in Yugoslavia. Doctor Lazic unrolled a large map of the country explaining to them it was occupied mainly by Italians in the western half, being divided the length of the country from Slovenia in the north to Macedonia in the south. The eastern half, with the exception of small areas occupied by Hungary and Bulgaria, was occupied by the Germans. However, the whole of the wildly mountainous centre of the country was partisan country. A small resistance force of the original Serbian army, known as Chetniks, under the control of a Colonel Mihajlovic and supported by the Yugoslav King and his government in exile in London, operated in the north. The communist group led by Josip Broz Tito had its headquarters in Bihac in Bosnia. They were known as the K.P.J. Chetniks numbered some 20,000. K.P.J. at this time, September 1942, probably 150,000. Against them were marshalled 280,000 Italians, 120,000 Germans and 100,000 others, mainly Bulgarians.

In Croatia the Germans had established a puppet regime, which formed a much-feared military force called the Ustasha, known as 'the Black Legion' as they wore black uniforms. In addition, they established a well-armed Home Guard, called the Domobran, of some 85,000 men.

If I remember that lot it will be a miracle, David thought, Paddy too consoling himself with the fact that he could always get David to repeat it all to him after the meeting.

"Well, you have a general idea of the forces involved, and you are probably saying to yourselves where the hell do I fit in," the brigadier remarked genially, "all will be revealed in due course, all will be revealed."

Dr Lazic continued. "Since the outbreak of war against Yugoslavia in April of last year - 1941 - and the occupation of the country, the Slav government in London appears to be concentrating their Chetnik operations against Tito's force, being more concerned with safeguarding their position against communism than fighting the

German and Italian occupiers. Secondly they appear to be actually joining forces with the fascist Ustasha and the Domobran. In other words we are providing aid to people who are using it to fight our comrades in arms - the partisans. We don't know any of this for certain, the brigadier will doubtless be giving you your tasks which will including establishing the veracity of these rumours which come by radio from Tito's headquarters and are therefore not entirely reliable since he may be making a case for greater assistance by spreading them. As one of your famous writers once said 'Nobody speaks the truth when there's something they must have.'"

He continued.

"Well, that's the overall briefing picture, the brigadier will go into your operational orders, I shall be giving you further information of the topography, the people and customs at a later date." He sat back. David had already revised his opinion of this man. He had delivered this succinct presentation without reference to a single note, in a fluent, controlled fashion, which indicated the command he had of his subject, which in turn conferred confidence in those who were absorbing it.

This first briefing concluded, the brigadier said, "Right, we'll have some coffee now, and then I am getting Toby to drive you in an open jeep to General Alexander's HQ. You will not be doing anything there - Toby has to collect some bits and pieces for me - but I want your red berets to be seen in high places, just to keep the pot boiling. After that go to Shepherds for lunch - a fair proportion of waiters there earn extra money playing at espionage. Then this evening we tap in to the radio messages being sent to Italy, having already broken their codes months ago."

Middle East HQ was an experience. Hundreds of people milling around wearing a vast array of arm-bands, red tabbed officers by the score, immaculately turned out military police in every corridor and door-way, countless doors with 'Knock and Wait' on them - "That's not very polite Sir is it?" said Paddy.

"What the hell do they all do?" was David's inevitable question to Toby.

"Well, when you consider that every single requirement of the 8th Army in the desert, from spare fly-buttons to a replacement heavy artillery piece has to come through here, and not only the 8th Army, there's an army in the Sudan and East Africa, in Palestine and Mesopotamia, there are even a couple of very odd bods going into Yugoslavia, the organisation and co-ordination of all these takes place here. I have heard estimated that behind every private soldier putting his bayonet into a Jerry's guts, or hoping to shortly, there are some fifteen support troops, artillery-medics, and head quarter staffs etc, stretching back to here. It is a mind boggling organisation when you come to think of it."

"I shall never say derogatory things about the base wallahs again," David assured him.

Shepherds presented them with another experience. Immaculate starched tablecloths, silverware on each table, so many waiters it was impossible to remember which were the four who were looking after your particular table. The place was full of well-fed looking staff officers, with here and there a much leaner and much more tanned major or lieutenant-colonel giving a clear indication he had just come from the desert. David still wore his City Rifles black crowns on his epaulettes; Paddy having the large black and green laurel leaves on a leather strap on his wrist. As they were finishing their meal, another Rifleman approached them, leaving the restaurant. He looked at David, looked a second time, and then bellowed "Chandler - it is Chandler isn't it?"

David looked up to see his old C.O. Colonel Brindlesby-Gore.

"Sir, how nice to see you, please sit down," a waiter was already providing an extra chair as they shook hands.

"And O'Riordan isn't it - and now Sergeant Major O'Riordan, well congratulations, you must both have been very busy to get where you are. And what the hell are you doing here - complete with red berets I note." They explained what they were up to, making sure they were out of earshot of the waiters. The conversation then developed into the inevitable 'How are Mark and Charlie' and so on. Mark was up for an M.C., Charlie was now a captain, second in command to Mark, who lost three of his officers, one killed, two wounded in the recent scrimmage. In several other parts of the restaurant other unexpected meetings were taking place, to end up as theirs did in a short while with "Well, I'll tell them all I've seen you, they will be surprised."

"Sir, I haven't asked after your brother. Where is he?"

"He transferred to the Ghurkha Rifles, or as his particular lot call themselves, The Goorkhas. He was at Peshawar but I believe he has now moved over to Imphal or regions adjacent. All that heat and mountaineering will slim him down a bit I fancy," he joked. "Well, I'll be off. Take care of yourselves," he shook hands with all three, adding quietly as he shook hands with Paddy, "Look after him Paddy won't you."

"I will that Sir," and thinking to himself, being called by your first name by the colonel must be something very few regular soldiers ever experienced.

For three days they had intermittent instruction from Dr Lazic, in particular studying the complex central mountainous region in which mainly they would be operating, the equally complex racial and religious divides of the population and the known positions of what were to be their adversaries. On Thursday 24th they had their briefing meeting with the brigadier. It was quite lengthy but boiled down to the main requirement of assessing just exactly how efficient the partisan movement was. They were told that communists formed only forty percent of the force - probably a little less. However it was organised and controlled by the K.P.J. - the communist party. Secondly twenty per cent of the organisation was female and there were very strict rules against sexual relations between the comrades, rigidly enforced. They were to assess how the bonding of the various ethnic, religious, and political factions worked, what the military planning succeeded in achieving and if possible what their post war aims were. They were to establish precisely what the Chetnik situation was, in general to provide as wide a range of information as possible from on the ground, not from headquarter sources. A substantial mission was being planned to go into the country at the end of April 1943 to organise major assistance, tanks, aircraft, command training and so on, based on whether their preliminary report indicated such large scale assistance could be justified. So that this mission can be properly briefed they would be collected by submarine from a beach south of Dubrovnik on or about the 25th March, and returned to Alexandria. They would be leaving in two days time. The brigadier's final words were, "No heroics, we want neither of you killed - understand?"

David smiled and said "On that Sir, you can rely utterly."

The next two days were spent getting their kit together, being given good advice by Dr Lazic. On the 26th Toby took them out to the airfield where the familiar outline of a Halifax was spotted on a dispersal point.

"We will collect your parachutes; the container with your gear is already on the aircraft."

When they reached the aircraft a loading party from the Royal Army Service Corps were positioning large rectangular loads down the centre of the fuselage.

"What have we got here?" asked David.

"These are cases of Italian Carcano 6.5mm rifles, captured from the Italians in the desert. As you will find when you get there, the partisans are armed with every conceivable kind of weapon, their main problem being to get the correct ammunition to fit the gun they hold. The Carcano is popular because they can capture 6.5mm ammunition from the Italian occupation forces, and from the Domobran. I think there are close on a thousand rifles in this drop - not a fraction of what they need, but every little helps as the old lady said."

At five o'clock they changed into their heavy battledress and in minutes were 'sweating like pigs' as Paddy described it, despite the benefit of a large ceiling fan in the room they had been allocated on the dispersal point. Worse was to come, they had to walk the hundred yards or so to the aircraft in a temperature around ninety degrees. Worse still, they had to climb into the aircraft which had been sitting on the dispersal point all day and had, as a result, reached an astronomical temperature within the fuselage. Rivulets of perspiration ran down their back in between the cheeks of their backsides and down their fronts provoking Paddy to observe, "Even my bloody undercarriage is getting soaked."

"It's all that high living you've been enjoying lately coming out."

"Well as long as the moisture doesn't give me arthritis in me wedding tackle I'll put up with it."

"That might be an advantage perhaps. Doesn't arthritis stiffen the joints? But then I understand that's an affliction you suffered more or less permanently a few weeks ago."

"Holy Mary, don't remind me. What am I doing here for God's sake?"

They literally 'sweated it out' for nearly three quarters of an hour before the massive Hercules engines burst into life, the Halifax lumbered off to the end of the runway, throttled up until it would seem the aircraft would be shaken to pieces, moved away faster and faster until it took to the air. When eventually it levelled off, the co-pilot came back to give them details of the flight and despatch information. It would take about four hours. When they were over the target, which would be well lit - there was no enemy within fifty miles...

"That's the sort of enemy I like," Paddy butted in.

"As I was saying, when we reach the target, the dispatcher," pointing to the two R.A.S.C. men sitting further up the fuselage, "will lift the cover off the hole. We have twelve loads which means we have to make three passes over the dropping zone as we can only despatch four loads at any one time. They will then step aside and on the fourth pass I will despatch you two. All clear?"

"What about our container?"

"That will follow you down."

"I bloody well hope so - I've got a bottle of scotch tucked away in there."

"In which case it may not follow you down."

The night was clear but dark. The flight itself was uneventful. They were not flying over Western Europe with its saturation of anti-aircraft installations doing their best to blast you out of the skies. Although part of the flight was over enemy held Greece and Macedonia they droned on without disturbance.

Half an hour before the target area - Bihac - the co-pilot came back again and helped them on with their parachutes, hooked them up, after which David and Paddy checked one another's straps, release gear and internal hooking, gave the thumbs up to the young flight lieutenant, and sat down again somewhat awkwardly due to the large pack on their backs.

It took about twenty minutes for the dispatchers to get their loads out of the aircraft, the plane having to make wide circular turns at each end to make the return drop. They both shook hands with David and Paddy and retreated to their seats forward whilst the co-pilot watched the despatch lights.

"Red light on." David stood by the hole, Paddy up close behind him.

"Green light on. GO. GO." and in less time than it takes to tell, David and Paddy were swinging their way down to a lightly snow covered D.Z. which looked quite inviting until they hit it and found it to be rock hard. Although a little bruised here and there they suffered no lasting damage. They were both surrounded by partisans slapping them on the back, each one trying to shake hands in welcome. The landing of these two British paratroopers was as symbolic as it was practical. They saw it as being a commitment from powerful allies to giving them help in their lone fight against the might of the German and Italian divisions ranged against them. They saw this descent from the skies as being the one way help could come to them in their beleaguered land-locked battle zone. Above all it meant they would be able to assist in the overall battle against the Axis, the more fascist divisions, which were sent to combat them meant more had to be drawn from other fronts. They were therefore not only fighting for their own liberty, but also aiding the overall fight against fascist aggression.

In the morning they were taken to the camp commandant's quarters who apologised for not meeting them at the drop due to being delayed in getting back from a brigade visit. In walking to the commandant's office the first thing they noticed was that no two partisans wore the same uniform, in fact a fair proportion of them were wearing Italian uniforms, others wore a Yugoslav tunic with civilian trousers, others just had a bandolier slung across their chest over a civilian suit. Footwear described a similar picture. Everything from knee boots to sandals, but mainly ordinary boots re-soled with pieces of old tyres cobbled on.

The second thing was, in passing a lean-to; they saw some thirty or forty men and women, carefully unstitching the panels of the nineteen parachutes, which had descended the previous night. It was explained to them that the fabric would be made into undershirts to help keep the fighters warm through the coming winter. The nylon cords were untangled and would be absolutely invaluable for securing loads on to mules and horses which were their only means of transport as they moved from one ambush point to another. The webbing straps attached to wooden frames would become panniers on the horses.

As for weapons, as Paddy remarked, it must be a quartermaster's nightmare. There appeared to be everything from shooting rifles through to pre-war Yugoslav army Mausers, Italian Berettas and Carcanos, and many others. The only standard, absolutely universal piece of equipment was the red star on the front of each person's headgear. No matter what form the headgear took the red star was on the face of it, despite the fact that less than half the partisans were communists.

The commandant was a burly, barrel-chested, close cropped man of around forty, David judged. He was accompanied by an attractive young woman in a well-cut tunic, breeches and knee boots. She could be straight out of Moss Bros was David's first thought. They were welcomed effusively by the commandant with bear hugs and a voluble speech in his own tongue of which they understood not a word, but which was translated for them by his assistant, speaking extremely good English.
"The commandant, Comrade Todor Mavric, welcomes you to Yugoslavia and is so pleased you arrived safely. My name is Livia, I translate for the commandant. The commandant has instructed me to ensure you receive all the information regarding our operations you require and to accompany you to translate for you when you visit our brigades in the field."
David replied. "Please thank the commandant for the very kind

reception he has given us. But we were hoping to visit the forward units, those in contact with the fascists." Anna translated to Todor, who smiled when he replied. She translated.

"Of course, we shall go to the forward units." David was perplexed.

"But I anticipated having to march many kilometres, and we could be in some danger."

The two partisans had a chuckle when this was translated. With a somewhat mischievous look she answered.

"I shall try not to march too fast for you, and I have just spent six months in an active service unit in which there were many women."

David and Paddy looked at each other, shrugged, grinned, David held his hand out and shook hands with Livia, Paddy followed suit, the commandant looked on smiling benevolently, dived into a drawer on his desk, pulled out a bottle of slivovitz and four small glasses, filled them up, handed them round, raised his glass and said,

"To England."

To which David replied,

"To the partisans."

The commandant and Livia threw their drinks back and turned not a hair. David and Paddy followed suit, Paddy upheld the honour of the British Army by appearing to have just drunk a small glass of lemonade, but when the fiery liquid hit the back of David's throat he had to fight a fight which under different circumstances would have won him a medal for the highest example of valour. As it was his eyes watered, his throat burned, he overcame a wild urge to spit the lot out but bravely swallowed, suppressing even the overpowering desire to cough his heart up, lowered his glass, hoped his eyes had not watered too much and managed to ask

"What was that drink?"

"Slivovitz, plum brandy," Livia replied.

"Comrade Mavric, if I remember nothing else of Yugoslavia I shall never forget that glass of slivovitz."

The commandant roared with laughter at the translation, shook hands with them again, the two took a pace back, saluted and left with Livia. They couldn't know, but the courtesy of those salutes by these two seasoned soldiers had a tremendous effect on Todor Mavric. He equated them with professionalism, which led him to believe he and his partisans would, in time, get the help they needed so that they would become professionals. Which they did.

For the next three months the three musketeers, as David had christened his little party, were passed from battalion to battalion operating in what was called the N.D.H. - the Independent State of Croatia. They took no part in the ambushes and attacks they witnessed, except on occasion helping to give covering fire to those making the assault. Fighting the Italians and the Domobran home guard units was considered to be hitting sitting ducks; the Italians invariably put up a bit of a fight and then retreated. Any who surrendered were relieved of their clothes, boots, weapons and ammunition and sent on their way. The Domobrans however made it a practice to fire two shots in the air as they were being approached, then dropped their rifles and automatically took their clothes off without being ordered so to do. David and Paddy had been told that this was standard procedure and had considered it a leg-pull. In the middle of October, with a foot of snow on the ground, they actually saw it happen. "God, I wish I had brought a camera," he laughed to Livia.

Two weeks later, they met a different enemy. Most strategic bridges, particularly railway bridges, were guarded by blockhouses mounted on either side if of any length, if not by a single post. Having reconnoitred a target comprising a single block house the group leader decided to attack it, destroy it and then do as much damage to the bridge and track as they could before melting back into the forest. They would attack just before dawn. David was not very happy with the plan. They had not been able to get close to the target, neither could they get a clear view of it with field glasses. The plan outlined was simple. Four men would crawl to the block house and throw grenades through the weapon openings and between the top embrasures. When they had exploded, a second group would charge the doorway with a heavy log to break it down. It would all be over in a couple of minutes, they could then get on with the bridge. David diplomatically put his fears to Livia. Firstly they could not clearly see how open the weapon slits were. It would be quite likely they would mostly have removable interior covers to keep out the cold, except for say two or three, which would be used by sentries on watch. Secondly, they could not see if there was a machine gun mounted on the roof behind the embrasures, which if it failed to be neutralised could play havoc with the retreating partisans as dawn broke. At the back of David's mind was the intelligence he had gained from his father of the virtual impregnability of their blockhouses in the South African war against a foe who lacked an artillery support capability.

Livia appreciated David's assessment of the situation but said she had no operational authority over Comrade Djokic, the leader of the group. She would, however, tactfully query the plan with him and suggest they carry out further reconnaissance after dawn. Whether or not the group leader was beginning, himself to have doubts, or whether he tacitly acknowledged the indirect authority of the commandant's representative, whatever the reason, he called the attack off. Soon after dawn signs of life appeared. Djokic, watching through his binoculars, spoke one word - "Ustasha." The blockhouse was not manned by militia or Domobran, but by members of the highly organised fascist Black Legion, constituting a very different nut to crack. They moved back into the forest to consider what to do next. The alternatives seemed simple. Either they attacked the blockhouse, in which case they could expect casualties, or they could find another, softer, target and lose the opportunity of killing the hated Ustasha and capturing their weapons. David spoke up.

"If Ustasha are guarding a bridge, it is because it must be important. If we capture a goods train going towards it, we could hide our men on the wagons, make the driver stop at the blockhouse, the guards will probably all come out to see what the problem is, we then attack. In addition, three or four men can climb on to the top of the driver's compartment to deal with any enemy on the roof of the blockhouse. They will be so close to the flat roof they could jump on to it and prevent anyone inside trying to get out that way. Others can bomb through the weapon slits."

Comrade Djokic thought this an excellent idea, but this being a single track railway they could not be sure from which direction the train was going to come so would not know in which direction to effect their ambush. Judging by the shine on the rails it was well used, therefore, suggested David; if they waited a mile from the blockhouse where the train faced the up-gradient they could afford to let one go should it come from the blockhouse on the down gradient. If a train had troops on it they would have to let it go anyway otherwise they would lose the element of surprise.

The leader slapped him on the back.

"Good idea, comrade major, we will do as you suggest." He outlined the plan to the others, and they moved off to the ambush point leaving the groups two cooks and four women soldiers to look after the mules.

Out of sight in the thick woods bordering the track they awaited the train. The partisans had been given strict orders not to break cover until the leader gave two short blasts on his whistle, these being masked by the noise of the engine being hard worked on the upgrade. Luck was with them, after just under an hour waiting on the snow-covered hill, they heard the train approaching on the upgrade. It had to negotiate a gentle curve some three hundred yards from the ambush point so that Djokic, David and Paddy could get a partial side-view of the types of trucks it was pulling. The first four, open topped, appeared to be empty, or partially filled perhaps with ballast. Their luck was holding, those four trucks could conceal all the attackers. They could hardly believe their eyes at the second four wagons. In each one there were three horses - twelve horses for the taking, they were worth a king's ransom in the mountains!

The train puffed its way slowly up the gradient towards the partisans. As the engine reached Djokic, he blew the whistle and out of the trees ran some forty partisans, some for the guards' van at the rear, the remainder to see what was in the front four trucks. Two Domobran guards and the train guard offered no resistance; the driver and fireman likewise stopped the train and stood at the controls with their hands high in the air. They knew they would not be harmed if they showed no opposition. Djokic quickly gave orders to get the horses off. The Domobran said they would do that, and could they join the partisans? They were both well built and in their early twenties, Djokic had no hesitation in accepting them, members of their units, and the Muslim militia, were defecting every day if they got the opportunity. The horses off, the men piled into the front four open topped wagons crouching against the side wall to escape being seen. Djokic, David and Paddy hid in the tender. As the train approached the blockhouse, all the men inside piled out to see why it was stopping. With steam hissing from half a dozen different places, with smoke swishing around from its chimney, a particularly dirty, noxious smoke as a result of the poor quality coal it was burning, there was for a moment or two, commotion and chaos compounded by the whistle signal from the leader at which all hell was let loose. The fight was short but bloody. Those eight men outside the blockhouse immediately became eight corpses. Two more in the blockhouse were reduced to pulp as a result of the grenades tossed in through the weapon slits. David and Paddy climbed from the tender on to the roof of the cab and from there jumped on to the blockhouse roof to see two Ustaha emerging from the stairway carrying a German MG34 light machine gun and a box of ammunition. Without a second thought they blasted them with their tommy guns and the battle was over.

Quickly they stripped the dead of their boots and trousers, they would not wear the tunics, collected the weapons and ammunition, particularly the greatest prize of all, the MG34 and its three boxes of cartridges, and were away to the rendezvous point. They covered the backs of the horses with blankets they brought from the blockhouse and loaded all the booty in a rudimentary pannier type manner on to them, then moved off at a steady pace due east into the mountains until it was getting dark.

It was a hard life. It was cold the snow was often deep. They slept mainly in barns gladly turned over to them by the peasant farmers who inhabited the mountain pastures. Often they slept out, when they had good cause to thank the Brigadier for suggesting they took gas capes with them, which kept them dry, since in that environment once you got wet you stayed wet until you could build a fire. Fortunately there was no shortage of wood!

And so, at the end of December they found themselves back at Bihac, warmly welcomed by Todor Mavric.

"You are to have seven days' rest over the new year," they were told, "so that you can get some decent food in you, get yourselves de-loused, I expect you can do with it, and sleep in a decent bed. You will then journey south and meet our brigades in Herzegovina and Montenegro before you are taken away from us."

Thinking of the bravery, the fortitude, the tenacity of the partisans they had lived and fought with over the past three months, the dangers, discomfort and hardships these brave people constantly endured in an unforgiving climate, David replied with absolute sincerity, "Part of us Comrade Mavric, a part of our hearts, will remain with you always," Livia having translated, David and Paddy were surprised to see tears running down the cheeks of the commandant and his assistant as they hugged each of the two British.

Chapter Thirty Five

On Monday 24th August Fred received an imposing looking - and feeling, envelope. Stationers at this stage of the war were extremely utilitarian to say the least. No longer could one purchase impressive letter headings so stiff they were difficult to fold, however this communication definitely appeared to be in that category. The two sheets of paper having been removed were headed:-

"Central Chancery of the Orders of Knighthood"
St James' Palace.

They informed Fred that his investiture would take place at Buckingham Palace on Tuesday 6th October and that he could bring two guests. They gave instructions as to where to report, dress of recipients and guests, where to take photographs after the investiture and a subtle hint that since the proceedings take in the order of two hours or more, to have a pee before you arrive. Orders and decorations should not be worn.

Under normal circumstances Ruth would have been excited beyond belief at the thought of going to the Palace and being in the same room as the King and Queen. She read the command, put her arms around Fred, and said, "I do hope I am well enough to come with you," to which Fred replied
"Of course you will - why it's over a month away, you will be as fit as a fiddle by then."

Nevertheless, when they saw the specialist on the following Wednesday, the 26th, Fred took him aside whilst Ruth was in the examination cubicle and asked him whether he thought she would be alright by then.
"I can't answer that Mr Chandler, but I can hazard a guess that whatever is the problem with Mrs Chandler now, she will be little different in five weeks' time, so I would say yes, take her. Often occasions like that can provide a catalyst which starts off the recovery process."

So it was decided that Ruth and Rose would accompany Fred on his great day. That evening Rose answered a telephone call from Ray Osborne. Ray had been notified in July that he had been awarded a bar to his M.C. for his numerous acts of bravery in dealing with unexploded bombs. "It's a consolation prize for making me left handed," he had joked to Fred. He called to say he had to go to an investiture on 6th October and could invite two guests, he wondered if Mr & Mrs Chandler would do him the honour. Rose explained the situation, he suggested therefore that perhaps Megan and Anni would care to come and give him moral support, to which Rose replied he should telephone them, they already knew of course that Fred had been requested to attend. Following this suggestion he telephoned them, they excitedly accepted the invitation, as a result, Ruth was surrounded by family at this great landmark in her husband's life.

There was some discussion as to how they should travel. Ray was to stay at Chandlers Lodge for a few days, although he was not officially discharged yet, he had no duties and was able therefore to make his own arrangements. Jack Hooper solved the problem, such as it was.

"As my contribution to this memorable occasion, I have hired a six seater Rolls Royce from Hooper's in Maidstone - no relation I assure you unfortunately, I might have got a discount otherwise. Anyway, it will take you to the Palace, wait with the carriages of the nobility and gentry, then bring you back to the Angel, where I and others will be waiting with a suitable festive board to welcome you home."

And that's how it worked out. Ruth and the girls were seated near the dais having clear views of the King, the Queen seated behind him as he presented the bravery awards, knighted the Knights, and went through the gamut of commanders, officers and members of the various orders. Three Victoria Crosses headed the investiture, two young airmen and a bearded sailor, with each of whom he spent some time. With all of the others he had a word or two of congratulation or enquiring in which theatre, or town in the case of civilians receiving George Medals, they had won their awards. Not one recipient left Buckingham Palace without a word or two from the King. As Fred said afterwards, that in itself was worth a medal to His Majesty.

When they arrived at the Angel, expecting to meet with Jack, Ernie and Karl, they found, as again Fred commented to Buffy Cartwright over the phone to Ramsey later that evening, half the bloody town there. John Tarrant had so organised it with Jack and Fred's Rotary Club secretary they would all pay for their own lunches for the privilege of being present to welcome back their popular and now honoured fellow-citizen. Fred and Rose kept a watchful eye on Ruth to ensure she was not becoming too stressed by it all, but apart from the fact she looked a little strained, she appeared to be enjoying this festive occasion. They enjoyed their meal, after which Jack stood up and called for attention. He gave a short speech saying how delighted they were that Fred had been honoured and how richly deserved it was. There were calls for "Speech. Speech," at which Fred rose.

"I thank you all for this grand and totally unexpected reception. So as not to risk being drummed out of the Rotary Club, or at the very least, being fined by the sergeant-at-arms, I shall make this a very short speech. There are two people who deserve this honour as much as I do. First is my wife who has had, for several years, to put up with never knowing when I am going to be in the house and when I am not, but has backed me all the way, often at great inconvenience to her own arrangements. We all wish you well love, and I thank you for your kindness and steadfastness over the years."

Immediately there was a scraping of chairs as spontaneously all arose with glasses high to drink to Ruth Chandler.

Fred allowed them to be reseated and settle down then continued with:-

"The second person I referred to is my friend, my co-director, a chap who doesn't known what nine to five is, a chap who never says I don't think we can do that, a chap who has the respect of and the highest regard of every man and woman in Sandbury Engineering, and the various ministries he has to deal with. I refer to Ernie Bolton."

Again, the chairs scraped back, glasses were raised, whilst a bemused Ernie sat back in his chair with his wife standing beside him on one side and his father-in-law, Karl Reisner, on the other, both weeping bucketfuls.

"Speech, speech," they chorused, all now well lubricated both with the wine provided and the festive atmosphere. Ernie rose to his feet.

"All I have done and am doing is trying to repay in small measure what the Guvnor has done for me, and not just the Guvnor but the whole family and Mr Hooper. David persuaded the owners of Sandbury Engineering to give me a job when I couldn't walk. Harry invented my 'Erniebike' so that I could get around. David saved Anni from the Nazis to become my wife. Mrs Chandler took her, and later my father-in-law, into their home as family, as did our dear Rose. If I could help to get the Guvnor to become the Earl of Sandbury it still would not be enough to repay him and his family for all they have done for my family. Thank you all."

He sat down to thunderous applause, as the local paper usually described the conclusion of the speech by the local M.P. when he visited Sandbury once in every five years, usually just before an election.

The celebration broke up. Fred anxiously asked Ruth if she was alright to which she replied she felt rather tired, but that it had been one of the most wonderful days of her life.

"Not the most wonderful?" queried Fred.

"No, the most wonderful was the day I married Sergeant Frederick Chandler, 2nd Battalion, The Hampshire Regiment."

He gave her a little hug. "Let's get you home so that you can put your feet up."

During October Ruth showed slight signs of improvement. On the day before she was due to see the specialist again, the 29th October, she got out of bed to go to the bathroom in the morning, Fred already having got up and was downstairs eating a hurried breakfast. As she started to walk she found she could not lift her left leg. Thinking it had 'gone to sleep' she sat back on the bed and rubbed it, stood up but still could not lift it. She could stand, but it would not move. Becoming a little frightened she called for Rose, thinking Fred would have left for the factory, however he heard her call and ran up the stairs as Rose appeared on the landing in her dressing gown and slippers.

"My leg won't move."

With one supporting her on either side they walked her along the landing hoping that whatever was causing the problem would free itself once she got underway. They had no success.

"I'll phone John Power. Help her in the lavatory, I will come back and we will put her back to bed. Have you any other symptoms love?"

"I've a very bad headache, but no pain in the leg."

"Right. I'll tell John."

When John Power arrived and had carried out the usual temperature, blood pressure etc tests, subjected her knee to the funny little hammer tests doctors seem to enjoy so much, then tickled her sole with the stick end of the hammer, he pronounced.

"I would like to talk to Doctor Fielding before I give you my views. You are seeing him tomorrow I believe?"

They confirmed this to be the case.

"Well, I'll try and get him to come here rather than your going to Maidstone. I will ring you later at the factory."

During the day Dr Power confirmed the appointment for 4.30 at Chandlers Lodge. When he arrived Megan, Anni, and of course Rose, were all there, deeply concerned at this new turn of events.

"What other unusual things have been happening to you Mrs Chandler?"

"I have had some flashing lights from time to time, but it's this headache - I keep taking aspirin but it won't go."

"Anything else?"

"I had a sort of lockjaw the other morning which frightened me, but it went off after a few minutes."

The two doctors walked Ruth up and down the bedroom while Fred looked on.

"Right, let's get you back to bed - could we have a word Mr Chandler?" Ruth grasped his wrist.

"Doctor Fielding, I want whatever you are going to say to say in front of me. Although I am not feeling well, I am not depressed as I was - I want nothing hidden from me." He looked at Fred, Fred nodded his agreement.

"Well Mrs Chandler, I shall not beat about the bush. I am sure now you have a brain tumour. I thought this was probably the case when you came to me in the first place but unfortunately I could only work on a clinical examination. One day we shall perhaps be able to get a picture of what is going on in the brain, to be able to exactly locate the tumour and even remove it, today we have only X-rays, which are of little help in this case. The tumour may spread or it may stay as it is, we cannot tell. We have no means of fighting it, all we can do is to relieve any pain it may give. I am terribly sorry to be the bearer of such bad news."

Ruth sat back against the pillows.

"Thank you doctor for being so honest," she paused. "How long have I got?"

"That I cannot tell you, no doctor could, but I think we are talking in terms of months."

"In that case, I shall make the most of what I have left. I have had a wonderful life, with a wonderful family. My great sadness is that I shall not see my two sons and my son-in-law again, nor they me. I have always hated this war and all the misery it brings to so many millions of people, why cannot I be allowed to die with all my family around me?"

That night, as she lay back on her pillows, with Rose and Megan seated beside the bed she said, "I think I can hear the church bells." Rose went to the window, opened it and was greeted by the first peal of bells the town had heard since before the threat of invasion over two years ago. In that time they had been silenced to be used as a warning countrywide that the invasion had started, now they were ringing out loud and clear, albeit in such a ragged fashion due to lack of practice, that any aficionados of the craft of bell ringing lying in the graveyard surrounding the bell tower would not just be turning, they would be revolving!

"I'll go and find out what is happening," Rose told them, and hurried off downstairs, returning to say that Mr Churchill had ordered all the bells in the country to be rung to celebrate the great victory at El Alamein. Rommel it would appear had been decisively beaten and was in full retreat. El Alamein and Stalingrad, being fought at the same time, marked the turning point of the war against Nazi Germany.

Over the next weeks, the family worked out a rota to include Moira when she could get away from her duties, Mrs Treharne who filled in at any time, Cecely on her afternoon off from Country Style and in the evening, Rose and Anni, so that there was always someone with Ruth or nearby at all times. In the second week in November Anni sat with her, it was quiet throughout the house, Rose being out with young Jeremy. Ruth had been dozing on and off, brought about by a combination of the illness and the sedatives she was being given. Suddenly she woke with a start saying to Anni, "I must have been dreaming, I was sure I was talking to Harry." She paused for a moment or two. "I wonder what the boys are doing now, I do wish I knew." Anni remained quiet for a short while.

"I have some news for you."

Instantly Ruth became wide-awake.

"Have you dear? Are you..."

"Yes, Doctor Power confirmed it this morning. Ernie and I are going to call her Ruth if you agree. Just plain Ruth, no other name. We shall want her to grow up exactly like you."

"Oh yes of course, how lovely, but what if it is another boy?"

"In that case we shall send it back to be exchanged."

Ruth laughed. It was her first laugh since receiving the dreadful news.

"I am so happy for you. I am so happy." She lay back. Anni could see she had dozed off again, took her hand and held it between her own hands for over half an hour, silently weeping for a while before she became calm. The thought of her own mother, dying all alone for all she knew, crept across her mind, at which she again soundlessly shed more tears.

The October gales were succeeded by a series of fogs in November. Ruth slept more but became immobile by the end of the month. The family decided that there would be no Christmas festivities, with presents only for the children. Fred got compassionate leave from his duties in the Home Guard, taking more and more time away from the factory. It was clear that Ruth was sinking. Christmas Day and Boxing Day passed like any other day. Every now and then she would have spells of lucidity, having, on one occasion, a long talk with Jack, reminiscing of the time before the war when they all went to Eastbourne together in his Daimler. "And you bought a new hat for the occasion - do you remember?" Jack reminded her. On the day before New Year's Eve she asked to see the children. They all came, including Cecely's two children. Maria came over from Chingford where she was on leave; she had been a regular weekend visitor over the past two months.

Ruth died at 8 o'clock in the evening of New Year's Eve, peacefully and surrounded by a loving, heartbroken family, but with the absence of her two sons, one in the freezing snows of the Balkan Mountains, the other in the humid monsoon heat of tropical Malaya - there could not have been a greater contrast.

Lord Ramsford had kept in constant touch with Fred as to Ruth's condition. He telephoned early on New Year's Day but was intelligent enough not to wish Fred a 'Happy New Year' until he received the news of Ruth. He was deeply saddened when he received it, "As will be my father," he added. "Please let us know the funeral arrangements Mr Chandler, we shall both attend and I would like to send flowers from Charlie who was very fond indeed of Ruth, in fact I have a feeling he considered her a surrogate mother, she was so kind to him. In the meantime I will pull all the strings I can to get David and Harry notified, although there would be no hope of getting them back in any way of course."

"No, we all realise that brigadier. It is going to be very hard for both of them."

The funeral was held on the following Thursday. The church was crowded with friends from Mountfield, from Sandbury, and from as far afield as Worcestershire and Aylesbury, in the persons of the Earl and Lord Ramsford, and the Maguires with Mary respectively. There were no fewer than four generals in the congregation, if you count the brigadier as a general, which he is - a one star general. Generals Earnshaw and Halton were there, as also was the French General Strich, whose life David saved at Calais over two years ago. Canon Rosser conducted the service giving a heartfelt eulogy of his dear friend Ruth Chandler, "Who was," he said, "to quote Horace, integer vitae scelerisque purus - Of unblemished life and spotless record." And so it seemed to all who knew her, except that Ruth herself might have had a wry smile.

So 1942 had ended in a major sadness for the Chandlers and 1943 was beginning with the thought in all their minds as to how the family would manage without Ruth's guiding hand. There was a general feeling of hope as a result of the great victories in North Africa and in Russia, nevertheless, they were only too well aware that there was a long way to go and many more battles to be fought before the men of the family were safely home again.

And not only the men.

They could have no idea of the death and destruction, which would, in the next years, be falling on them in their corner of England from the evil Hitler's secret weapons. Thousands of flying bombs and rockets would fail to reach London and fall into the Kentish countryside, many shot down by our own anti-aircraft batteries and fighter planes with the belief it was better for them to explode in the countryside than in built-up London. And so it was, except that they did not always explode in the open countryside.

John Milton has said, 'With hope, farewell fear,' but he also pronounced:-
> 'Where there is an equal poise of hope and fear...
> I incline to hope rather than fear.'

The fact is that John Milton in 1650 probably had both hopes and fears, but they would be nothing to compare with the everyday hopes and fears of the Kentish people at the end of 1942. Nevertheless, their hopes now were built on a far sounder foundation than had been the case a year ago, they had cause to hope, it was no longer a case of blind hope. 1943 would not provide an end to their suffering, but it would surely bring nearer the day of their returning to a normal family life, without fear, nor the need for hope.

But there was still a long way to go.